W9-ARV-921

THE NEW DAY DAWNS
People of the Frozen Earth,
Book One

To the Patrons
of Peabody Public Library —
Happy Reading —
Grace Ann
Schafer

People of the Frozen Earth, Book One

THE
NEW DAY
DAWNS

Grace Anne Schaefer

GASLight Publishing,
512-528-1727
PO Box 1025,
Leander, TX 78646

ISBN: 0-9754796-0-1

Cover art: Kim Downing
Cover and Book design: Jonathan Gullery

Library of Congress Control Number: 2004096675

Visit us on the web: www.peopleofthefrozenearth.com

Dedication

This book is dedicated to my grandmother, Annie Pickle, who encouraged me every step of the way and pretended she understood what I was talking about when I told her the story of Mach and Horda. I believed I could because you believed I could. Nannie, I miss you.

I also dedicate it to Bessie Mae Simpson. Aunt Bess, thanks for remembering and believing in me.

My mother, Frances Maroneey, doesn't like the genre, but she has always been one of my biggest fans. That means a lot. Thanks, Mom.

My baby daughter, Anja, what can I say? You encourage me just by competing with me. I literally don't know what I'd do without you. (I don't always know what to do with you either, but that's another story.) Thanks, Pooh.

And last and most of all, I dedicate this book to Kenn, who believes I can do anything I want to and makes me believe it too. I'm so glad I married you. You are my rock. Thanks again.

><> Grace Anne Schaefer

Acknowledgements

This project began many long years ago and there are many people who helped me finally finish it.

I especially thank Daniel Lee who didn't always tell me what I wanted to hear. Jo Blome and Cathy Winkley never seemed to doubt, and I thank them for their faith in me. I am grateful to both the encouragers and the doubters who were my students at Leander Middle School. I wouldn't have done it without them.

Dr. James Shepherd answered all my questions about blood poisoning and ovarian cancer. That's why Meiran had uterine cancer instead.

Jodi Thomas, author extraordinaire and exceptional friend, gave me the encouragement I needed to finish. She has truly shown me what it means to be a friend.

Kelly Carpenter, my "second daughter," grumbled and shook her head, but she helped me with my dreams. I don't know how I'd survive without her.

Traci Maynard, my "other daughter," pushed and fussed and yelled at me. She dried my tears and listened to me whine, but she never let me give up. Fred and Sam, her husband and daughter, deserve more credit and thanks than anyone will ever know because they allowed us to work on this project in their home.

Miriam Ruff showed me what it really meant to be an editor.

Kim Downing created the original cover art. It was a wonderful thing to see my imagination translated into a picture.

Jonathan Gullery of Budget Book Design turned the pretty picture into a book cover and all the manuscript into a book. I thank him for his patience and humor.

Scott Monroe took the author photos. We nearly froze, but it was worth it. He did a great job. They don't look too much like me.

Litho Press of San Antonio, Texas, put everything together into a real book.

This would still be just a dream without each of my friends and family who helped make this book a reality.

Preface

In the ancient days before the Ancestors kept the stories, the People of the Frozen Earth lived in the vast wasteland that is now called Siberia. Seeking a better life, they moved south across the land bridge into a New World, traveling through what are today Alaska and Canada. Just under two thousand years ago, this semi-nomadic People settled in the basin between the foothills at the eastern edge of the Rocky Mountains and the flat tableland of the Western Great Plains in the area now known as Wyoming, Montana, and the Dakotas. Strong and proud, they lived, loved, hated, laughed, cried, and died in the fullness of Mother Life's time.

Prologue

Adrenalin surged through Mach's veins, erasing a pleasant dream of Horda's amber eyes and urging him to complete wakefulness. What had woken him? His eyes flew open, and he tensed his muscles silently, preparing to face his unknown adversary.

Mach stared across his feet into bright amber eyes. *Ah, Horda, she was here after all.* Surprised and delighted, he almost reached out to his love before he realized here she was just a dream; she could not join him on his Great Travel. Then the diamond-shaped pupils registered in his consciousness. His fingers tightened automatically around the hilt of the fine flint knife on his belt as he stared back at the big-toothed cat sitting silently beside his feet. Not just a cat, no. It was nothing less than Father Death himself who waited there.

"Greetings," Mach said softly, though his insides shivered like aspen leaves in an autumn wind. "Have I taken your home as shelter from the snow storm?"

The big cat glared at the young warrior but did not move. Encouraged by the cat's lack of response, Mach inched to a sitting position. "I didn't think cats liked fire." He looked at the embers winking in his fire pit without ever taking his eyes from the animal. "Of course, that isn't much of a fire anymore, is it?" He edged his free hand to the pile of twigs kept at the ready. Slowly, casually, he placed two handfuls of twigs and dried grass on the pit. When the flames renewed themselves, he added a medium-sized branch.

11

"Were you cold? I was. That's why I came in here. This cave was empty when I chose it, but I'll be happy to share it with you if you'd like. That's a mean storm blowing out there." He added another chunk of wood to the growing fire. "Don't you think the storm seems a little fierce for this early in the season?"

Mother Life, what am I doing carrying on a conversation with a big-toothed cat?

Mach fought the bubble of hysterical laughter rising in his chest. He must keep calm. The cat growled deep in its throat, as if provoked by his words, and it swatted one enormous paw at the flames dancing in the fire pit. He tensed.

I'm going to the Frozen Wilds ... just one more young warrior lost on his Great Travel ... never see Horda again ... never tell her I love her ... mate with her ... carry our little ones in my arms and teach them the ways of the People of the Frozen Earth.

Mach's fear of failure was greater than his fear of the cat. "No!" he roared, jumping to his feet and raising his knife as the great cat leaped. "You will not cheat me of my dreams!"

The cat's fetid breath scorched his face while its claws tore his scalp and twisted in his ebony-colored hair, ripping a swatch out by its roots. Adrenalin, perhaps even more than his warrior's training, powered Mach's arm; he drove his knife into the animal's chest again and again. "I will not walk the Frozen Wilds! I will go home to Horda. I will carry our little ones in my arms. You will not cheat me!"

The cat twitched and heaved, trying to get free, then it collapsed on top of Mach, almost pinning him to the rough cave floor. As he lay there panting with exertion, the blood from his wounds mingled with the cat's, Mother Life and Father Death together as one. Then, with a strength born of his newfound conviction, Mach flung the carcass aside and scrambled to his feet. "I love Horda," he repeated, more softly now. "You will not cheat me."

Chapter 1

Mine.

Horda peered through half-closed eyelids at the rays of the setting sun. They glittered red and blue in Mach's ebony hair and kissed his powerful bronze shoulders — as she wished she could. She smiled to herself.

Mine.

The hustle and bustle of the gathered People of the Frozen Earth faded from her hearing. Her fingers traced the beads on the small leather pouch the handsome young warrior had fashioned for her from the bones and skin of the big cat that attacked him in the long lonely days of his Great Travel.

After living as many winters as the fingers of four hands and completing his Great Travel, the time had come for Mach to choose a mate and take his place as a Father of the Frozen Earth. The necklace, braided from his own hair, declared to the tribe his intention to court Horda. Her heart, as she stood silently by the cook fire, made its own declaration — to choose him.

Other men also courted her, the chief's eldest daughter. Horda accepted the attention of each of her suitors and even enjoyed it, but only Mach made her heart beat faster and filled her with feelings of love and desire.

Ah, Mach, I can't remember when I didn't love you. Please love me, too.

An increasingly familiar warmth washed through her body, and she quickly bent to tend the stew so he wouldn't see the softening of her features as he walked past her father's campsite for the third time that afternoon.

Even before she understood about mating, she had loved Mach. He had been her gentle playmate and friend. Now, old enough to choose a mate, she dreamed only of mating with him. A smile played on her lips, and once more she stroked the fine cord braided from his ebony hair. He had presented gifts to no other eligible maidens.

Please, don't let him change his mind, Mother Life. Let him bid for me.

She raised her eyes and found him watching her, and a slight blush crept up her cheeks. He nodded to her as she met his gaze, but he didn't return her smile — not quite. At times like these he reminded her of an eagle — proud, almost regal, ever watchful. It made him even more desirable. She longed to call out and tell him she would soon be finished so they could walk, but she didn't quite dare, not with so many others around.

Though Gathering provided the time for choosing mates, not all the taboos governing unmated behavior were relaxed. She contented herself with watching the handsome young warrior walk away. She knew he'd return, and they would walk together then.

❋

Still lost in thoughts of Mach, Horda became aware of an unnatural silence. Looking around, she saw all the people looking in a single direction, toward a ragged band approaching the entrance to the camps. One man dominated the handfuls of others. Wrapped in a tattered, dirty bear fur and moving with long, measured strides, he looked more animal than human — not a bear, though. No, more like a mountain lion, poised and waiting to pounce.

Horda's eyes widened and her blood ran cold. *Mother Life, protect us.* As many warriors as she could count on the fingers of five hands stood behind the ragged leader, and all were heavily armed with spears, shields, and war axes. Looking behind them, she felt angry sympathy rise to struggle with her fear. Bowed beneath huge packs and almost unrecognizable from their loads, one hand count of women stood at the edge of the group. What kind of men carried only their arms and overburdened their women so cruelly? A raiding party?

All thoughts of Mach flew from her head when the monstrous leader's cold eyes met hers. Fear clutched at her stomach. She returned to her work, peering at him through her lashes as he led his strange entourage toward her. Horrid black scars like those sometimes caused by uncleaned wounds crossed his cheeks with fearful symmetry. His silver-black eyes roamed up and down her body before he grinned and licked his thick lips, as if anticipating a tasty meal. A predator, yes, and one to be feared.

Questions darted in and out of her mind with lightning quickness. Who were these people? What were they doing at the Gathering, a festive time for her people? Why was their leader staring at her so crudely? Even a child would never be so bold; had he never learned proper manners?

Barely suppressing a shudder, she felt her skin crawl beneath his continued scrutiny. She stirred the antelope stew and kept her eyes averted. Even so, she sensed the man's approach as if she stared straight at him. When he neared the cook fire, her heart hammered in her ears, and her feet itched to run. She raised her head and watched him signal his people to stop beside her father's fire. Then he walked directly toward her. The smells of rancid bear grease, sweat, and dirt overpowered the good aromas of the stew and the sage brush fire and nearly overwhelmed her. She longed to be a child again so she could run and hide behind her mother's tunic.

Mother Life, doesn't he ever bathe?

Three fingers more than three hands old and finished with the rituals that preceded the choosing of a mate, Horda cer-

15

tainly understood the man's lewd interest. She also sensed he enjoyed her discomfort. She reminded herself, though; she was the daughter of the chief. She would not allow him to intimidate her, nor would she show her fear. She raised her eyes to meet his stare. Though she stood as tall as most of the older men in her tribe, she was surprised to find her eyes almost level with the stranger's.

Mother Life, he looked bigger and taller when he surveyed the camp. Is it all an illusion, or am I right to be afraid of this man?

Framed by the grotesque scars, his hawk nose intersected the sharp plane of his high cheekbones before it beaked down toward his chin. His eyes, as they bored into her, shimmered like the deep ice at the center of the river in winter. How could they seem to radiate both heat and cold at once? It was more than a little unsettling, but she would not be rude. She would wait for him to speak first.

Once more the man's eyes roamed up and down her body like dirty fingers. She gritted her teeth and commanded herself not to fidget beneath his gaze. Her eyes flashed her distaste, but that was all she allowed to show.

"Greetings from Zaaco, Chief of the People of the Frozen Earth. I trust you had a pleasant journey." Horda's knees almost buckled when her father's voice rumbled the traditional greeting from behind the stranger. Giving no indication he heard, the man's hard eyes continued to bore into Horda's. Zaaco spoke again, more sharply this time. "Perhaps you did not hear me. Who are you? Why have you joined our Gathering?"

It was a rude question, but not entirely without merit, Horda thought, still staring at the repulsive man. In recent memory, Gathering had included only the bands of the People of the Frozen Earth, but she knew it hadn't always been that way. She vaguely remembered stories about other Peoples attending Gathering before Zaaco became chief ... in the time before the last war. But that was long ago.

With an insolent half smile, the man flipped the ratty bearskin over his shoulder to reveal a short, scarred muscular body clad only in a frayed woven grass breech cloth.

Mother Life, his legs look like peeled tree stumps.

Finally, almost as an afterthought, he turned to face the old chief. "I am Bear Claw, Chief of the People of the Tall Grass. These are some of my people." A negligent wave of his hand acknowledged the ragged men and women waiting huddled beyond Zaaco's camp. Bear Claw's accent was harsher, and his tones more guttural, than those of the People of the Frozen Earth, but his words were familiar. Horda had little trouble understanding him. He gestured toward the packs the women carried. "We've come to trade. We understand this is your time of mating."

He turned to gaze again toward Horda before he continued. "You have many beautiful women. We have few. Many People of the Tall Grass departed in the last long, hungry cold. Most were women and children." He shrugged and smiled a cold smile at Horda, as if that explained enough.

Horda suppressed a shiver.

"I'm not sure I understand," commented Zaaco, still standing his ground.

"We'll trade for some of your women." He leered. "Then we'll make our own little ones. Our tribe will be strong again."

Out of the corner of her eye, Horda watched her father fight to keep his face blank. When he spoke, his voice sounded strained. "Our women are not available for trade."

Surprise or anger shimmered in Bear Claw's eyes, but his voice did not reflect either. It was the same harsh, cold tone that sent shivers up Horda's spine. "Now I don't understand. Isn't this your time of mating?"

Zaaco nodded but did not speak.

"Then how can you say you won't trade? You haven't seen

our goods. I assure you they're fine and different from the things your people make." Bear Claw's voice rose angrily.

"You're correct this is the time of mating among the People of the Frozen Earth, but we don't trade our women," Zaaco said with finality.

But Bear Claw ignored the chief's words. "I told you we brought fine trade goods. You have more women than you need, and we have far too few. We'll all benefit."

Zaaco shook his head slowly. "Perhaps I did not make myself clear. Trading for women is not the way of the People of the Frozen Earth. Our women belong only to themselves. When the time comes for them to mate, the men court them and make bids to show they can care for them. The women choose the men with whom they will mate. There is no barter."

"Why?"

"Why?" Zaaco almost shouted.

Horda fought to keep from smiling at the stormy look on her father's face. He didn't like having his authority questioned and certainly not by an ignorant stranger.

"Sit beside my fire, and I'll explain." Although Zaaco's words sounded cordial, his face reflected his anger. "My daughter will serve us wild rose tea."

Bear Claw's eyes gleamed as he stared at Horda once more, then he seated himself beside the fire. No, not seated, Horda thought, more like crouched. Again the image of the mountain lion sprang into her mind, and she frowned to herself.

Maybe if she ignored the man, at least as much as protocol allowed, he would take his band and go away. She gave the stew a quick stir then prepared and offered Bear Claw a tea brewed from the dried buds of the wild rose. As she served him, though, he caught her hand, squeezing her fingers against the horn until she almost spilled the scalding liquid on both of them.

Her amber eyes shot sparks, but she managed to keep her face blank and ignore the pain spiraling up her arm. Eyes gleaming, Bear Claw smiled coldly and then released her hand almost dismissively. In spite of her resolve to give him no satisfaction, she glared back at him and flexed her numbed fingers. Bear Claw chuckled. It was not a pleasant sound.

Zaaco's brown eyes darkened, and his lips tightened until the wrinkles around his mouth thinned into a straight line, but he did not vent his fury. He had been a chief long enough to know when to fight and when to hold his ground. Horda smiled encouragingly at her father as she handed him his horn of tea. Though anger still flashed in the depths of the old chief's eyes, he spoke softly, "Thank you, daughter. You may leave us."

Wanting to hear what came next, she protested, "But the stew needs —"

"Set it aside and leave us."

"It will not be good if it isn't tended properly," she argued.

Zaaco insisted, "I want you to leave us alone."

Horda knew when to give in herself. "Give me a moment. I'll take the stew to Elko's fire so it won't be ruined."

Zaaco shook his head but said no more. She pulled on protective deerskin hand covers before lifting the bison-stomach cooking bag and carrying it away.

Bear Claw watched her go. "She is beautiful, but she must learn obedience. I am a strong warrior and the Chief of my people. If she were mine, I could teach her to obey." Like Zaaco, he now spoke softly, but his tone carried an unmistakable threat.

"And I will be glad to trade for her," he continued. "Something about her calls to me. I like the spirit flashing in her unusual eyes, and I anticipate great pleasure in taming her. What do you want for her?"

Anger, pain, and a touch of fear flashed behind Zaaco's eyes, but he was strong, like a bison; he allowed none of them to reach his face. "I have already told you she is not mine to trade."

Bear Claw frowned. "She is your daughter."

"Yes."

"She has a mate?"

"No."

"Then I want her."

Zaaco spoke softly but firmly. "That is her decision, not mine. But you should know — our men view women as earthly counterparts of the benevolent Mother Life. They are special." Bear Claw scowled disgustedly, but Zaaco ignored him and went on.

"Through them our tribe continues, so we must treat them with care and love. Women help us and lighten our burdens as we travel the earth filling our horns of time. We do not own them nor do they own us. We are all one People of the Frozen Earth."

Zaaco watched the anger swirl in Bear Claw's icy eyes for a moment before he continued. "We have rules governing mating. Men and women court at Gathering time. Men bid for the women they've chosen by bringing food, furs, hides, and tools to show their ability to care for them. Usually the men and women reach an agreement before the men make their bids, though this is not always the case. And the men have the right not to bid for any of the women they court. As for the women, they have the right to accept or reject any and all bids."

"Bah." Bear Claw spat in the dirt at Zaaco's feet. "This is foolish prattle. Women belong to the men, first the father, then the mate. Men trade for the women they want, and the women have no say. It is the way of the People of the Tall Grass."

"Then clearly your ways are different from our ways."

"Our ways are better. It is too much trouble to have to court some lowly woman."

Zaaco forced himself to smile and speak respectfully. "Some day, if we are looking for mates, we may trek to your Gathering. If that is so, we will trade with you, as is *your* custom."

Bear Claw tensed at the sarcasm concealed behind the old

man's soft words. "We need women now, and we will trade for them." His tone left no room for argument, but Zaaco stood by his people, and his beliefs. He spoke calmly, hoping his reasonableness would forestall any further discord.

"I have told you repeatedly, we do not trade our women, and we will not consider doing so. You have joined our Gathering. If you wish to participate, you are welcome, but only if you agree to our rules. You said you brought fine trade goods. I urge you to use them to bid for the women of your choice."

Bear Claw started to spit again, but the black look in Zaaco's eyes stopped him. He snarled, "Foolishness!"

"This is our Gathering," repeated Zaaco.

Bear Claw's eyes roamed around the camp, then settled on Horda, now working beside Elko's fire. A frown twisted his gruesome scars. His voice, when he spoke, was almost thoughtful. "I don't understand why — perhaps it is the fire in her eyes, or ..." he paused to lick his blubbery lips again "... her ripe body, but I must have your daughter. It is a waste of time, but I will try your way."

Rising, Zaaco replied, "Then you are welcome to join our Gathering. We wish you a pleasant and prosperous time. One of my warriors will show you where your people may camp."

Bear Claw rose without acknowledging the old man's words. Turning away he muttered, just loudly enough for the chief to hear, "I *will* have your daughter, old man."

Zaaco chose not to respond to the younger man's softly spoken threats. He would alert his own warriors in case of trouble, but he would not force a confrontation, at least not now.

The People of the Frozen Earth held that life was sacred and never to be taken lightly, and Zaaco embraced that belief. He also believed, though, that they were the strongest tribe of the Great Plains and could fight for what they cherished. They had avoided war for almost three hands' turnings of the seasons, but the last time they fought, they had annihilated two groups who united to conquer them.

That time and many times before, they had proven their strength by claiming victories in the bloody battles others forced them to fight. Zaaco knew they were still strong, and to him the avoidance of war proved their position of strength rather than weakness. It was important to know when not to fight, as well as when to engage the enemy. His warriors held themselves ready, well-equipped, and well-trained, for whenever such a time to fight might arise.

Such thoughts made Zaaco think back across his long life. He had been a warrior barely in his prime the last time any others truly challenged the People. When that war finally ended, he became the Chief — the youngest chief to lead the People of the Frozen Earth. The seasons had turned one finger less than three hands since then. He looked at his hands now scarred and roped with veins, and he rubbed the vague pain that never completely left the knuckles of his left hand. Though he had grown old, he was still strong.

Zaaco smiled sadly. In those younger days, Horda had been a little girl with big amber eyes and long brown braids that always refused to remain smooth. Now she was a woman grown, and Bear Claw wanted her. But the chief sensed violence seething in Bear Claw, and he feared the peace of the People of the Frozen Earth would soon be shattered unless he sacrificed his daughter to the cruel man's lust. But the decision is hers, he reminded himself, surprised at where his thoughts had led. It is our way.

Chapter 2

Anger flashed through Horda, but she kept her voice deliberately soft. "You have no say in my choice of mate." Meiran's mouth tightened, but she said nothing as she busied herself, spreading the antelope hide ground cloth beside her shelter fire, then sitting and smoothing the wrinkles from her knee-high moccasins and straightening the fringes of her buckskin tunic. Horda waited, breathing hard. Sometimes her mother could be as stubborn and as difficult to speak with as a she-bear.

Finally, hunching her arms protectively around her lower body, Meiran replied simply. "I'm your mother."

Horda struggled to match her mother's quiet tone but did not quite succeed. "I know that. But it doesn't give you the right to choose my mate."

"Horda, sit down. You aren't thinking clearly. You need to listen to your elders." She waited until Horda dropped unceremoniously to the ground before she continued.

"I am the number one mate of the Chief of the People of the Frozen Earth." Meiran smiled as she patted the ornate coiffure, which she often told Horda made her the most beautiful of the women. "And you are the eldest daughter. Many men seek to claim you. You must consider each man carefully, as the correct choice will increase your father's power."

Uncharitably, Horda remembered her mother became the number one mate only because the two older mates walked the Frozen Wilds. "My father has all the power he needs."

"How can you say such a thing, you foolish girl? No one ever has all the power they need. And your father grows old." Meiran clucked softly under her breath, more like a bird than a she-bear now. "An alliance with the People of the Tall Grass would strengthen his position. Your mating with Bear Claw will stop the threat of war with them."

Horda bit her lips and lowered her eyes. She did not want her mother to see how deep the fear and revulsion ran in her when she thought of the foreign chief. To her young eyes, Bear Claw appeared almost as old as her father and certainly, with his fearsome tattoos and scars, much uglier. Her nose crinkled at the memory of the smells of rancid fat, sweat, and dirt that swirled around him like a dirty fog. Gingerly and almost absentmindedly, she flexed fingers still tender from his crushing grip. She had seen cruelty in his eyes. She sensed he enjoyed inflicting pain. The thought of mating with him caused her to shiver visibly.

Meiran took her daughter's silence as consent and continued, "I know your father is supposed to be the chief for the rest of his life, but," she continued ominously, "someone may try to shorten his days to take his place as leader. I see no way for you to refuse if Bear Claw bids for you."

Horda longed to snort like an angry bison or shriek like a frightened big cat, but she didn't dare. Her mother, always mindful of position, pushed her to choose a mate whose power was assured, no matter what the People said about her own right to decide.

Meiran paused to consider. "If some way can be found to refuse Bear Claw's offer, I suppose you might choose Norlon. No one except the chief, of course, has more power than the Medicine Man." Warming to her favorite topic, Meiran's black eyes gleamed. "Think of the honor and power which will be yours as Norlon's number one mate. Why, young as he is, he is already an accomplished healer. Some people actually prefer to take their illnesses to him." Since before last Gathering, her mother had tried to convince her to choose Norlon. Horda frowned and pretended to listen to the familiar words, but she couldn't focus on them. "Some day he will become the Medicine Man of the entire tribe of the People of the Frozen Earth. That would really be even better for your father and me than having you mated to this Chief of the People of the Tall Grass."

Anger and frustration boiled within Horda's gut, and it was only with great effort she brought her voice under control. "Ma, I told you before the last Gathering I wouldn't choose Norlon. He's my friend, nothing more."

Meiran's mouth turned down at the words, but after only a brief moment she nodded. "It doesn't really matter. I'm sure Bear Claw will bid for you, so then you can choose him."

"I'll certainly choose death before I choose Bear Claw." Horda's words were soft, but they carried an unshakable determination. Stubborn as a she-bear herself, her father would chide her.

"Oh, really? How childish! Whom would you choose?" Meiran's lip curled and she shook her head. "The brash young toad, Mach?"

"If he chooses me, I will." Horda felt her anger drain away at the mention of the man's name, and she knew a smile played across her face. No matter. It was best her mother knew something of her heart, although she dared not mention Mach had effectively chosen her by not offering gifts to any other maidens.

Meiran glowered. "If you are so selfish, our entire world will burst into war. You owe it to the People of the Frozen Earth to stop such a war from happening. Bear Claw wants you, and he intends to have you — one way or the other." Meiran's voice softened until it was cajoling. "Little Bear," she said, trying to use the childish nickname to smooth things over, "you're scarcely more than a girl. You must listen to your elders. I know you've almost completed the Rituals of Womanhood, but you don't understand power and position yet. Not really."

"I understand Bear Claw is cruel and will take pleasure in hurting me."

"You foolish girl. You've hardly spoken with him, so how can you say such a thing? I'm sure he wouldn't purposely hurt you, any more than one of our own People. He wants you very much. He told Zaaco. Think of it. You'll be the mate of the Chief of all the People of the Tall Grass. You'll have much power. That alone is worth the choice." Refusing to meet Horda's eyes, Meiran repeated softly, "He wouldn't dare hurt you. Your father wouldn't allow it."

Icy fingers of fear grasped Horda's insides. Her bruised fingers throbbed, reminding her of the pain Bear Claw was capable of inflicting. "Not now, perhaps, but what will happen when he takes me far away to live with his people? Who'll stop him from hurting me then?" Tears filled her eyes. "Ma, I'm afraid of him. I can't choose him."

"And I am afraid of war. You were but a young child when our people last fought. You don't remember it, but I do. The pain, the terror. You can stop it with this one act." Meiran snapped out of her reverie and glared at Horda. "You alone can prevent it. Not to choose Bear Claw is selfish, and you must consider the consequences for everyone of that decision. And anyway, you're the daughter of the chief of all the People. Even without Bear Claw, Mach is an entirely unsuitable choice."

"I love him, Ma."

Meiran ignored Horda's words. "He has no power to share. He's very young."

"He has but one less winter than Norlon."

Meiran waved away Horda's words as if they were pesky smoke wafting its way out of the small sleeping shelter. "He's barely a warrior. He's daring, true, but he has no real sponsor. His father's only the second chief in a middle band. At best he'll become the leader of a second-rate band. Bear Claw, on the other hand, is the chief of a whole tribe just like your father."

Meiran smiled dreamily. "Unlike Mach, he has real power. Even Norlon has power of a sort — he was born to it. He's a medicine man. He will be Medicine Man. His place in the Inner Band is assured. Can't you understand? You must choose well. You owe it to me."

Horda bit her lips to stop her angry words. She knew the warrior Council already looked on the young Mach with favor. They found him strong and daring, a natural leader. Didn't her mother know Zaaco, the chief, planned to sponsor Mach himself? She repeated, "I love Mach, Ma, no one else."

"Ha! Love. What do you know of love? You belong to the Inner Band while he barely walks the edges. You have all the special treatment afforded the daughter of the chief. Can you deny you enjoy the advantages and friendships your position brings? You'll give it all up if you choose that young boy." Meiran's voice softened. "And you may not understand it now, but love between mates grows. You'll learn to love the man you choose, even if you don't now."

Horda's long hair curtained her face so her mother couldn't see the tears trickling down her cheeks. Advantages? Yes, she dressed well in fine leather garments, but for the past hand of winters she sewed her own garments from hides she herself prepared. She'd continue to do so, regardless of whom she chose.

True, members of the Inner Band ate well, but at the last three Gatherings, she'd been named the best gatherer in the Inner Band. At the two Gatherings before Mach began his Great Travel, he'd been recognized A Most Able Hunter, and she was sure his time alone only sharpened his skills. The two of them would eat well, no matter which band they joined.

Friendships? Many people pretended to be her friends because she was the chief's daughter. Too often she heard her *friends* discussing her — her unusual eyes the color of fresh honey and her strange hair, lightened by the sun until it bore the colors of the prairie grasses at Gathering. She absentmindedly smoothed the curling strands away from her face. They would never stay in the smooth braids the others admired so much.

She couldn't remember a time when Mach, two winters older than she, wasn't her friend. Her earliest memories of Gathering were of Mach patiently teaching her the games the other children seemed to play so effortlessly. Of Mach helping her find the best hiding places during games of hide and seek. Of Mach watching when she raced, and of Mach cheering — not because she won, since she seldom did, but because she didn't give up knowing she wouldn't.

More tears pooled in her eyes and trickled down her cheeks. Time separated them. They grew apart. A hand plus one of Gatherings ago he entered the First Hunt Rituals of Manhood and left her behind in childhood. But she never stopped watching him, remembering, and hoping.

Then three Gatherings ago, two older boys from a distant band caught her alone. Tangling their fingers in her strange hair and pulling as if they meant to rip it out, they told her she didn't belong to the People of the Frozen Earth but was a foundling from another tribe. They taunted and insulted her, touching, pinching, and poking until she fell and wrapped her arms around her head, trying to protect herself. Her tears and cries excited them to greater cruelty, and they tormented her without letup.

Mach appeared from nowhere. Taller than most men of the tribe even then, he caught the boys by the scruffs of their necks. "Hiyah! What are you doing?" He shouted and shook them until their teeth clicked together before dropping them into a heap at his feet.

"We're only playing with the foundling," huffed the braver of the two boys, scrambling to his feet. "We aren't hurting her." Several strands of light brown hair were wrapped around the fingers of his right hand.

Mach glared and caught a hank of the boy's ebony hair, giving it a mighty yank. "Ouch!" The boy rubbed the roots of his hair.

"I'm only playing. I'm not hurting you," Mach mimicked, giving another tug. He looked pointedly at the hairs tangled around the boy's hand. "And I didn't even pull any out." Raising himself to his full height, Mach said, "This foundling is a woman, Mother Life's emissary on earth. As a Man of the Frozen Earth, it's your duty to protect her and care for her — not harm her."

The boys shuffled to their feet and studied the toes of their moccasins without replying.

"Such behavior could be called before the Council." Mach glared, and the color drained from the boys' faces.

"We didn't know. We ... ah ... heard someone ... say ... she was a foun —"

"Silence!" Mach's voice was quiet, but it held an authority well beyond his years. He allowed the boys to fidget uncomfortably for a few moments before he continued. "Perhaps if you apologize politely and never let such a disgraceful thing happen again, I won't call the Elders' attention to your behavior."

Horda's mouth curved into a gentle smile at the memory; never once had Mach mentioned her status as the Chief's eldest daughter. The boys stammered apologies then tripped over themselves and each other to put as much distance between themselves and Mach's wrath as they could.

She'd almost been afraid herself, but when Mach knelt beside her, only gentleness remained in his manner. She could still feel how tenderly his rough fingertips had dried her tears. And hear his soft voice telling her how different and beautiful he thought her hair. How special she was. Lightly, like a spring breeze, he had brushed the tangles back from her face and smiled into her eyes. In that instant she gave him her heart. And she never wanted to take it back.

Advantages as a member of the Inner Band? None she would miss.

True, more men than the fingers of both her hands courted her in her time of choosing a mate. Even some whose manner showed they found her unusual hair and eyes distasteful sought to ally themselves with her father by mating with her.

A wry smile lifted the corner of her mouth. Seeing Emol's face when she walked away from the Bid Ceremony on Mach's arm would give her great pleasure. Emol, fat and lazy, with only three fewer winters than her father, led one of the small outer bands. Under his weak guidance, his people had grown as slovenly as he. He boasted she'd have to choose him because he was a ranking leader, and already he spoke of the positions he would seek for his sons. No, she certainly wouldn't mind disappointing him.

She thought about all the other men of the People who sought to mate with her. She knew little more than the names of most. They were simply men of the tribe. She had no feelings for any, but one...

Pain nibbled at her heart and erased her smile. Norlon's handsome young face framed by his smooth black braids shone clearly in her mind's eye. Both members of the Inner Band, Horda and Norlon's friendship began when they were small children. She trained with his father to be a healer woman, while Norlon prepared to become the tribe's Medicine Man. Because of their studies, they remained close even after Norlon entered the Rituals of Manhood. She liked him, even loved him, but she wasn't in love with him. In her heart, she knew Mother Life didn't intend her life to be bound to his.

Norlon completed his Great Travel at the previous Gathering and could have chosen a mate at that time. She had hoped he'd decide to choose another woman, but he didn't. She'd spent the past turning of the seasons avoiding him more carefully than the mores of the tribe required.

Norlon accepted her behavior without asking her any questions. She missed him, but as a friend; her heart, her soul, belonged to Mach. He would understand that, wouldn't he? Her mother certainly didn't. And her father? She wasn't sure.

Then thoughts of Bear Claw crashed into her mind. Did her mother speak the truth? Would war result if she didn't choose him? Could she take such a chance?

Meiran's voice rambled on, and Horda's thoughts returned to Mach's handsome face. The carved bone beads grew warm between her breasts, and a single tear traced its lonely path down her cheek.

Oh, Mother Life, please help me know what's right.

Chapter 3

The sun's first rays lightened the indigo sky to pewter as Horda walked the river path to fetch water. The early mists swirling around her moccasined feet made her feel she was strolling above the clouds and chased her worries away.

Lost in her daydream, she did not see the tall, lithe figure of Mach until she was beside him. She gazed at him. His ebony hair glistened in the morning sun, and the muscles of his arms rippled when he reached to take the water bags she carried.

"Greetings, Mach." She tried to keep her tone pleasantly neutral, as if he were only a friend.

His deep mahogany eyes danced. "Greetings to you, Horda. I trust you rested well with pleasant dreams."

"I did. And you?"

"Yes, my sleep was restful and my dreams were pleasant." Though his tone matched hers, his eyes hinted at a shared intimacy. "By your smile, I trust you're thinking good thoughts this day."

Do my thoughts betray me? Horda wondered silently. The mere sound of his deep voice sent shivers up and down her spine. A blush crept up to tint her cheeks. She'd told her mother she would choose this man, but he hadn't made a true bid for her. Perhaps he never would. Then her problem would be solved, at least as far as her mother was concerned. But Horda knew if he didn't bid for her, the emptiness would be unbearable, and she'd walk the Frozen Wilds with Father Death. Hmm, at least

Bear Claw wouldn't worry her then.

Horda found with all these thoughts racing around in her head, the words she wanted to share with Mach had disappeared, and her tongue had somehow tied itself in knots.

Mach smiled, then prompted, "Do I dare hope you think of me?"

"Not exactly," she managed.

He quirked one eyebrow and persisted, "No? Then what made you smile so prettily?"

"I was just thinking."

"About us?"

His hopeful face forced the truth past her lips. "No, about the mist."

"The mist?" He sounded vaguely disappointed.

She took a deep breath and said in a rush, "I thought walking through the mist must be like walking on the clouds." Her cheeks grew hotter, and she knew her blush had grown even darker. "I'm sure you must believe me a fool to think such things, but I do. The thoughts are comforting, and they allow me to forget everything else."

A grin curved Mach's mouth and danced in his dark eyes. It made her blush even hotter, this time with the anguish of shame. He was laughing at her. He saw her for the crazy dreamer she was, and he would never bid for her. Tears gathered in her eyes, and she turned quickly to run away.

But Mach reached out and caught her hand to stop her flight. Gently he turned her around and forced her face up until she looked into his eyes. His grin melted to a tender smile that transformed the hard planes of his warrior's face into something much softer — the face of a lover. "Then I'm a fool because I too dream of walking above the clouds."

She looked into his deep mahogany eyes and thought she would drown in their depths. Her jaw tingled where his fingers touched it. She gulped, "You do?"

"I do." A bright jay landed on a boulder and paused to scold the young couple invading its territory. Mach watched it fly out of sight before he looked once more into her eyes. "Sometimes I wish I could fly like the birds. I try to imagine the freedom they feel soaring high above the earth."

"You do?" Her voice squeaked. *Oh, Mother Life, was that all she could come up with?*

But Mach seemed not to notice her discomfort. He nodded solemnly and explained, "Once I talked to a man who came from behind the mountains. He told me about places where the peaks reach up beyond the clouds and touch the sky. I want to go there someday."

"Would it really be possible for us to go there? To walk so high we were above the clouds?" She bit her lip. She shouldn't have said that. He hadn't even bid for her, and she was talking as if they'd walk together for the rest of their lives.

Mach shrugged and said with a trace of bitterness, "The man swore he told me the truth, but when I repeated the stranger's words, my father laughed and insisted such a thing wasn't possible."

Then his voice softened again, and he caught her cool hands in his large warm ones. "I still want to see for myself whether the stranger spoke the truth. Someday I'll find out. We will go together to see if we can truly walk above the clouds."

Horda's heart twisted even as her eyes widened in delight, but she did not speak. It was almost too much to hope for.

He rushed on. "At this Gathering, I'll be recognized as a Father of the Frozen Earth. My skills as a hunter and a warrior aren't questioned, but I'm not a chief. I know other more powerful men court you, but I want you to be my number one mate. I will take care of you. I love you. I've always loved you."

Mach's smile faded when he saw tears sparkling in Horda's eyes. She reached up quickly to touch the line of his jaw and assure him all was well between them. "I would be happy to accept your bid. I wouldn't care whether we walked the earth or above it so long as we walked together."

"You would?" His voice was hopeful, but disbelief etched small lines in his broad forehead. "Why are you crying then?"

She sobbed. "Because I'm afraid."

"Of me?"

She sniffed and shook her head. "You saw the Chief of the People of the Tall Grass?"

"Yes."

"He wants me. He has said so."

"Do you want him?"

"No."

Now he reached out and hugged her tightly. His size made her feel small and delicate, even though she wasn't. He tilted his head down and gently breathed against her mouth. Trembling, she pressed her lips against his.

Mach laughed aloud. "Then don't choose him. Choose me."

"I want to choose you, but I'm frightened. My mother says Bear Claw will have me — one way or another. She says if I don't choose him, he and his people will cause a war. She says —"

Tiny sparks of anger flared in the depths of Mach's eyes, but he kept his voice calm. "I don't believe it. It's not that you're not worth it, but we have too many warriors for him to defeat. He knows we would slay his men, leaving the rest of their band defenseless."

"His warriors number more than a hand of hands."

Mach's light laugh sounded forced. "And our warriors number more hands than you can keep track of without a counting cord. Surely even he can see such a war would be over before it began."

Hope flickered in her heart. "Do you really think so?"

"I do. Don't trouble yourself any more about it."

Horda barely managed to keep herself from tapping the toe of her moccasin on the packed dirt as she watched Zaaco eating his morning yampah root porridge. How could anyone eat so slowly? When he appeared to be considering a second helping, she decided she could wait no longer. "Fa, I need to talk to you."

Zaaco scraped the last bit of his porridge from the wooden platter. A teasing light danced in his dark brown eyes. "So sit down and talk." He picked up his drinking gourd filled with yarrow tea and blew gently before testing the heat of the brew.

Horda cast a nervous glance toward her mother. She whispered, "I'd rather walk beside the river with you."

Following her look, Zaaco gulped down his tea. Wiping a hand across his mouth, he said, "My mates and my daughters, I thank you for the morning eat." He grinned at Horda and murmured conspiratorially, "Come on, then."

They walked in silence until they were almost out of sight of the camp. Zaaco paused and plucked a stalk of grass, which he stuck in the corner of his mouth. "I don't think your mother can hear you now, Horda. What troubles you?"

A guilty blush crawled up the young woman's face. "I didn't mean —"

Her father chuckled. "Your mother's a fine woman, but she sometimes gets overexcited about things, especially those which don't really concern her. What's the matter?"

"Fa, I'm choosing a mate at this Gathering."

The old chief rubbed his face and wiggled his eyebrows in a perfect parody of surprise, dropping the grass stalk as an added touch. "Really? I wondered why so many young and old bucks cluttered our shelter area. Is that the reason? My little daughter is choosing a mate?" He furrowed his brow and pretended to ponder. "I don't think she's old enough. Are you sure?"

"Fa, don't tease me." But Horda laughed in spite of herself.

"Why not? It may be my last chance. I certainly won't be

allowed to tease a grown woman, at least not in front of others."
He grew suddenly more serious. "I've seen at least two hands'
count of men hanging around. Which one are you going to
choose?"

Horda ducked her head. "Ma wanted me to choose Norlon."

"Norlon will soon be the Medicine Man of all the tribe. I
know your mother would like that." He grinned at her. "And
you've always been friends. He'd be a perfect mate for you."

"I don't want to choose him. I don't love him."

"Love grows. Its absence at this stage is not necessarily a
problem."

"But I love another."

"Ah, now that could be a problem." A comic look of dismay
twisted Zaaco's features. "It isn't Emol, is it? You don't plan to
choose him, do you?"

Horda smiled. Her father's opinion of the fat and lazy chief
was well known within the family. "No, Fa, it isn't Emol. I don't
even like him."

"Well, good. That shows some intelligence anyway. Now, I
suppose you're going to tell me you love that little ..." He paused,
narrowing his eyes, then went on, "well, actually not so little,
toad Mach, and you want to choose him even though your
mother has told you how totally unsuitable he is for the daughter of the Chief of all the People. I believe she must even have
said something about him being the leader of a second rate band
or some such nonsense." He grinned down at her.

Horda gasped. "How did you know?"

"It's my business to know these things, daughter." Zaaco
nodded before admitting, "Your mother does babble. I imagine
she's told me the same things she told you."

"Oh. Then you know." A small frown puckered Horda's
smooth brow, then she turned away from her father. What more
was there to say?

Zaaco caught her arm and forced her to face him. "Know

what?"

"That she's decided I must choose Bear Claw."

"No," he said softly, "she didn't tell me that." Only a muscle twitching in Zaaco's wrinkled cheek betrayed his distress. "Do you want to choose Bear Claw?"

Reluctantly, Horda met her father's eyes. "No, but she says if I don't choose him I'll cause war. She's afraid, and so am I."

The old chief spoke slowly. "The woman chooses her own mate. No one, not even her mother, has the right to force her choice."

Anguish sharpened her voice. "Even for the good of the tribe?"

She watched uncertainty flicker in Zaaco's eyes. Finally the chief spoke. "The People of the Frozen Earth are a peaceful people. We've learned through many turnings of the seasons that all of us working together make our survival possible. Life is a gift and shouldn't be wasted because once it is gone, it cannot be called back. Even so, we accept the fullness of time and know every living thing's time has an end.

"Mother Life forbids aggression, so we avoid war. But even so, the People of the Frozen Earth aren't weak. We remain ready to defend ourselves — our warriors are well equipped and well trained, in a variety of weapons — spears, knives, hatchets, war sticks, the small spear throwers, and the slings. Long ago we proved our super ..." At Horda's growing smile, his voice trailed off to silence.

"Is that the speech you give the boys when they enter the Rituals of Manhood?" she chided him. "Remember, I'm a woman."

He tweaked her nose. "Don't be fresh. All I'm telling you is we've lived in peace for almost three hands' turnings of the seasons because others know we're victorious when they force us to fight."

Horda felt the hope flaring within her. It warmed her and made her feel strong. She would not have to choose the foreign chief because the People's warriors could and would fight those who threatened their way of life, including Bear Claw and the People of the Tall Grass. Impatient words bubbled up, but she pushed them back. There could be strength in silence, too.

Now Zaaco's eyes looked beyond his daughter, to something only he could see. He chose his next words even more carefully than before. "But we cannot only think of ourselves. All our lives the People of the Frozen Earth are taught each person must do whatever is needed to ensure the survival of all. We strive to give our little ones an understanding of and appreciation for each person's role in doing that. It is the duty of each of us to do whatever is necessary to keep all of us strong. We must survive, not just as individuals, but as a tribe."

Now the hope faded, leaving Horda's hands and heart icy once more. Tears filled her eyes and threatened to spill down her cheeks. "Are you telling me to choose Bear Claw?" she asked, her voice almost a whisper.

Staring into her father's eyes, she thought the silence would stretch forever. His wrinkled face creased with lines of sadness, and he brought his hand up as if to wipe them away. When he finally spoke, it was so softly she had to lean close to hear his words. "It is not my right to tell you whom to choose as your mate."

Horda's anger flared — anger at her father for saying so many different things. Anger at herself for not understanding, for feeling so lost. "Even for the good of the tribe?"

"Who can say which alliance would be best for the tribe?" Zaaco answered.

"Even if I were to agree, the People of the Tall Grass are so different from us. They treat their women as pack animals. They don't wash often, and it's summer." She wrinkled her nose in an almost childish expression of disgust. "Imagine how they smell in the winter."

Zaaco smiled once again. "You're right. It's not a pleasant thought. But perhaps the right woman could teach them the joys of bathing."

Remembering Bear Claw's fierce eyes and his demanding tone, remembering the men's cruelty and the women's submissive stance, Horda shuddered. "I doubt anyone could teach them anything."

Zaaco remained silent now, his features impassive.

Suddenly she burst out, "Why won't you tell me what I should do?"

"Because I don't know."

"You don't know?"

"No."

"I don't understand."

"Even though I am many turns of the seasons old, I do not know everything. This Bear Claw and his band came into our camp only yesterday. I don't know him, nor do I know his intentions beyond what he has told me. I sense there's much he hasn't said. Perhaps many other warriors and women wait in the hills to attack us. Our scouts are out looking, of course, but their survey will take time.

"If there are no others, the danger that Bear Claw can cause significant damage to the People of the Frozen Earth at this time is small. But who can say what they will do in the future?" He shrugged. "You, daughter, must make your own decision about whom you'll mate."

Horda nervously caressed the necklace she wore.

"You want to choose Mach even though he is young and has no power?"

"Yes."

"You and he will live in one of the outer bands. If the People of the Tall Grass attack, most likely they'll attack those bands first because they're the farthest away from our numbers. You know that?"

She nodded.

"Mach's not weak. Any band he's part of will fight

admirably, I'm sure." He paused and seemed to consider his next words. "You know he plans to dance the Dance of the Sun this Gathering?"

Horda's eyes flared with both pain and fear. She hadn't known. The Dance of the Sun was an important rite of passage for the elite warriors of the People. It was a way for them to receive helpful visions and prove their courage. But it was also a difficult ordeal, and sometimes it was deadly. Mach's life would be at stake.

Zaaco reached out a comforting hand to his daughter. "The seasons have turned many times since one so young considered such a bold move. Already Mach strives to prove himself worthy of a position of leadership."

Horda bit her lip and swallowed the words of fear clogging her throat.

"Even so, Mach may never make his way back to the Inner Band. If he doesn't, his number one mate won't either." His dark eyes searched her lighter ones for understanding.

"I know, and I don't care." Horda clasped her hands before her and looked pleadingly at her father. "Mach is special, and I know he'll take care of me. I want to mate with him no matter which band we belong to."

"Has Mach spoken to you?"

Horda blushed furiously at the memory of their hugging and sharing of breath. At the time those actions had seemed perfectly reasonable, but now she realized they were completely against the strict pre-mating rules of the tribe. Avoiding her father's eyes, she whispered, "Yes."

Zaaco frowned but did not question further. "I have but one request, then — as your chief."

Reluctantly she met Zaaco's eyes, almost afraid to hear what he had to say. "What?"

"At least consider Bear Claw. Perhaps he's not as bad as he seems."

Horda sought words to describe her revulsion, but before she could speak her father went on, "And Norlon cares for you ... a great deal I think."

Horda looked down at her beaded moccasin. "I swear by Mother Life and Father Death I haven't tried to encourage him."

"I didn't think you had, daughter." Zaaco touched her shoulder. "Sometimes these things just happen."

"I don't want to hurt him, Fa, but I don't want to choose him. He's special to me, but more like an older brother ..."

A brother. The faces of his elder sons, each gone from his cook fire for more than one hand of fingers, sprang into Zaaco's conscious mind. And he could hear again the piping voice of tiny Horda reporting real and imagined slights committed by the teasing boys — two grown into men and one gone to the Frozen Wilds. Zaaco laughed and said, "I didn't think you even liked your brothers most of the time."

A telltale blush heated her face. "I wanted to, truly I did, but they always teased me so and —"

"They did like to tease the little girl, didn't they?" Zaaco pulled her into his arms and hugged her. "Ah, well, your brothers aren't the problem any longer, are they?"

She shook her head. "What should I do, Fa?"

Zaaco considered her question. "Be kind to him. Yet you must discourage him — don't give him false hope."

"I never intended to give him any hope at all." She chewed her lower lip.

"I think you must speak with him."

"Must I?" she asked, with just a touch of desperation in her voice.

"Yes, daughter, you must." Zaaco's voice was firm but kind.

"Do I need to speak with the others?"

"Let them find out at the Bid Ceremony." He paused, and a tender smile lighted the harsh planes of his face. "Don't get me wrong, you're a lovely young woman, but I think you know many of those men hope to use you to find favor with me."

She nodded but remained silent.

"Well, I'm glad it didn't work." He hugged her tightly and spoke with an unusual raspiness in his voice. "I love you, little girl, and I'll miss you."

Tears prickled the back of her nose, and she threw herself into his arms — a small child, just a little longer. "I love you, Fa," she whispered against his neck. Looking up, she forced a smile. "I'll talk to Norlon."

"And don't turn Bear Claw down just yet. Get to know him before you make your final decision known. Perhaps you'll find he's a fine man."

And perhaps bison will fly like eagles, she thought, but she reluctantly promised, "I won't turn him down, not yet."

They walked together back to the encampment. At the first tents Zaaco caught his daughter's arm. She waited as he cleared his throat. "Horda, although I cannot tell you what to do, I must tell you this much. I don't believe your young Mach will be a second-rate leader." The hazy expression in his eyes told her he looked beyond at things she could not see.

After a long pause, he spoke again. "I didn't expect it to begin so soon, but changes are coming to our People. Our whole way of life must adjust, or we'll disappear like the smoke from the morning fires. Someday when the People need him the most, I believe Mach will walk in my moccasins. I don't know whether you'll walk by his side or not. Perhaps ..."

Not a shaman, Zaaco didn't seek visions and dreams, but Horda knew he often did, in fact, see beyond the present. It was part of what made him such a good chief. Still, she was no less confused than when she sought her father's counsel. She wondered whether it was pride or fear that caused the shiver now tracing tiny fingers up and down her spine.

Chapter 4

During the first moon after the fall harvest, but before the blizzards walked the land, all bands of the alliance that made up the People of the Frozen Earth journeyed to the central Gathering grounds. Gathering served as a combination legislative session, marriage brokerage, fair, vacation, military training camp, special school, and celebration of life. The People looked forward to it throughout the year and welcomed the change it brought from the monotonous routine of their days.

Gathering was also a time of choosing mates, so the taboo forbidding private contact between unmated couples was relaxed. Fearing she had already avoided one such contact far too long, Horda sought Norlon, the young medicine man, before the morning sun reached above the tallest trees. She found him beside his family's cook fire, surrounded by the people his father trained. A bright smile lighted his dark brown eyes when he saw her, gentling the sharp planes of his high cheekbones, and piercing her heart with the pain of what she must do.

Though the words nearly choked her, Horda forced the traditional greeting past her stiff lips. "Norlon, I trust you are having a happy Gathering."

Sensing her distress, Norlon's smile wavered and his face grew solemn, but his voice remained steady. "Yes, I am. I trust you, too, are enjoying an exceptional time."

Sadness darkened the amber honey of her eyes to brown, and her voice grew small. "No, Norlon, I am not ... exactly."

He studied her face, pain flickering in his eyes at what he saw there and then said simply, "Would you walk with me? Perhaps, a talk with an old friend will help improve your Gathering."

Tears gathered on her eyelashes, but she refused them permission to fall. They would only make this worse. She nodded her assent then led him slowly away from the hustle and bustle of the cook fires to the path beside the river. The world was alive with the vibrant sounds of the gurgling river, whirring insects, and twittering birds, but the silence between them stretched, grew taut, and then uncomfortable.

Horda sought the words to refuse this gentle young man, but none seemed right. Finally, in desperation she simply blurted, "Norlon, you spoke the truth. You are my friend ... my dear friend."

Only the tightening of the skin around his eyes betrayed his pain. "But not your love."

A single tear traced its way down her rounded cheek. "No, not my love," she admitted.

"Men, older and more powerful than I, seek the hand of the chief's eldest daughter. I knew in my heart you wouldn't choose me." He paused, and for an unguarded instant his strong features revealed the heartache raging within. Then he forced his expression to become smooth and said levelly, "But I had hoped."

"I'm sorry, Norlon, truly I am." Horda's voice broke. "I love you like I have always loved you. Like I will always love you."

"Like a brother." His words were tinged with a bitterness she didn't expect.

"Like a friend," she said, desperate to make it right between them.

His dark eyes bored into hers. "What difference does the word make? Neither is a mate, is it?" Abruptly he turned back toward the camp.

She knew he expected no answer to that question, but she

felt she owed him one. Gently she called out, "My mother wanted me to choose you."

"It's not her right to choose your mate." His back was still toward her, but he stopped where he was. Then turning stiffly, as if trying to control a deep-seated anger, he growled, "Why are you telling me this?"

His pain was hers now, and she fairly cried, "You are my friend. I wanted to give you time to prepare yourself."

"Prepare myself to see the woman I love choose some lazy old chief who only wants her for the prestige she brings him?" He snarled, "Never as long as I live will I have time to prepare myself for that."

Her words were hesitant. "I am not certain whom I will choose."

"Maybe not, but you know you won't choose me." Norlon glared at her for a moment, and then realization dawned. "By the Father's dirty teeth. You plan to choose the young calf Mach, don't you?" It was almost an accusation.

Horda could hardly push her words past the lump in her throat. "I planned to choose him, but now I don't know."

Norlon's pain deafened him to her words, and he raged. "You're choosing a nobody, one who just returned from his Great Travel. He has no status, no prestige. He hasn't even completed the ceremony. Is that really better than what I could give?"

The tears Horda had tried so hard to stop ran down her cheeks, and she sobbed. "I love Mach, but now I'm afraid to choose him."

Horda's tears cooled Norlon's anger. He saw and heard the anguish she was feeling, and his features softened. He reached out to her. "What do you mean? Why are you afraid to choose Mach?"

"B-b-bear Claw shows interest in me."

"Bear Claw? Why would you even consider him? He is dirty and rude, and from what I've seen he is cruel. His women are little more than beasts of burden. Have you taken leave of your senses?"

"He threatens war."

"War? What are you talking about?"

"I heard him talking to Zaaco. His tribe lost many people last winter, and they have more men than women. His tribe trades for women, as if they were furs or tools, and he wants to trade for me. When Zaaco explained they had to bid like everyone else, Bear Claw told him how strong and well armed his warriors are and how willing they are to fight. He said he would have me." Though tears still ran down her cheeks, Horda's voice did not falter until she ran out of breath.

"You're worrying yourself over nothing. I'm sure it won't come to war," said Norlon.

Horda shook her head. "I'm not so sure."

"Well, even if it did, I'm sure your father would tell you we are prepared to fight," said Norlon.

"Yes, but —."

"But nothing. It's settled."

"I talked to him. It's not."

"What do you mean?"

"I tried to get him to tell me whether I should choose Bear Claw or not."

"And?"

"And he told me how many well-trained warriors we have and how few they seem to have."

"See, nothing to worry about," Norlon grinned.

"But then he told me how it's the duty of each Person of the Frozen Earth to do everything he can to ensure the survival of the tribe."

"Oh," Norlon frowned. "Then it sounds like he's telling you to make up your own mind."

"Even I understood that much."

"I don't see what the problem is."

"I'm scared of Bear Claw," she said. "That's the problem."

"I'm sure our warriors can defeat him."

"But how many of our people will walk the Frozen Wilds because of me?"

Norlon shook his head. "I cannot answer your question. I can only tell you I think you'd be making a bad mistake to choose him. One look at the way he treats the women they brought with them should tell you that."

"They are even thinner than the men, and dirtier, too." She wrinkled her nose in memory of the stench surrounding the People of the Tall Grass.

"I have heard the men shouting at their women, and I believe they hit them."

Horda's eyes widened, and she shuddered. "Hit them?" Though small children were swatted to get their attention when they misbehaved, the People of the Frozen Earth did not tolerate physical abuse — in any form.

"Whether you reconsider choosing me or not, you must think long and carefully before you choose Bear Claw. I believe he's more dangerous to his women than he is to our warriors."

"Honestly?" Hope flared anew in Horda's eyes.

Norlon nodded solemnly.

"You really don't think I should choose him?"

"It's not my place to tell you whom to choose, but I would fear for you for the rest of your life if you chose Bear Claw." At the look of hope suffusing her face, Norlon knew he had truly lost her. With no other words left to say, he turned from her and walked away.

❁

Horda watched the sun paint oranges, pinks, and purples across the pale blue evening sky before it sank behind the jagged peaks of the mountains. She touched Mach's necklace and smiled.

Thank you, Mother Life, for today.

Free since helping prepare the morning eat at sunrise, she had finished decorating her new doeskin moccasins with tiny bone beads and porcupine quills for the Bid Ceremony. Now it was time for the evening eat. She shouldered the pouch containing her beading tools and moccasins and started back to her father's campsite.

She flung her arms wide to embrace the beautiful sky. If she hadn't hurt Norlon and worried about Bear Claw, it would have been a perfect day. But it was still a good one, and she was grateful for it.

Although Gathering didn't officially begin until sunrise tomorrow with the Ceremony of the Great Traveler, tonight they would have guests for the evening eat. Maybe, just maybe, Mach would join them. She wrinkled her nose. She certainly hoped Bear Claw wouldn't.

As she walked to the campsite, her mood improved. The evening breeze wafted the luscious smells of special foods being prepared for the Feast of the Great Traveler to her. They tickled her nose and aroused her stomach. The savory aroma of bison hump roast baking with dried sage leaves and wild onions in its own rich juices made her mouth water. The sweet scent of cammas molasses candy mixed with fresh rose blossoms brought happy memories of childhood flitting through her mind and made her smile.

Bits and pieces of conversations from the gathered bands along her route kept the smile on her face. She listened as the men talked and — she thought privately — boasted about hunting, Great Travels, fishing, women, and the games of chance they loved. The women seemed to brag just as much, but it was about their children, preserving food, tanning leather, childbirth, breeding, and, of course, men. Her happy laughter mixed and mingled with theirs to float on the evening air like the wood smoke from the evening cook fires.

❋

The Mating Ritual contained many steps. In the first step, the men presented small gifts to the women in whom they were interested — a finely tanned hide, an especially fine snare or trap, a sharp flint knife, an assortment of small tools, feathers, or carved beads of bone or stone for decorations, or, like Mach, adornments they had crafted. These first gifts demonstrated the man's special skills and gave him the right to court the young women of his choice. Men might present such gifts to three eligible women.

Most marriageable young women received one hand of the small gifts. Horda, however, had received gifts from two hands plus two men in the first few days the bands had gathered. Actually, Bear Claw's gift of a small finely woven basket made two hands plus three. As much as she would like to believe otherwise, she knew she received so many gifts only because of her position as the chief's daughter. Still, the attention made her feel good, and she enjoyed it.

During the first days of Gathering, each of Horda's suitors visited Zaaco's fire and sat beside her and the chief talking, laughing, flirting, and bragging — some too much, she thought. After tomorrow, courting would begin in earnest, and she would be expected to spend time with each of these men, getting to know him better. She grimaced. She didn't want to know any of them any better except Mach, but she had to behave in a manner befitting a Woman of the Frozen Earth. She embraced the ways of her people, and she would not do otherwise.

❋

When the warrior had shown the People of the Tall Grass where to camp, he had briefly explained the time of Gathering and the basic customs of the People of the Frozen Earth to the newcomers. But they had fidgeted, ignored him, and talked among themselves as if he were not there. Bear Claw had spent the entire time glaring at him like a lion targeting its prey. The young man had summed it up quickly and left, with much unsaid.

Bear Claw had spent the first night and most of the next day awake and alert, watching the people who milled about. When the day's shadows grew long and thin, he took some soaproot, headed down to the river, and proceeded to scrub himself clean.

His warriors had followed, hooting in derision at his actions. Bear Claw was not amused, and he brought their laughter and teasing to a quick end when he cracked two of their heads together. "Wash," he commanded.

"Wash?" They stared at him with their mouths open.

"Yes. We want their women." When they showed no signs of understanding he growled, "They won't choose men who stink."

"Washing robs us of our powers," protested one.

"Do these men seem weak?" asked Bear Claw.

The warriors considered all they had seen. "No."

"Then wash."

"The People of the Tall Grass don't wash," argued one of the warriors.

Bear Claw's fist slammed into the man's nose, breaking it and sending blood spurting. The chief eyed the rest of his warriors menacingly; they quickly splashed into the river to do his bidding.

Back at his campsite, now that Gathering was officially beginning, Bear Claw dressed himself in a freshly woven grass breechcloth and then sat motionless while one of the warriors framed his fearsome tattoos with red and yellow lightning slashes and painted his body with signs and symbols of bravery and daring. As darkness gathered, he muttered curses and waited impatiently while one of the women greased his long hair and fashioned it into the elaborate braids and roaches his people wore. Then he frowned. The Men of the Frozen Earth had not painted their bodies nor did they wear elaborate coiffures. He knew he looked splendid ... but would Horda think so?

Because he had not listened to the warrior's explanations, Bear Claw was unsure what to expect, or even what was expected of him now. His temper stretched tighter and tighter, until not only the woman, but also the men, scurried away, lest they end up permanently maimed.

Glaring across the open area of the camp, Bear Claw watched Horda and her family receiving the men who had declared an interest in mating her. They laughed and talked and shared food and drink. What right had they to enjoy what he wanted? His anger burned hotter. He didn't want to waste time on all this preening nonsense. Trading for her would be so much easier. Stealing her would be even better. Then they could go home.

The evening drums spoke softly, breaking his reverie and causing him to look around the camp. The People of the Tall Grass huddled together in a small cluster. Everywhere around them were the People of the Frozen Earth. His men, the strongest and best fighters who remained in his tribe, looked ragged and insignificant among these well-dressed, well-fed people. Shivering in the warm air, he reminded himself what folly it would be to raid the camp and take the women. He would bide his time, for now.

Pulling himself up to what he hoped was an imposing height, Bear Claw left his camp and stalked across the open area to Zaaco's fire. He stood glowering down at Horda and Mach, who were sitting beside the old chief.

Zaaco looked up and smiled. "Greetings, Bear Claw, I trust you're having a pleasant Gathering."

"Humph," muttered Bear Claw.

Zaaco waited for Bear Claw to speak a greeting. When the silence dragged on, Zaaco cast a look at Horda and Mach then spoke again, "I'm enjoying this Gathering. Each year there are more people and more things to see and learn."

Bear Claw looked out at the many flickering cook fires spread across the Gathering grounds, and said abruptly, "There are more people than I expected."

Once more the silence yawned. Zaaco tried again to start a conversation. "Most of the bands of the People of the Frozen Earth come to the Gathering each year since it is the time of many celebrations for us. Gathering officially begins with the Day of the Great Traveler. Did the men explain the Great Travel to you?"

Shaking his head, Bear Claw's cold gaze speared Horda and Mach.

"Completing the Great Travel finishes the Rituals of Manhood. The Rituals begin when the boys have three hands of winters and continue for three turnings of the seasons before the Great Travel.

"Then each man-child walks alone into the unknown, making a great circle of our land. He carries a small pack of tools and supplies and must survive on his own skills with very little help from the people of the outer bands until he returns to the meeting grounds for the next Gathering.

"Many of our young men fill their vessels of time and drink the bitter nectar blended for them by Father Death. Only the strongest return to be accepted into the tribe and granted the rights and responsibilities of manhood at the Ritual of the Great Traveler. You see, men are Father Death's counterpart on Earth, and our lives are always more likely to be forfeited than the lives of our women." Zaaco swallowed a smile as Bear Claw finally turned to look at him.

"Who is this Father Death?" asked Bear Claw.

Horda and Mach exchanged surprised looks. Neither could imagine not knowing such a basic thing.

But Zaaco was tolerant. "The Most Powerful Spirits of the

People of the Frozen Earth are Mother Life and Father Death," he explained. "Mother Life gives all the good things that come to the People. Father Death dispenses punishment — deserved or undeserved. These Most Powerful Spirits are the forces behind all that happens to the People, and they are the guides for our actions."

Bear Claw broke in. "We don't separate our deity. The Great Mystery controls our lives."

"I see," Zaaco commented noncommittally. "For us, Mother Life and Father Death are everything. And just as men are Father Death's counterparts, women are the earthly counterparts of Mother Life. It is through the women the tribe continues since they have been chosen to give birth to the little ones. It is the men's duty to care for the women and protect them so the tribe doesn't pass away forever. Mother Life and Father Death expect no less."

Bear Claw frowned. "That is ridiculous. The men are more important. We provide. Without us the tribe would starve and be no more. Women, though quite pleasant in our sleeping furs, are of little importance beyond caring for the men."

"Really?" Zaaco frowned as if he did not understand the younger man's words.

Bear Claw preened, warming to his subject. These people placed too much value on their women. He would set them straight soon enough. "Yes, the Great Mystery is a man. He has given His strength and power to men. It is only through the warriors that a tribe gains strength. The warriors alone provide power and all good things. The Great Mystery provides women to see to the needs of men. They are nothing more." He folded his hands on his stomach and nodded to show he had finished speaking.

"Have your men discovered some way to bring little ones by themselves?" Zaaco asked.

"Of course not," snapped Bear Claw.

"Have your men found some way to stay young and strong forever?"

Bear Claw's rage flashed in his eyes. The old man only pretended to listen to his words and his beliefs. And now he twisted them to make Bear Claw look foolish. His eyes flashed, and he shook his head, but he refused to speak another word.

Zaaco's face remained impassive, but his eyes bored into Bear Claw's. "I wonder how long your tribe or any tribe can remain strong without women."

Anger burned in Bear Claw's face, darkening his scars. And he clenched his fists so tightly the veins popped out all up and down his arms. Within his heart, Bear Claw admitted to himself bitterly, his and his warriors' presence at this Gathering gave truth to the old chief's words. But he would not be made a fool of, not by this man nor by any of these people. He turned and stalked away from the campfire without even speaking to Horda.

Chapter 5

The first formal activities of the Gathering — the Day of the Great Traveler — honored those who had just completed their Great Travels.

Bear Claw emerged from his shelter early and scowled as he saw several young men hurrying back to camp, still wet from the river. He knew some of them had bathed only the day before. Did these people intend to wash their skin away? Well, he would not do it; he was more than clean enough. And if he washed, he'd have to renew his paint, a very time consuming endeavor. No, it would not do. Instead, he went back in the shelter and kicked one of the sleeping women. "Get up, woman. I want something to eat."

The soft sounds of voices punctuated by laughter accompanied Mach's steps that morning as he headed toward the assembly area and blanketed him in a feeling of well being. Home. He was home. Besides marking the official beginning of Gathering, this Day of the Great Traveler was his official entrance into manhood. Soon would come the Bid Ceremony. Then, Mother Life and Father Death willing, Horda would be his mate.

Everyone was dressed in fine ceremonial clothing. Some of the men wore fringed leather tunics dyed the colors of the rainbow and lavishly adorned with tiny shells, porcupine quills, feathers, and the carved thighbones of birds. Others wore the ornate chest protectors made of hardened bones with shells, animal teeth, and polished beads of stone and bone worked in intricate designs. All wore beaded knee-high moccasins, fringed leggings, and breechcloths of the finest buckskin leather. The variety dazzled his eyes and made him smile.

As he adjusted his own chest protector and smoothed his leather breechcloth, the image of Bear Claw's grass breechcloth popped into his mind. That, plus all the paint and grotesque tattoos, made Bear Claw more a comic character than a fearsome warrior in Mach's eyes. He could not imagine doing such hideous things to his face — for any reason. True, after the Dance of the Sun he would have his own scars to show, but it wasn't the same. Was it? Best not to dwell on it now.

Mother Life. He hadn't realized how many women were here, or how beautiful they were. Well, most of them. He smiled. Though ornate and attractive, the men's clothing could not compare with the delicate beauty of the women's. For these ceremonial tunics, the women made fine thin leather from the skins of fawns or bison calves, then dyed it in gentle pastels before sewing it. The tiniest shells, feathers, bone and stone beads, and porcupine quills embroidered the bodices, sleeves, and hems. His smile broadened into a wide grin that lit up his face. Though he hadn't seen her, he had no doubt Horda would be beautiful.

Meiran walked toward Mach and nodded a cool greeting. The dark circles beneath her eyes and the unnatural paleness of her skin shocked him. She looked as if a strong breeze would blow her away. Was she ill? Perhaps he should say something to her. He was about to speak when he saw the top of her head and forgot his words. He smothered his chuckles with a sudden coughing fit.

That woman. How could she walk upright? Her hair was braided and coiled with traditional shells and beads, but she also had a bird — a whole stuffed bird, its nest, and what looked like a clutch of eggs — perched precariously atop her head. He turned and watched her totter away. He fervently thanked Mother Life he had noticed before he said a word.

Trying to be gracious, even in his thoughts, Mach reminded himself everyone had taken special care dressing their long hair on this occasion, and that there were many ornate styles decorated with feathers, shells, leather thongs, and beads. He touched his own long braids into which his mother had woven eagle feathers and shells. But still ... He looked back over his shoulder at Meiran to see if her bird had flown away yet and chuckled.

He had only seen one hairdo as elaborate, but where? Suddenly his eyes narrowed in horror. It had been on a man — Bear Claw! First Meiran, then Bear Claw. Surely Horda wouldn't allow her mother to do anything so ... unusual ... to her hair. *Mother Life.* He certainly hoped not. He wouldn't know what to say then.

With one last tug at his breechcloth, Mach hurried to the common area. Dawn marked the beginning of ceremonies, and everyone had to be in place before the sun's first rays touched the Circle of Light. Today they would honor many of the young men of the tribe — not only the ones who had so recently completed their Great Travels, but also the ones who had ended their Great Travels in the Frozen Wilds, and the boys who would begin their Great Travels when this Gathering was done. It wouldn't do to be late, and he pushed through the crowd with a renewed sense of haste.

Mach joined the other returned Travelers assembled on the low hill at the right-hand side of the meeting ground. He looked around the crowd of milling young men for his father, who would be waiting with the fathers of each of the previous year's Great Travelers. Not finding him, his thoughts returned to Horda.

Although he could not see her, he knew she waited behind

the hill with the other young women who were eligible to mate and the boys who would soon begin their own Great Travels. Neither of these groups would be seen until much later in the ceremony.

"Hey, Mach. Over here," called a voice from the crowd. It was Thuro, a young man taller than Mach, but slightly thinner and darker-skinned. Originally the two had been competitors and wary of each other, but they had learned to trust and depend on one another after the elders had paired them in the activities of the First Manhood Rituals. Through the turnings of the seasons, their friendship had deepened, and now they were closer than most brothers.

"Greetings, Thuro."

"Nuroo wants you over here."

Mach bit back a testy response and simply nodded. He knew his place in line as well as Thuro did; they had certainly practiced enough. But this was the actual ceremony, and they were all a bit nervous.

"Did you see her?" Thuro whispered, as Mach drew close.

"Which one, Wilda or Horda?" Irritation forgotten, Mach teased his friend.

"Neither." Thuro looked around. "They weren't walking around the assembly area, were they?"

Mach grinned at Thuro, rolling his eyes in mock exasperation.

"No, of course not," Thuro answered, more to himself than to his friend.

"Of course not," agreed Mach. "Then who was I supposed to see?"

"Meiran."

Mach chuckled again. "I thanked the Mother she didn't stop to talk to me. I don't think I could have kept a straight face if she had."

"I thought she might fall under the weight of that bird nest thing on her head."

Mach's face abruptly sobered. "She doesn't look well, though. Could you tell?"

"I didn't notice," admitted Thuro. "I didn't see anything but the bird."

"It was rather ... dominating."

"Ha! That's putting it mildly. Her hair's worse than that Bear Claw's."

"Well, it certainly is different." Mach frowned as Bear Claw arrived, leading the People of the Tall Grass into the natural amphitheater surrounding the assembly area.

"Speaking of a bad spirit," said Thuro, "there he is."

"I see him."

"I've heard rumors, but Horda won't really choose him." Thuro frowned. "Do you think?"

"I —"

"To your places, and stop talking," Nuroo, Norlon's father and the tribe's current Medicine Man, commanded, cutting off Mach's reply.

The sun's first golden ray peeked over the horizon of the eastern sky, and the tangy scent of dew on the trampled grass mixed with the wood smoke from the morning cook fires. Mach sniffed appreciatively. It was a comforting mixture; it smelled like Home. Home ... If Horda chose Bear Claw, would he ever have not just a shelter, but also a Home?

Mother Life, don't let her choose him. Let her choose me.

The musicians waited on the small rise to the left of the meeting ground. Now the first notes sounded from their elderberry flutes and ram's horns, and the measured beat of the log drums called the Assembly to order. Gathering had officially begun.

Mach's back straightened, and he forced himself to concentrate on the day ahead.

Wearing the chief's fine cloak of matched white wolf skins,

Zaaco stepped to his place in the Circle of Light, the raised area from which he presided over all the formal ceremonies of the People of the Frozen Earth. He was accompanied by an array of glittering sunbeams, now pushing their way above the prairie horizon and splashing their pink fingers across the sky's pale blue. The music escalated.

Looking around, Mach silently counted. Only five hands of returned Travelers. Ten hands plus two fingers of boys left, but only five hands of men returned.

Father Death, so few. The others gone as I almost was. Gone forever to dwell in the Frozen Wilds. Mother Life, thank you for being merciful to me.

The Fathers' March began. Mach watched the fathers march across the open area toward Zaaco. All carried the traditional gifts of spear thrower and quiver, though some would never be used in this world. He acknowledged Mahlo, his own father, with only the smallest gesture, a happy crinkling around his eyes. It would not do to break the formality of the occasion with anything more.

As the fathers arrived, the young men stood silently waiting. Finally, the ram's horns blared a welcome, the log drums boomed, and the smaller drums sounded the rhythm of the march. Regal in his cloak of black bear fur, Nuroo solemnly led the Returned Travelers to the open area surrounding the Circle of Light. When all were in place, Zaaco began the slow, dignified roll call of all who had made the Great Travel, no matter what their outcome.

Zaaco's voice, deep and resonant, resounded across the open area, "Suto, son of Sumo and Kaila."

There was a beat, then, Sumo, an old man dressed in slightly shabby clothing, stepped forward and faced Zaaco and Nuroo — alone.

Zaaco said, "Father Death, you saw fit to fill this man's young warrior son's vessel of time. We pray you welcomed him into your kingdom and will keep his spirit safe to walk with you through the mists of forever."

Sumo bowed slowly to the chief. Then he placed an ornately carved spear thrower and beaded quiver decorated with blue jay feathers and the milk teeth of a bear cub on the ceremonial travois. The gentle morning breeze fluttered the feathers and clicked the teeth, a breath of life, almost, for the boy who would never be a man.

As the sun rose, the light glittered off the tears running silently down Sumo's face. Mach felt his heart constrict with the old man's unspoken pain. He had found the remains of his only son. He knew better than to question Father Death, but the loss seemed such a waste. He longed to reach out to Sumo and comfort him, but he could only watch as the man, back bent but head still held high, returned to his place among the other fathers. His stoicism, Mach thought, did both himself and his departed son credit.

Then, as he looked out across the rest of the crowd, he felt the stab of a different sort of pain – one bordering on anger. Bear Claw, the Chief of the Tall Grass, sneered at the old man as he returned to his place. It didn't matter that he was a stranger here and never knew Sumo's son. Why didn't he show the respect this man deserved?

Zaaco's deep voice drew Mach back to where he was. "Mach, son of Mahlo and Woda."

This time there was no pause. Mach and Mahlo stepped forward together, meeting at the edge of the Circle of Light. Mahlo's face remained solemn, but his eyes gleamed up at the son who had now become a man. The two bowed to each other formally, and Mahlo offered Mach the gifts he carried. Though Mach fought to keep his face solemn, he could feel a grin trying to lift the corner of his mouth when he saw the signs for hunter of the bison and teller of stories his father had carved on the small spear thrower.

Then his eyes softened as he noticed the tiny shells and downy eaglet feathers his mother so carefully traced into the lines of the quiver. He knew he would never actually carry it on a hunt because the jingling of its tiny beads would scare away his quarry. Ah, but he would always treasure it because it showed how much his mother cared for him. The past year must have been as hard for both his parents as it had been for him. Never before had he truly realized how much they loved him. Mach touched the gifts to his chest to show his appreciation.

Mahlo opened his arms, and Mach walked into them and clung to his father while Zaaco spoke. "Mother Life, we thank you for sparing this brave young warrior so he could continue to walk with us. May his days be long and his hunts successful. May he grow old around the fires of his own hearth and watch the sons and daughters of his sons and daughters grow to adults long before he walks in Father Death's kingdom."

With another hug, Mach and Mahlo parted, and each returned to his own place. Against his will, Mach's eyes moved to Bear Claw's face, searching for signs of derision, but the Chief of the People of the Tall Grass now watched the proceedings through unreadable eyes.

Zaaco continued to call the names of the young men. After he was done, the log drums beat the slow, measured heartbeats of the March of the Dead. Two members of the Council of Elders lifted the ceremonial travois and led the procession to the mouth of the Frozen Wilds. The entire Council led the people in the songs and prayers for the dead Travelers. When they were done, they left the belongings of those honored warriors for Father Death, so he could present them to those who had joined them.

After this ceremony the lost warriors were not forgotten, but they were relegated to a place of less importance. The willow flute trilled a bird song. The small drums beat a gentle rhythm, and the music rose from the sad, haunting notes of the death songs to the high-spirited songs that celebrated life. The day belonged once again to the living, and to the young men returned from their Great Travel. They now took their positions as leaders, guiding the procession back to the assembly area.

Mahlo and the other fathers ritually embraced their sons one more time before returning to the rest of their families. After the embrace, Zaaco, with only the slightest playful twitch of his lips at Mach, officially proclaimed the young men adults and afforded them all the rights and responsibilities associated with adulthood. The People of the Frozen Earth looked with pride on their new men, and they basked in the glow and in the warm sunlight, listening to the triumphant music played just for them.

Mach's blood quickened when the mood changed yet again. The music was still triumphant, but it took on a softer tone with an insistent and subtly suggestive beat hinting at the delights of mating. Mach watched eagerly while the parade of eligible young women began to march, bow, and sensuously weave its way through the assembled crowd toward the young men.

A smile lighted Mach's eyes when he finally saw the golden glint of Horda's hair in the middle of the procession. Some of the young women danced close, flirting and teasing him, but he moved not a muscle in response. It soon became apparent to all who watched that he saw only Horda, whose eyes were fixed solely on his.

But in an instant, anger, jealousy, and fear gnawed Mach's insides, and his face visibly hardened. Bear Claw had shifted his position ever so slightly, placing himself directly in Horda's path. Mach watched the older man smile suggestively at the woman they both had chosen. Rage threatened to explode from every inch of his body when Bear Claw reached toward her.

Didn't Bear Claw realize the insult implied by his action? The young women could touch and tease the men during the march without censure, but for a man to reach out, to touch at this point ... Mach tried to convince himself it was simply that

Bear Claw didn't know the mores of the People of the Frozen Earth. But was it he didn't know, or simply he didn't care? Mach clenched his fists until his knuckles turned white. He willed himself to remain still as stone.

Horda's eyes, though, never left Mach's face. Without losing the rhythm of the march, she stepped around Bear Claw and continued unerringly toward Mach.

The anger drained from him, all but forgotten, and his face relaxed into a welcoming smile, when she finally reached him and twined her body around his. So quickly no one could be sure whether they had seen it or not, Mach winked and smiled at his chosen. Taking her place across the Circle of Light from Mach, Horda returned his smile.

Now the young people stood in two lines before the assembly — proud, to be sure, but still slightly self-conscious. Mach's eyes never left Horda's face while Zaaco offered prayers of gratitude for the young people standing before him. The People sang songs of thanksgiving and praise, and Nuroo offered prayers. Zaaco spoke of the importance of the families the young people would found. More songs were sung before Zaaco offered the prayers of hope. The People of the Frozen Earth delighted in the beauty of their young men and women, but they also saw in them the key to the survival of the People — they were the fathers and mothers of the next generation, the future.

The prayers for the couples completed, there remained only one last group to be honored in the Ceremony of the Great Traveler. A haunting melody called Mach from his dreams of the future with Horda back to his own past. The drums remained silent while the plaintive notes of the willow and elderberry flutes soared in counterpoint to the sad and lonely notes of the thighbone flutes.

Mach watched the last marchers approach, the boys whose Great Travels would begin when Gathering ended. They stepped across the meeting grounds and took their places in the empty space between the young men and women.

A thousand recollections of loneliness and fear chased each other through Mach's memory as he watched these boys, and he silently offered a heart-felt prayer of gratitude for the successful completion of his own Great Travel. A sudden twinge of anxiety teased his thoughts at the coming Dance of the Sun, but he resolutely pushed it from his mind — at least for now.

The boys stood straight and still, allowing only their eyes to betray their fear and excitement at their coming ordeals while the music wove its melancholy spell around them. As Zaaco called all the names and formally introduced the boys to the People, Mach's thoughts wandered to the things he felt they should know — things he longed to speak, though he realized he could not. No words could make them understand until they lived the experiences for themselves.

But what a price some would pay for their ignorance. The gentle wind suddenly sent shivers down Mach's spine as he thought half of the boys standing before him would walk the Frozen Wilds by the next Gathering.

He tried to return his attention to the proceedings — to the prayers Nuroo offered as he introduced the boys to Mother Life and pleaded with her for her protection on their coming travels. To the callings Zaaco made to Father Death as he requested his mercy and begged for each of the boys to be allowed to return a man. Once again Mach fought his urge to cry out, to warn the young men to be careful. It would not do to show such weakness.

The words finished; the music began again. The small drums beat a simple tattoo, sounding much like multiple hearts beating in a synchronized rhythm. Then the sad, lonely voices of the littlest flutes sang the boys back to their parents for a last brief sojourn in the Land of Childhood.

The people once again cheered the new men and saluted them. Nuroo offered a final prayer — a benediction and grace

— for their futures. The triumphant music that had introduced them now swelled, accompanying their dance of thanksgiving and joy. They had been tested and found victorious. They were men.

The Ceremony of the Great Traveler ended as the new men led a parade of the entire tribe across the meeting area to the camps where the Feast of the Great Traveler awaited. There would be much celebrating throughout the day, and laughter and excited talk filled Mach's ears with a happiness he had never before imagined.

Chapter 6

The Feast of the Great Traveler opened the courtship rituals. At this time the normal restrictions governing contact between unmarried members of the opposite sex were relaxed. Looking over possible mates, the young people laughed, talked, and flirted among themselves with great delight.

Mach joined Horda in the crush of people heading to the feast. "You're beautiful, did you know that? Your tunic exactly matches the lightest color of your hair."

She smiled shyly. "I'm glad you like it. My mother and I worked hard to get exactly the right shade of dye."

"It was worth it. I think it's perfect." He took her hand, and they made their way together among the crowd.

Mach stopped, though, as he spotted Sumo and Kaila standing silent and alone in the otherwise happy crowd. His intention to give them some small measure of comfort flooded back. He whispered to Horda, "I must speak with them."

Horda's smooth brow furrowed as she followed Mach's eyes to the melancholy pair. "Why?"

"Suto, their only child, is gone. I found his remains. I must try to ease their grief."

A new understanding and compassion flickered in the honey-eyed depths of her eyes. "I'll go with you."

Heads down and faces now solemn, the young couple made their way to the grieving parents. Stopping before the older couple, Mach and Horda waited to be acknowledged.

Sumo looked up in surprise when Kaila gently poked his ribs with her elbow. "Greetings ... ah, Mach, isn't it?" Sumo's voice creaked like it had not been used for a long, long time. After another gentle jab to his ribs, he continued, "My mate Kaila and I trust you will have a ..." He took a deep breath, cleared his throat, squared his shoulders, and finished, "... fine Gathering."

"Greetings, Sumo, Kaila," Mach responded. "You know Horda, Zaaco's daughter."

Horda reached out to touch the older woman's wrinkled hand. "Greetings. Mach has news for you. We hope it will bring you comfort in your time of grief."

"News?" Kaila straightened and a tiny spark of hope flickered behind her eyes.

Horda immediately regretted her choice of words. Mach shook his head and spoke gently to the older woman. "Not news so much as information. I found Suto and prepared him for the Frozen Wilds. I sang the songs to ease his journey."

The tiny spark of hope in Kaila's eyes flickered out, drowned by the tears that filled them. Sumo wrapped his arm around his tiny mate's slumped shoulders. Silence stretched before he spoke. "How did our son meet Father Death?"

Mach looked directly into the older man's face. "He went bravely, as a warrior should. He had his spears in his hands when I found him."

"Do you know ..." Tears now trickled down Kaila's shrunken cheeks, but she forced herself to continue. "... what took him away?"

"He had been hunting."

"Hunting? What do you mean?" Sumo's voice sharpened. "My son was an able hunter."

"Yes," Mach acknowledged. "He was."

"Then explain yourself."

"He trapped an antelope."

"An antelope? He had killed many antelope." Sumo angrily

waved away Mach's words.

"Yes, he did." Mach's voice remained calm. "But this time, the earth tricked him. He fell on his quarry."

Sumo's eyes searched Mach's, but he didn't interrupt.

"It was one of those things that should not have happened, but because Father Death willed it, it did happen. When Suto fell, the antelope's horn ripped him open." Mach pushed his palms against his own abdomen. "He could not help himself, nor could I help him. He embraced Father Death lying in the shade of a tall pine tree with his spears and arrows in his hands."

"Did he still live when you found him?" Kaila asked softly.

Mach considered his answer for less than a heartbeat. "Yes."

"Did he suffer?" Tears still flooded Kaila's eyes and shimmered on her wrinkled cheeks.

Mach spoke as he sought to ease her grief. "I'm sure he suffered, but he was brave. He recognized me and sent you a message before he went."

"A message?"

"Yes, his last thoughts were of you, his parents. He asked me to tell you this: in his time alone, he realized how much he loved and respected you. He asked me to beg your forgiveness for leaving you alone. He said Father Death needed him."

Almost imperceptibly the tiny woman's hunched shoulders relaxed, and she wrapped one arm around her mate's waist. "I'm glad he wasn't alone. Though sometimes trying, he was a wonderful son. We will never forget him."

Sumo studied the younger man intently, trying to discover if the words were true. Mach kept his eyes steady on the old man's, while inwardly he prayed forgiveness for his gentle lies. Sometimes a lie could be more kind than the cold reality of truth. The moment stretched – one heartbeat, then two – before Sumo took the young man's hand in his. "Thank you for taking time in your special day to bring our son's words to us."

"If I'd been in his place and he in mine, I'm sure he'd have done the same," Mach said.

"Perhaps ... perhaps," said Sumo. "Go in peace, Mach and Horda." Standing straighter, with a small, sad smile on his time-worn face, he gently dismissed the young couple and turned to embrace his mate.

The young couple left without another word. Once they were out of earshot, Horda said, "I'm glad Suto realized how wrong he had been."

Mach looked sharply at her. "What did you know of Suto?"

"My father worried about him. He said his wild ways frequently caused trouble and that he shamed his parents by his words and actions."

Mach nodded. "I stayed away from him when I could."

"I know it was hard for you to talk to his parents, but I'm glad you gave them his message." She smiled sadly at Mach. "I didn't realize how much those words would mean to them."

Biting his lip, Mach admitted, "Um, actually Suto met Father Death before I found him."

Horda's eyes widened. "But —"

"Perhaps I was wrong, but when I saw how sad Sumo and Kaila looked, I couldn't help myself. I didn't plan the words I spoke, but, Mother Life forgive me, once they began I couldn't stop them any more than I could stop Suto's walking the Frozen Wilds."

She reached up and gently smoothed the troubled line between his brows. "Don't fret. You spoke the words he should've spoken ... the words he would've spoken if he had grown up. Maybe his spirit gave them to you to ease his parents' suffering."

"Maybe." He didn't sound convinced.

Horda watched the conflicting emotions battle across Mach's face. She said nothing, though, offering only the quiet support of her presence. Finally the pain faded away, replaced by an affectionate smile.

"Thank you." He looked around again at the crowd. "You know, I'm suddenly very hungry. Let's get something to eat."

Although she was still worried about Bear Claw, Horda knew she had to follow her heart, at least for this one day. She smiled and took his arm. "Yes, let's." Together they walked the paths among the cook fires.

At the first fire, the cook, an older woman with a wrinkled face, thin grey braids, and twinkling eyes, had baked a bison hump roast in the fire pit, together with cow parsnip roots and pond lily bulbs. "Greetings, Mach, Horda. Try some of this." She served two small portions.

"Greetings to you, Almar. It sure smells good. You know, I dreamed about your bison hump roast last winter."

"You did?" The cook handed the small wooden platters to the young couple.

"Yep, during a blizzard when I only had a little pemmican left. I dreamed about the roast you fixed for the last Feast of the Great Traveler." Mach took a bite. "It tasted just as good in my dream as this does." He rolled his eyes and smacked his lips.

"Oh, how you talk." The older woman shook her head, but she looked pleased. "Are you sure it was the one I fixed at the last Gathering?"

He appeared to consider. "Well, it might have been the Gathering before."

"Or the one at any of the four hands Gatherings of your life. I have a counting cord to keep track of my Gatherings," said the woman with a laugh. "Or maybe it was the bison roast of another of the cooks?"

"Nope." Mach enjoyed another bite. "I remember your smiling face from my dream. Besides, no one makes a roast like you."

"Oh, go on with you." The old woman gently punched Mach's arm.

He grinned and leaned closer to whisper in her ear.

"Anyway, no one else makes bison hump roast as good as yours."

"Bison hump roast is my specialty."

"I know." Mach cleaned the platter. "You've really outdone yourself this year. I think this was the best I've ever eaten."

"Thank you." The cook accepted the empty platter with another smile. "Would you like some more?"

Mach looked longingly at the cook pit. "I'd love some more, but I'd better not. This is our first stop. We don't want to hurt anyone's feelings because we filled up on the best first. Thanks, anyway." With a wave, he and Horda walked away.

Horda whispered, "You do that very well."

"What?" asked Mach, sniffing his way to the next cook fire.

"Flirt."

"Flirt?" He stopped to stare at her.

"Yes, flirt." She kept her face solemn, but her eyes danced.

"That woman is older than my mother's mother." Mach looked over his shoulder at the old woman serving another couple.

"Doesn't matter," said Horda.

"Of course, it matters. And anyway, I wasn't flirting."

"Well, maybe not exactly flirting," conceded Horda before she mimicked softly, "I remember your smiling face. No one else makes bison hump roast as good as yours."

"Well, they don't," he protested.

"I believe you." She smiled a dreamy smile. "You really don't see anything unusual about what you've done, do you?"

Their arrival at the next cook fire forestalled his answer. "Greetings, Mach, Horda."

"Greetings, Suka. What are you cooking today?" asked Mach with a cautious sniff.

"I prepared an antelope haunch with wild onions and yampah roots. Would you like some?"

"Of course." Mach held out his hands for the small platter Suka prepared. He took a tentative bite and grinned in surprise.

"Hey, this is delicious."

"Not quite like last year's, eh?"

"I didn't say that," he protested.

Horda silently watched the exchange and ate her sample of the food.

"You didn't have to," said Suka. "I remember the fowl I fixed at the last Gathering. I made up a new recipe, but it didn't work quite the way I planned. My fowl truly tasted foul."

Mach hooted. "I wanted to say that, but I'm much too polite."

Suka poked him in the arm. "You just didn't think of it. Anyway, it's past time for me to find a specialty."

Mach chewed slowly and swallowed. "This is really good. I vote you've found your specialty."

"Maybe," said Suka.

Mach savored another bite. "What's the tangy taste? Dried sage leaves and cow parsnip?"

Suka nodded. "You have a good sense for what's in any recipe. Maybe you should be a cook."

"I *am* a cook." Mach drew himself up to his fullest height. "I survived on my own cooking for a turning of the seasons."

Suka poked his well-muscled shoulder. "Looks to me like you did more than survive."

He chuckled before solemnly admitting, "I didn't exactly feast most of the time."

"No, I didn't think you did. Most Travelers don't." Though her mouth still smiled, her eyes were serious. "But you survived."

Mach shrugged. "I added my contributions to other cook pots as often as possible."

"I'll bet you did." Suka beamed at the handsome young warrior and his chosen.

"Let me tell you, there are some real cooks in the outer bands." He rolled his eyes, and Horda heard the laughter in his voice once more. "Though I don't think I've ever eaten any better antelope.

Suka chuckled. "Or been any more surprised, I'm sure."

"I didn't say that." He sounded politely outraged by the suggestion.

"You didn't have to. I watched your face when you tasted my food. You were prepared to pretend you enjoyed it, just like you did last year."

"I did not pretend," he protested, as he and Horda handed Suka their empty platters.

"Mach," Suka chided. "You know you aren't supposed to lie."

"I did not lie." He raised himself to his full height and stared down at Suka. Horda chewed the inside of her cheeks to keep from giggling. "If you recall, I told you your fowl was 'interesting,' and it was."

Suka laughed at him. "No, I guess you didn't. It was interesting, though, how I could ruin perfectly good birds." He smiled but said nothing further.

"Go on, you two," said Suka, "before Mach's mouth gets him into some real trouble." They waved good-bye and walked away.

When they were out of Suka's hearing, Horda shook her head. "It really doesn't matter."

"What doesn't matter?" Mach asked following his nose to another cook fire.

"How old the woman is — you just charm her, whether she's that old lady I don't even know or the number one mate of Elko, who'll probably be the next chief."

"But I've told you, I wasn't trying to charm either of them," said Mach with a frown.

"I know. I think that's the best part of the whole thing."

"What do you mean?"

"You really think women are special." Her voice was soft

and wondering.

"Of course. Doesn't everyone?"

Horda smiled. She knew she couldn't explain her feeling without sounding stupid and inane, so she said, "I'm glad you're courting me."

He grinned and hugged her. "Me, too. Hey, I smell simmering thimbleberries in camas molasses. Come on, I'll bet there's fry bread too."

Horda followed him to the next cook fire, marveling at both his charm and his seemingly endless appetite.

Bear Claw watched the young couple make their way around the cook fires and waited for a time to interrupt. He found his opportunity as Mach and Horda finally passed near his camp. "Greetings. I trust you're having a pleasant time." Bear Claw managed to make the traditional greeting sound like an insult.

Neither Mach nor Horda wanted to respond to his words, but manners forbade their ignoring him. Mach spoke first. "Greetings. Yes, my Gathering's been more than pleasant. I trust you're enjoying your first Gathering."

"I must admit I find parts of it strange, but the food is delicious. I've never seen so much at one time."

Mach said, "We seldom see this much either. Next to the feast on Mating Day, this is the biggest feast in the turning of the seasons."

Horda spoke for the first time. "We eat well. At least we seldom go hungry, but we don't often prepare so much. Actually it's somewhat wasteful, though it's delicious."

Bear Claw ignored her and spoke directly to Mach. "Is it proper to congratulate you on the completion of your Travel?"

"Ah, well, yes, I guess it is."

"Then I congratulate you. It must have been quite an ordeal."

"It wasn't too bad." Mach lowered his eyes so Bear Claw couldn't read his true feelings.

"You're too modest. I understand sometimes one man returns for every three boys who leave."

"It's rare there are that many who walk the Frozen Wilds."

Bear Claw raised an eyebrow inquiringly. "Two boys leave and one man returns?"

"Too often such is the case," Mach admitted.

"You must be very skillful."

"And very lucky because Mother Life protected me."

"Ah, yes, luck. How often we overlook the part it plays in our lives." Suddenly Bear Claw turned to Horda. "I owe you an apology."

"An apology?" Involuntarily Horda took a half step back.

"I saw the other young women touching some of the men. I didn't know my touching you would be viewed as an insult."

She looked into his strange silver eyes. They glittered like the frozen river beneath the winter sun, and she shivered inwardly. They were the coldest eyes she'd ever seen. How could she ever choose such a man even for the good of the tribe? She forced herself to be polite. "I understand. I was just surprised. I didn't expect it."

"I assure you I didn't mean to dishonor you. Please accept my apology. You see I'm trying to learn your ways."

"No harm came from your action."

His mouth curved into a smile though his eyes remained cold. "Mach, I'd like to visit with Horda for a while. With her permission, of course," he added, almost as an afterthought.

Horda longed to cling to Mach's arm and tell Bear Claw to go away, but she knew she couldn't. The mores of the tribe bound her to consider his bid for her even if her entire being screamed for her to refuse his attentions. She had to walk with him and talk. She had to give him a chance, but Mother Life, she didn't want to. Was that wrong?

Her tongue felt like it was made of clay. It didn't respond when she tried to speak. She finally cleared her throat and forced herself to answer politely. "Of course, I'll walk with you. Mach, will you excuse us?"

Hurt, dismay, and disapproval warred on Mach's face, but he knew the mores as well as she did. He said simply, "Certainly. Horda, I'll see you later. Thank you for sharing the feast with me."

"I enjoyed it very much." Her eyes caressed his face before she turned back to Bear Claw.

Chapter 7

Horda and Bear Claw walked a short distance in silence. She racked her brain for something to talk about, but her mind felt like it was stuffed with the fluff from the spring cottonwood trees. In desperation, she blurted the next thought that came to her mind. "Do the young men of the Tall Grass go on Great Travels?"

"Not exactly," said Bear Claw. "As I understand it, this is part of the Ritual of Manhood, isn't it?"

"Yes."

"We travel, but not until after we are men. We go on a vision quest before our initiation, but ours only lasts a few days. We walk away from the home camp, and we cannot return until we find our spirit guide." He smiled his first real smile. "I never knew for sure whether I found a spirit guide or imagined it so I could go home and eat."

"Eat?"

"Unlike your People, we aren't allowed any supplies on our travels. We fast until we receive our vision, then we go home and are welcomed into adulthood. We have a feast, though nothing like this one, where we receive our marks of honor."

"What kind of marks?"

He touched the ugly scars on his face. "These tell the other members of our tribe I am a man."

Horda swallowed her smile. "I'm sure I'd notice without them."

"Now, you would." He smiled at her again, but this time it was more of a leer. She watched his silver eyes gleam while she felt her face burn. He chuckled at her obvious discomfort. "When I received them, they separated me from the other boys who hadn't completed their quests."

"Oh." Searching for something appropriate to add, she could only come up with, "Did they hurt?"

"The chief said they didn't."

She smiled knowingly. "But of course they did. How did he make them?"

"Well, first he knapped a new chert knife while I watched. Then he sliced my face in the pattern I had chosen. Finally the elders rubbed dye, ashes, and fat into the cuts to be sure the marks would remain distinct and not blur or go away."

In spite of herself, Horda gasped. Bear Claw was unmoved.

"It's very bad for a mark of honor to go away," he explained. "The warrior loses his manhood if it does." He absently rubbed his right cheek. "Yes, it hurts very badly, especially if the fever demon feasts on it."

"And the fever demon feasted on yours."

"Yes, it did. How did you know?"

"I didn't know for sure," said Horda, "but it makes sense. I'm just surprised any of your face remains."

"Why?" asked Bear Claw in genuine confusion.

"Nuroo teaches us to wash all wounds and keep them clean."

"That would take away the marks," Bear Claw protested.

"Not always though it does help keep the fever demon from feasting on them."

"Really?" asked Bear Claw.

"Washing doesn't always stop the demons completely, but it seems to help." Horda was surprised to find she enjoyed talking with Bear Claw. He really didn't seem so frightening when he wasn't eyeing her like a tasty bite.

"Your ways are very different from our ways."

"They are. So tell me about your ways."

"What do you want to know?"

She furrowed her forehead, trying to decide what was most important before she said, "Everything, I guess."

Bear Claw chortled. "Will this walk last several days, little Horda?"

Embarrassed by his laughter she snapped, "Of course not."

"Ah, I seem to have upset you again. I didn't mean to." He reached out to touch her hand. "Could you tell me everything about the People of the Frozen Earth in one conversation?"

Chagrined, she said, "No, I'm sure I couldn't. I've spent all my life being taught about my People."

"See what I mean? Pick one thing you want to know. I'll tell you about it."

"Tell me about your family."

"Family?"

"Do you have mates and little ones?"

"No."

"You have many winters. Haven't you ever had a mate?"

"I have joined with a number of women."

Horda's eyes widened, but she managed to keep her voice level. "You must have rituals governing those joinings. Tell me about them."

"Nothing to tell. We don't have any ritual. I pick the woman I want and join with her."

"Don't you have some kind of ceremony?"

"No."

"You don't pledge yourself to her?"

"Of course not."

"You don't promise to take care of her?"

Bear Claw scoffed. "She takes care of me as long as I want her. Women exist only for men's comfort and pleasure. I explained that to your father."

Horda grimaced. "I don't think I'd like your tribe very much." It wasn't polite to say, but it was at least honest.

"You'll get used to it," Bear Claw snapped. It was not a hope, just a statement of fact. Seeing her anguished look, though, he softened his tone. "Tell me about your mating rituals."

She took a deep breath and recited, "Gathering includes the Mating Rituals, which are conducted by men and women chosen for their knowledge and understanding of themselves and their mates. To lead these rituals, a person must be nominated by his or her own mate and then selected by the Council of the Elders. It is a great honor to lead the Rituals of Mating because they train the future mothers and fathers of the tribe."

She frowned when Bear Claw grinned at her. She realized she sounded like one of the teachers, but somehow she wouldn't allow herself to stop. He needed to hear these words. He had to understand what she expected of her mate. And she didn't want to leave anything out or make it too simple. Maybe he'd decide she wasn't worth the trouble.

Please, Mother Life.

"During the first sessions, the men and women meet separately. Everything about the mate is discussed, from duties and expectations to goals and dreams. Both partners must understand how mating changes their lives. Next, the young men and women, with both sets of teachers, talk about the same things together. It helps everyone learn to communicate and compromise. Those sessions end when the couples actually pledge themselves to each other. Finally, the couples dress in new ceremonial clothing and voice the Mating Vows before the Spirits and all the assembled People. They are joined for the rest of their lives."

Bear Claw scowled. "What do you mean 'for the rest of their lives'?"

"Everyone understands they belong to each other. They take care of each other."

"Take care of each other?" he asked doubtfully. "I don't

understand what that means."

"It means the man takes care of the woman and provides for her. He helps her if she needs help. Just as she does everything she can to make his life more comfortable and easier."

"How does the man take care of the woman?"

"He provides meat and pelts and helps with the fruits and vegetables when he has time. He helps with the children and protects her and them. This strengthens the entire family. We believe our strong tribe results from our strong families."

"Children?" squawked Bear Claw in horror. "The man takes care of the children?"

"Sure," said Horda with a grin. "They're his, too."

"No, they are not," said Bear Claw firmly. "The children belong to the mother, and she takes care of them. The man doesn't have anything to do with them."

Horda opened her mouth to argue, but Bear Claw's glower closed it.

"What if the man tires of his mate?" asked Bear Claw suddenly.

"Tires?" Small frown lines pleated Horda's brow.

Bear Claw laughed harshly. "Yes, tires. Decides he doesn't want her any more."

"We don't do that," sniffed Horda with all the arrogant anger of innocence.

"By the Great Mystery," growled Bear Claw. "I've had many women. I tire of them. They tire of me. We go our separate ways."

Horda shook her head. "If one partner doesn't uphold the mate, there are ways to release the bonds, but that doesn't happen often."

"Your father has three mates I've seen."

Horda nodded. "He had a hand of mates, but two walk the Frozen Wilds."

"So three mates? Why doesn't he put aside the ones he's

tired of?"

"I don't think he's tired of any of them."

"Then why does he have so many?" insisted Bear Claw.

"One reason," said Horda patiently, "is because we have more women than men."

Bear Claw glared. "So what? Women are useless, and even a young man would have a hard time servicing so many mates."

Horda refused to be baited. She continued, "Another reason is men have needs that cannot be met by women who are breeding or nursing." She felt a blush crawl up her cheeks at the sensitive topic, but she refused to lower her eyes.

Mother Life, what have I said?

Bear Claw hooted at her stricken expression. "Neither hinders my pleasure."

Shocked, Horda realized she had nowhere to go. The People of the Frozen Earth's belief that little ones should be protected and given every chance of survival even before their births would only provide Bear Claw another chance to mock.

Oh, Mother Life, I cannot convince him, and I cannot choose him. What am I to do?

She closed her mouth and stared silently at this stranger.

Bear Claw's foreign ideas confused and upset her. Even though she'd enjoyed talking to him before, she realized anew how very different his beliefs were from her own. Even if she didn't love Mach so, she doubted she'd ever be happy mated with Bear Claw.

Looking around, she suddenly realized the Gathering Grounds lay out of sight around the bend of the river. She stopped and opened her mouth to suggest they turn back, but before she could do so, Bear Claw reached out and pulled her into his arms.

"What are you doing?" More surprised than frightened, she pushed against his chest, smudging the painted designs.

He laughed harshly. His silver eyes gleamed while his hands

fumbled at the neck of her tunic. "Enough talk of mating. I want you."

"Me?" It was the only thing she could think to say.

"Yes. I choose the woman I want, and I join with her. I want you. I will mate with you."

"Now? Like this?" She struggled to free herself from his grip.

"You know I do. You heard me tell your father."

"But — that is not our way."

"It is mine, and it is simpler." He grasped her breast through her tunic and gave it a painful squeeze.

"Stop it!" Anger gave her strength. She twisted away from Bear Claw's groping hands. "I can't join with you this way, and I don't want to! It violates the taboos of my tribe. You'd be punished."

"Punished?" His laughter rumbled deep in his chest. "What are you talking about?"

"It is taboo to join outside the ceremony."

"My people don't have a ceremony."

"But mine do. And you'll be punished for forcing me."

"Forcing you?" His laugh was harsh, entirely without compassion or mercy.

"I told you I don't want to join with you."

He lunged, grabbing her once more in his rough embrace. "It doesn't matter what you want, little one."

"Yes, it does! You're in the midst of *our* Gathering. You must abide by *our* ways. If you force me to join with you against my wishes, my father, the Chief, will use a dull flint knife to cut off your man parts."

For the first time, Bear Claw hesitated. He loosened his hold on her slightly. "My man parts?"

"And you'll be forced to carry them in your hands when you march naked around the camp, to show everyone the price a man pays for forcing himself on a woman. Then you'll taste the

Wrath of Fire."

"What's that?" Bear Claw looked at her with all the disdain he could muster, but his eyes betrayed the real fear that lay beneath.

"They'll burn you alive in the assembly fire and leave your remains in the ashes to be burned over and over forever."

Bear Claw's arrogant tone returned. "And what would they do to *you* if I said you led me on, but changed your mind and cried I forced you?" He grinned lewdly. "After all, you did walk out here with me of your own accord."

She did not blink. "Then they wouldn't cut off your man parts . . ."

He laughed his harsh laugh again and tightened his grip on her arm, pulling her against himself once more.

". . . but we would taste the Wrath of Fire together."

He hooted. "Burn you? Oh, I doubt it. You're the chief's daughter. You're honored. They wouldn't dare."

"Who I am doesn't matter. All the People of the Frozen Earth are equal, and even our smallest children know the mating urges are natural and enjoyable — but only within the sanctity of the recognized mate. The laws and taboos are part of the earliest ritual training."

Mother Life, I'm lecturing him again, but I don't know any other way to make him understand.

"The mating urge isn't a beast which cannot be controlled, but rather a river of life to be channeled and used productively to guarantee the survival of our People. Sexual promiscuity is the result of the irresponsibility of both partners, and both are punished for it. If I'm found guilty of such an offense, I'll also be punished."

"By the Great Mystery! You're serious, aren't you?" Bear Claw sounded genuinely incredulous.

Though fear of this strange man and what he might still do to her shook her insides, her voice was strong and firm. "Yes, I'm serious."

There was a brief, tense pause; suddenly Bear Claw seemed to reach a decision. Throwing back his head, he guffawed. "Scared you, didn't I, little one? You're such a solemn thing. I was teasing you, just as I've seen you tease your men. You didn't think I was serious, did you?"

She looked at him doubtfully but refused to answer.

"You didn't honestly think I'd dishonor you." It was a statement as much as a question.

"I didn't think so, or I wouldn't have walked with you," she said calmly.

"I'm trying to learn your taboos and customs, but clearly it'll take me a little time. Don't judge me too harshly. And please, accept my apologies for my little words. Won't you?"

His mouth smiled down at her, but a cold fire burned in the depths of his eyes.

It's not your words that beg an apology, Horda thought to herself, but as she had been trained since birth to accept apologies freely offered, she could not tell him that. Still, she nearly choked on her response. "I accept your apology."

"Then it is settled." Horda did not find the words reassuring. Bear Claw frightened her more than ever now. She understood the lust burning in the cold depths of his eyes and sensed he meant to have her no matter what choice she made. Oh, Mother Life, that she were a child again so she could run screaming back to her father's camp and find comfort in his embrace. But she was not, so she forced herself to stand her ground.

A sudden commotion on the path drew both their attentions. Emol lumbered into view, puffing and groaning from the strain of his exertions. Horda released the breath she didn't know she'd been holding. She had never thought she'd be glad to see that fat old chief for any reason. How strange life could be sometimes.

"Greetings, Bear Claw and Horda," wheezed Emol, oblivious to the lightning crackling between the other two. "I trust you're having a pleasant Gathering."

"Yes," snapped Bear Claw, clearly not pleased by the interruption.

The silence stretched while Emol waited for Bear Claw to greet him. Smoothing ineffectually at the wrinkles in the stained tunic stretched over his bulging stomach, Emol finally said, "Ah, you know I've expressed an interest in Horda."

"You have?" Bear Claw's mouth curled into a surprised sneer.

"Yes, I have," said Emol sharply. "I'd walk with her. We need time together."

Horda swallowed her smile. Emol's little piggy eyes had narrowed at Bear Claw's sneer. She imagined fat, lazy Emol trying to punch the Chief of the People of the Tall Grass and chewed the inside of her cheeks to stop her laughter. That would be a fight. Emol would surely win if he could sit on top of Bear Claw.

She wanted to leave both men and go back to camp — alone — but she didn't dare insult Emol so grievously. Besides, she certainly didn't want to remain here with Bear Claw a moment longer, and this gave her the excuse she needed to withdraw. She still disliked this fat chief intensely, but she smiled winningly at him.

Bear Claw turned mocking eyes on Horda. "I enjoyed our ... ah ... visit."

"Thank you." She pretended not to understand his innuendo.

"I look forward to continuing our *discussion* soon." He touched her hand.

Her skin crawled, but she didn't pull her hand away. Nodding to Bear Claw she walked away beside Emol without another word.

Searching for words to fill the silence after she and Emol discussed the weather, the hunting, and the Feast, Horda gratefully heard the thigh bone flutes and log drums calling the people to order.

"It's time for the First Hunt," she commented softly, in an effort to hide her relief. "Hurry, we don't want to miss it."

"Humph," snorted Emol. "What difference does it make?"

She blinked. "Don't you need to be there to wish the boys of your band a good hunt?"

"No boys," he muttered.

"You don't have any boys entering the Rituals of Manhood?" She looked at him questioningly, hoping for more information. Truly, she hadn't known.

Emol hedged, "We did have a boy last Gathering."

She feared she had embarrassed him. "I'm sorry. I thought all the bands had boys of an age to enter the Rituals."

"Not all," he wheezed. "We are a small band, and trouble follows us. Many young ones meet Father Death in the long cold of winter." He shrugged acceptingly. "It can't be helped. Food becomes scarce, and little ones depart easily. It's the way."

She turned toward the assembly area so he could not read the disgust in her eyes. Little ones departed easily if no one took care of them. It seemed more young ones departed his band than any other, and his band was very small to begin with. She knew the Council had forced young couples to join him in the past, but that they no longer did so. He was always whining about some problem, either real or imagined. For example, no other band had found game or other food scarce for many turnings of the seasons, but he complained his band never had quite enough. And he never seemed concerned about trying to fix things himself rather than depending on the charity of others. It made him a weak leader. She told herself it wasn't any of her concern right now.

"Ah, let's hurry anyway," she murmured. "Zeephro,

Treema's eldest, is beginning the Rituals. I need to see him before he leaves." She walked briskly toward the Gathering Grounds without looking back.

"Wait!" Emol panted, waddling behind her at some distance. "I would visit with you some more."

Plunging into the throng of people moving toward the Circle of Light, Horda pretended not to hear his words. "I enjoyed walking with you," she called over her shoulder. "I will see you again." She hurried away to find her brother.

"Humph, I will teach you manners when you are my mate," he muttered. This time Horda truly did not hear what he had to say.

❈

"Zeephro." Horda saw her little brother far ahead of her and hurried to catch up. "Zeephro, wait!"

He paused and frowned. "Horda, I'm in a hurry."

She laughed. "I know. This is the most important time of your life so far, so I won't keep you but a short span." She hugged him and touched her lips to his forehead. "My, Little Brother, you're almost grown up."

He leaned against her before he remembered his dignity and gently pushed her away. "I'm almost as tall as you," he protested. She caught one of his hands and pulled him back so she could look into his clear amber eyes, just a shade lighter than her own. Her other hand smoothed one of his already smooth ebony braids and gently tweaked the shells and beads at its end.

"Yes, you're almost grown," she acknowledged, looking at his hands and feet grown huge in the past moons. When they fit his body, he would be taller than their father. She reached in her pocket and pulled out a small relic worn smooth by the hands of many owners. "I just wanted to wish you the best." She pressed the bone into his hand.

90

His mouth dropped open at the object, and he blinked rapidly.

"You knew I'd give it to you."

"No, I didn't."

"Zephat gave it to me to hold when he went to the Dance of the Sun. My father allowed me to keep it because I was the eldest after Zephat walked the Frozen Wilds, but it truly belongs to a warrior. You know I only held it to keep its magic strong for you."

Zeephro's eyes grew shiny, and he blinked quickly to keep his tears from falling. Legend said he held in his hand the heartbone of the first kill of his ancestor, his father's father's father's father's father — a hunter still revered in the stories of the winter cook fires. "Thank you."

"Luck and happiness, Little Brother." She smiled down at him.

"Zeephro, hurry up," shouted Brash, from still farther up ahead. "Zaaco is about to begin."

He stood on tiptoes and touched his lips to hers. "Luck and happiness to you, Big Sister." Then he was gone to join the other boys standing on the brink of manhood.

Horda blended with the throng in the assembly area, waiting in the open under a cloudless blue sky for the Ritual of the First Hunt to begin.

Zaaco looked at the new men and the boys with three hands of winters. With the slightest nod, he stepped into the Circle of Light and raised his arms. "On this the Day of the Great Traveler, we have celebrated with the feast that officially ends the Rituals of Manhood begun four winters ago for the men on my left."

He paused dramatically and looked at the assembled people before he continued, "One thing that keeps our tribe strong is that the People help the People, no matter which band they belong to. These new men, on their day of celebration, must take time for their first official duty to help the future. They will assist the boys on my right, boys born three hands of winters ago, in the Ritual of the First Hunt, their first Ritual of Manhood."

He lowered his arms and waited while the men on his left joined the boys on his right. He smiled to himself to see Mach and Thuro form a group with Zeephro, Brash, and a hand of other boys.

When all the groups were formed, Zaaco looked to Elko, a short, powerfully built man with a barrel chest and bronze skin darkened to burnished copper by the summer sun. His ebony braids flashed with red highlights and his dark-brown eyes twinkled despite the solemn expression on his warrior's face.

Zaaco's voice boomed across the assembly. "Elko, as the Master of the Hunt, it is your duty to train these men-to-be in the skills they will need to ensure our People's survival through all the winters to come. Do you accept this sacred duty?"

Elko's voice was deep and firm. "I do."

Zaaco's eyes swept the older warriors chosen to help with the training. "Do you, the hunt master's chosen helpers, accept the sacred duty you have been given?"

"We do." The older warriors' deep voices echoed Elko's acceptance.

A slight smile wrinkled the corners of Zaaco's eyes. "Do the new men of the tribe accept their own sacred duty?"

"We do." One of the new men's voices slipped into the higher registers, smudging the dignity of the measured response. Fortunately, no one laughed aloud at the unexpected squeak.

"Then go and bring back meat for the eats of this Gathering. May the game be plentiful." Zaaco lowered his hands in dismissal, and the People chanted their approval and encouragement.

The hunters exited, and the noise died away. Zaaco raised his arms once more. "For the rest of us, let the games begin."

Gaiety and excitement filled the rest of the day, a triumphant tribute to Mother Life, who allowed the People to continue their way of life. The young people and many of the old men played games with inflated deer and antelope bladders. Others ran races or challenged each other to throwing contests using bones or spears. Wagers were won and lost and won and lost again. Through it all, laughter and excited talk filled the warm air.

Though Horda walked and talked and even laughed with the many men who courted her, her thoughts were still confused and angry, swirling between the man she loved and the man she felt obligated to choose. It definitely cast a pall over an otherwise beautiful day.

The festivities concluded when the sun dropped behind the mountains, painting the sky with bright streaks of oranges, yellows, purples, and pinks. Just before the colors faded, the men and men-to-be returned from the First Hunt laden with fresh meat.

"Horda, Horda," called Zeephro, "I made the cut that killed one of the deer. By myself. Mach told me how, but I did it all by myself!" His voice was positively bubbling; at the moment sounding more like an excited child than the man he was learning to be.

Horda grinned. "I'm proud of you. That's wonderful."

"Brash fell down, but he still ran the deer I killed."

"Fell?" Something about his tone put her healer woman training on the alert. "Was he hurt?"

"I don't guess — he still chased the deer right to me."

Horda looked at Mach who stood behind her brother and his friend. "Was Brash hurt when he fell?"

"I don't think so," Mach said looking at Brash, who shook his head. Mach laughed down at Horda. "Don't be such a mother hen. Men on hunts take falls. It happens. And he said he wasn't hurt."

"Sorry," she whispered. "They're still little boys to me."

"Don't let them hear you say that," cautioned Mach. "They're becoming men."

"In four turnings of the seasons," she reminded him tartly.

"Doesn't matter," he said. "Today they began."

An unwanted thought popped into her mind again, and fear trailed its icy fingertips up and down her spine. Would most of those boys be dead before they became men? Would Zeephro, her own brother, be one of them? She shivered. The tribe's growing, she told herself firmly. But, oh, what a waste that would be. *Please, Mother Life, be merciful, to all of them.*

"I couldn't have made the kill without Brash's help," Zeephro declared, catching Horda's hand and pulling her attention back to him.

"No, I'm sure you couldn't have." She squeezed his hand affectionately in return.

"They make a good team," Mach said.

"Like you and Thuro." She smiled up at her beloved.

He nodded.

One last prayer officially ended the Day of the Great Traveler, and most of the people headed, sated and happy, to their tents for some well-needed rest. Horda, though, knew she would not rest, torn as she was – her heart still chose Mach without hesitation or condition, but her head screamed that such a choice could lead to a devastating war for all her people.. What was she to do?

Chapter 8

The rising of the moon brought the beginnings of preparation for the next day's activity, the solemn and dangerous Dance of the Sun. Mach returned to Zaaco's camp where he sought Horda's company. "Tomorrow I will need you," he declared formally.

Pain flickered in her eyes. "Almost, I'd forgotten. Must you do this thing?"

"Yes."

"But why?" Her eyes pleaded with him even more than her tone.

"I must prove myself."

"You proved yourself by completing your Great Travel. You're still young. You could wait to do this." Forever, if necessary, she told herself. "And many great warriors never perform the Dance of the Sun at all."

Indulgence flickered in his eyes then faded. "I'm aware of that, but I must dance, and I don't choose to wait."

"You could be hurt."

"I could be." A gentle smile softened his harsh features. "Would the danger be any less at another Gathering?"

"I don't know. You could prepare yourself better if you waited."

"I have prepared myself now. I made my decision during the long cold after the big cat attacked me." His eyes looked beyond her at a past she could not see. "I sought Mother Life's guidance, and this is where it has led. I must do this for her as much as for myself."

"I'm not prepared. I don't want you to —"

"I do this to be worthy of you."

"You're already worthy of me. This will not make you more so."

"I believe it will."

"I don't want you to do this, and I've said so — many times. How, then, can you claim it's for me?"

Taking a deep breath, Mach explained, "I'm young, with only two winters more than you. I was declared a man today, but others still talk because I dare to court you, the daughter of the chief."

Impatiently she waved his words aside. "I know this. I don't care."

Mach ignored her interruption. "Leaders and second leaders of our tribe court you. Even the future Medicine Man courts you."

Tears filled her eyes. "I don't care!" she repeated stubbornly.

"Bear Claw wants you to choose him. He wears those scars that show his courage."

"And are hideously ugly," she shot back angrily.

"No one can question his bravery."

"Because of some stupid scars?" Could a few scars really blind this man to Bear Claw's true character?

Mach's dark mahogany eyes stared into her soul. "Can you tell me now you will choose to spend the rest of your life with me?" he asked.

Turning away, she bit her lip. Two fat tears ran down her cheeks. He caught her arm and gently turned her to face him. Silently his eyes searched hers.

"I *want* to choose you." She finally forced the words past the lump in her throat. "Mother Life, it's all I want.

"But?"

"But I'm frightened —"

"See, what I mean." Mach took her cold hands in his warm ones. "Many people look at me beneath their slitted eyes. How dare I, a young pup, challenge others who are older, and who have proven themselves here or in another place, for your hand? The Dance of the Sun offers me a way to show them my bid is not just a whim, but that I am worthy to be the son-in-law of the Chief, the mate of his eldest daughter. I do this thing for you and for myself. The tongues will stop wagging, and we can be together."

Tears still glittered in her eyes, but she kept her voice strong. "I do understand why you feel you must dance, but even after it's finished, I cannot promise I'll choose you."

Pain flickered in the depths of his dark eyes, but his only outward reaction was a deep breath and a squaring of his shoulders. He didn't want to argue with her. "Will you be my helper?" was all he said.

"Your helper?"

"I'm trying to help you make up your mind." He grinned. "Will you do it?"

"I'll try."

"Trying isn't enough. There'll be blood."

"I know."

"You mustn't faint."

Horda drew herself to her full height and glared at Mach. "I've studied to be a healer woman since I had seven winters. I've seen more human blood than you." Her eyes glittered fiercely. "I do not faint at the sight of blood, even yours."

He chuckled. "Does that mean you'll help me?"

Her glare softened to show her love. "Yes."

"Good." He leaned down to touch his forehead to hers and share her breath. "I must go. Zaaco and Nuroo will be waiting to help me prepare."

He turned away before he saw her shudder — a fearful gesture, even now that she had promised to be there for him.

Mach left her and joined the men chosen to assist in the ritual Dance of the Sun. They entered the sweat lodges to purify themselves for the coming day.

❀

Horda sat beside her father's fire, dreading the trial to come. Then her thoughts turned inward to the bloody ordeal of a Gathering long past. She could hear the drums long since silent, beating the fearful rhythm of the Dance of the Sun in her head again. They pounded over the insistent noise of the muffled moans of Zephat, her favorite brother, and the tortured wails of Xyla, his mother.

Once more she became a child too tall and too old to be carried on Zephat's broad shoulders, but done so one last time nonetheless. She felt his soft hair, so like her own, blowing beneath her fingers. Saw his mother's anguished face while his words echoed through her memory. His gentle voice explained once more how he had to dance to prove himself worthy of being Zaaco's son. He shared his breath with Horda and laughed at her fears before he went to prepare. She had sobbed then, and did so again now.

She pressed her fingers to her eyes until the swirling reds and blacks and greens and yellows covered the memory pictures — almost. She could still see Zephat secure the tethers in his own flesh. Once more his body lifted into the air. Once more Xyla screamed as one tether tore free, ripping the muscles and tendons and causing the men to lower Zephat's body to the ground. Once more his blood bubbled and spurted from the fearsome wound into a puddle in the dust beneath his body, fast going limp.

Nausea swirled in her stomach as the memory of the bitter salty smell of blood burned her nostrils once more. Remembered pain clutched her throat while his lifeblood filled his vessel of time. The fever demons crawled into the gaping hole in his chest and burned away his gentle spirit before Father Death came and carried him to the Frozen Wilds.

The Dance of the Sun tore away more than just Zephat's shoulder. It tore a hole in the heart of his mother Xyla, Zaaco's first mate, and left a void which robbed her of her own life force. The soft, laughing woman who comforted Horda's childish hurts also departed that day, though her body walked the earth through the long cold of winter to the time of early green.

Even after more than two hands' turnings of the seasons, Zephat's passing remained an empty place in Horda's soul, which only pain seemed able to fill. She shivered. Zephat and Mach mixed and mingled in her heart.

"Oh, Zephat —" The cry ripped from her soul.

"What's wrong with you?" Meiran's face twisted, and her voice sharpened. "Did you see a spirit?" She looked around the camp cautiously.

Horda sought a reply that wouldn't anger her mother. She couldn't tell her the truth, and no safe answer came to mind. She remained silent.

"What's wrong with you? Have you done something to shame me?"

"I'm tired." The words came unbidden, but their truth washed over Horda like rain. Fatigue dragged at her limbs until she could hardly remain upright.

"Then go to your furs. Tomorrow comes earlier than usual." Meiran turned away, loosening her hair in preparation for sleep. Horda stood beside her mother, silently begging for comfort while remembered pain slashed her soul.

Meiran turned back. "You haven't moved. There's something wrong."

"Mach ..." Horda couldn't force the rest of the words into the open.

"What has that young pup done? Did he force himself on

you? Has he shamed you? He'll be punished, you know. Doesn't he understand you're meant for Bear Claw?" Meiran's angry voice rose sharply.

Fear pushed words through the lump in Horda's throat. "No, no, it's nothing like that. He's done nothing wrong. Why do you always assume the worst? It's just that he'll dance tomorrow."

Meiran frowned. "What are you babbling about?"

The tears filling Horda's eyes almost drowned out the hateful words. "Mach will dance the Dance of the Sun tomorrow."

Meiran's features softened.

"I'm afraid, Ma," whispered Horda.

"You mustn't even think such a thing," Meiran scolded, as if simply wishing should make it so. "The spirits may punish you for speaking such nonsense."

Her words were brave, but within Meiran's head danced the echoes of another voice admitting fear for one who danced. The cold hand of Father Death twisted inside her, pursing her mouth and darkening her eyes. The Dance of the Sun sent both Zephat and his mother to walk the Frozen Wilds. She was determined it would not claim her daughter, too.

"Mach is strong and brave," she continued loudly, so all the hovering spirits could hear her confidence. "He's worthy to dance the Dance of the Sun. He'll bring great honor to the tribe."

Horda was still racked by doubt. "Zephat was strong and brave and worthy, but still he fail —"

Whispering angrily, Meiran clutched her daughter's arm, "Would you call the evil spirits down on him? What are you thinking?"

"But I'm af —"

"Nonsense! You must prepare yourself for the morrow by praying to Mother Life and Father Death. You must be strong, for all of us. It's your duty as the daughter of Zaaco."

Meiran turned abruptly away, but not before Horda saw

the fear in her eyes. Mother Life, her mother was frightened, after all. But there was nothing more to say, so, biting her lip to prevent her anguished cries from escaping, Horda went to her sleeping furs.

But the furs did nothing to calm her. Wide-eyed and afraid, she prayed silently until long after Zaaco returned from the sweat lodge. Finally, she drifted into sleep, but it was restless, haunted by terrible specters of unnamed disasters. Crying, she clawed through the dirty cobwebs of her dreams toward wakefulness.

"Shh, shh, little girl, it'll be all right." Zaaco was sitting beside her, petting her heaving back as he had when the bad dreams of Zephat's Dance of the Sun had wakened her.

Horda wrapped her arms around his neck and clung to him like a tiny opossum clings to its mother. "Oh, Fa, it was awful. There was blood ev —"

"Shh, don't give your dream reality by speaking it aloud," he scolded, but his tone was gentle, soothing.

"But, you have to do something." Tears ran down her face and pooled in the corners of her mouth. "He thinks he has to do this to be worthy of me. I tried to tell him I fear I must choose Bear Claw anyway, but he won't listen. You must stop him."

Zaaco didn't ask of whom she spoke; he already knew. His fingers dried the tears from her cheeks before he spoke. "You know I can't."

Her head lowered, and she sobbed.

He placed his right index finger beneath her chin and raised her head until she looked into his eyes. "You know this is between Mach and Mother Life. He knows you're torn. He accepts you may choose another, but he still feels this is what he must do. You can understand that, can't you?"

Reluctantly Horda nodded.

"It will be all right."

"Will it?" Her words sounded little louder than a whisper.

"Can you promise Father Death won't interfere? Can you promise Mach won't end up like Zephat?"

Pain flashed in the old chief's eyes. "I sat with Mach in the sweat lodge. I prayed with him and talked with him while he prepared himself for the coming ordeal. I flaked the black stone skewers and explained how the cuts will be made. I prepared the rawhide tethers we will use. I've done everything I can to help him."

Her amber eyes darkened. "Can you promise he won't be like Zephat?"

"I've done everything in my power to keep him safe. Tomorrow Nuroo will make the cuts with his own hands. I'll check the cuts and secure the thongs. I can do no more."

Her eyes widened in surprise. The Medicine Man did not normally make the cuts himself. Nor did the Chief check them. But she felt the stubbornness weighing on her like a stone. "Will that be enough? Can you promise, Fa?"

Her questions hung in the air between them. He rubbed his face. "Did you pray?" he asked, seemingly changing the topic.

Though she longed to demand an answer to her question, she finally settled for answering his, "Yes, but ..." How could she tell her father she felt that no one seemed to hear her prayers?

"Do you want to go to the sweat lodge to prepare yourself for this ordeal?"

"What?"

"You must be as strong as Mach if you are to help him. You could go to the sweat lodge to prepare yourself."

"But I haven't completed the ritual training."

Zaaco sighed. "You've been asked to bear a woman's burden. You are permitted to use the sweat lodge to prepare yourself."

"I didn't know."

"Now you do."

She hesitated. Her father offered her comfort. She knew little about the sweat lodge because she wouldn't study it until she went through this year's rituals. She needed its comfort, but she was afraid. "I don't know how to."

"I'll help you."

"Thank you."

They rose from the furs, and together they walked to the squat round lodge covered with four layers of woven prairie grass mats. Zaaco's voice was soft and comforting. "When everything is ready, take off your clothes and rub your body with this." He handed her a bundle of sweetgrass. Then bathe in the steam.

"Next, sprinkle these," he continued, giving her a bundle of sage leaves and juniper twigs, "on the coals in the fire bowl. Then, pray for the strength and courage to meet the coming ordeal. The smoke will purify you and carry your prayers to Mother Life and Father Death. When you have found your strength, come outside and wash in the cold water I will leave for you. Then dress and sleep until I call you."

As he explained each step, he placed several round stones in the fire pit and covered them with dried cedar wood, pine cones, and juniper kindling. Then he offered the ceremonial flint to the four directions and struck the fire. When the wood and pine cones crackled merrily, he sprinkled dried sage leaves over the flames. "The sage cleanses the stones just as it cleanses you," he told his daughter.   Together they carried water to the pit and waited for the stones to heat. After a short while, Zaaco used the hardened wood tongs to lift one stone from the flames. He carefully dripped cold water on it and watched the droplets dance away to steam.

"It's time," he said, filling two hardened wood racks with the heated stones. They carried the racks inside, and, chanting the ancient prayers, Zaaco placed the stones around the center pit. Horda carried the rest of the stones while her father carried coals to the tiny fire bowl inside the lodge. She watched him feed it sweetgrass and cedar shavings and saw his smile when the fuel burned quickly to ash. At last he poured water over the stones and watched the white steam fill the small enclosure. When the air had turned to a white mist, he stepped outside. Everything was ready.

"You stay in the lodge until you are purified. You must rise above your fears."

"I will try."

"You must do more than try, daughter. You must succeed if you expect him to succeed." He raised the door covering of the small sweat lodge and waited for her to enter.

She caught his arm and asked once more. "If I do these things, can you promise me that Mach won't end up like Zephat?"

She watched Zaaco fight to speak the lie. Finally he sighed heavily and said, "You know I can't. We can only trust Mother Life to protect him. Pray for strength to face whatever must be faced."

She nodded sadly and closed the door covering.

Chapter 9

The chilled air whispered of winter's coming, and a lone owl screeched in the darkness, hunting its prey. Horda barely noticed either. Looking around the semicircle of assembled People, she fought to hold her serenity, hard-won in the past night's sweat lodge and prayers. The moon slipped behind the mountains to the west, but the assembly waited in place, waited for the sun to push its golden rays above the rim of the plains to the east and cover the black bowl of the sky with the vibrant blue of the new day. Then the ceremony would begin.

The twinkling stars above and the tang of sage and cedar smoke from the ceremonial fires intruded on her thoughts and brought the story of the ancestors' campfires in the Frozen Wilds to her mind. She shuddered once again. Would Mach walk with those ancestors when this terrible ritual ended? She raised her eyes to the majestic poles rigged with rawhide ropes, each taller than a hand of men. Soon Mach would be lifted by those ropes to offer his strength, his bravery, himself to ... to what? Horda gritted her teeth against the touch of Father Death and forced herself to pray yet again to Mother Life.

In counterpoint of white wolf and black bear cloaks, Zaaco and Nuroo took their places beside the ceremonial fire pit at the base of the poles. Though his face remained stoic, Horda found silent comfort in her father's eyes. She stood up straighter and squared her shoulders. She would prevail against her doubts and offer Mach the support he needed.

The sun's first pink fingers teased the plains to the east, and Zaaco raised his arms to signal the beginning of the ceremony. The log drums began to beat. The men who would assist Mach in the Dance of the Sun marched forward in a tight circular formation, their footsteps echoing the beat. Mach, at their center, stood two hands' width taller than the rest. His eyes found Horda's in the crowd. One mahogany eye half-closed in a slight wink and almost brought a smile to her face. Not mischievous, though, it seemed to be more a plea for her understanding and her strength. She allowed the hard set of her face to soften and forced the tiniest smile to curve her lips in response, and she saw his clenched fists relax.

Bear Claw also watched her, but it was from across the circle. His scarred face looked even more frightening in the flickering firelight of the early dawn hours. After a glance, Horda forced herself not to look at him at all, though she continued to feel his stare on the back of her neck. Instead, she kept her eyes steady on Mach's.

Nuroo began the solemn Songs of the Sun. The warriors echoed his words. Horda's heart matched the fearful rhythm of the drums, but her eyes did not waver.

"Who comes before this assembly of the People to pledge himself to the Sun?" Zaaco's formal tones reverberated through the gathering.

The circle parted, and Mach stood alone, bathed in the first golden rays of the new day. "I, Mach, pledge myself to the Sun."

"Why dare you make this pledge?"

"I owe my life to the Sun. I offer my life back to the Sun."

A murmur of approval whispered through the crowd at the simple yet eloquent answer.

The morning grey of the sky turned blue as the sun crawled above the horizon. Horda's eyes widened, and her heart lightened when a playful breeze bathed Mach in the fragrant smoke of the ceremonial fires. A good omen at last!

Please, Mother Life, keep him safe.

Nuroo lifted the first obsidian skewer from Norlon's outstretched hands. Stately, measured steps brought him to Mach who waited, silent and still. Only the twitch of a muscle in the old Medicine Man's jaw betrayed his tension. Reaching up, he made a deft, sure cut in Mach's chest, inserting the blade under the pectoral muscle above his right nipple. Pain flared in his mahogany eyes, but the young warrior made no other response. Nuroo stepped back.

After straightening the cords, Zaaco attached the rawhide tether to the blade, before pulling it the rest of the way through Mach's flesh and securing it. Mach did not flinch. Zaaco stared approvingly at the young man before he, too, stepped back. Nuroo then repeated the procedure on the left side. Droplets of blood flowered around each wound but did not trickle down Mach's sides.

Though her eyes remained steady and her body straight and still, tears burned the back of Horda's throat. Swallowing hard, she gritted her teeth for fear she would dissolve into sobs. *Focus,* she told herself. *Focus on the ceremony itself.*

Raising his arms and beginning the first chant of dedication, Zaaco left Mach alone in the Circle of Light. A hand plus three other warriors took their places beside the rawhide cords of the tethers in Mach's chest. The log drums whispered. Then Mach began the slow steps of the Dance of the Sun. Twisting and turning, he moved around the poles while the other warriors prevented the rawhide cords from tangling around him.

The sun rose higher. Its rays gilded the sweat and blood staining Mach's chest. Mach's steps followed the widening Circle of Light, drawing the tethers tighter and stretching his wounds wider. His face reflected only his intense concentration; the streams of blood-tinged sweat pouring from his body gave silent testimony to the pain he suffered. The beat of the drums grew louder and more insistent, guiding Mach's feet to move faster and faster to match their rhythm.

Horda concentrated on sharing her strength with Mach as her eyes followed him around and around the circle. The sun climbed the sky above the assembly area. The playful breeze fell, and the heat rose. Although she had avoided looking at him, a slight movement by Bear Claw caught her attention — doubt and fears of a future mated with him nibbled at her consciousness, eroding her frail confidence. Now her insides quivered and quaked like aspen leaves in the winds of an autumn storm. As if he could sense her distress, Mach's steps began to falter, and Horda almost cried out to him. Instead, she firmly scolded herself for her selfishness and pushed her fears away, rededicating her strength to her beloved.

The Dance continued as the sun crawled higher and higher. Now the drum beats slowed to match Mach's shuffling steps as the awesome ordeal lumbered toward its next level. Zaaco raised his arms, and the warriors tightened the cords embedded in Mach's flesh. Then stepping back, they drew the rawhide cords tauter still.

When the sun hung at its zenith, Zaaco lowered his arms to his sides. Farther and farther back the warriors moved, until Mach's body rose above the ground — suspended only by the tethers and skewers in his chest.

Mach's face twisted in agony as the warriors worked the cords and continued the steps of the dance. His body spun slowly around and around and back and forth, a fearful pendulum marking the passing of time. Bear Claw's shocked expression caught Horda's attention for just an instant, and she thought she saw respect or admiration glimmering in the icy depths of his eyes. So, there was understanding behind the scornful façade.

Quickly banishing all thoughts of Bear Claw, she watched only Mach as the terrible tension that kept his body rigid drained away, allowing him to sag like a soft leather doll with too little stuffing. Once more her tears formed a hot lump in her throat, and she fought to focus her thoughts away from the present to the future.

Please, Mother Life, to days that really will be.

As she fought for control, the awful spectacle before her dimmed. The pungent smell of sage burning in the ceremonial fires around the assembly wafted away and was replaced by the fresh, crisp scent of new grass slightly bruised beneath her feet. The harsh chants of the warriors and the incessant pounding of the log drums faded and gave way to the gurgling sounds of a small stream and the chattering of birds.

The searing heat of the late summer sun faded to a soft warmth caressing her hot face; the dry winds softened to gentle breezes and brought cool relief. The harsh golden brown stalks and seed pods became pale green shoots of spring grass intermingled with forget-me-nots and primroses nodding in the wind. She wondered how early springtime had found its way into the grisly Dance of the Sun, but she was grateful for the respite, and she refused to question too closely.

Horda walked the narrow path beside the water and found Mach waiting for her. They did not speak though they touched and shared breath. His mouth covered hers, sipping her essence. Tentatively, then more eagerly, her tongue touched his, and he pulled her toward him, crushing her body against his own. She drew back suddenly afraid of hurting the fresh wounds she expected to mar his bronzed chest. Shocked by their absence, her hands traced the faded scars raised against his muscles. She laughed as he quivered beneath her touch, but neither spoke. What was there to say?

She saw his eyes darken with desire and, remembering Bear Claw's lustful pawing, felt a sudden anxiety sweep through her body. Ah, but this was not Bear Claw, this was the man her heart cried out for every minute of the day. She leaned against his solid strength, feeling her own desire reach out toward him, and her anxiety fled completely. Mach's roughened warrior's fingers gently traced the beaded and quilled designs on the bodice of her tunic. His eyes asked permission, and hers granted it without hesitation.

Her skin heated against his fingers as they unlaced her soft doeskin tunic and pushed it off her shoulders. His large hands delicately cupped her breasts before he lowered his head to taste them. As his lips caressed her skin, her insides melted into hot honey, and her legs threatened to give way. But legs were unnecessary; the two sank slowly to the ground to join on a bed of soft spring grass laced with blue forget-me-nots and bright pink primroses. Together they climbed the hills of pleasure and danced among the clouds. Each time they neared the earth, they climbed again to play above the clouds and savor each other's essence.

Slowly the sun crept toward the jagged teeth of the mountains. The shadows of the tall trees fell over their resting place. Soon they would have to part although she wanted this moment to go on forever. Her hands grew clumsy; tangling the thongs of her tunic; smiling, Mach reached over to straighten and secure them for her. He shared her breath once more then mysteriously faded away, leaving only the crushed spring grass to mark his passing. A strange peace settled over her, and she knew she had reached a decision. She would walk the Frozen Wilds before she chose anyone but Mach.

Dazed, she blinked — surprised and more than a little embarrassed to find herself in the midst of the assembly of the People. Hot blood still pounded in her veins. Her tunic chaffed nipples that were exquisitely sensitive. Her secret woman place felt warm and full and tender. Her legs seemed too weak to support her weight. Once more she blinked, trying desperately to focus her eyes.

Before her the warriors gently lowered Mach's body back to the earth and cut the rawhide ropes free from the tethers embedded in his flesh. Forgetting propriety, she allowed a smile to curve her lips. The Dance of the Sun had ended. Mach's flesh had not ripped. Unless the fever demons feasted on his wounds, he would not walk the Frozen Wilds. He would be her mate. Her heart sang.

The drums beat quietly, and the flutes sang softly. The warriors began the dance of victory around Mach's supine body. Horda silently thanked Mother Life for protecting him and Father Death for sparing him before she joined the women in the outer circle of the dance. Tears of joy streamed unchecked down her face.

Oblivious to all save Mach, Horda didn't notice Bear Claw watching not the ceremony, but her. Anger heated his body and knotted his muscles. His face twisted into a mask of rage, and his fists clenched. He knew from her expression he had lost her, and his wrath became palpable to all around him. The warriors standing beside him instinctively moved away. Bear Claw stalked out of the assembly without a backward glance.

In the central area, Zaaco gave the signal and a group of young men lifted the exhausted Mach to their shoulders. Nuroo led the group from the assembly area. Horda and his parents followed close behind. Fresh droplets of blood bloomed around the skewers to mix with the sweat still trickling down his sides. Once inside Mach's family shelter, Nuroo carefully washed away all traces of blood and sweat from Mach's chest before removing the tethers. Then he packed the wounds with dried alum roots, buckthorn leaves, and chamise oil. He wrapped Mach's chest with soft strips of fawn leather.

Swallowing a moan, Mach obediently raised his head and drank the strong willow tonic Nuroo offered. When he finished drinking, he saw Horda, and a smile lighted his tired face. Her heart fluttered when Mach's right eye dipped in the familiar half wink.

"We will leave you alone," said Nuroo gruffly, lowering

Mach's head to the furs. "The tonic will make you sleep until morning."

Mach nodded and closed his eyes, not watching the others file from the shelter.

❄

Outside Nuroo spoke to Zaaco while Horda listened unashamedly. "The wounds are clean. The obsidian didn't chew his flesh, and the tethers didn't tear it. Unless the fever demon feasts on him, the worst is over."

Zaaco hugged Horda, and they breathed twin sighs of relief. "Where did these come from?" As he pulled away, Zaaco lifted sprigs of blue and pink flowers from Horda's shoulder.

A blush tinted her cheeks, but she kept her voice steady. "They look like forget-me-nots and tiny primroses, but neither blooms in late summer."

Eyeing the flowers, he frowned. "They're fresh. I wonder where they came from." He began to crush the flowers in his fingers.

"Don't!" Horda cried, clutching his arm.

"Why not?"

"I'd ... I'd like to keep them," was all she could muster. She lifted the remaining flowers to her nose. Her body tingled with the memory of her vision, and another blush heated her face. "It's just ... I ... I want to remember this day."

Zaaco raised his eyebrows, and he stared questioningly at his daughter. When she didn't respond, he decided to say no more.

She smiled and silently tucked the tiny flowers into the leather pouch on the necklace Mach had given her. Truly, it was a day to remember.

Chapter 10

Gathering was not just a celebration, but a time for learning, as well. It included sessions where everyone who had lived more than two winters studied or taught the history and beliefs of the People of the Frozen Earth. For two hands plus one finger of Gatherings, Meiran had led the sessions for the children who had completed one hand of winters. Three Gatherings past, Horda had been chosen to help her mother.

"We must hurry. The children will soon be here." Struggling to spread her deerskin robe, Meiran fought for breath.

Surprised by the pain she read in her mother's eyes, Horda asked, "Are you all right?"

"Why do you ask?"

"You're so out of breath and you look pa ..." Horda's voice trailed away at Meiran's glare. "I'm sorry. I just wondered," said Horda lamely.

"I'm fine, just in a hurry," assured Meiran dismissively, with an insincere smile pasted on her face. "Spread the robe. I'll sit over there with the sun behind me."

Bear Claw's appearance at the session surprised Horda and made her more than a little uncomfortable. He smiled one of the smiles that didn't reach up to warm his eyes and said, "I want to learn more about the People of the Frozen Earth, so I thought this would be a good place to be. You don't mind, do you?"

Meiran looked at her daughter. When her motherly frown

did not elicit an answer, she tried a pinch, instead. It made Horda hiss, but the young woman remained stubbornly silent. Meiran took control of the situation, her voice taking on the unnaturally bright timbre that always set Horda's teeth on edge. "Of course, we don't mind. I think it's a wonderful idea. You're more than welcome to join us."

As ungraciously as she dared, Horda muttered, "Stay in the background. This session is for the children."

"I'll be quiet," promised Bear Claw mockingly.

Horda ground her teeth to stop her angry reply as the other young women of the tribe brought the laughing, chattering children for their lesson.

"Children, gather around and sit down so you can all hear my words," invited Meiran, now clearly in her element. A playful breeze ruffled the carved bone beads and shells decorating her elaborate coiffure. She patted a spot beside her for Horda who, eager to set a good example, immediately sat down. Still talking among themselves, the children swiftly found places in a semicircle before Horda and Meiran. Bear Claw drifted closer, but he obediently stayed in the back, out of the children's view.

"I trust you're having an enjoyable Gathering, children," said Meiran formally.

As prearranged, Horda led the children's reply. "Yes, we are. We trust your Gathering is also pleasing."

"Yes, thank you." Meiran bowed to the children. "Now, let us begin. At the last Gathering, you learned about the first band. Does anyone remember?"

A bright-eyed little boy said, "In the days before time, the first fathers brought their mates out of the snow and ice of the Frozen Wilds. They walked across the water from North Lands where the cold winds blew all the turnings of the seasons. They wandered and wandered to find plants and animals." His face had screwed up with the intense concentration of memory, but now that he had gotten the whole thing out, he looked pleased.

She smiled. "Very good, Lonzar. Who helped them?"

"Mother Life," volunteered three little girls simultaneously.

"Yes, and how did she help them?"

One small girl raised her hand.

"Sula."

"She told the animals to let them catch them so they could eat them and use their skins and bones."

"That's right. What else?"

Another boy said, "She told the sun to shine so the plants and animals could grow big and strong for her people. Then she taught the first band which plants and seeds to eat and use for medicine."

"You're correct," Meiran nodded. "What does she do for us now?"

"The same stuff," sniffed the little boy.

Meiran's face betrayed her disapproval of his terminology, but she smoothly said, "You're nearly right. She's responsible for all the benefits we receive." Seeing puzzled looks on the children's faces, she added, "That means Mother Life gives all the good things to us."

"All of them?" asked one of the little girls.

"All of them. She gives us food and clothes and shelters and medicines."

"Does she give us little ones?"

"Yes, she gives us little ones, too." Meiran's face sobered. "Now, does anyone remember about Father Death?"

She looked at all the solemn, little faces before one brave girl said, "He punishes us when we're bad and sometimes even when we aren't. He takes people with him to live in the Frozen Wilds beyond the sky. My ma's ma went with him since last Gathering. We cried when we found out, but my fa told us we could see her campfire if we looked real hard at night." The little girl's lip quivered. "I don't think she was bad though."

"No, she wasn't bad," said Meiran quietly. Horda longed

to reach out to comfort the child with a touch, but the moment passed and was lost. Meiran continued, "At their birth, Father Death gives each person a vessel for time. As the person's life passes, Father Death fills the vessel. For some, many turnings of the seasons pass while their vessels fill slowly. Your ma's ma was blessed. She lived a long time and knew and loved many of her children's children before her vesse ..." Meiran's voice broke off.

Horda saw pain beneath the tears in her mother's dark eyes. "Ma, are y —"

A fierce glare silenced Horda. Meiran took a deep breath and continued as if nothing had happened. "Others are not so blessed. Accidents or illnesses fill their vessels quickly." She shrugged. "Sometimes it seems Father Death chooses people just because he wants them. Other times anger takes people away. We must be careful not to anger him. How do we keep from angering him?"

Horda looked again at her mother. Meiran's face looked different somehow, but Horda couldn't quite pin down why; her voice, however, carried the same note of authority as always. The tiny beads and shells in her hair clicked and jingled softly as she looked at each child in turn, waiting for a response to her question. Perhaps Horda had only imagined the reflection of pain in Meiran's eyes. And the tears? What was she thinking? Horda nearly laughed out loud — her mother did not cry, ever. She must still need rest from yesterday's ordeal.

The children looked at each other, but none willingly volunteered an answer.

Meiran persisted. "No one knows how we keep from angering Father Death?"

All the little heads shook back and forth.

"Then I'll tell you. We, the People of the Frozen Earth, believe work helps keep from angering Father Death. We share whatever work needs to be done. Right now, all of you are learning signs, hunting, preserving food and hides, tanning leather, and cooking. Isn't that so?"

All of the little heads bobbed. Dawna, one of the small girls said, "I caught bunches of fish all by myself before we came to Gathering."

Meiran swallowed her smile and said, as only a mother could, "You did?"

"Uh huh. I helped my ma dry them with hers. I'm going to eat them this winter."

Lonzar frowned at Dawna and whispered loudly, "You won't be able to tell your fish from all the others your mother caught and dried."

"I will, too."

"Will not. She'll just tell you they're your fish, and you'll believe her."

Horda tensed to intervene, but a shake of Meiran's head kept her still. Dawna whispered back triumphantly, and just as loudly, "I put the mark for my name on my fish. I can read it, so I can pick out my very own fish myself. So there, Lonzar."

Horda saw a genuine smile lighten Bear Claw's face as he listened to the children arguing among themselves, but she did not let him know she had seen.

Meiran waited silently until the whispers ended. "That's very good, Dawna. You make Mother Life and Father Death very happy because you're working to see you don't starve."

Not to be outdone, Lonzar said, "My ma showed me how to make yampah porridge."

Meiran smiled, "I'm proud of you. You're learning to cook so you can if you need to."

He ducked his head, a blush creeping up his cheeks. "I didn't do very good. I burned it."

Horda giggled, and Meiran laughed outright. Meiran said, "Don't worry, Lonzar. It takes practice. Horda used to burn the porridge every time she made it."

Lonzar's eyes widened. "She did?"

The children all looked at Horda as if they could not imagine a grown-up young woman having the same problems learning tasks they did. Horda met Bear Claw's appraising eyes. Maybe he'd decide he didn't want her at all if she couldn't even cook porridge.

"She did, but she learned to do better. As you will." Meiran nodded sagely then stated, "Of all the work we do, one task and only one task is reserved for the warriors of the tribe." She stared solemnly at the small faces surrounding her. "What is that one task?"

"Making the spears and axes and the other things for war," cried one of the first little girls.

"That's right. Only the making of weapons for war is men's work." At Meiran's words, Horda quickly looked anywhere but at Bear Claw — best he should not see her fear.

"Why?" asked one brave little girl.

Meiran thought silently for several seconds before she finally admitted, "I don't know why. I think it's because the men fight and use the weapons, but I really don't know. I'll ask Zaaco before we meet again. I do know why we all learn the other tasks though. Do you?"

"Because we might need them," suggested Lonzar.

"That's dumb," said one of the girls named Challa. "Anyway, *I* won't need them because I'm very special. I'll always have someone to take care of me."

Meiran frowned at Challa. "Actually it's not dumb, Challa. People can't always depend on others to provide for their needs if they want to survive. All work is important and valuable. For the People of the Frozen Earth to survive, everyone must work. The work you're learning now has to be done, whether it's done by a man or by a woman."

A little boy with two front teeth missing smiled up at Meiran. "All of us learn all the work because we might need it someday to survive. Right?"

"That's right." The smile on her face suddenly froze in place, and she twisted back and forth, as if trying to find a more comfortable position. Mach and Thuro's approach brought an audible sigh of relief to her lips. She clapped her hands. "Now, I can tell you need to run, don't you?"

It was more a statement than a question, but all the little heads nodded eagerly nevertheless.

"Mach and Thuro will take you to run and play."

Excitement rippled through the group as the little heads turned to look. Young men just returned from their Great Travels conducted the play groups. Some saw it as a burdensome duty, but Mach had always made time to play with the little ones and had been a great favorite with them even before his Great Travel.

Meiran clapped her hands again, calling the children back to attention one last time. Obediently they looked at her. "Before you go, I want to tell you that next time we meet we'll talk about laziness, cruelty, and the Wrath of Fire. Oh, yes, and I'll try to learn why only men make weapons of war. Is everybody ready to leave?"

"Yes," chorused the small children.

"Then have a good Gathering. Horda and I will see you tomorrow."

"A good Gathering to you," the children shouted before running to the young men who waited to take them to play.

"You do that very well, Ma," said Horda softly.

"Yes, you do," added Bear Claw, coming up to join the women.

Though pain now visibly darkened her eyes, Meiran forced a smile. "Thank you."

Horda asked, "How do you always know what to tell them?"

Meiran thought a moment before she replied. "I don't, but it seems to get a little easier each Gathering. When I first started, I didn't do very well. I told them too much about too few things.

They're children. This is early training. They need to know a little bit about a lot of things. I can't go into too much detail on any one topic or I'll lose their attention." She laughed before she continued, "And when they start to wiggle around, I pray for the young men to hurry."

"They came at the right time."

"I try to train them, too," admitted Meiran, surreptitiously rubbing her lower back. "Do you want to conduct the session tomorrow?"

"Me?" Horda blinked. "Ah, I don't think so. I'd rather just listen."

"Suit yourself."

Bear Claw said, "Your daughter gave me a lesson yesterday when we walked together. She also is very knowledgeable about the People of the Frozen Earth."

"I know," said Meiran, "but she's a little unsure of herself. I think the children make her nervous."

"I think I make her nervous," said Bear Claw, boldly eying Horda while smiling an almost gracious smile at her mother. It made him look like a snake to Horda, but Meiran seemed not to notice anything amiss.

"Perhaps," agreed Meiran.

Anger painted roses in Horda's cheeks and compressed her lips into a tight line. How dare they talk about her as if she wasn't there?

"Thank you for sharing this time with me," said Bear Claw formally to Meiran.

"You're welcome. I hope your Gathering remains pleasant." Her tone clearly dismissed him.

Looking meaningfully at Horda he said, "I'm sure it will. I wish you both a pleasant Gathering and look forward to tomorrow's lesson." Then he turned and strode away without so much as a backward glance.

At three hands of winters, Doria, Meiran and Zaaco's younger daughter, had begun the first Rituals of Womanhood. But as she ran to her mother and sister, straight black braids flying behind her, she seemed much younger. "Ma, Horda, did you see Mach?"

"Yes, I saw Mach," said Horda softly. Meiran sniffed.

"I didn't expect him to come for the children. Did you?" Doria asked, her voice bubbling with conspiratorial enthusiasm.

"It's his task," said Meiran shortly.

Doria's soft doe eyes swam with unshed tears. "I know, but I thought he'd be excused today of all days. He just did the Dance of the Sun."

"Nuroo said the obsidian skewers made a big difference," Horda told her. "They didn't tear his flesh like the old flint ones. He said the cuts almost seemed to close themselves when he pulled the skewers from the flesh. His wounds are healing well."

Meiran opened her mouth to rebuke Horda for her graphic description, but Doria managed to jump in first. "I'm glad. He's not only the best-looking man in the tribe, he's also the nicest."

Closing her mouth without comment, Meiran shook her head in exasperation.

Doria plopped down between her mother and sister and grinned. "Oh, I almost forgot. I just learned the neatest stuff. You won't believe it."

"Probably we will, since we learned it too," murmured Horda under her breath.

"Don't discourage her," mouthed Meiran, rubbing her back again. More loudly, she said, "Why don't you tell us what you learned, Doria?"

Dark brown eyes sparkling, Doria proclaimed, "I learned about the most joyous ritual of the People of the Frozen Earth. The Ritual of Womanhood. It's celebrated only at Gathering, and it teaches me to be a woman and a mate."

"Imagine that," muttered Horda.

A soft pinch from Meiran silenced her. Meiran turned back to her younger daughter. "Tell us more."

"I'm going to have moon cycles. That bleeding makes it so I can have little ones."

"You already knew about moon cycles," said Horda, frowning at the younger girl, who already showed signs of becoming a traditionally beautiful woman. Sometimes in spite of herself, Horda envied Doria's straight black hair, her dark brown eyes, and her square face accented by high cheekbones and a flat almost bridgeless nose.

"I know I did," sniffed Doria, "but I didn't know it had anything to do with little ones. Did you know that, Ma?"

Meiran smiled, "Yes, Doria, I knew." Meiran's hand on Horda's shoulder stopped whatever sarcastic words she was about to say.

"Once I begin my moon cycles, I go to the next part of the ritual where I study the Mysteries of Life and Death. That sounds kind of scary, doesn't it?" Doria didn't pause long enough for either to answer. "When I finish learning about them, I'll be ready to choose and be chosen by the man who'll be my mate until his death."

Remembering her vision during the Dance of the Sun, Horda absently touched the little leather pouch containing the forget-me-nots and tiny primroses and felt her face grow warm. She wondered if she'd ever be able to talk to Mach about what happened — no, what seemed to happen — between them. She hadn't even had a chance to tell him she had made her decision. He didn't know she'd chosen him. Oh, what if he'd changed his mind in the meantime? If he had, she knew she'd walk with Father Death. Guiltily, she forced herself to listen to her sister's babblings.

Understanding dawned in Doria's eyes. "You already know all of this. Don't you, Ma?"

Meiran nodded.

"Horda, you know it too since you're choosing a mate at this Gathering." Her tone had turned accusatory. At her older sister's hesitation, she demanded, "Answer me. Don't you?"

Horda remembered she really cared for her little sister ... very much. She reached out and pulled her into her arms for a hug. "Yes, Squeak, I know it too, but I thought it was scary at the time. Sometimes I still do."

"You did?" Doria asked hopefully.

Meiran turned suspicious eyes on her older daughter.

"Ah, I still do," Horda amended quickly. "Anyway it won't hurt me to hear about it again." Horda wondered if mating would be as wonderful as her vision or as frightening as she had once imagined.

"It won't?" Delight and genuine hope danced in Doria's dark eyes.

"No, it won't." It definitely wouldn't, Horda thought to herself, since she was totally confused right now.

Doria proceeded to explain everything she had learned to her mother and sister. When she finished, she smiled mischievously at Horda. "Have you decided which man you're going to choose?"

Horda couldn't bring herself to tell her mother and sister before she told Mach. She studied the grass at her feet and shook her head.

"Well, I wish you'd hurry up and decide," announced Doria. "I hope you don't choose Bear Claw. He's scary looking with all those things on his face."

"Now, Doria," scolded Meiran. "Those 'things' on his face are marks of bravery in his tribe. And I think he really wants Horda to choose him. He's even learning our ways. I believe we'd find he's nice if we got to know him better."

Horda looked at her mother in amazement. Did she really believe her own words? How could they be so different?

"I don't care how much he learns. He scares me. I don't like him at all, and I really don't want my sister to choose him," Doria said. Then she grinned. "But if you do choose him instead of Mach, can I have Mach?"

"Mach will choose a mate at this Gathering," Horda informed her, trying to change the subject. Meiran glared at her.

"He will? Oh." Doria frowned, suddenly deflated. "I hoped he'd wait for me if you didn't choose him."

"Maybe you can be his number two or number three mate, since you're so much younger," suggested Horda helpfully.

Doria's smile returned. "That's a good idea. That wouldn't be too bad. I really like him. He's nice. He smiles at me and talks to me. I'm glad Father Death didn't take him from the Dance of the Sun. I want to go down to the river. Okay?" Her ability to shift direction in midstream was mind-boggling.

"You may go." Meiran hugged her younger daughter and softly warned, "Stay away from my group of children, though. Mach's much too busy for you to bother him now."

"Oh, Ma." Doria pulled free of her mother's arms and raced away.

A hint of a smile fought the pain in Meiran's eyes, but her voice was solemn. "It seems I'm destined to lose at least one of my daughters to that young pup."

"Yes, Ma, it seems so." Horda kept her voice noncommittal.

"Your father says he's a fine young man."

"I think so."

"He said you could do worse, much worse."

"I'm sure I could."

"Are you going to choose him?" asked Meiran bluntly.

Horda's thoughts raced and she hedged. "I want to, but I'm worried. Bear Claw frightens me. He doesn't respect our ways."

Meiran clucked softly under her breath. "How can you say that? He doesn't know our ways, but he is trying to learn them.

He told me you and he discussed them. What more do you expect of him?"

"Ma," cried Horda. "I didn't say he wasn't learning our ways. I said he doesn't respect them."

"You foolish girl. You can't know that. You're just being stubborn."

Horda clenched her teeth so she wouldn't tell her mother more specifically how and why Bear Claw frightened her. She knew Meiran would scold her and claim his actions were her fault.

Black eyes searched amber. Meiran patted her coiffure and said, "Well, I really think you should choose Bear Claw for the good of the tribe. But your father forbade me to speak of it. You must make up your own mind."

Horda took a deep breath and admitted, "Yes, Ma, I must, and I've decided to choose Mach."

Meiran's eyes widened in dismay. "Perhaps our warriors are strong enough to defeat Bear Claw's people," was all she said, her tone dripping, though, with her disapproval.

Horda bit her lip. "Mach doesn't think they'll attack us while we're all together at Gathering."

"Now Mach's an authority?" asked the older woman. "Perhaps he's correct. Who can say?" She tried to rise from the grass. Pain twisted her features, and the slightest moan escaped before she clamped her lips tightly shut and pressed her hands against her abdomen.

"Ma, are you all right?"

"Of course, I'm all right," snapped Meiran. "I just sat too long in one place."

Taking a deep breath and gritting her teeth, Meiran stumbled to her feet. Then Horda saw the ominous red stain soaking into her mother's robe, and her face went completely white.

Chapter 11

❋

"Ma! What's wrong?" Fear for her mother flared as bright in Horda's mind as the stain on Meiran's robe.

Fear, pain, and a number of other things she couldn't identify flickered briefly in the older woman's eyes, then vanished as she muttered, "Haven't you ever had an unexpected moon cycle?"

"An unexp —"

Taking refuge in anger, Meiran retorted, "Stop repeating everything I say! Get the robe and help me to the camp, you goose! Do you want the whole Gathering to see my embarrassment?"

Horda wrapped the deerskin robe around her mother and took her arm.

Mother Life. Her arm felt as fragile as a hatchling bird's wing. Her head barely reached Horda's shoulder. Had Horda grown so much, or had her mother shrunk when she wasn't looking?

Finally the interminable walk to Zaaco's camp ended. Meiran stood beside the banked embers of the cook fire and allowed Horda to unwrap her.

Cold terror twisted Horda's heart. Drops of bright red blood, like huge summer raindrops, dripped onto her feet. This was more than a moon cycle. Biting her lip, Horda fought a daughter's panic and sought refuge in her healer woman training. Remedies to stop the bleeding floated just beyond her consciousness, teasing her.

Think, she commanded herself angrily. She had seen blood pour from a woman's body once before at a birth gone wrong. That woman's lifeblood had drained away until it emptied her body and filled her vessel of time.

Don't think of that. Remember the remedies.

Horda closed her eyes and prayed for strength. "Ma, are you expecting a little one?" she asked timidly. Without responding Meiran sank to the ground. As the silence stretched, Horda's panic built. "I don't know what to do, Ma. I'm going for Nuroo."

Meiran turned vague pain-filled eyes to her daughter. "No. Come back here." Her black eyes focused and flashed. Her fragile fingers gripped Horda's arm with surprising strength. "I'll be fine. You must never tell anyone about this. Do you understand me? I forbid it!"

"Ma, you're sick, and I'm scared. You may be losing a little one. You need more help than I can give you."

Meiran's bitter laughter chilled Horda's heart. "I need more help than anyone can give me." She struggled to a sitting position and gestured for her medicine pack. Her voice echoed her usual arrogance. "You forget I, too, have some training as a healer woman. I can help myself. Give me my pack."

Not knowing what else to do, Horda complied, and Meiran rummaged briefly before putting a dried leaf in her mouth. Slowly she chewed and swallowed.

"Was that lobelia?" The sight of the strong narcotic plant caused Horda's voice to shake with fear.

Ignoring her daughter's question, Meiran resumed searching through her pack.

"Ma, was that lobelia?" Horda's voice rose as she repeated the question.

"Bring me some fresh spider web," said Meiran. "I have leaves of the white alder, common yarrow, and alum root." She sniffed the alum root. "It isn't quite fresh, but I think it will still do."

The lines pain had etched in Meiran's face were already smoothing, and her eyes wore the dreamy, faraway look Horda realized she had worn often in the days of the past moon.

Swallowing the hot lump of fear in her throat, Horda forced herself to speak firmly, with an authority she didn't really feel. "I asked you a question. I will not do anything else until you answer it."

Horda's insistence finally penetrated Meiran's pleasant haze. "What? Were you speaking to me? How dare you use such a tone?" Meiran's own tone didn't match her words — she sounded half-asleep.

Horda took a deep breath, fighting her panic and frustration, and tried to make her voice more respectful. "I asked if that was a lobelia leaf."

"You weren't supposed to know."

"Ma, why?" Horda wailed. "Did Nuroo give it to you?"

Meiran's downcast eyes answered for her. Horda cried, "You're forbidden to dose yourself with lobelia. It's too dangerous. You could kill yourself without meaning to!"

A bitter laugh escaped Meiran's drugged lips. "I don't intend to kill myself."

"But —"

"I do not intend to kill myself," Meiran repeated more firmly.

"Then why are you using it?"

Meiran's mouth snapped shut, and she resumed searching her pack.

"Ma, this is more than an unexpected moon cycle, isn't it?"

Meiran didn't answer, but fat tears welled in her eyes and rolled down her cheeks. Cheeks, Horda suddenly realized were shrunken instead of plumply rounded. When had that happened?

Mother Life. How long had it been since she had really looked at her mother? Horda realized Meiran's vessel of time had almost filled. She would soon walk the Frozen Wilds.

Horda reached a quick decision. Even if it meant disobeying her mother's demand for secrecy, she would go for help to save her life. "I'm going to get Nuroo, Ma. He'll be able to help you."

With surprising strength, Meiran caught Horda's arm, forcing her to stop. "No!"

"Damn your pride, Ma ..."

"I said no. He can't help me. His father couldn't help my mother, and he can't help me." Meiran knuckled the tears from her eyes. "You can't tell him or anybody else. I'll carry on as long as I can. I know what to do."

"What do you mean 'his father couldn't help your mother'?"

Meiran blinked and rubbed her face sleepily. "Long ago, when I was just about your age, my mother began to bleed when it wasn't time for her moon cycle. My father worried and fretted. The Medicine Man, Nuroo's father, dosed her and packed her and treated her with everything he had, but nothing helped. Shortly before the Gathering where I chose your father, the pain defeated her, and she walked alone into the Frozen Wilds to meet Father Death.

"Nothing could be done then. Nothing can be done now. It's a thing which grows inside some women but not in others." Meiran wiped the tears from her face and tried to smile. "When it first started, there were a few drops of blood and little twinges of pain. Later I could feel it growing inside me — like a little one." Her face grew dreamy again.

"I think I always knew it wasn't, but I pretended I had another chance to give your father a little warrior. Then blood, like a moon cycle, flowed even while the thing inside me grew hot and heavy." She shook her head. "It never quickened. And then the pain came with the blood — squeezing and pulsing — but not all the time. Sometimes the blood stopped, and it went back like it first began. Then I could almost forget it was there." She closed her eyes and breathed deeply.

Finally, her voice weaker, Meiran continued. "Now the blood gushes like a flood, and the pain feels like rats with teeth of fire eating away my insides. The lobelia quiets it for a little time. That's why I dose myself. I don't know any way to stop it or even slow it, but I can quiet it so I can endure it. It won't go away until I am gone." She clutched her stomach.

Horda reached out to her, but Meiran pulled back and continued talking in that strange, teary voice.

"I pleaded with Mother Life to let me see you well-mated. If it makes any difference to you, the lobelia helps her grant my plea. After Gathering, I'll go to Father Death. My usefulness to the tribe is ended. My vessel of time is almost full. I won't fight any longer." Meiran's eyes darkened, and, streaked with tears, her face looked pathetically fierce. "But you, Horda, must help me. I won't be pitied like my mother was."

Horda felt her mother's pain as if it ate her own body. Though she and Meiran, different as night and day, were not truly close, she loved her mother and had always hoped some day they might find a way around their problems.

Taking a deep breath and squaring her shoulders, she said, "I can't remember how to stop the bleeding. I'll help, but you'll have to tell me what to do."

Blinking, Meiran looked up and appeared surprised she was not alone. "I thought you went for the spider web. I need it. I can feel the bl . . ." She stopped speaking suddenly, and for an instant her eyes cleared. "I just need it quickly. I have some in the shelter. You go get it, and I'll fix the rest of the packing."

Horda left. When she returned, her mother fanned the nearly dead embers of the cook fire. Fresh tears streaked her once proud — haughty — face. "I can't make the fire burn. It won't get hot, and I'm cold ... so cold." She shivered and wrapped her arms around herself.

Without speaking, Horda took dried leaves and grass from the nearby supply and fed the embers of the fire. When it began to crackle, she added wood and set the water over the flames. "What do I need to do while the water heats?" she asked.

Shivering, Meiran closed her eyes and held her hands over the flames. "Did you get the spider web?"

At Horda's nod, Meiran instructed, "Make a packing with it. It'll stop the bleeding. I have the rest of the plants in my pack." She blinked and wrinkled her forehead in concentration. "No, they're not. I took them out, didn't I? Where did I put them? I think they're over there." She pointed to a mound across the enclosure.

"What do I need?"

"Leaves of white alder, common yarrow, and alum . . ." Meiran's voice faded into silence.

Horda's heart pounded. Surely she wasn't weakening, not so quickly. *No, the lobelia made her drowsy. Please, Mother Life, let me be correct.*

Horda found the plants beside the discarded pack. More ominous than the carelessly dropped medicine plants was a trail of blood marking Meiran's aimless movements. "I've got them, Ma, but I don't remember what to do. You'll have to help me." She tried without success to keep her voice calm.

Meiran opened her eyes and gestured toward her pack. "Grind the white alder, yarrow, and alum root together into a powder. Mix it in a little warm water to make a paste. Then rub the paste into the combed flax and sp ..." Meiran's eyes drifted shut, and her voice trailed away to nothing.

"Mama." The childish name slipped out before Horda could stop it. "What else? I told you I don't know what to do. You can't fall asleep." Tears streaming down her face, Horda shook her mother's cool, clammy arm but gained no response. She withdrew in horror, then ran out of the family area crying, "Oh, Nuroo, come help me! I don't know what to do. Please, help me. Nuroo!"

Mach who was helping Thuro with the young ones heard

Horda's cries. "That's Horda!" he exclaimed. "You watch the children." Before Thuro could even nod, Mach had raced off to help Horda.

Concealed behind some cottonwood trees, Bear Claw watched the young warriors tend the children. He, too, heard Horda's cries and headed to her even as Mach began to run. The strongest runner in his tribe, and closer to the source of the distress than the young warrior, Bear Claw smiled. He would surely beat the young pup to the tender doe — and then she would be his.

However, he had underestimated the man. Mach reached Horda first and wrapped his arms around her. "Shh , shh. What's the matter? What happened?" Bear Claw stood behind a clump of grass.

"My mother's bleeding," she gasped. "I'm afraid Father De — " Sobs stopped her words.

"Bleeding? How much?"

"Too much," Horda gasped.

Sensing Horda's despair, Mach took control of the situation. "Stay with her. Keep her warm. I'll find Nuroo." Mach raced away, and Horda turned back toward her father's camp.

Cursing silently, Bear Claw followed Horda and watched her pile sleeping furs on the still form of Meiran. Such a lot of trouble. Couldn't the senseless girl see the woman would soon walk the Great Beyond — if she didn't already?

Horda chafed her mother's cold hand, babbling to keep her fear in check. "I'm sorry, Mama ... I couldn't remember what to do ... You couldn't tell me ... I had to call Nuroo ... He can help you ... I'm sorry ... Please, forgive me ... I'm so sorry ..."

Meiran's breathing grew slow and ragged, and Horda's heart nearly stopped. "Please, Mama, ... I have never dealt with this sickness ... Please ... Wake up and tell me what to do ... I'll send Nuroo away if you help me . . ." Scalding tears trailed down her face. "... Please ..." Meiran sighed but didn't waken.

The scent of blood filled Nuroo's nostrils even before he lifted the sleeping furs from Meiran's lower body and found the pool growing there. Opening his pack, he removed a large stone cup and a carved bone pestle. Scooping the plants from the ground where Horda had dropped them, he put them into the cup and quickly ground them to powder. "I need a little warm water."

Still clutching Meiran's hand, Horda did not respond.

"Now!" Nuroo barked.

Mach jumped to obey. He dipped a horn of the simmering water and handed it to the Medicine Man, who promptly emptied most of it onto the ground. Then Nuroo put the powdered plants into the horn and stirred them gently with the bone implement before adding a large wad of combed flax and cleaned spider web. "I'll need soft leather to clean her when I'm finished."

Not knowing where else to look, Mach raced to his father's camp. Sniffing appreciatively and humming a cooking song under her breath, his mother stood over the cook fire, stirring a bison stew for the evening eat. Mach skidded to a stop. "I need soft leather for Nuroo to clean Meiran."

"You what?" shrieked Woda, totally taken off guard.

"I need soft leather for Nuroo to clean Meiran. She's bleeding."

"What happened? How was she hurt?"

"I don't know," admitted Mach. "I just know her lower body is covered in blood, and Nuroo needs soft leather to clean her."

"Why didn't her daughter give him leather? It should be her job, not mine." Even as she protested, Woda handed him two of the fawn skins she used for washing and drying.

Mach took the leather and ran, but he called over his shoulder. "Horda is dazed. She isn't much help right now."

"Wait, you can't go back there. Stop!" Woda called. "Meiran's my friend. I'll help Nuroo with her. You shouldn't go back there; it isn't proper. Come back here!"

But Mach ignored his mother and allowed his long legs to carry him across the Gathering grounds. Following closely behind him, Woda muttered under her breath about the improper behavior of the younger generation in general and her son in particular.

Mach pushed his way through the people gathered around the chief's camp. The crowd called out questions. "What's wrong? What happened? Was Meiran injured?" He didn't answer.

Nuroo was kneeling on the ground beside the blood-soaked furs that partially covered Meiran. He'd just finished packing her womb. "Good. You're back." He held out a blood-covered hand for the fawn skins. "Did you bring soaproot?"

"Ah, no, I didn't think about it," Mach answered.

"See if Horda has any.".

Mach went to Horda who stood a small distance away, staring at her mother. He touched her arm. "Horda, Nuroo needs some soaproot."

"Soaproot?" Horda turned to him with a confused look.

"Yes, do you have any?"

Anger flashed in her eyes. "Of course, we have soaproot. What do you think we are? Savages?"

"No, Sweet, no, I know you're not savages. Nuroo didn't bring any soaproot, and he needs some."

Her anger was replaced by bewilderment. "Nuroo? Nuroo's mates can give him soaproot; I don't have to. They always keep plenty of it."

Mach's face twisted with confusion. "But, Horda, your mother needs —"

Horda smiled up at him, her expression peaceful, and her eyes a bit blank. "It's okay. My mother will be fine. She was cold and tired, that's all. Now she's sleeping comfortably."

Bear Claw watched the young couple with disgust. Spitting in the grass, he growled, "By the blood of the Great Mystery!

Slap her. Force her to look at her mother. She'll see the woman isn't sleeping comfortably."

"Slap her?" Mach squawked, his voice a mixture of outrage and incredulity. "I most certainly will not!"

"I need the soaproot now," called Nuroo, cutting off Bear Claw's reply.

Bear Claw stepped into the camp and grabbed Horda by the shoulders. Shaking her vigorously, he hissed, "Look at your mother, woman! See? She's not sleeping comfortably."

"Yes, she is," Horda insisted, closing her eyes.

"You stupid woman," he persisted. "People do not just sleep drenched in their own blood." Though she struggled against him, he was more powerful than she. He grasped her chin and forced her head in the direction of her mother's blood-covered body. "Open your eyes!" he commanded.

Her body trembled, and tears rained down her face, but she refused to look. Bear Claw slapped first her left cheek and then her right, snapping her head back and forth and leaving angry red prints where he made contact.

Her eyes flew open in response, and Bear Claw continued, relentless. "Help Nuroo. Though I don't think there is any hope, your mother will surely go to the Great Beyond if you don't." His cold eyes gleamed at her stricken look.

"But- But, I don't know what to do." The words were barely intelligible through her sobs.

"He needs soaproot. Find some!" Bear Claw shoved her toward the shelter. "He may need other things, too. Get them when he asks."

Horda's shoulders shook with sobs, but she went into the shelter without another word.

Mach's mahogany eyes blazed with anger, frustration, and hatred. His hands clenched into fists, although he dared not throw a punch in the chief's camp. His voice was low and dangerous. "You didn't need to hit her so hard."

Muttering an obscene oath, Bear Claw wheeled around and fixed the younger man with a cold smile. "Didn't you want her to help Nuroo?"

Mach's fists clenched and unclenched as he sought to keep his voice level.

"Answer me!" thundered Bear Claw.

"Of course. I tried to —"

"You tried to," Bear Claw mimicked. "You tried to talk her into doing what needed to be done."

"It was better than hurting her." Mach glared at the foreign chief. His knuckles turned white, but he knew hitting Bear Claw would only hurt Horda more. He forced his hands to relax.

Bear Claw's voice became an insulting rumble. "Boy, you have much to learn before you become a man."

A thousand angry retorts buzzed through Mach's brain before he admitted to himself Bear Claw spoke the truth, at least in part. Not breaking the stare, Mach replied, "Yes, I agree. I do have many lessons yet to learn, but I have already learned one important lesson you obviously haven't."

"Oh, do tell," Bear Claw replied, his voice dripping with false sweetness.

"I don't find pleasure from inflicting pain on those weaker than myself."

Something flickered briefly in the icy depths of Bear Claw's eyes, as if in acknowledgment, but it quickly disappeared. Before either one could say another word, Nuroo interrupted.

"Mach, Zaaco's with the Council. Bring him. Quickly!" Without a backward glance, Mach ran from the camp.

Chapter 12

"Why didn't you call me sooner?" Zaaco's voice carried an unaccustomed sharpness.

"Mach called me only a short time ago." Nuroo spoke calmly but firmly. "Meiran's blood poured from her body like a raging spring flood. It took all my effort to stop it. There was nothing you could have done, and I didn't have time to call you until now."

Zaaco's eyes glittered with unshed tears. "Will she be all right?"

Nuroo remained silent so long it seemed he wouldn't answer. Zaaco opened his mouth to repeat his question, but Nuroo waved a hand before admitting, "I don't think she'll awaken."

"What?"

"She's lost so much blood she can't have much left. Her heart beats slowly, and her breathing is shallow. I don't see how she can recover." Nuroo passed a hand wearily over his face. "Do you remember her mother?"

Zaaco's eyes showed his confusion at Nuroo's seemingly abrupt change of topic, but he answered, "Not really. She walked into the Frozen Wilds shortly before Meiran and I mated. What does that have to do with Meiran?"

"I helped my father treat her." Frustration roughened the Medicine Man's voice. "We tried everything, but nothing helped. One day the pain became more than she could bear, and she walked away."

"That was a long time ago. What does that have to do with Meiran?"

"I believe Meiran has the same sickness. From what your mate Treema told me, she's been ill for quite a time. She's been dosing herself with lobelia."

"And I didn't realize?" Zaaco's simple words, phrased as a question, conveyed a heavy guilt. His voice caught. "Of course, I knew something was wrong, but she kept denying it. She grew too thin, and I questioned her, but she insisted she'd grown as fat as a bear before its winter sleep and needed to lose flesh. I accepted her words and didn't ask more."

"She didn't want you to know."

"Why?"

"She didn't want anyone to know. Horda only discovered Meiran's illness because the blood flowed out of her like a river." Nuroo recounted the happenings of the afternoon for the chief.

"But why?" Zaaco repeated like a confused child.

"Meiran didn't want pity."

"But why didn't she come to you?"

Nuroo reached out and touched his old friend's arm. "Because she remembered her mother. She knew I could do nothing."

Desperation brought anger to Zaaco's words. "Of course, you could do something! You're the Medicine Man of the whole tribe. You know more about illness than anyone else."

"Yes, I do," acknowledged Nuroo. "But I also know there are some illnesses I cannot help. Perhaps I could have kept her from bleeding so much and prolonged her time a short while, but I couldn't cure her any more than my father could cure her mother."

Resignation dimmed the light in the chief's eyes, and his voice went flat. "She's going to walk the Frozen Wilds with Father Death."

"Yes."

"When?"

"Only Father Death knows the answer to that. I think soon, but unless her blood flows freely again, she may linger. I'll keep her comfortable as long as she's here."

"Can I do anything?"

"Sit with her. Talk to her, whether she's awake or not. Let her know you care. She will sense your presence, and it will ease her pain. And ..." Nuroo paused briefly, as if hesitant to speak the words, "... look to your children."

"My children?"

Nuroo nodded. "Especially Horda."

"Horda?"

"She feels guilt at not being able to save her mother. She refuses to believe it's not her fault Meiran is beyond aid."

Standing a small distance away from Bear Claw, Mach listened to Nuroo and Zaaco. After a short while, Bear Claw, who was also following the conversation, said, "I don't understand the problem."

"Meiran's going to the Frozen Wilds." Mach said.

"So?"

It wasn't the response Mach expected. Speechless, he gaped at the older man.

Bear Claw said, "Meiran herself told me the People of the Frozen Earth accept the fullness of time and realize everything which lives will finally be claimed by Father Death. She said when a person's vessel of time is filled, it is his or her obligation to meet Father Death bravely and avoid his anger which can spill over to fill the others' vessels too soon."

"That's true," agreed Mach, "but —"

Bear Claw didn't let him finish. "Then why all the fuss? The Medicine Man himself said he couldn't do any more for her. Why don't you just let her go?"

"She is important to us. We care for her."

"But she's just a woman."

Mach understood Bear Claw, though not in the way the foreigner intended. His cold voice readily conveyed the rage building inside him. "We will 'just let her go,' but she's a mother of the People of the Frozen Earth. She's the mate of the Chief. She deserves our respect and care until her time is over."

Bear Claw spat on the ground. "You're a fool. Women do not deserve respect."

Mach's tone turned dangerous. "No wonder your tribe is so near extinction."

The jab hit home. Suddenly speechless, Bear Claw's face flushed crimson, and his hands fisted. Mach turned and strode to Horda's side, leaving him to stare at the place where he had been.

❊

Zaaco, Horda, and Doria sat beside Meiran, offering what comfort they could: a warm fur, a pat on the arm, a gentle hand to soothe her brow, soft words of love. In the quiet time after the moon dropped behind the mountains, she grew restless and fretful without regaining consciousness.

Shortly before dawn, when only the morning star still glowed in the eastern sky, the blood poured from her body once more. Nuroo worked frantically from the onset, but nothing slowed the flow. Father Death descended then, refusing to allow Mother Life to grant Meiran's request to see Horda safely mated. With a slow, soft sigh, Meiran embraced him.

Treema and Selah, Zaaco's remaining mates came to prepare Meiran for the Frozen Wilds, but Horda would have none of it. "No, go away. I'll take care of her!" she cried.

"Child, you cannot do this alone. Allow us to help you," Treema said gently.

Tears streamed down Horda's face. "I failed her in life; I cannot fail her in death. I will do this myself."

Treema reached out to the young woman. "You didn't fail her."

"Yes, I did. If I'd known what to do, she wouldn't be gone."

Little Selah, normally so timid, now hugged Horda tightly. She said simply, "Don't you understand? It was her time."

Horda leaned into her warm arms for an instant before straightening her back. "She was fine yesterday."

"No, she wasn't," insisted Treema. "She knew her vessel had nearly filled. In the moon before Gathering, she admitted her pain to me. She chewed the lobelia leaves so she could bear it. She only hoped to last through this Gathering, to fulfill her duties, to see you mated."

Horda fell sobbing into the older woman's arms, her muscles relaxing with the now unstoppable flow of tears. Treema smoothed her hair and offered the comforting sounds a mother would. Together they watched Selah wash Meiran and rub her body with oils and herbs. When the time came to clothe her body once more, Treema gently withdrew from Horda's embrace. "Come, child, I need to help Selah."

Silent tears trickled down Horda's cheeks as the women dressed Meiran in the new ceremonial dress she would have worn on Horda's mating day. When Treema loosened Meiran's long black hair, though, she looked a silent question at Horda. Taking a deep breath, Horda stepped forward and took the comb from Treema's outstretched hand. "Please." Treema and Selah withdrew, allowing her time alone.

Horda worked dry-eyed, fixing for the last time one of the ornate hairstyles her mother had loved so much. "Mama, I'm sorry I can't give you the one with the bird's nest," she whispered while her hands fashioned the braids. "It wouldn't set correctly, and the eggs would be crushed." A dry sob racked her body. "Mama, I loved you. I know I didn't please you, but I'm just not like you. I tried, I really did. But Bear Claw scares me so badly, and I love Mach so much. I just can't choose anyone but Mach. I'm sorry."

A single tear dripped onto Meiran's hand and glittered in the early morning sun. Horda gently patted the twisted braids and jingled the little shells and beads one last time. "Good-bye, Ma. Walk softly in the Frozen Wilds. Someday I'll see you ag . . ."

Horda's voice trailed away self-consciously as Zaaco placed his hands on her shoulders. Sobbing, she burrowed her face into the hollow of his neck. "Oh, Fafa!"

He smoothed her hair and cuddled her against his chest. "Sometimes she was difficult, I know, but we'll miss her anyway, won't we, daughter?"

"Oh, Fa," she cried. "It isn't fair!"

"No, but neither Mother Life nor Father Death ever promised fairness."

"I didn't even know she was ill."

"Neither did I, daughter." Zaaco swallowed the hot lump of tears in his throat. "Neither did I."

Horda found a measure of comfort in her father's strong arms and familiar scent as they clung together, lost in silent memories. Finally Zaaco whispered, "Please go find Doria. I would like a little time alone with Meiran before the others come."

Horda held Doria's hand and stared blindly across the prairie as the morning sun gilded the dewdrops clinging to the grass. A thousand thoughts flitted through her mind without pause or consequence save one: *My mother is gone. My mother is gone.*

Each time the phrase repeated itself, Horda's heart lurched within her chest, and fresh pain penetrated the frozen shell of her body.

After a time, Zaaco joined his daughters. He said softly, "The people will be here soon." Because it was Gathering and Meiran was the honored number one mate of the Chief, every member of the tribe from the oldest to the youngest would pay their respects and remember her with stories.

Please, Mother Life, let the callers speak to Zaaco and Treema. Don't let them talk to me.

But she knew she couldn't escape the duty, no matter how guilty or sad she felt. The empty words of comfort often comforted the speaker more than the hearer, and she owed it to the rest of the tribe to at least try.

So, dry-eyed, with her head held high, Horda stood beside Zaaco while the People filed past in an unbroken line. Numbly she listened to the memories and accepted the words offered to her. Solemnly she spoke the words expected of her. Only Mach, standing apart from the others but in her direct view, seemed to realize how tenuous her hold on composure was. Each time she began to falter, he smiled comfortingly or gave his half-wink of support. Each time she saw him, she nodded and straightened again.

Bear Claw stood apart from the others and watched the exchange between Mach and Horda for quite some time. He did not join the line of people waiting to speak with the family, but he also did not cause a scene. Finally, a disgusted look twisting his face, he turned his back and walked away.

At long last, the visitation ended. Zaaco took his place at Meiran's feet while Nuroo stood beside her head. The muffled drums and wailing flutes once again began the March of the Dead, and Zaaco led the procession to the gates of the Frozen Wilds.

A real place as much as a symbolic one, the Frozen Wilds encompassed a rocky gorge set some distance from the living areas of all the bands. It was a desolate area, home mostly to a gentle wind that carried the voices of the dead back and forth through time. Raised daises built into the rock served as the final resting places for those newly departed.

Horda and Doria walked directly behind Zaaco. They carried Meiran's most treasured possessions, the items she would need for her journey into the new world. The rest of the People followed in reverent silence. When they arrived, the men placed Meiran's body on the rock while the women surrounded her with her treasures. Together they sang the songs of life and death, spoke of the departed, and prayed for Father Death to welcome her into his kingdom. After a final song of farewell, the musicians began a new melody, an up tempo march that would lead the People away from the Frozen Wilds and back to Gathering. Horda took one last look behind her at where her mother lay then joined the rest of the People as they left the gorge.

❊

The People of the Frozen Earth believed life belonged to the living, and Gathering was perhaps the greatest celebration of that belief. As a result, by the time the sun reached its zenith, the scheduled events had resumed completely. Meiran, though certainly not forgotten, was placed in the mists of memory, at least for most people. That afternoon, though, Horda sat alone and silent beside the cook fire, staring into its depths and thinking, remembering, regretting.

Bear Claw seemed oblivious to her mood as he joined her. "I'd like to walk with you."

"Not today," she said.

Anger shimmered in the depths of his silver eyes. "I understand it's bad manners to refuse to spend time with a man who's declared his interest in you."

She forced a smile. "I'm not refusing to spend time with you. You're welcome to sit beside the fire with me, but I don't feel like walking today."

He sneered. "You'd jump up and walk if Mach asked you."

"Mach has better manners than to intrude on my grief."

"Your grief?"

"My mother has gone to walk the Frozen Wilds. Surely you

didn't miss that."

He looked around nervously before cautioning, "You mustn't speak of such things."

It was not the response she expected from him. "Why not?"

He lowered his voice. "The spirits don't like it."

Now she was totally confused. "What are you talking about?"

"By speaking of those gone, one may tie their spirits to this world and stop their journey to the Great Beyond. When such a thing happens, the spirit becomes restless and bitter and causes trouble for the living."

"I don't believe that," she said bluntly. "Father Death came for my mother, and he's already taken her to the Frozen Wilds. She can't come back."

"But if you grieve too long, the Great Mystery — ah, Father Death and Mother Life — may become angry."

"I hardly think either of them would think one turning of the sun too long to grieve. Besides, they want us to honor and respect our ancestors."

"Why?"

Why? Was this man truly stupid? How had he ever become a chief if he understood so little? "Why what?"

"Why honor and respect one who is gone? What difference can they make?" He looked genuinely puzzled.

"They teach us. We remember the good they did and try to do the same things. We remember the ways they made life easier or better and the lessons they taught us so we don't have to relearn them."

He grinned. "What if they didn't do anything good? What if they were stupid? What if everything they did was bad or wrong?"

In spite of her grief, she smiled. "Everyone does some good, but if we have trouble recalling good, we remember the person so we'll know how not to act and what not to do."

His laughter rumbled. "Little Horda, you always find an answer, don't you?"

Abruptly her face sobered. "No."

Oh, Mother Life. If I always had an answer, I'd have been able to save my mother.

Tears welled in her eyes.

Disconcerted at Horda's sudden shift in mood, Bear Claw said quickly, "I didn't mean —"

"Please, I'm not good company right now. I don't want to be rude, but I'd really like to be alone." Fat tears trailed down her cheeks. "I trust you'll have a fine Gathering."

He looked at her for a long moment, as if weighing his response, then he turned and walked away without another word.

Bear Claw had hardly gone when Treema hurried into the camp, moving things around and building up the cook fire. She looked in the direction he had gone. "He's a bad one."

Horda nodded listlessly.

"The men should fall on him and his warriors and defeat them. They'll bring trouble to the People of the Frozen Earth. You mark my words."

"Treema, they're different than we are, but they haven't really done anything wrong," protested Horda.

Treema pursed her mouth. "If a rattlesnake crawls into our midst, do we wait for it to strike before we destroy it?"

A rattlesnake? Yes, that was a good comparison. Shivers of fear traced their way up and down Horda's spine, but she said nothing. The question answered itself.

Chapter 13

The sun crawled past the zenith of its second turning since Meiran's death, and Gathering continued. Having been Meiran's helper for three previous Gatherings, Horda would conduct the rest of the lessons for the children with one hand of winters. Still caught up in her grief and nervous about the session, her steps dragged on the way to meet little ones. When she arrived, she saw that Bear Claw, too, waited for her.

Please, Mother Life, not today. Please, don't make me deal with him now.

The children scrambled to take their seats in the semicircle when they saw her. Forcing her lips into a smile, Horda took her seat and said, "Draw closer so you can all hear my words."

There was a bustle of movement until the little ones were settled. Then she said formally, "I trust you're having an enjoyable Gathering, children."

Mach's strong voice led the little ones' reply. "Yes, we are. We trust the rest of your Gathering will also be pleasing."

Tears filled her eyes when she saw the young warrior take a place at the back of the group. He'd told her he'd help with the session, but she had been afraid he'd be too busy or decide not to.

Thank you, Mother Life.

She finally managed to say, "I hope it will be. Thank you. Now, let us begin." Bowing her head, she wiped her eyes before continuing. "At the last meeting you discussed the first band, work, Mother Life, and Father Death. Do you remember?"

The little heads nodded, but the solemn faces watched her closely without answering. Taking a deep breath, she asked, "Doesn't anyone want to remind us what we learned?"

Lonzar finally blurted, "Meiran said she'd find out why men make weapons."

Horda smiled sadly. "Yes, she did. I asked my father."

"Zaaco, the chief," supplied Lonzar.

"Yes," agreed Horda. "But he said it's tradition. Mach, do you know why?"

Startled, Mach stared at her. She watched a blush crawl up his face. Why had she embarrassed him?

He cleared his throat and swallowed before he said, "Ah, I think it has to do with Father Death and Mother Life, but I don't know either. Sorry."

Horda said, "That's okay. I'll tell you what, we'll keep asking. I'm sure someone remembers why this is so. I'll try to find out before Gathering ends." She forced a smile as the youngsters nodded their agreement. "Today we'll talk about laziness, cruelty, and the Wrath of Fire. You all know the People of the Frozen Earth are hard-working people. You remember we share all our work."

The children nodded.

She asked, "Does anyone know what it means to be lazy?"

"I do," said Challa. "It means not doing your part."

"Yes, that's exactly what it means."

Challa tossed her long honey-colored curls over her shoulders and preened. "But I'm special, so my fa does my part for me. He's sorry because my ma departed a long time ago. I'm not lazy, though, because I don't ask him to do things. He just does them because I'm his special little one."

Horda and Mach exchanged a look. Horda thought the child both lazy and spoiled, but she decided it would be wise not to mention either fact. "Does anyone know what it means to be cruel?"

Dawna, a little imp with straight black hair and sparkling eyes, raised her hand. "It means hurting someone or something on purpose. It's not nice."

"Yes, that's what it means, and it certainly isn't nice. It's about the worst thing a person can be."

Bear Claw frowned at Horda, as if he knew her words had been meant for him. She pretended not to notice.

"There are several ways to be cruel. Who can tell me some of them?"

"Hitting, pinching, kicking, throwing rocks, biting." Several children called out the most obvious answers.

"Yes, but there are other ways of being cruel which hurt just as much, but they don't show. They hurt only on the inside. Do you know what I'm talking about?"

The children looked at each other, but none ventured an answer. Bear Claw's frown turned to a glare, but Mach smiled encouragingly. Horda took a deep breath and asked, "Have any of you ever teased or made fun of anyone?" Several children nodded. "That's a way of being cruel because it hurts the person inside. The People of the Frozen Earth don't believe in purposely hurting anyone — inside or out."

Challa grinned. "I like to tease people. It makes me laugh, and I feel good when I laugh."

"Yes, laughter does make us feel good, but does it make the person you're teasing feel good?" Horda asked gently.

"I don't know. I never asked them," admitted Challa.

"Perhaps you should," suggested Horda. She paused for the children to think about her words. Then she asked, "Does anyone know what happens to people who are lazy or cruel?"

"Nobody likes them," said Lonzar.

Horda smiled, genuinely this time. "That's certainly true, but if they continue being lazy or cruel, more than that happens."

The children waited expectantly for her to continue. "Well, children are taught to share the work and be kind. If they don't, they're first scolded. Little ones may be swatted or miss some special treat because they didn't do their work or they've been cruel."

Several small heads nodded before Challa lifted her head and declared, "My fafa never swats me because I'm special."

Horda bit her lip to keep from suggesting a swat might do her some good occasionally. Smiling Mach winked at Horda above the children's heads.

"Well, um, this is perhaps the most important thing I'll teach you this Gathering," Horda cleared her throat. "Adults who are lazy or cruel are first warned their behavior is wrong. If they don't change, they're banished from the band for a time. It can be anywhere from three moons to a turning of the seasons. Do you know what it means to be banished?"

Lonzar, ever the outgoing sort, spoke for all the children. "Nope, but it doesn't sound nice."

"It isn't. It means the person must survive alone away from all the bands."

"Like a Great Traveler?" the young boy asked.

"Yes and no," Horda answered, addressing the group as a whole. "Great Travelers are alone, but they may visit the bands and trade foods. The banished have their hair cut as short as possible, they are branded, and they must not be seen by any of the People for the entire time they're banished."

"They cut their hair off short?" asked Challa. Horda nodded. "Ohh, I'd hate that. My fa says my hair is beautiful." Challa fluffed her long hair and smiled. Horda watched the sun gleam in its golden highlights and realized Challa's hair looked much like her own. Why hadn't she noticed before?

"Do they ever come back?" asked Dawna timidly.

Horda smiled at her. "Yes, if they survive when their time is up, they're welcomed back into their band."

"Good."

"What if they don't behave any better?" Lonzar asked.

"That doesn't usually happen, but if it does, they overflow their vessels of time and taste the Wrath of Fire."

"You mean they'll be burned to death?" squeaked Challa.

"Yes. But not just burned to death. They're burned in the Assembly Fire with all their possessions for the rest of time. Their spirits are banished to the outer darkness beyond the flames forever.

"When people walk the Frozen Wilds with Father Death, we believe they receive rewards and will someday be reunited with their loved ones in the World Beyond." Thoughts of Meiran brought tears to Horda's eyes, but she refused them permission to fall. "People who taste the Wrath of Fire can never be reunited with their loved ones because they burn forever."

"How do they do that?" Challa asked.

"Because we never remove their ashes from the fire pit, those people and everything they had burn over and over each time the Assembly Fire is kindled. Their spirits burn in eternal torment separated both from their loved ones and the cooling embrace of Father Death."

Challa wrinkled her nose and crinkled her face like she was imagining what that would be like. Finally she said simply, "That sounds bad."

"Yes, I think it would be horrible, but we can keep it from happening to us if we are careful to obey the rules and do the best we can."

Horda breathed a sigh of relief when she saw Thuro. "Today we talked about laziness and cruelty. Tomorrow we'll talk about other things which cause people to taste the Wrath of Fire."

"Don't forget to find out about the weapons," commanded Lonzar.

"I'll certainly try." Horda smiled at the children. "Are there any questions?"

Silence reigned, though several of the children fidgeted as if they wanted to speak. Horda said, "Then are you ready to go play?"

"Not yet," said Dawna. Her brown eyes filled with sympathy. "Yesterday, I wanted to tell you I was sorry Father Death took Meiran away, but my ma wouldn't let me. She said I was too young."

At Horda's stricken look, the little girl said, "I didn't mean to be cruel. I'm sorry. Don't punish me!"

Horda held out her arms and pulled Dawna close. "You weren't cruel, and you certainly won't be punished. That was a very nice thing to say."

"But you're crying."

"Yes, I seem to be." She sniffed. "And I can't stop."

"Do you miss Meiran?" asked Lonzar.

"Yes."

"I do, too. She fussed at us sometimes, but she was usually nice," he said.

"Yes, she was."

"She always smelled pretty — like flowers."

Horda smiled through her tears. "Yes, she did."

"How'd she do that?" asked Dawna, her fear of punishment now forgotten.

"She gathered flowers as long as they bloomed. When she had fresh blossoms, she rubbed her skin and hair with the petals, and in the winter when no flowers bloomed, she put dried flowers in the warm water in the bath pit." Horda wiped her eyes. "She hated it when she once ran out of dried flowers before spring."

"I'm going to do that too," Dawna said with a decisive nod.

"I'll always remember her," vowed another small girl.

"Me, too," echoed several others.

"Me, too," whispered Horda with a small sniff. She couldn't bring herself to say more.

Mach took charge, clapping his hands. "Okay, it's time to run and play. Thuro's here, so please go with him, but stay away from the river. I'll join you in a little while."

With pats and hugs, one by one the children left Horda.

Mach remained behind. "You did well."

"Not really. I talked too long, and I cried too much," she said.

He reached out and gently wiped the tears from beneath her eyes. "I didn't think so."

She gave him a watery smile. "But you're not one of the children. Anyhow, I'm glad you could help me. Thank you."

He shrugged, "I wanted to be here because I was afraid you'd find the session difficult."

"I did."

"It didn't show. You didn't need me at all."

"Oh, yes, I did." *Oh, Mother Life, I need him more than I can ever tell him.* She silently shook her head and closed her eyes to keep more tears from falling.

"Are you all right?"

"No, not yet. But I will be. I'm going back to the shelter. You go on and do what you need to." With one last touch, she turned and walked away.

In all this time, Bear Claw stood silently watching from the back. Now, seeing the exchange between the young couple, he glowered and spat on the ground, but he did not move. He would wait until the time for action arrived.

❈

Mach watched Horda walk away before going to help Thuro control the small children. Delighted to be freed from sitting still, they ran and chased each other. Some walked ahead of Thuro and others followed behind him, but they all seemed to gravitate toward the river.

Thuro yelled to the ones farthest ahead, "Come back. Don't

go near the river." The children didn't seem to be paying attention. Trying to keep sight of everyone and gather them all together, he realized he needed help. "Mach, hurry," he called. "We're leaving you behind."

"I'm on my way," Mach yelled back. "Little Ones, don't get too close to the river. The current's strong here." He hurried to catch up.

One of the girls tugged at Thuro's hand, distracting him. He bent down until his eyes were level with hers. She whispered, "Is your name Thuro?"

"Yes." He smiled encouragement. "What's your name?"

"I'm Dawna." She peered up at him through her stubby eyelashes, and a smile lighted her broad features. "You're almost as tall as the sky."

Taken aback, Thuro laughed self-consciously. "Not quite."

"You're taller than he is." She solemnly pointed to Mach still some distance behind them.

"Well, yes. I guess I am."

"My fa says he's the tallest man in the tribe, but I won't let him say that anymore." Her eyelashes fluttered in a little girl's version of coyness.

Thuro didn't seem to notice. "Why not?" he asked innocently.

"'Cause you're taller and much handsomer." A small sturdy hand reached out to touch the finely chiseled line of Thuro's dark bronze jaw. She grinned an impish smile and ran to join the other girls.

Thuro was stunned into immobility. A frown marred his handsome face as Mach finally caught up to him. "What's the matter?" Mach asked.

"I don't understand why we have to watch these children," muttered Thuro uncomfortably.

"Because it's our assigned task. Anyway, it's fun — kind of." Mach looked ruefully at the children running in so many different directions. "Hey. Don't go near the river!" he called again.

Thuro grimaced, "Oh, yeah. It's great fun — like walking on cockleburs."

"What's wrong with you? I thought you liked the little ones."

"I did. I mean I do. It's just ... do you know that little girl?" Thuro pointed in the general direction of the group.

Mach looked at all the wriggling, giggling, little girls and shook his head. "Which little girl?"

"The one with straight black hair and dark eyes."

Mach chuckled. "Thuro, almost all of those little girls have straight black hair and dark eyes."

Thuro's eyes searched the group. "I can't tell which one now, but I think she was flirting with me."

"Flirting?" Mach roared with laughter. "She has one hand of winters. What makes you think she flirted?"

A blush crept up Thuro's bronze face to the roots of his raven black hair, but he repeated Dawna's words for his friend.

"My, my, it does sound like you ha —"

A loud splash and screams interrupted Mach's teasing words. Mach and Thuro ran to the river in time to see a small boy disappear into the swirling water.

"Lonzar fell," one of the children called to Mach and Thuro. The rest looked on in wide-eyed horror.

Without considering his wounds from the Dance of the Sun, Mach waded into the fast-moving water and began swimming. With the help of the current, he quickly reached the area where the child had disappeared. Diving beneath the surface, he searched until he ran out of breath. He allowed the current to carry him a little farther downstream before diving again.

On shore, Thuro spotted the child's body bobbing in the swirling water and called, "He's to your left. About five arms over and ten arms downstream. In the whirlpool."

Mach didn't waste breath replying. He stiffened his body and allowed the current to carry him to the whirlpool. Panic swirled in his stomach when the turbulent water claimed his body. Would he have enough strength in his arms and shoulders to break free?

He forced himself to remain calm. He spread his arms to catch the small body when it tumbled past him. Something bumped his hand. His numb fingers managed to close on the tiny tunic. He gripped it hard, pulled the boy toward his body, and tucked him safely under one arm. Lungs ablaze, Mach fought toward the surface before trying to free himself from the vortex.

On the bank, a crowd had formed — anxious men and women drawn by Thuro's cries. They spoke hurriedly to each other, eyes fixed on the river. Others searched for lines of braided sinew and wooden floats. Bear Claw stood on the bank, but he did not join the others.

Instead, he smiled inwardly. *Stupid, stupid Mach forfeiting his life for a useless little one. Both will surely drown in the raging water, and then Horda will be mine. It is almost too good to be true.*

After an eternity, Mach's head broke the surface of the water. He drank great gulps of air before the current sucked him down again. But with the air, reason had returned, and he forced himself to relax. Perhaps if he didn't fight it, the whirlpool would spit him out. He felt the water lift him and Lonzar toward the surface once more.

The watchers on the bank were now joined by the sinew lines, with Thuro in front holding the loose end. As Mach's head bobbed above the churning water, he twirled the line and shouted, "Mach! Here!"

Miraculously Mach heard Thuro's cry and saw the weighted line land in the water, just beyond his reach. He lunged and gripped the line, wrapping it around his forearm and clutching it for dear life.

Thuro and the others pulled Mach and Lonzar's limp body toward safety, one short tug at a time. As they neared the shore, Thuro jumped into the shallow water. Mach relinquished the child to his friend, but he kept a firm grip on the line with his remaining strength.

Thuro climbed onto the bank and stretched out the child's limp body. He pounded the small chest gently before listening for a heartbeat. There was only silence. Turning Lonzar on his side, Thuro pounded his back, less gently this time. Water ran out of the little nose and mouth, but the child remained limp and still. Thuro continued to pound his back, pleading under his breath for Mother Life to spare the child.

Zaaco watched him work for a while before he shook his head sadly. He touched Thuro gently on the shoulder. "It's too late. The child is gone. He walks with Father Death in the Frozen Wilds."

Dimly, Thuro heard the old chief's words and a woman's keening cry though he acknowledged neither. Instead, he turned the child on his stomach and demanded, "Breathe! Father Death, give him back. You can't have him, he's too young. Breathe! By all we hold dear, Lonzar, you have to breathe!"

Thuro's litany of prayerful curses continued as he firmly rubbed the boy's back in motions like breathing. Each time Thuro pushed forward, he forced more water from the child's lungs.

A choking cough finally rewarded his efforts. Water gushed from the child's mouth and nose, followed by rasping breaths and a strangled cry. Thuro smiled, but he didn't stop his motions until the boy began to breathe more easily. He stepped back reluctantly surrendering his place to Lonzar's mother.

Zaaco clapped the young man on the back. "You saved the child's life. You brought him back from Father Death."

"No, Mach saved him," Thuro said looking around for his friend.

"Mach brought him out of the river, but you saved his life."

Thuro finally located Mach lying spread-eagled on the river-bank. His heart turned cold with fear. Had Mach drowned? Was everyone so worried about the boy they allowed Father Death to steal Mach's life away? Thuro raced to Mach and began to vigorously pound his friend's apparently lifeless back.

Mach sputtered and tried to sit up. "What are you doing?" he barked.

"You're not drowned!"

"Not quite, but is that any reason to beat me to death?" he asked with a mixture of gratitude and indignation. He flexed his shoulders and rubbed the healing wounds left from the Dance of the Sun. He knew they would ache more tonight.

"I thought you walked the Frozen Wilds."

"I wasn't sure I wouldn't for awhile. I couldn't break free of the whirlpool. If you hadn't thrown the line ..."

Embarrassed, Thuro helped Mach to his feet.

Bear Claw, still standing apart from the rest, watched the scene with his emotions now written plainly on his face. Anger. Frustration. Disbelief. The young warrior and the child still lived. The praises Mach received after the Dance of the Sun would pale in comparison with those now heaped upon him, and where would that leave Bear Claw and Horda? His expression hardened even more. It was nothing more than a small setback. Horda was his. He would have her — no matter what it took to get her.

A white-faced Horda stood quietly at the edge of the crowd. Thuro saw her first and turned Mach toward her. "Your chosen waits."

A smile like a sunrise lighted her features when she saw him standing upright. She ran to his side, and he placed an arm around her shoulders. Neither thought about propriety; given the circumstances, it was hard to believe anyone would object.

Together Horda and Thuro eased Mach through the crowd

of well-wishers to his shelter. Thuro helped him change into dry clothing while Horda waited outside. When Mach was fully dressed, Thuro raised the door covering and called to her. "You can enter now. I'll act as chaperon."

Horda's amber eyes swam with tears. "I was so frightened."

Mach tiredly held out his hand. "No more so than I. Come sit beside me."

When he took her hand, her tears traced trails down her cheeks. "I thought surely you would walk with Father Death," she admitted. "I didn't think you could escape the whirling water."

"I couldn't," Mach admitted. "Thuro saved me."

She turned a bright smile toward Thuro. "Then I must thank you."

Thuro looked at the ground, embarrassed by the attention. "I didn't do anything except throw him the rope. He's the hero. He saved the little boy."

"Yes, he did," whispered Horda, "but you saved him, and for that I'm grateful."

"The little boy shouldn't have been in the river anyway," croaked Mach. "Does anybody know what happened? We told them to stay away, but there were so many of them, and they were all running in different directions. Do you think the Council will punish us? We were right behind them. I didn't dream one of them would fall in." He stopped suddenly, realizing he was babbling.

In spite of herself, Horda laughed. "Children rarely stay where they're put."

"Nor do what you expect," added Thuro sourly.

"Well, do you think we'll be called before the Council?" asked Mach again.

"I think you're about to find out," Horda said.

Zaaco's deep voice rumbled from the entrance of the shelter, "I bring you greetings."

"Greetings, Zaaco," croaked Mach.

"May I enter?"

"Please, do," he responded politely.

Zaaco's eyebrows rose when he saw his daughter in Mach's shelter. His disapproving look spoke volumes. Support was one thing; being in his shelter was quite another.

A blush tinged her face. She stuttered, "I, ah, I will g-go now."

When she left, Zaaco turned to the young men. The silence stretched uncomfortably among them. Finally Thuro could stand it no longer. "Zaaco, may I speak?"

"Speak."

"She, ah, wor ... I mean, 'er, we, 'er, I came with Mach to, ah, change out of his wet clothing and, ah, she, 'er, waited outside." Thuro took a deep breath and finished in a rush. "After he changed, I offered to act as chaperon so she came inside. I'm sorry if I offended you."

Zaaco's expression didn't lighten as the two young men exchanged dismayed looks. By the Father's sharp, dirty teeth, not only were they in trouble for the child falling in the river, now Zaaco was angry because they had invited Horda into the shelter.

"I'm truly sorry, Zaaco," Mach said. "She worried about me, and I rejoiced to be alive. We didn't think it would hurt for her to sit with me for a little while."

After what seemed half a lifetime, Zaaco spoke. "It's not usual for another young man to act as chaperon." Thuro and Mach didn't say anything, but the chief noted they looked properly chagrined. "But it's not usual for young men to save a child from the river either," he continued.

"Mach warned the children to stay away from the river," said Thuro. "We were right behind them. We don't know how he fell in."

"Children move very quickly." Zaaco smiled. "Your actions

both put him in the river and saved him from walking the Frozen Wilds this day. The Council will see both of you after the sun sets. Until then, Mach, you need rest. Did you break open your wounds?" He eyed Mach's chest.

"No." Mach rolled his shoulders, feeling the muscles creak. "My shoulders are still sore, but they aren't bleeding or anything."

"Good. Then I'll take my leave. I wish you each a pleasant Gathering with a little less excitement from now on." He turned and left the shelter.

Mach and Thuro looked at each other in dismay. "So are we in trouble or not?" asked Thuro.

"I don't think so, but I'm not sure," said Mach. "What do you think?"

"He asked about your wounds and sort of smiled at the end," said Thuro hopefully.

"But we have to appear before the Council," reminded Mach.

"He said for you to rest."

"Maybe they want us strong for our punishment."

"I don't think so." Thuro's brow furrowed. "Do you really think he's going to punish us?"

Mach yawned. "How would I know? I'm in the same position as you."

"What are you going to do?"

"Rest. That is what he ordered." Mach rolled himself into his sleeping furs and was snoring a few moments later. Unsure what else to do, Thuro lay down and joined his friend, hoping they both would be spared.

Chapter 14

The sun had neared the mountains when Bear Claw arrived at Zaaco's camp. Without preamble he announced, "I would walk with Horda."

Zaaco ignored the man's rudeness and said simply, "Greetings, Bear Claw, I trust you're having a pleasant Gathering."

Bear Claw stared at the old man without replying.

Zaaco smiled tolerantly, "Would you sit beside my fire and have tea?" He waited until Bear Claw was seated. "It's the way of the People of the Frozen Earth to exchange pleasantries first, and to make polite requests rather than issue demands, especially when speaking with the chief."

"I'm not of the Frozen Earth. The People of the Tall Grass don't waste time with such nonsense as empty talk."

"Ah, but you and your people are attending our Gathering. You and your men hope to be chosen by Women of the Frozen Earth. You must act, as if you were one of us." Zaaco prepared tea for his uninvited guest.

Bear Claw's face flushed. "I don't understand your ways."

"Nor do our women understand yours." Zaaco smiled and held out a drinking horn. "Would you like some honey for your tea?"

"I don't want tea. I want to walk with your daughter."

Only Zaaco's eyes showed his anger at Bear Claw's continued rudeness. "Ah, yes. You want to walk with my daughter."

"Yes."

"I understand you attended some of the sessions today," said Zaaco, seemingly changing the topic. "I commend you for studying our ways."

"I've nothing better to do."

"Perhaps practicing what you learned would be a productive way to spend some of your time."

"Are you going to call your daughter?"

"No."

"Why not?" Bear Claw's voice rose with barely concealed anger.

"I would, but she's not here."

"Then where is she?"

Zaaco shrugged. "I'm not really sure. Two hands plus two other men court her. I believe she must be spending time with one of them."

Jumping to his feet, Bear Claw thundered, "You could have told me long ago, Old Man. Why did you waste my time?"

Zaaco shrugged and said mildly, "You said you had nothing better to do."

Turning away, Bear Claw snarled under his breath, "By the blood of the Great Mystery, Old Man, I'll have your daughter."

"Only if she chooses you." Though Zaaco's words were mild, his voice carried an unmistakable authority.

Clenching his fists, Bear Claw whirled to face the old chief, but before he could speak, Zaaco cut him off. "I trust you'll enjoy the rest of our Gathering." The dismissal was obvious, and even Bear Claw understood it. He stomped away from the encampment; his fists still balled.

Watching Bear Claw disappear into the crowd. Zaaco realized he had made an enemy. The battle lines were now drawn. How many warriors did Bear Claw have waiting? Were there enough of his own people to guarantee success in a war? And even if the numbers were in their favor, how many of Zaaco's own people would go to the Frozen Wilds before the battle was done? Was his daughter's happiness, as much as it meant to him, worth the price the tribe would pay? So many questions. So few answers.

⊛

Finally freed of Emol's unwelcome attention, Horda took the long way back to her father's camp, the way past Mach's family camp. Although the fading sunlight warned her the evening eat was near, she hoped to catch a glimpse of Mach. The mere thought of him brought a smile to her lips. Instead of her beloved she saw Woda, Mach's mother, carrying food. She stopped at the entrance to the sleeping shelter and called softly, "Mach, Thuro, I bring you greetings."

Horda smiled at the rasping snores answering Woda's call. It wasn't surprising, given the gentleness of her voice, but it still amused Horda when the older woman seemed perplexed and fidgeted with her load. Horda knew she should leave but was curious about what Woda would do next.

After a moment, Woda called into the shelter again. There was a snort, a mumble, a brief silence, and then the snores resumed. Woda looked around uncertainly.

From across the encampment, Mahlo laughed heartily. "You know your son can sleep through herds of wild bison, woman, that's not how you wake him."

Eyes blazing, Woda turned on her mate. "What would you have me do?"

Mahlo's said matter of factly, "Go in and shake him like you always have. He's still your son."

"But ... I can't just . . ."

Mahlo covered the distance between them in a few short strides. "Why not? What's the problem?"

A tear glistened on Woda's round cheek, and her voice cracked with a mother's pain. "He could have walked the Frozen

Wilds with Father Death today."

"Yes, he could have. And on many other occasions. Thank Mother Life he didn't."

"No, he didn't, but today it is different."

Mahlo looked deeply into his number one mate's eyes. "We've always known he's special, so why is he suddenly different now?"

Woda burrowed her head against his chest. "Now, everyone else knows he's special, too. He no longer belongs to us. He belongs to the tribe."

Mahlo didn't argue with his mate's words; he simply held her close.

Though vaguely ashamed to witness so private a scene, Horda shared Mach's parents' feelings, and it made her feel closer to them. It would not do to linger any longer. Retreating quietly, she made her way back to her own camp.

Horda found Zaaco sitting beside their cook fire, a bowl of stew in front of him. "Greetings, Fa."

The chief appeared not to notice her until she touched his arm. "Oh, greetings, daughter. Have you eaten?" He gestured vaguely toward the cooking bags.

"No, I'm not hungry, but —"

"Sit down and eat something. It'll soon be time for Council." He picked up his own bowl.

Horda dipped herself a bowl of stew and sat on the ground beside her father. She stared into the bowl and chewed her lip, searching for the right words to tell him about the scene she had witnessed between Mach's parents. Finally she took a deep breath and said, "Fa, Mach and Thuro are still sleeping."

"What?" Zaaco's brows beetled. "Have you been in their shelter again, daughter?"

A blush heated her cheeks, but she kept her eyes on his.

"No, no ... I had walked to the other side of the Gathering grounds with Emol when one of his mates called him back to his camp. He hesitated to leave me, but I assured him I'd find my way back to our camp."

Though Zaaco kept his face stern, his eyes twinkled mischievously. "And you just happened to learn Mach still slept on your walk straight across the grounds."

Her cheeks burned. "I didn't say I walked straight across the camp," she muttered.

"No, you didn't." Zaaco's laughter rumbled. "So tell me how you know our heroes still sleep, despite the hour."

"I heard Woda calling them, but they didn't answer. Then I saw her and Mahlo talking, but neither of them went inside to wake them."

"The sun's nearly gone. Council begins shortly, and they know those boys mustn't be late. Why didn't they wake them?"

"I don't know."

Zaaco stared at her, unconvinced.

"Well, yes, I do know," she admitted finally, but said no more.

Zaaco raised his eyebrows. "And are you going to tell me, or do I have to swat it out of you?"

Sheepishly she met her father's eyes. "They are in awe of their son."

Shaking his head, Zaaco rose from his place beside the fire. "Hero worship. Phfft! I was afraid it was something like that."

"I was afraid you'd be angry at me, but I thought you needed to know," she said softly.

He gave her a smile. "Although I don't approve of you watching Mach's shelter, daughter, any more than I approve of Thuro as a chaperon, you have given me information I need. I will stop this nonsense before it goes any farther."

He hurried away toward Mach's family shelter.

The People of the Frozen Earth assembled in the natural amphitheater where the formal Council meetings were held. Grass torches soaked in bear fat discouraged the mosquitoes, but they cast a smudgy glow over the area. The men and women of the Council of Elders already occupied places of honor on the left and right sides of the raised area at the front. Horda had found a seat near the middle of the crowd beside one of the torches when Mach and Thuro filed into the gathering. On time, she noticed. Zaaco must have been very persuasive.

Bear Claw and his people huddled near the back. Though Mach nodded a greeting, Bear Claw only stared stonily in return.

Zaaco's rumbling voice caught everyone's attention. "There are places for many of you at the front. Mach, Thuro, please take your seats quickly; we need to begin."

This assembly puzzled Horda. Except for Zaaco's calling Mach and Thuro heroes, she knew nothing about this meeting. She watched Mach and Thuro exchange dismayed looks when they thought no one was looking. Surely they'd be censured. They moved to the places Zaaco indicated for them as slowly as they dared.

After all were seated, Zaaco rose and looked across the assembled people until their rustling movements ceased. "Most of you are aware of what happened today." A murmur of agreement whispered through the assembly. "As is the custom of the People, the young men care for the children during play time.

"Today Mach and Thuro cared for the children with one hand of winters. They walked beside the river so the children could run and play." Solemnly, Zaaco looked at Mach and Thuro who squirmed and tried to look away. Quietly, Zaaco recounted the facts of Lonzar's near-drowning. Then he allowed himself a small smile. "Join me, Mach and Thuro."

Feet dragging, they ascended the dais to the chief and stood before the assembled People like deer startled by a hunter's torch. Zaaco touched hands with each of them before he continued. "As you can see by their faces, they don't know whether they're to be praised or punished. I intended for them to wonder." He gave each a stern look before he continued. "Perhaps they could have been more alert to their duties, although they were only a few steps behind the boys and did warn them to stay away from the water.

"Who can say what more they could have done? Lonzar is safe, as are the rest of the children. I believe their time of anxiety will be punishment enough for any wrong they may have committed." He watched relief melt the tense features of the two young men, and he smiled across the heads of the assembled people at his daughter, who was sighing with relief.

Bear Claw snorted softly from the back of the assembly, but those around him pointedly ignored him. Mach sensed the silver eyes boring into him, and they raised the hairs on the back of his neck. But Zaaco was talking to him, and he needed to focus.

"You're to be praised for your quick actions which saved young Lonzar from entering the Frozen Wilds this day." Zaaco placed his hand on Mach's shoulder and smiled up into the younger man's eyes. "You, son, with no apparent thought for your own safety or regard for your wounds from the Dance of the Sun, jumped into the raging water in an attempt to save the child. Had you not acted quickly, he would surely have been carried away and drowned."

Treema stepped up beside her mate and placed an ornate necklace of turquoise, obsidian, and bear teeth in Zaaco's outstretched hand. He held the necklace up so all could see it. Gasps of surprise rippled through the assembled People. It was part of the chief's treasure. Zaaco turned to Mach and signaled him to bend down. The necklace slipped easily over his head and settled on his broad chest.

Zaaco spoke. "Mach, wear this with the gratitude of the People of the Frozen Earth. Today, you demonstrated the highest belief of our people. Our future is in the young. You refused to allow one to depart needlessly. On this day you proved yourself an exceptional Man of our People. We thank you."

Treema then placed an almost identical necklace in Zaaco's hand. He raised the new necklace above his head and waited for the People to admire it before signaling the sweating Thuro to bend down.

"Thuro, wear this with the gratitude of the People of the Frozen Earth. Your quick thinking and actions saved not only the child, but also your friend Mach from the Frozen Wilds. You, too, have proven yourself an exceptional Man of the People of the Frozen Earth. We are grateful to you, as well."

Zaaco stepped back, leaving the two young men alone in the center of the speaking platform. The assembled people chanted, clapped, and stomped to show their approval. Mach and Thuro exchanged embarrassed looks. They longed to sit down, but politeness required them to respond to the chief's words. Before the noise faded, Mach whispered to his friend, "Do you want to speak first?"

"Not a chance."

"Coward," he chided gently. Mach stepped to the front of the platform and waited for silence. "To say I'm honored by this ceremony seems too small. But I don't have other words to express my thanks." His speech set off another round of joyful noise.

Finally the people quieted, and Mach continued, "As Zaaco said, I didn't consciously think before I jumped into the river. I thank you for the honor, but the praise belongs to Mother Life, who helped me, and Father Death, who allowed both of us to survive."

Mach turned to Thuro and placed his hand on his shoulder, pulling him forward. "But I especially want to thank my friend Thuro. He located Lonzar in the whirlpool for me. Though I caught him quickly, the raging water held both of us captive.

I'm grateful Thuro kept his head and pulled us to safety. He's the one who deserves the honor, not me." Mach took a step back.

Once more the people shouted, clapped, and stomped. Mach smiled as a blush darkened Thuro's bronze cheeks.

Bear Claw spat in the dust. Rage seemed to pour from his body, and the people beside him could no longer pretend he was not there. They moved as far away as they could in the crowd.

Though his handsome face still flamed, Thuro moved not a muscle until the noise ended. Then he turned to Mach. His teasing words belied the solemn look in his eyes. "I thought I'd say I agreed with you and sit down, but you took care of that." Laughter rippled through the assembly.

Thuro fingered the fine necklace Zaaco had given him. He cleared his throat and smiled nervously. "I don't deserve this honor though I'm grateful for it," he added quickly, lest the people think him unappreciative of their efforts. "I knew I couldn't swim well enough to battle the river current, but I'm glad Mach could." Thuro smiled when Mach fidgeted under his words of praise. "Without his strength, we couldn't have saved Lonzar. I thank Mother Life for showing me a way to help Mach and Lonzar and Father Death for allowing me to help them. And I thank all of you for the great honor you've given me."

Zaaco rejoined the two young men, each of whom stood over two hands width taller than he. Before dismissing the assembly, he looked up at Mach and Thuro. "When I had your winters, I was the tallest man." He shook his head in mock dismay. "The People are changing."

The People laughed dutifully, but Horda couldn't help thinking there was more to his words. The People *were* changing, and they might have to change still more. The question was would they be changing for the better?

Chapter 15

Horda waited on the edge of the milling throng to greet Mach — and Thuro, she reminded herself — when he, er, they came her way. Wilda, one of the other young women who would soon mate, stood anxiously by her side.

Eyes gleaming, Wilda pounced on Thuro when the young men approached. "Oh, Thuro, I'm *so* very proud of you. You're absolutely wonderful! Undoubtedly you're one of the bravest men in the tribe." Eyelashes fluttering, she pressed her body against his and gushed up at him, "Not only that, you're surely the most *handsome*. Any woman would be proud to have *you* for her mate."

Both excited by and uncomfortable with her bold display, Thuro took a small step back and looked for Mach and Horda, but they had been carried away by the crowd. He found he was more afraid now than when he pulled Mach and Lonzar from the river.

A short distance away, Horda smiled up at her beloved. "I'm proud of you."

"Come walk with me away from this crush."

Nodding, she took the hand he offered. Together they threaded their way through the well-wishers, accepting congratulations without pausing, until they made their way outside the lighted area. Walking in the cool night beside the gurgling river, Mach spoke first. "I'm grateful for all this, but I really don't deserve the honor."

"Of course, you do. You pulled Lonzar from the whirlpool."

"But Thuro pulled me from it."

"*You* saved the boy. Thuro couldn't have saved him if you hadn't jumped into the water first. You're a hero. My father said so in front of the assembly. Surely you're not calling him a liar." She spoke gently so he wouldn't take offense.

But Mach stopped and looked at her with a kind of pain in his eyes she hadn't seen before. "Can't you understand? I'm not a hero. I didn't jump in to save him."

Horda tried to hide her surprise. "Then why did you jump in?"

"I jumped in to save myself. I feared the punishment Thuro and I would receive if the child drowned. We were responsible for him."

A frown crinkled her brow. "You what?"

Shamefacedly Mach admitted, "I jumped in because I feared what would happen to me if I allowed the boy to drown."

"What could have happened?"

"I could have been banished for up to a year ... well, I don't think I could have stood that." He rubbed his face and looked into her eyes. "I hated my Great Travel. I looked forward to visiting the bands any chance I had, and I stayed as long as I could when I did. Sometimes I didn't think I could stand being away any longer."

She squeezed his hand sympathetically. He pulled her into a hug. Horda didn't resist. She clung to him like she would never let him go and silently shared the deep pain the young man had felt. She saw his dark eyes turn even darker, and he looked back across the night past her, picturing things she could not see.

"The silence became a living thing trying to devour me. I truly didn't think I would survive without someone to talk to until the big cat attacked me. After I killed the cat and almost lost everything, I understood how much I had to lose. I learned to look inside myself for strength. Somehow I always found enough to go on, but I always feared I wouldn't.

"From that time on, I thought about things I never gave much thought to before. Things I'd been taught all my life but hadn't really understood until then. Things like life and love and happiness. Like Mother Life and Father Death and our way of life and you — always you."

She held her breath, not daring to interrupt him. His eyes lightened. "I thought about children. They're so special, and they really are our link to the future. I can hardly wait to hold my own little ones in my arms." A teasing grin lifted the corner of his mouth. "I hope we have many children, Horda. I want to carry them on my shoulders and play with them and tell them stories and train them in all our ways."

His grin faded, and his voice turned somber. "If Lonzar had drowned and I had been banished, I don't think I could have found the strength to survive. So you see, I'm not a hero. I saved the boy for my own selfish reasons."

Sympathy softened Horda's features. "Mach, you didn't think all this before you jumped into the river. You didn't set out to be a hero, which makes you one all the more. I think you're being too hard on yourself." She smiled up at him and touched her forehead to his chest.

Hope lit his dark mahogany eyes. "Do you honestly believe that?"

"Yes, I do." She shared his breath and smiled up at him. He couldn't wait any longer; his mouth claimed hers. Softly his tongue explored her lips, and he felt her shiver beneath his grasp. He whispered, "Are you cold?"

"No." Daringly she tasted his tongue then nibbled his lower lip.

His hands slipped beneath her hair and traced small, gentle circles on the sides of her neck. Now he was the one who shivered as he struggled to retain control. His words came out raspy, "We shouldn't ... do this —"

Her lips quieted his words. She whispered, "No, we — should — not," but her body did not share the conviction. Desire coiled in her stomach, and she no longer cared what was proper. She leaned against his body and covered his mouth with tiny butterfly kisses.

Reluctantly, he raised his head and forced himself to take a step back so he could look into her eyes. "Since the day of the Dance of the Sun, wanting you has been a fever demon eating my insides."

A small, wondrous smile curved her lips. She hadn't dreamed alone. She stepped back into his arms and said simply, "I know." She drank his essence and molded her body against his, trying to absorb him into herself. Breathlessly she repeated, "Oh, I know."

Once more he pulled back and stared into her amber eyes. "The Mating Ceremony is soon. We must stop."

Bear Claw's cruel face swam before her mind's eye, and she pulled Mach's head down once more so she could share his breath and blot out the unpleasantness.

Mach kissed her eyes, the tip of her nose, and her mouth before he whispered brokenly, "Oh, Horda, — if we don't — stop this — now, — I won't be able to stop."

Once more Bear Claw's fearsome image drove her forward. "I don't want you to stop." Boldly she rubbed herself against Mach's body and nibbled at the tender underside of his jaw.

"Are you sure?"

The love she felt for him blazed through her body, burning away all thoughts of Bear Claw and war. This man belonged to her. Now and forever. She nodded. "Oh, yes, I'm sure."

The white light of the moon washed the scene with smudges of pastel color and cast faint shadows on their bodies. His hands unlaced the thongs of her tunic and slowly, almost reverently, pushed it off her shoulders to land in a heap at her feet. She kicked it aside. He stared, delighted at the sight of her naked body frosted in pale shades of honey by the moon.

He traced the coral nipples of her small breasts and watched in awe as they grew firm against his fingers. Goose bumps caused her to tremble.

"Are you cold?" he asked again.

"No."

"Do you want me to stop?"

Her voice was a breathless plea. "No." She melted against him in a fierce embrace. He lowered his head to drink her breath, and her tongue sketched the lines of his mouth before he deepened the kiss. She brought her hands up to caress the broad muscles of his chest, and she gently kissed the new scars left by the Dance of the Sun. Now he was the one who shivered.

"Are *you* cold?" she whispered mockingly.

He grinned, his entire face lit with pleasure. "Not hardly."

They lowered themselves to the cool grass, which bowed down under their weight, softening their bed and tickling their noses with its sharp aroma. Heat from the warm earth caressed their bodies, binding them together.

As a single being they climbed the hills of pleasure and danced above the clouds. Higher and higher they climbed until Horda thought she could stand no more. Then spent and satiated, they cuddled together in their fragrant bed of grasses and protected each other from the cool air.

The cry of a night bird suddenly called them back to reality. Mach jumped, startled. "Mother Life, what have I done? At the Dance of the Sun I dreamed of this, but I didn't mean . . ."

Horda smiled dreamily, still wrapped in the moment. "You've done nothing."

Mach looked at her uncomprehendingly.

"Well, you did nothing alone," she clarified. She gazed into his eyes. "I shared your dream, and now it's a fact. Together we joined. We are mates."

"I don't understand."

She opened the small leather pouch on the necklace he had given her and shook its contents into her palm. Then she dropped the dried flowers into his hand.

Squinting in the moonlight, he poked at them. "What are those?"

"They're a gift from the Mother," she said.

He rolled his eyes in exasperation. "All living things are a gift from the Mother, Horda."

"These were a special gift. They're forget-me-nots and tiny primroses. They only bloom in early spring while the snow is melting."

"So . . ."

"So, my father found them clinging to my tunic after the Dance of the Sun."

He whispered, "We lay on beds of these in —"

"My vision," she finished softly. "And I think in yours. The Mother gave us to each other."

Quietly she recounted what she had experienced during the Dance of the Sun. His eyes widened at her words, and he closed his hand on the flowers. "We had the same vision?"

She nodded. He leaned close to hear her words. "I decided then I truly had no choice about whose bid I would accept."

He turned and collected his clothing. "Are you telling me good-bye?"

Surprised — and frightened — by his reaction, she took a deep breath before she spoke. "What do you mean?"

Eyes blazing, he faced her once more. "I mean is this your way of telling me good-bye because you've chosen Bear Claw?" She opened her mouth to protest, but he pulled her to his chest in a savage embrace and whispered roughly, "Because if it is, you can forget it. I'll never let you go. The Mother gave us both the vision to show us we belong to each other. You're mine and I'm yours. Do you understand me?"

She finished dressing before she answered, "Yes, I understand you." She kept her voice meek although she knew a smile danced in the depths of her amber eyes. She hoped he noticed it. She pulled his head down so she could sip his breath. "I couldn't find the words to tell you my choice, so I showed you. I choose you, with everything that I am."

He hugged her even closer, and his tongue traced the lines of her lips. "Say it again."

"I choose you. May Mother Life forgive me if my choice causes a war, but I don't want to live if I can't belong to you."

He dropped the little flowers back into the pouch on her necklace and smiled down at her. "You do belong to me," he said fiercely. "Mother Life gave you to me at the Dance of the Sun. We belong to each other. Now and always. No matter what."

He bent his head and kissed her. Hand in hand they walked the path back to her father's camp.

Chapter 16

Though Wilda's attention had been enjoyable, now Thuro was embarrassed watching her accept the praises the People continued to heap on him. He felt even less a hero than before.

Still, her attention evoked other feelings, and he tried to sort them out. She was tiny, reaching not much higher than the middle of his chest, but she was beautiful in the way of the people — high cheekbones, a flat, almost bridgeless, nose, and light copper skin. She looked so fragile he felt he ought to gather her in his arms and protect her from everything.

Her tiny hands smoothed her waist-length blue-black braids and jingled the shell beads and ornaments adorning them each time attention moved away from her. She made people notice her. And she'd almost told him she'd accept his bid if he offered one. He felt a stirring of desire every time he thought of her. Suddenly he decided. He'd bid for her. He'd make her his.

"I've always known Thuro possessed exceptional bravery," she cooed, looking up through her sooty lashes at one of the elders. "It didn't surprise me a bit when he saved both the boy and Mach."

Thuro felt his face flame as the elder gently reminded Wilda that Mach had made it possible for him to save the child. Guilt rose up in him like gorge. "Thank you for your kind words," he interrupted quickly, "though I know I don't deserve them. Without Mach, the child would certainly have drowned." Before Wilda could utter another word, Thuro caught her hand and hurried from the assembly area.

They hadn't gotten far when she dug in her tiny heels in an effort to slow his headlong dash. "Thuro, honestly. Where do you think we're going in such a rush?"

"I don't care, as long as it's away."

Wilda smiled conspiratorially. "I know you're shy, but this is your chance. Don't you see how your quick actions today will affect your future?"

"No, I don't. I didn't do anything anyone else couldn't have done."

"But they didn't. *You* did." She made it sound so obvious he wondered why he was having trouble accepting it. Watching his muscles quiver, she traced the fine necklace on his chest with the tip of her right index finger. "You're a hero. It'll make a difference in the winters to come."

"I tell you I'm not a hero."

Wilda fluttered her eyelashes and simpered up at him. "The tribe says you are. Surely we all aren't wrong."

Dawna had watched Thuro pull Wilda through the crowd. When they finally stopped, she gathered her nerve, walked up, and touched Thuro's hand. Grinning broadly, she announced, "Not only are you tall, you're smart."

Thuro leaned down and frowned in mock ferociousness. "Don't you start on me, too. If I hadn't been talking to you, Lonzar might not have fallen into the water."

Dawna giggled and said as seriously as she could, "You weren't talking to me when he fell in."

"Well, I'm not a hero," insisted Thuro.

"Zaaco said you are." Dawna grinned her snaggle-toothed smile. "Don't you want to be a hero?"

"Not particularly," he admitted.

Wilda stamped her foot. "Thuro, I can't believe you're saying such things." She glared at the little girl. "Of course, he wants to be a hero. Anyone in his right mind wants to be a hero.

Now, go away and leave us alone."

Thuro leaned down to Dawna, who looked about ready to cry at Wilda's harshness. "Thank you for your words," he said sincerely, touching her hand. Dawna held his hand an instant before she nodded and hurried back into the crowd.

Thuro wrapped his arms around Wilda and gave her a hug. "I guess that tells me what you think of my mind." Turning her around, he looked into her eyes and asked, "Why did you say anyone would accept my bid if you're so sure I'm not in my right mind?"

Hugging him, Wilda hid her triumphant smile. "Because I'm sure you'll come to your senses. You've been recognized as one of the young leaders of the tribe. You and your mate will have your choice of bands."

The smile froze on his face as her words brought the guilt back. He had to find Zaaco before he lost his nerve. "Don't be too sure," he whispered and slipped away.

❄

Mach and Horda met Thuro just outside Zaaco's shelter.

"What are you doing here?" asked Thuro impatiently.

A guilty flush heated Mach's face, but he kept his voice even. "Horda and I walked beside the river. Now it's time to retire, and this is her shelter."

"Oh, right, I guess I forgot."

"So what are you doing here?" asked Mach pointedly.

"I ... ah ... need to talk to Zaaco."

Mach's face showed his surprise. "Why?"

"Mach, I'm an imposter. I didn't do anything but throw you a rope. You saved the boy. They're calling me a hero, but I'm not. I'm really not. I must talk to Zaaco before this goes any further."

"You, an imposter? The boy and I would have drowned if it hadn't been for you, so what does that make me?" Mach's own doubts showed in his eyes. "Anyway, I only saved him to save myself from disgrace." Mach's voice rose with frustration. "I must talk to Zaaco, too."

They didn't have long to wait. Pulling his long grey braids into a semblance of order, Zaaco stepped from his sleeping shelter. Although hazed with sleep, his eyes flashed at Mach and Thuro. "Boys, is this discussion so important it can't wait until morning?"

Mach and Thuro both opened their mouths to speak though not a word escaped from either.

"You woke me to stand gaping like fish on the bank of the river?" Zaaco turned to his daughter and thundered, "Do you know why these young calves are here?"

Horda barely managed to keep a straight face; she could hear the mirth behind the thunder, something the others would be too tense to notice. Carefully solemn she replied, "Yes, Fa, I know."

"If they aren't going to tell me, will you?"

She didn't have to; at that moment, both young men found their voices. In unison they said, "I'm here because I don't deserve ..." They stopped and looked at each other. Thuro gestured for Mach to continue. Taking a deep breath, Mach poured out his feelings like water from a vessel.

Zaaco listened without interrupting before he turned to Thuro, who added his own version of the story. When he finished, Zaaco said nothing. He stood by the entrance to his shelter, looking at neither one of them, yet somehow at both. The silence grew deafening. Finally he said, "Do you presume to tell me the Council made a mistake by honoring the two of you?"

Mach and Thuro took inordinate interest in their own moccasins and refused to meet the old chief's eyes. They knew no matter what their answer, it would be the wrong one and neither quite dared to take the risk.

"Mach, did you or did you not jump into the river and catch

the boy in the whirlpool?" Zaaco lowered his voice until it almost sounded gentle.

"I told you —"

"Just answer me yes or no. Did you stop him from being drowned by the raging water?"

"Sort of."

Zaaco's dark eyes impaled him like a fish on a hook. "Yes or no?"

Mach murmured, "Yes."

"Thuro, did you or did you not guide Mach to the boy in the river and then pull both of them from the river with a line?"

"But I didn't —"

"Yes or no?"

"Yes, I did," muttered Thuro, "but —"

A sharp look from Zaaco silenced the rest of his protest. "I see." After a moment, Zaaco gestured toward the banked fire. "Sit down. I need to tell you a story. Horda, you may join us if you wish."

The young people exchanged surprised looks but sat beside the banked fire. Once more the silence stretched.

"Long ago, like both of you, I returned from my Great Travel. I chose my first mate Xyla, a woman of rare and delicate beauty, whom I loved very much." He smiled sadly. "I doubt either of you boys remembers her, though Horda might."

Horda nodded. "She was Zephat's mother."

"Yes, she was."

"I remember her," she said softly, "and I loved her too."

Zaaco wandered the hallways of his mind, gently fingering memories for a brief time before he chose the ones he wanted to reveal. "We had been assigned to one of the smaller distant bands. Three of our warriors and I hunted away from the camp one day in late autumn. A war party of another people attacked our winter shelter. They killed the other men and made prisoners of the women and children." His voice sharpened like a good flint knife. "My friends and I returned to find the attackers preparing to rape my mate. Because we surprised them, we were able to kill every one of them."

He paused and looked at Thuro and Mach before he continued in a softer voice. "I hacked their bodies to pieces long after their lives ended, and I'm ashamed to say I enjoyed it very much."

Surprise registered on all the young faces, but no one dared interrupt.

"I forgot all I had been taught about taking life. When I began, I didn't think about anything but their hands on my mate. Before it ended, I reveled in their cries and the smell of their blood. I only stopped hacking their bodies when several of our men pulled me away." Zaaco stopped speaking and stared into the darkness. "The tribe honored me for saving the women and children."

"You did save the women and children," said Thuro.

"But I didn't do it to save them. I told you I forgot everything I had been taught. I killed them for my own selfish reasons, and I therefore didn't deserve to be honored."

"You stopped a threat to the people."

"But I didn't intend to. I only intended to save my mate and feed my vengeance. I felt like an imposter," insisted Zaaco.

"I understand that," said Mach. "What did you do?"

"Do? I didn't do anything. I wasn't quite so bold as you two. Because so few of us survived, we returned to the Inner Band for the winter.

"My bad feelings festered inside me like an uncleaned wound, and I growled and snarled at everyone. Finally the old Shaman, Nuroo's father, learned the cause of my distress. Maybe he figured it out because I acted like a cross between an angry child and a bear with a thorn in its nose." Zaaco smiled. "More likely it was because Xyla told him."

"Whatever the reason, he sat me down and talked to me. He

asked if I believed heroes thought 'Today, I'm going to do a brave thing so everyone will know I'm a hero.' Even through my anger, I laughed at the picture he painted with his words." The others chuckled, trying to imagine Zaaco in that position.

"Yes, it's amusing, but I finally understood his point. Heroes usually do brave things for totally different reasons than others recognize, but it doesn't matter. What matters is the end result. In my case, we defeated the savage warriors and saved the women and children. In your case, Mach, you pulled Lonzar from the whirlpool. Thuro, you pulled both Mach and Lonzar from the river. Why you acted as you did really doesn't matter. You did what needed to be done when it needed to be done."

Zaaco stared at Mach and Thuro for what seemed a long time. Finally he asked, "Do you understand what I am saying?"

Mach and Thuro nodded though their faces showed they didn't fully accept Zaaco's words.

"I never said your hearts would believe my words. I just want your heads to understand why we did not make a mistake by honoring you today." Zaaco laughed softly. "Perhaps by the time you stand in my place and try to explain heroism to young men not yet born, you'll accept my words with both your heads and your hearts."

He stood and gestured to his daughter. "Now, I think it's time for all of us to retire. Morning will come early."

"Ah, I'd like to share some news with you," Thuro said.

Zaaco swallowed a yawn, "You may speak if it doesn't take too long."

"It won't," Thuro promised. "I just want you to know Wilda told me she'd accept my bid."

Only the tightening of the skin around Zaaco's eyes and lips betrayed his dismay to Horda. "I'm sure Wilda has many fine qualities," he offered without voicing his congratulations.

Thuro waited, unsure how to react. It was not quite the response he expected. The silence stretched unbroken until

Zaaco pointedly yawned. Mach poked his friend in the arm, then they wished the chief a good sleep with pleasant dreams and made their ways to their respective shelters.

Zaaco draped his arm around Horda's shoulders as they watched the young men leave, and his soft laughter rumbled across the quiet night. He said nothing about Thuro's choice of mate, only, "Oh, daughter, can you believe I actually worried they'd turn arrogant with their honors?"

Golden sunbeams danced across the lightly frosted grass to greet Horda when she stepped from the sleeping shelter the next morning. The cool breeze tickled her nose with rich morning smells and whispered of the long cold to come. She smiled and hugged herself in the crisp air. Mach loved her and she loved him. They belonged to each other. The faint tenderness of her woman place sent guilt creeping up her spine, but she pushed it away by promising herself no one would ever know they joined before the ceremony.

"Horda, what are you doing?" called Treema from the cook fire.

Horda jumped as if Treema had poked her with a long thorn. "Just looking at the morning." She hurried to the cook fire.

Treema looked around in surprise. "It's beautiful, but I'm in a hurry, so come and eat. I want to attend the session Bear Claw's women are holding. They're going to teach us to make baskets to carry water."

Realizing only Treema remained beside the cook fire, she said, "I'm sorry I overslept."

Treema leveled a stare at her. "It was very late when you sought your sleeping furs last night."

Horda fought not to fidget under the older woman's quiet gaze. "All the attention yesterday upset Mach, and we walked beside the river discussing his feelings. When we came back,

Thuro was waiting, and they talked to my father about heroes," she answered.

Treema didn't lower her eyes from Horda's.

Horda felt a blush tinge her cheeks. *Treema knows. Somehow she knows, and she is going to accuse us. I can't lie to her if she asks. Oh, Mother Life, we'll be punished for sure.*

Treema gave the yampah porridge one last stir. "Everyone's eaten except you and Zaaco. He went off with some of the warriors, but he said he'd be back soon." She smoothed her hair and said, "I'm leaving, so it's up to you. Don't let the porridge burn."

Horda hadn't done that lately, but she smiled nonetheless. "I'll try not to."

Suddenly solemn, Treema reached out and touched the younger woman's arm. "Be careful." She left before Horda realized the caution did not refer to the porridge.

❁

Stirring the porridge frequently, Horda finished her morning eat before Zaaco returned. Still bustling about the cook fire, she ladled yampah porridge with roasted meat into her father's wooden eating dish.

Zaaco's eyes twinkled with a mischievous glint. "The porridge smells good, Horda. Your mate will be glad you finally learned not to burn it."

It seemed she would never escape that part of her past. "Oh, Fa, you know I haven't burned the porridge in a long time."

"Humph." Zaaco cocked an eyebrow at his oldest daughter.

"Well, at least not since we came to Gathering."

"Unless I'm mistaken, this is the first time you've cooked porridge since we came to Gathering."

Horda smiled innocently at her father. "Then I'm sure I haven't burned any."

"No, daughter, you certainly haven't." Zaaco's rich laughter

186

rumbled in his chest. Then his eyes darkened, becoming guarded. "So tell me, have you decided to choose Mach?"

Wariness replaced Horda's smile. "I tried to choose Bear Claw because my mother thought I should ...."

"But ..."

"But I'm afraid of him, and I don't want a mate who frightens me."

Zaaco stared into space until Horda wondered if he had heard her response. She opened her mouth to repeat it, but he waved her to silence. After a moment, he said, "For the tribe, I wish Bear Claw was a different man — a man you could choose." He shook his head as if to dispel his apprehension. "Of course, if he was a man you could choose, you wouldn't need to choose him for the good of the tribe."

"Fa, I'm sorry I can't choose Bear Claw. I really wish I —"

Zaaco waved her to silence again and stared deeply into her eyes. "Daughter, I'm torn just as you are. It's been many turnings of the seasons since we fought a war, but I know our warriors are still powerful."

He looked away, and she strained to catch his words. "If you chose Bear Claw, perhaps others would feel forced to choose Men of the Tall Grass. I don't believe they treat their women well." He laughed bitterly. "No, that's an understatement. They appear to be cruel to their women and to each other. Your lives would be more dreadful with the Men of the Tall Grass than any fight which may result from you not choosing Bear Claw."

Tears clogged her throat. "Are you giving me permission to choose Mach?"

Zaaco's laughter sounded forced, but his voice was gentle. "Permission, daughter? You never needed my permission."

His dark eyes bored into her lighter ones.

He knows something, but, Mother Life, what? With great effort, she kept her face impassive and her eyes level. If he would not voice his thoughts, then neither would she encourage him.

He continued softly, "You'll make your own choice, as is our way. But even though you've made your choice, please continue to spend time with the others who court you. It would not be seemly to spend all your time with Mach."

Guiltily she nodded. Seemly, no, but it would be wonderful.

Chapter 17

"Greetings, Zaaco. Though Meiran's untimely death saddened all of us, I trust you're once again having a pleasant Gathering." Zaaco had barely finished his morning eat before Wilda showed up at his camp. Not only that, she was managing to make the polite greeting sound like a flirtation. Zaaco gave Horda a questioning look; she shrugged almost imperceptibly behind the other woman's back. She had no idea about the visit either.

"Yes, thank you," Zaaco replied formally. "And you?"

"Oh, yes, I'm having the best Gathering ever." Wilda's dark brown eyes sparkled. "Such terrible excitement, what with the visitors of the Tall Grass, Mach participating in the Dance of the Sun, Lonzar falling into the river and Mach and Thuro saving him, and ... ," She paused only long enough to toss her head, jingling the ornaments in her hair. "... and all the men who show interest in me. It's a truly wonderful time."

Zaaco's features hardened into an unreadable mask. "I hardly find the death of my number one mate and the near drowning of two people wonderful."

Puzzlement appeared on Wilda's face, marring her features momentarily. "I already expressed my sorrow about Meiran. Her death saddened the People." Then her brow cleared. "But neither Mach nor Lonzar drowned," she added cheerfully.

Horda glowered when Wilda smiled up at Zaaco. The nerve of this woman!

"The most exciting part of Gathering will be the Bid Ceremony," Wilda continued as if this were news. "I know Horda must be excited too. She has even more men courting her than I do. Of course, she is the daughter of a powerful chief. Her position makes her even more desirable as a mate, don't you agree?"

Horda's lips pressed into a tight line, and her hands clenched. Wilda acted as if Horda's father's position was the only reason any man would court her. To his credit, Zaaco said nothing.

Wilda tossed her head so the beads and shells in her braids tinkled merrily again. "I'm so excited; I can hardly wait for the Rituals of Mating."

"My daughter is a fine young woman. A number of good men court her," Zaaco said stiffly. Wilda pushed the bounds of propriety by discussing such things with a man other than her own father or the leader of the Rituals, and it seemed she was the only one who didn't know it — or didn't care.

Zaaco, though, was unfailingly polite. "Would you like some porridge or tea?"

Horda jumped as though her father had poked her; she should have been ready to offer hospitality without his prompting. She wondered why Wilda was at the chief's cook fire. Wasn't Thuro enough for her? Did she want Mach too?

Until this Gathering, Wilda had made no secret of the contempt she felt for Horda. She made snide remarks about Horda's hair, her eyes, and her size, all so different from the rest of the tribe. There were the whispered comments and the taunts. So why the pretense of friendship now? Mother Life, did it have nothing to do with Mach? Was she trying to get Zaaco to court her?

Seating herself closer to Zaaco than was entirely proper, Wilda simpered, "I've already eaten, but I'd enjoy some tea. It's awfully cool this morning."

Horda practically threw the horn of tea at Wilda and earned a reproving look from her father, but Wilda seemed not to notice. She leaned even closer to the chief. "Zaaco, I want to discuss an important matter with you."

Zaaco allowed himself a brief smile. Ah, the point at last. "I thought perhaps you might."

"May I speak?" Patting her elaborate coiffure so the shells and beads again tinkled merrily, she smiled and fluttered her dark eyelashes.

Horda sat down. She didn't want to miss a word of this. "You may speak."

Wilda spared Horda the briefest of glances before leaning closer to Zaaco. "Um, privately?"

Horda bit her tongue to keep from laughing. The old chief's features froze in shocked disbelief. *Uh-oh. You've made him angry. If you're wise, girl, you'll leave now before he explodes.* Wilda drew back with a look of genuine surprise.

Coolly Zaaco repeated, "If you have words I should hear, you may speak."

Wilda glared at Horda. Horda smiled back, enjoying her growing discomfort.

Keep glaring, girl. Now you know how it feels to be on the receiving end. Anyway I'm not leaving my father alone with you. There's no telling what such a stupid one as you might do.

Wilda pasted a smile on her face and fixed her attention on the chief. "Thuro's very brave. He's a recognized hero of the People."

Zaaco leaned close to the young woman's ear and almost whispered, "You may not have noticed, but I presented the awards to Mach and Thuro myself."

Wilda opened and closed her mouth like a beached fish. Horda coughed to cover her laughter and quickly bent to stir the leftover porridge.

Wilda gulped most unbecomingly before she continued,

"Yes, yes, of course. Um, well, because of his heroism, I'd ask a favor on his behalf."

Zaaco arched one eyebrow like a wooly caterpillar. Obliviously, Wilda rushed on. "I mean, since Thuro's so brave and valuable, don't you agree he should be assigned to the Inner Band? That would be a just reward for his actions, don't you think?"

Horda could hardly contain her gasp of surprise. *The stupid girl asks for special treatment for Thuro and herself. I never thought she was particularly bright, but this ridiculous.*

Though the day was warm, Horda could see icicles dripping from Zaaco's words. "Thuro has been justly rewarded."

"Yes, the necklace is beautiful, I'd be the first one to say that, but one so brave should be near to help protect the chief."

"I'm not in the habit of falling in the river." Zaaco's features were completely impassive, but Horda nearly laughed out loud at his response.

Finally doubt clouded Wilda's smooth face. "No, no, I know you aren't, but Thuro's brave in many ways. He thinks quickly and would protect you from dangers."

"Is that so?"

"Of course, you're growing older and soon you will need hel —"

It was absolutely the wrong thing to say. Zaaco's face darkened like a storm cloud, and his voice thundered across the entire camp. "Do you think I need a young pup just returned from his Great Travel to protect me? I, the Chief of all the People of the Frozen Earth?"

Heads turned. People stopped in their tracks and abruptly hurried away as they recognized who was doing the yelling. Wilda realized she was the focus of attention again, but this time it was definitely not attention she wanted. "Well, ah, I only meant, if you needed help, it would be good for Thuro to be close by," she muttered feebly.

"And you? What would you gain by Thuro's being appointed to the Inner Band?" Zaaco's voice had turned deceptively mild. Horda knew it was not a good sign; the temper he worked so hard to control was ready to explode.

"I?" Wilda lowered her eyes. "I'd gain nothing."

"You wouldn't expect to join the Inner Band with your mate?" Zaaco waited in silence until Wilda raised her eyes to meet his. Horda almost felt sorry for her. She was like an animal caught in a trap.

"Ahm, Thuro's not my mate."

Horda watched her father's dark eyes bore into Wilda's soul. "Didn't you agree to accept his bid?"

"Nothing is final yet." Wilda mumbled the words and lowered her eyes.

"This is unselfish of you." Zaaco's broad smile didn't reach his eyes. "You petition the Chief for special treatment for a man who's not your mate and, as far as you know, doesn't plan to bid for you. My, my, you *are* generous."

Mistaking the sincerity of his words, Wilda preened once more.

Zaaco persisted, "But then who'll receive Thuro's bid? What lucky girl will live with him in the relative ease of the Inner Band if your pleas are heard?"

Wilda shook her head until the shells and beads jingled. "I really don't know."

Zaaco's tone sharpened, "Horda, do you know for whom Thuro will bid?" Wilda jumped, as if she had forgotten Horda was still there.

"Ah, Fa, I thought he told you last night Wilda would accept his bid." Horda breathed deeply to keep her glee from showing in her voice. Wilda was caught in a lie. "If he doesn't bid for her, I don't know for whom he'll bid," she added.

Horda watched Wilda scramble for control of the situation. A large smile brightened her face. "Did he tell you he planned to choose me?" She tried a small laugh, but it came out more a sob. "Really? I didn't know. My, how exciting. I'd love to belong to the Inner Band. Oh, yes, if Thuro chooses me, I'll be delighted to live here with him."

Although he didn't move a muscle, Zaaco's bearing became infused with all the powerful dignity of a Chief. His words were uncompromising. "Thuro told me he spoke with you last night."

"Well, yes, we did speak briefly after the ceremony." Wilda seemed to wither under Zaaco's penetrating gaze, and she stuttered, "But, ah, he didn't actually bid for me. Nothing's final until the cer —"

"Don't lie to me." His quiet words cracked like thunder.

"Well, he hasn't actually brought his bid before me," Wilda said defiantly.

"But you told me you didn't know whom Thuro would choose. He told me you informed him you'd be happy to accept his bid."

"But he did not —"

"Be gone from my presence." He thundered.

"Please, Zaaco, you must allow me to explain."

Horda felt an uncomfortable mixture of pity and delight when her father pointed away from his camp. "Wilda, you've explained more than enough. People are invited to join the Inner Band. They do not petition to join it."

"But I just —" Wilda's voice quaked.

"I said be gone!"

Tears ran down Wilda's cheeks. She turned Horda. "Horda, help me, please."

Horda blinked in surprise. "Me? What can I do?"

"Make him listen to me."

"It's not my place."

Wilda didn't stop. She turned back to Zaaco and begged, "Oh, please, you must lis —"

"The only thing I must do is decide whether or not to punish Thuro for your insolence. Now go!"

Weeping and muttering, Wilda left "Why won't he listen? Thuro deserves to be part of the Inner Band. And *I* deserve to belong, too. Why won't he give me a chance to explain?"

As much as Horda disliked Wilda, she pitied her for this mistake. She certainly wouldn't want to be in her moccasins right now.

Zaaco shook his head and called, "Horda?"

"Yes, Fa?"

"I don't know what's happening to the young people of today. Find Thuro, but do not mention what happened here."

She had to ask. "Are you really going to punish him?"

"If he sent her with that ridiculous petition, the Council will decide." Zaaco struggled to control his temper. "I suspect he has no clue what she's done."

❊

Horda raced to Thuro's family camp. Breathless, she found some of the women of the band preparing for the second morning sessions, but no Thuro. A premonition urged her to Wilda's family camp.

She was right. There was Thuro, holding a sobbing Wilda in his arms. Even though she knew Wilda could bring forth floods of tears on a moment's notice, the sobs sounded genuinely heartbroken.

"You must tell me what's wrong," she heard Thuro beg. "I can't help if you don't tell me what happened."

Wilda only cried harder and burrowed her head against his broad chest. Thuro's handsome features twisted with helplessness. "Please stop crying now and tell me what's wrong."

"You will h-h-hate me."

"Come now, it can't be that bad. I seriously doubt you could do anything to make me hate you." Thuro hugged her and patted her back. "After all, you're my chosen."

Wilda sniffed and rubbed her face against the leather of his tunic, but she didn't answer. Thuro looked around in desperation and spotted Horda standing silently at the edge of the camp. "Horda," he called, "please help me. Do you know why Wilda's so upset?"

Horda walked over to the couple before she answered. "Not exactly," she said, keeping her voice low.

"Not exactly?" Thuro's face mirrored his confusion. "Tell me what part you do know."

"My father, the Chief, wishes to see you now."

Wilda's sobs grew to a howl. "Don't leave me!"

"Now? He wishes to see me now?" Thuro still cuddled the young woman. "But what does this have to do with Wilda?"

"I can't say. But Zaaco said to bring you to him now, Thuro."

"You can't leave me — I'm too upset." Wilda grasped his tunic. "You must walk with me until I'm calmer. The Chief will have to understand." She peered up at Thuro through spiky eyelashes.

Obviously undecided, Thuro looked to Horda. "Will he wait a little while?"

Horda bit her lip then shook her head. "I think you'd better come now. He's awfully angry."

Thuro's brown eyes widened. "Angry? At me? I don't understand."

Horda looked meaningfully at Wilda. "I don't think he's angry at you, but he told me not to explain the reason for his summons."

Dismayed, Thuro looked down at his chosen. "I'll return as soon as I can."

Wilda stamped her foot like a small child. "That old man crooks his little finger, and you run to do his bidding. It's not right. This is an important time for us."

Now shocked more than confused, he said evenly, "He's the Chief of the People of the Frozen Earth, and he summoned me. I will go."

Tears streamed down Wilda's face though her eyes flashed. "This is her fault. Can't you see how jealous she is? She wants to cause trouble between us."

Disbelief turned to cold anger in Horda's heart. She thought of a handful of piercing comments, but she swallowed them all and said, "My father has commanded Thuro's presence, and I brought his summons. You would do well to heed us both." She turned and headed to the edge of the camp without looking back. She knew Thuro was wise enough to follow.

Thuro stared at his chosen. "I'm truly sorry, but my Chief waits for me. I'll be back as soon as I can."

Behind them, Wilda's tears stopped immediately. Horda could just make out her petulant wail as they left. "It's not fair! Why couldn't you wait just a little longer to find him?"

❁

"Greetings, Zaaco, I trust your sleep was pleasant," said Thuro, entering the chief's camp for the second time in as many days.

Zaaco speared the young warrior with his dark eyes, and Thuro fidgeted under the scrutiny. Coldly Zaaco said, "My sleep was pleasant. Brief, but pleasant. Yours?"

"My sleep was pleasant enough," mumbled Thuro. "Ah, Horda said you wished to see me?"

"Yes." But he said nothing more, and Thuro fidgeted again. Horda watched the scene with growing sympathy. Thuro opened his mouth to speak again, but a shake of Horda's head warned him to wait. Finally Zaaco spoke, "You desire to join the Inner Band?"

"I what?"

"You have great strength to protect a chief who grows too old to protect himself, and an appointment to the Inner Band would be a fitting reward for the young hero who saved Mach and Lonzar with his quick thinking. Is that not so?"

Thuro shook his head, confusion written on his features. "You already rewarded me more than enough for my small part in the rescue of Lonzar and Mach, and I told you last night I don't deserve to be called hero."

"So you did," agreed Zaaco. Again he was silent. This time, though, he seemed to be waiting for Thuro to speak.

The young man cleared his throat nervously. "I'd lie if I told you I never thought of someday belonging to the Inner Band," he commented. "In fact, I believe that's every young warrior's dream, wouldn't you agree?"

"Yes, but not every young warrior has the nerve to seek such an appointment," said Zaaco frostily.

"I have never done so," Thuro said vehemently.

"Hmm," Zaaco commented. "Did you or did you not tell me Wilda had said she'd accept your bid?"

The apparent change of subject confused the young man again. "Um, yes, I told you ..." his voice faded.

"I sense more words wait to be spoken," coaxed Zaaco.

"Ahm ... not exactly," admitted Thuro.

"What do you mean by 'not exactly'?"

"Well, she said any young woman would be pleased to accept my bid ..."

"And?" prompted the chief.

"And I decided to bid for her."

"You decided to bid for her?" echoed Zaaco. "That is all?"

But Thuro's face was suddenly a mixture of realization, embarrassment, and dismay. Reluctantly he raised his eyes to meet Zaaco's unflinching gaze. "No, not exactly all," he confessed.

"Tell me the rest," demanded Zaaco.

Taking a deep breath, Thuro said, "Wilda seemed delighted I'd been recognized as a hero, and she bragged to anyone who would listen about how brave and strong I am. I didn't like it."

He shook his head. "No, that's not true. I liked her thinking me brave and strong, but her words bothered me, and I told her so."

Zaaco nodded and asked, "Did she say anything else important?"

"Yes, she said ..." Abruptly he stopped, finally seeing the connection. "She said my mate and I would have our choice of bands."

Zaaco nodded thoughtfully. "I see. You may go."

"I don't believe it," Thuro muttered, more to himself than to anyone else.

But the chief acted as if the words were meant for him. "It's a terrible thing to lie to others, Thuro, but it's much worse to lie to oneself." He stared into the young man's soul. "Do you understand me?"

Thuro nodded somberly, his face flushed with embarrassment. "Am I going to be punished?" he asked tentatively.

"Not by the Council. Now excuse me — I need to check on the sessions." Zaaco headed toward the other side of the Gathering grounds.

Thuro turned to Horda. "She really came here?"

"Yes."

"And she actually asked Zaaco to appoint me to the Inner Band?"

"Yes."

He shook his head in disbelief. "She's very upset. I must comfort her."

Though Horda longed to caution him about Wilda, she sensed he would defend her. Love was truly a mystery sometimes, as she well knew.

Chapter 18

The evening eat completed, Horda swept around the cook fire with a twig broom when Bear Claw strode into the camp.

"I would walk with you," he said without preamble.

"Greetings, Bear Claw. I trust your day was pleasant." She smiled at him, hoping her politeness was not wasted.

"Pleasant?" He started to spit in the freshly swept dirt, but Horda's frown stopped him. He hesitated before he said, "By your Mother Life, I don't see what's so pleasant about this Gathering. It's a waste of time."

"A waste of time?" Though Horda's normal delight in Gathering had been weakened by her mother's death and by Bear Claw's presence, his words still mystified her. "Bear Claw, how can you say such a thing?"

"All I see are people running around talking and pretending to work without accomplishing a thing."

Horda smiled at his surly expression. "You've summed up Gathering pretty well."

"I have?" He glared. "Then what's the purpose of it?" he demanded.

"Well, you see, our bands live far apart. Most of us don't see each other from one Gathering to the next, so this is a time for all of us to visit, catch up on the news, learn new things, make new friends, and start new families. That's why there's so much talking." And, Mother Life, she was doing it again. Every time she spoke with the foreign chief she sounded like a session leader lecturing her group.

Still, this was a topic she could talk about knowledgably, and one she liked to discuss. "Gathering is also the main time of the Council Meetings," she continued. "Do you understand our Council of Elders?"

She watched as first one emotion and then another fought for supremacy on his face. Clearly her words interested him, but just as clearly he hated to admit it. She let the silence draw out until he decided which would win. Grudgingly he muttered, "No."

She swallowed her smile. Perhaps there was hope for him after all. And lecturing by her father's cook fire was certainly better than walking with him, she told herself. "The Council of Elders is really three Councils: the Council of Men, the Council of Women, and the Council of Both Men and Women. The complete Council includes a hand of the oldest men, the Chief, and the number one mate of each man. The Medicine Man also belongs to the Council, though none of his mates do.

"The groups meet together and separately. They deal with problems concerning hunting grounds, food supplies, band splits, and anything else the bands cannot settle for themselves. They also resolve disputes or problems between two or more bands."

"Instead of fighting?"

Horda nodded solemnly. "Instead of fighting."

Bear Claw thought a moment, then grinned. "The men outnumber the women."

She smiled back. "Yes, they do. They have slightly more votes when the whole Council meets."

He nodded his approval and waited for her to continue. "You already know we teach lessons about our ways to the children. That also makes for a lot of talking."

"Yes, it does."

"And you've seen the Ceremony of the Great Traveler and heard about the Ritual."

201

"Yes."

"There will also be other Rituals during Gathering. There are the Rituals of the Taboos, Manhood, Womanhood, the Bid, and First Mating. All our people take part in each of these — either as teachers or participants. Perhaps one reason you're not enjoying our Gathering is you don't really have a part in it."

Bear Claw grunted. "I've noticed."

She thought for a moment. "Perhaps there's something you could teach my people. Your women are teaching our women to make baskets. What do you know you could share with our people?"

Bear Claw's tone was flat and bitter. "Nothing. I discussed hunting with some of your warriors, but they no longer hunt the way my people do." He laughed, but there was no joy in it. "They've improved our methods."

"Ah, then perhaps you could be involved in learning new things," she said gently, "things you could bring home to your people. Everyone who's learned a new or easier way to perform a task shares the knowledge at Gathering. We all learn new ways to cook and preserve foods, tan finer leather, raise better crops, catch more fish, and kill more game. Those lessons and the training sessions are the 'pretend work' you mentioned. People remember these things more easily if they practice them."

"Of course." She couldn't tell whether he truly agreed with her words or was being sarcastic.

"You'd be welcome in any of those sessions."

Anger flashed in his silver eyes. "When I work, I do the work. I don't pretend."

Undaunted, Horda smiled at him. "I'm just trying to help you enjoy your Gathering more."

"Humph," snorted Bear Claw.

"Oh, here's Mach. He asked to walk with me." Horda was careful to keep the relief from her voice.

"I want to walk with you, and I was here first." Bear Claw

spoke through gritted teeth.

Horda's smooth brow furrowed in pretended innocence. "Then why did we stay here talking?"

"Because you were telling me about Gathering."

"Well, we could have walked and talked at the same time, couldn't we?"

Bear Claw glared and muttered, "By the blood of the Great Mystery, woman ..."

"I'm sorry, but I must go now. I wish you a pleasant Gathering. And I'm sure I'll see you tomorrow." She waved and hurried to Mach's side.

With Horda gone, Bear Claw spat in the smooth dirt, but it did nothing to improve his mood.

Carefully avoiding being alone, Mach and Horda walked among the camps. "Greetings, Mach, Horda," Thuro called from Wilda's family fire. "Come join us."

"Thuro, we have things to discuss," Wilda hissed loud enough for the newcomers to hear.

Thuro caught her hand and grinned. "So, we'll discuss them with Mach and Horda. They're interested in the same things."

"I hardly think that's proper," sniffed Wilda with a toss of her head. "This is private."

"Perhaps we should continue on our way," Horda suggested, trying to extricate Mach and herself tactfully.

Wilda almost smiled. "Yes, that would be —"

"Nonsense," boomed Thuro. "We're discussing the Bid Ceremony."

Mach had already taken a seat by the fire, seemingly oblivious to Wilda's discomfort. He tugged Horda's hand until she sat down, too. Then he said, "I understand congratulations are in order, Wilda."

Wilda frowned. Horda poked Mach gently in the ribs.

"Ouch! What was that for?" he whispered.

She said, "Men are congratulated. Women receive good wishes."

He laughed. "I know that, but I think she deserves the congratulations. She's mighty lucky to have caught my friend Thuro. In my educated opinion, he's the best catch of this Gathering's Great Travelers."

Thuro joined in the laughter. "Next to you, my friend."

"Next to no one."

Horda looked at Wilda. "Perhaps we should find higher ground."

Wilda looked blank. "Why?"

"The bison dung seems to be getting a little deep around here. I'd hate to get any on my moccasins."

Wilda looked around in confusion. "There haven't been any bison in our camp."

The young men began to chuckle, which did nothing to improve Wilda's mood. Horda marveled at the woman's stupidity, but she tried to ease her discomfort. "I'm sorry, Wilda," she said. "I couldn't resist the way Mach and Thuro were bragging about each other."

"You were teasing?" Wilda frowned.

"Yes," Horda said. "I didn't mean to upset you."

"Well, you did. First, you push in where you aren't wanted; next you make fun of my chosen." Tears welled in her eyes and began to roll down her cheeks. "Now you're laughing at my expense. It's not fair."

It *was* fair, Horda thought, remembering Wilda's taunts all those years ago, but she said nothing.

Thuro put his arm around Wilda and murmured gently, "I'm sorry, Sweet, but you must calm yourself. They didn't push in where they weren't wanted — I invited them. And Horda wasn't making fun of you."

"She wasn't?" sobbed Wilda.

"No, I wasn't," Horda offered.

"No, she was just making fun of Thuro and me." Mach chuckled.

"I was not," snapped Horda. This conversation was making her uncomfortable; she wished she hadn't said anything in the first place.

But Mach wasn't going to let it go. "Then what were you doing?" he asked with a grin.

"I was just sort of ... ah ... um ... teasing you?"

Mach's face sobered. "Teasing — making fun. Different ways of saying the same thing."

"When you put it that way, it sounds cruel." Horda frowned, contemplating the situation. "I didn't mean to hurt anybody, but you sounded so smug telling each other how great you are like no one else knew. It just slipped out."

Mach's dark eyes sparkled. "Oh, do you mean you already knew we're the best two warriors of this Gathering's Returned Great Travelers?"

Horda realized he was now teasing her and fishing for a compliment at the same time. She decided to play along. "I kind of had a sneaking suspicion that might be so."

"Does that mean you're considering his bid?" Thuro asked boldly.

Horda bit her lip. She had promised her father not to tell anyone she was accepting Mach's bid. She knew she could trust Thuro, but Wilda ...

Before she could reply, Wilda said, "Oh, Thuro, she can't possibly accept Mach's bid. That would cause war with Bear Claw and the People of the Tall Grass."

Everyone knew her words were meant to hurt Horda. Silence fell around the young people like a heavy winter snow.

Thuro, looking for a safer topic, finally said, "Well, Mach, we don't have to help with the little ones tomorrow."

"That's because the little ones don't meet tomorrow," Horda

commented. "They're going to some kind of pottery thing in the afternoon with Dara and her helpers."

"I'm just grateful for a respite," Thuro muttered.

"I still say they aren't too bad," said Mach. "I'm helping Elko in the First Rituals. Honestly, though, those boys are worse than the children." He rolled his eyes expressively. "I don't know if boys are more stupid now or if I've just forgotten how dumb we were."

Horda laughed. "I'd wager you've just forgotten."

But Wilda didn't seem to get the joke this time, either. "Mach and Thuro certainly aren't stupid."

"Probably not," agreed Horda, "but then they no longer have only two hands plus two of winters."

Thuro laughed. "Thank you, Mother Life. I'd hate to go through all of that again. My luck might not hold this time."

"Double that for me," said Mach fervently. "I used all my luck surviving that one."

"Of course, you'd survive," said Wilda with a face that looked like she'd bitten into a sour fruit. "You two talk like luck brought you through."

"Well, Wilda," said Mach, "there was a great deal of luck involved."

"Nonsense," she snapped. "You're the most skillful warriors in the whole tribe. You told me so yourself."

"And you believed us?" Thuro asked with amusement. "We were bragging for our women. We're no better than many others."

Mach shook his head. "Haven't you heard surviving the Great Travel is a finger of skill and a hand of luck?"

"Pooh, I won't listen if you two insist on talking such nonsense," Wilda said disdainfully.

She rose to leave, but Thuro caught her hand and pulled her back down beside him. "Listen to him," he said earnestly. "Mach speaks the truth — not nonsense."

Wilda's face clearly said she didn't believe his words, but she didn't dispute him.

Horda saw her chance to make a graceful exit. She rose, saying, "Morning comes early. We should be going."

"It does grow late," Wilda agreed a bit too quickly for politeness.

Reluctantly Mach and Thuro stood and touched hands.

"Good sleep and pleasant dreams, Thuro and Wilda," Mach said.

"To you, my friend," said Thuro. "Sleep well and dream happy, Horda."

"You and Wilda both," responded Horda.

Still sitting beside the fire, Wilda's silence said more than any words she could have chosen.

Chapter 19

When the morning eat was finished and the cook fire banked, Horda called, "Treema, I want to see Dara before the morning pottery session. She may need my help with the children this afternoon."

"You're turning into a regular mother hen. Dara has three little ones of her own. She can handle the group." Treema came out of the sleeping shelter with her weaving materials and a half-finished basket.

Horda frowned. "Challa can be a handful. She has a terrible mouth."

"Are you serious? She's such a pretty little thing. She reminds me of you at that age. I never realized she wasn't as well-behaved as she looks."

"Maybe I'm being too critical, but I think she's terribly spoiled. Most anything we talk about she says she won't need to know because someone will do it for her since she's so very special." Horda shook her head. "Oh, I don't know. She only has a hand of winters. It's probably a stage and she'll outgrow it in time."

"I certainly hope so, but be careful what you say — to her or about her." Treema chewed her lip thoughtfully.

"Why?"

"Well, you know her mother departed before she had completed her first winter. I don't know what happened, but Khollo seems ... Well, he's awfully protective of that little girl; just don't be too critical."

"Thanks for the warning. I won't even mention her by name," Horda said.

"That's probably best."

"Actually, I'm going to the session to try to find out how Dara fires those vessels without breaking the bottom points."

"Good, then you can teach me." Treema stared at her weaving materials. "I'm still going to the basket sessions with the Women of the Tall Grass. Those waterbaskets will be useful if I can ever learn to make my weave tight enough."

Horda grinned. Treema had many skills, but weaving wasn't one of them. She didn't have the patience required to keep each strand of grass separate and tight. Even among the People of the Frozen Earth, whose weaving was loose and somewhat misshapen at best, hers ranked among the flimsiest.

"Oh, I almost forgot," Treema said. "I need to see Mara about the Rituals of the Mate. I'll be back sometime before midday." With a wave, she grabbed her weaving and left.

Horda picked up her wet clay and was halfway across the Gathering Grounds when Nuroo's furious voice caused her steps to falter. "I cannot believe *you*, of all people, Elko, allowed something so unnecessary to happen." She'd never heard the Medicine Man sound so angry.

"Horda!" Nuroo's roar stopped her and brought goose bumps to her arms.

Mother Life. Was he angry with her? She thrust the bundle of clay into someone's hands and hurried to the Medicine Man. "Yes?"

"Find Norlon. Now!" He spared another glare at Elko before continuing.

Questions bubbled in her throat, but Nuroo's eyes told her answers wouldn't be forthcoming. She turned to search for Norlon and found him by her side. "I never heard him shout like that before," Norlon whispered. "What's going on?"

"I don't know."

Together they faced the Medicine Man. "We are here," said Norlon. "What do you want us to do?"

"Treat this boy's wound," snapped Nuroo. "I must check the other boys in the First Rituals of Manhood to be sure they aren't food for the fever demons." He stalked away, followed by Elko and Zaaco.

"Can you walk?" Horda asked the pale boy.

He nodded, but when he placed his weight on his right leg a moan escaped his lips. Horda and Norlon carried him to Nuroo's area of the camp and lowered him to the bed of furs beside the fire. When he was seated, she looked closer at the boy and said, "You're my brother Zeephro's friend Brash, right?"

The boy nodded.

"Well, Brash, I'm sure we'll fix this problem in no time."

Pain had leeched much of the bronze from the boy's face, allowing the bright crimson slashes of high fever to shine on each cheekbone. "Thank you," he whispered.

Lifting the boy's breechcloth, Horda fought to hide her shock and dismay. Angry red streaks radiated from the thigh up onto his torso and down almost to his knee. The ugly green pus of putrification oozed from the original wound and wafted the sickly sweet smell of death to her nostrils. She no longer questioned Nuroo's anger. Such a small wound — no longer than her hand was wide and no deeper than her smallest finger — could have been treated so easily if it had been looked at when it was new.

Memories tinkled in her mind. She remembered hearing, *"Brash fell down." "Was he hurt?" "Don't be such a mother hen. Men on hunts take falls. "He said he wasn't hurt."*

The alarm in Norlon's eyes matched that in her own heart. Almost certainly Father Death would claim the boy.

Carefully keeping her voice steady, Horda asked, "How did this happen?"

Brash forced a laugh, but it came out sounding more like a sob. "On the first day we hunted deer. They chose me to be one of the runners. Thuro said I ran as fast as Mach did at my age." Pride gleamed in his fever-bright eyes. "I did a good job. Everyone said so. No one knew I jabbed a stick in my leg before I ran the deer. I din' let it bother me. I kept focusin' on my task like Elko said."

"You ran a deer with a stick in your thigh?" asked Horda incredulously

Brash nodded. "I din' have time to take it out then. The deer would of got away."

"Why didn't you seek help after you ran the deer?" asked Norlon through gritted teeth.

Brash shrugged. "I din' need help. I pulled the stick out. It kinda ripped the skin, but it was just a little wound. I thought it would be okay. It din' hardly bleed at all. The men bragged about me runnin' the deer."

"I asked you if you were hurt that day." Horda fought to keep her voice calm. "Why didn't you tell me about the stick?"

"I told you why," said Brash. Fear flashed in the shiny depths of his eyes, and he clenched his hands. "I'll be all right, won't I? I need to get back to the First Rituals. I want my father to be proud of me."

Horda and Norlon exchanged a look that spoke volumes about their fears. Norlon turned away and prepared the herbs and implements to treat the wound, while Horda tried to comfort and reassure Brash.

"I'm sure he's already proud of you. And, yes, you'll soon be fine," she said evenly. Most likely Father Death would cure him when he walked the Frozen Wilds, but she wasn't going to tell him that. Sometimes it is better not to tell the whole truth. "We're going to treat your wound," she said. "Some of our treatments will be painful, but it can't be helped."

"That's okay," whispered Brash. "I can stand pain. It's been hurtin' a lot for the last couple of days, but I din' cry."

"Why didn't you tell someone when it started to hurt?" asked Horda.

Brash took a deep breath and shook his head before he said, "I couldn't. My fa would of called me a cryin' one. I soaked it in the river, but it din' help much. Elko saw me limpin' today."

Horda asked, "Then what happened?"

"Elko asked me questions. I pretended I din' know what he was talkin' about, but he pulled up my breechcloth and looked at my leg. Then he started cursin' and yellin' for somebody to get Nuroo. When Nuroo got there, he started cursin' at Elko and hollerin'." Brash's brown eyes looked enormous. "I never heard them curse before. An' both of 'em seemed awful mad. Are they gonna' punish me?"

"No, they aren't going to punish you," said Horda firmly. She bit her lip. *Although Father Death may claim you in spite of everything we do.* "Elko and Nuroo are angry because your leg would have been much easier to treat when it first happened."

"Oh." Brash closed his eyes tightly, but he couldn't stop the tears that trickled down his face.

"I've fixed a tonic of lobelia for the pain and willow to lower the fever." Norlon lifted Brash's head so he could drink from the bowl. When every drop was gone, Norlon nodded his satisfaction. "In a short time you'll feel drowsy, and then we're going to wash your wound with goldenrod water. We'll try to be gentle, but this will hurt. I'll give you a piece of leather to bite on."

Norlon waited quietly until Brash's eyelids drooped. Then he fitted the small piece of soft leather between the boy's teeth.

"Yell if you need to," said Horda. "Chewing the leather helps, but sometimes yelling helps even more."

Brash offered a wan half smile.

Horda and Norlon lathered their hands with soaproot and rinsed them in the hottest water they could stand. "Are you ready?" Norlon asked her.

Horda grimaced, but she nodded her head. Taking a deep breath, Norlon whispered, "Me neither, but here goes."

She picked up the bag of boiled goldenrod water, and Norlon wrapped a piece fawnskin around combed milkweed. She slowly poured the water into the festering wound while he gently scrubbed the area. Brash's eyes popped open to show white rings of panic. He chewed the leather and moaned quietly, but he did not yell, and his leg did not move.

"You're doing fine," soothed Horda. "This will only take a little longer, and then you can sleep."

"I don't think we've ever had a patient lie so still," said Norlon. Brash's brown eyes flared with pride at the compliment, burning away most of the panic.

"Nor be so quiet," crooned Horda. *If only he'd told someone when this happened, he wouldn't be going through this now.* She kept her face smooth and her words soft so they wouldn't betray her angry frustration. The treatment would have been simple, and he'd still be running deer today instead of dying. "I'm so proud of you. You're really brave, Brash."

Tears pooled in Brash's eyes, and he chewed frantically on the leather while Horda poured the warm goldenrod water and Norlon scrubbed away the bits of bark and dirt still embedded in the pus-filled wound. Neither wavered from their task though Norlon held his breath and Horda averted her head to avoid the sickly sweet smell of Brash's rotting flesh.

A half smile curved Brash's lips and a sigh of relief escaped when Norlon said, "Okay. No more water."

Brash took the leather out of his mouth. "Are you finished?" A wide yawn split his tear-streaked face.

"With the first part." Horda smiled at him. "You did well. A true warrior. I know that must have hurt."

"It was't too bad," yawned Brash.

Horda fought a yawn herself. "Are you sleepy?"

"A little," admitted Brash. "I hadn' slept musch lately."

"Go ahead and sleep. We'll only be looking at your wound for a while."

"Lookin' at it?" asked Brash

Horda spoke encouragingly. "We must decide what to do next."

"Oh." Brash yawned again. "It don' hurt so bad. Maybe you won' need to do nus'in' else."

"Nice try, Brash." Norlon teased the boy gently. "Don't you want us to test your bravery a little more?"

"Ah, no. Na'really," confessed Brash.

"I don't blame you," Norlon replied. "Neither would I."

"Please don' tell my fa I hurt mysef'," said Brash suddenly. Norlon was confused. "Why not?"

Tears gathered in the corners of Brash's eyes. "He awready thinks I'm a cryin' girl-child. I wann'ed him to be proud of me, but I don't guess he ever will."

Horda watched anger flare in Norlon's eyes, but he kept his voice level. "I personally don't see anything wrong with girl-children, I mean, after all, Horda's one of them." Horda was pleased to see a smile light Brash's eyes when he looked at her. "Anyway, unless your father is really stupid," Norlon continued, "he could have seen for himself that you aren't a girl-child simply by lifting at your breechcloth. I don't have any trouble recognizing boy-children. Do you, Horda?"

Horda shook her head, and Brash giggled.

Norlon's anger was growing. "You may be a lot of things, Brash, but you're as far from a cryin' one as I've ever treated. I could name some warriors who made bigger fusses over much less painful treatments. I'm proud of you."

"Honest?" Brash's voice reflected hope and doubt.

"Honest." Norlon raised his right hand. "Warrior's solemn honor."

Brash grinned and raised his hand. "Accepted." But then the

boy's face abruptly sobered. "Do you hafta tell Mach I hurt myself?"

"Mach?" Norlon was puzzled at the seeming change of topic, but Horda understood. *Mother Life, Mach's going to blame himself ... Just like I am. But what more could we have done than ask the boy if he was hurt?* Examine his body! shouted her conscience. "Brash and my brother hunted with Mach and Thuro that day," she explained quietly.

"I kind of lied to Mach — and Horda," Brash said in a little voice. "I said I was't hurt. I really din' think I was." He sniffed. "Mach won' be proud of me ennymore."

"Oh, Brash," said Horda. "Mach'll still be proud of the way you hunted. The fact you're hurt doesn't change that."

"Honest?"

Horda nodded. "Honest. He'll just wish you'd told someone sooner so the fever demons wouldn't have found you now."

"I wanna get well so I can keep up with the First Rituals."

Norlon took the boy's hand and spoke gently, but firmly. "Brash, I'm not going to lie to you. Your wound requires lots more treatment. It may take a long time for you to get well."

"Oh ... I guess I knew that ..." His voice caught, but he forced a smile. "I was ... just hopin'."

Brash's eyes showed Horda a knowledge she hoped he did not possess. *Oh, Mother Life, was there nothing more they could do?*

❂

Without touching the ugly wound, Horda and Norlon examined it from every angle. Brash watched them for a while, but he soon lost interest and appeared to doze. "It's on his bod —" whispered Norlon.

Horda pointed to the tree near the shelter area. They walked to it. "I'm not sure he's asleep," she whispered, "and I don't think he should hear this."

"No, you're probably right. Tell me what you know about his wound."

"No more than he told us," she admitted. "He said he wasn't hurt. Mach said Brash told him the same thing. We accepted his words."

"That's all you could do, Horda," said Norlon. "It isn't your fault."

"I know that, but if I'd insisted on examining him —"

"Maybe ... maybe not." Norlon shrugged. "It's an ugly wound though it's small."

"What are we going to do?"

Norlon frowned. "The infection's on his body. Even if we cut off the leg, it wouldn't stop it."

"No, it wouldn't," she agreed.

"His only hope is if we can burn the infection out."

Horda grimaced. "We can't burn all those lines up his body and down his leg."

"No, we can't." Norlon glared helplessly at the dozing boy. "We must discuss this with Nuroo. I'll find him now."

"Wait," said Horda. "He'll come here when he's finished with what he has to do. Let the boy rest a little ... I don't think the extra time will make any difference."

Chapter 20

Horda and Norlon had barely taken seats beside the dozing Brash when Nuroo appeared. Anger still vibrated from the Medicine Man like heat waves on a mid-summer day, but he was all business. No one spoke as Norlon poured water for his father to wash his hands. Nuroo looked at the wound carefully before probing it with a cautious finger. Brash moaned softly at the touch but didn't open his eyes. Nuroo shook his head then motioned Horda and Norlon to follow him back to the tree.

"You did a good job cleaning it."

"We tried," said Norlon. "I just wish we could have cleaned it when it happened."

"This is so senseless," Horda said. "I asked him if he was hurt the day of the First Hunt, but he said no."

Nuroo growled. "Senseless, but it's not your fault."

Horda protested, "I should have examined —"

A reluctant smile lifted the corner of Nuroo's mouth. "You often lift men-to-be's breechcloths at the First Hunt?"

"Of course not." A blush heated Horda's cheeks before she realized Nuroo's words were meant to ease the tension.

"I didn't think so." Abruptly sobering, Nuroo slammed his hand against the tree. "But the boy should have told someone. Someone should have noticed."

"He tried to keep anyone from noticing," said Norlon. "He told us he didn't want them to think him a coward."

Nuroo snorted. "Misplaced bravery. At least none of the

other boys carry secret wounds."

"I'm glad of that," offered Horda. "One's quite enough."

"More than enough." The Medicine Man sat down beneath the tree. Horda and Norlon took places on either side of him. Nuroo looked at Horda a moment then asked, "What should we do next?"

Horda blinked. "Ah ... Norlon and I thought ... ah ... Why are you asking me?" she blurted.

Nuroo chuckled deep in his chest. "You've followed me around most of your life and studied formally for more than two hands' turnings of the seasons. You're a woman about to choose a mate. You'll be the healer woman of your band. Why shouldn't I ask you?"

Mother Life, he really was asking her. But what if she made a mistake? She took a deep breath and squared her shoulders. *I won't make a mistake.* "Norlon and I decided we should burn the infection, but we can't burn away all the red streaks."

Nuroo nodded thoughtfully. "Umm. We'll burn the original wound, but that won't help his body fight the fever demons already invading it. What will we use?"

"Norlon gave him a tonic of lobelia and willow."

"Why?"

Norlon opened his mouth to answer, but Nuroo waved him to silence. Horda smiled slightly; this was her test. "The lobelia relaxes him and dulls the pain so he won't fight the treatment, and the willow fights the fever demons and the pain. Together they give his body a chance to heal itself."

"Good. What else did you do?"

"We washed the wound with goldenrod water and scrubbed away as much of the evil mess as we could."

"Then?"

"We looked at it."

"Why?"

"To decide what to do next."

"And?"

"We decided we should burn it," Horda said with a frown.

"After that," prompted Nuroo.

Once more Norlon opened his mouth, and once more his father waved him to silence. Horda thought for a moment then smiled triumphantly. "We should make a packing of prairie flaxseeds and figwort leaves to draw out the fever demons."

"You've both done well." Nuroo smiled at Horda and Norlon. "How much lobelia did you give him?" he asked his son.

"Three leaves ground with a finger of willow bark brewed into hot tonic."

"Good, that'll shield much of the pain. Norlon, heat the fire stone. Horda, explain to Brash what we're going to do. Tell him the tonic dulls the pain."

"Do you want me to wake him up?" she squeaked. "I thought you wanted him to sleep through the treatment."

Nuroo arched one bushy eyebrow at her. "Do you really think he'll sleep through our burning his wound?"

Embarrassed, she mumbled, "Ah, no, I don't guess he will."

"Neither do I. Some pain, probably intense, will break through the shield, and he'll be more frightened if he doesn't know what's happening."

"I'm sorry, Nuroo. I should have realized."

Nuroo frowned. "You asked a question, and I answered it. It wasn't an unreasonable question, and it certainly wasn't an unreasonable answer. Let it go, Horda."

Relieved by Nuroo's words, she met his eyes. "I'm really sorry; it's just I'm frightened. He's very ill."

Nuroo said, "I've seldom treated anyone so consumed by fever demons."

Anger flared in her eyes, and she shook her head. "Unnecessary," she said.

Nuroo said, "Yes, but wringing our hands won't cure him,

so let's get to work." She squared her shoulders, and he nodded. "After you've told him what we're going to do, I want you to sit by his head and help keep him still." Still doubtful, Horda followed Nuroo back to the dozing boy.

❋

Norlon pointed to a small round stone heating in the embers of the fire, but Nuroo indicated the warmed waterbag instead. "Wash your hands," he instructed.

"We just washed," said Norlon.

"Again." Nuroo handed soaproot to each of them and took some for himself.

When all three were scrubbed clean, Horda moved close to Brash and gently touched his arm. "Brash, I need to explain something to you."

Brash sniffled and opened fever glazed eyes. "What?"

"Nuroo's back, and he and Norlon are going to treat your wound." Brash started to rub his eyes, but Horda stopped him. "Try not to wake up any more than you have to," she cautioned. "The tonic Norlon gave you will dull the pain, but we want you to understand what we're going to do so you won't be frightened."

"I'm not scared." Brash's lower lip quivered slightly.

"Oh, I know you aren't scared now," said Horda as cheerfully as she could, "but sometimes when people wake up suddenly, they're confused, especially if they don't know what's going on. That can be pretty scary."

Brash tried to focus his eyes. Finally he gave up and closed them. "What are they going to do?" he whispered.

"They're going to burn away the fever demon feeding on your wound so your body can heal."

His eyes popped open. "Burn it?" he squeaked.

"Burn away the fever demons," said Norlon.

"Oh." Brash nodded, and his eyes drifted closed once again.

"I guesh tha'll be awright," he mumbled.

"Horda, sit beside his head. Norlon, take his feet." Donning protective bison skin mitts, Nuroo used fire-hardened wooden tongs to lift the hot stone from the flames. He eyed it for an instant before placing it in the center of Brash's wound.

Nuroo's movements looked too gentle for the violent response they prompted. A scream exploded from the boy's lips, and his body arched in a futile attempt to escape the stone. Norlon firmly held his feet while Horda braced his shoulders and crooned comfortingly.

The acrid smell of burning flesh quickly overlaid the sickly odor of rot emanating from the putrid wound. The liquids in the wound sizzled and popped against the heated stone. Nausea clawed the back of Horda's throat, but she fought it and continued crooning to the boy who could not possibly hear her over his own tortured screams.

Brash seemed to shrink before her eyes. It was as if the combined heat of the stone and his raging fever consumed his flesh until he was no more than a rigid rack of bones held together by a battered bag of skin. Frightened, Horda watched the life force flicker in his glazed eyes. His bronzed complexion blanched, leaving only the obscene fever slashes across the grey planes of his suddenly skeletal face. It seemed an eternity passed before Nuroo lifted the still smoking stone from the wound and dropped it back into the fire. Brash's screams subsided, becoming a moan. His body collapsed away from Horda and Norlon's restraints, then he lay silent and still.

Horda's eyes widened. "Is he ...?" She couldn't bring herself to complete the question.

Nuroo shook his head. "Unconscious." Pulling off his mitts, he used an obsidian knife to gently probe the streaks around the original wound. Brash moaned again.

Still fighting the nausea that burned the back of her own throat, Horda watched Norlon stumble away. She searched for words to divert Nuroo from the sounds of Norlon's retching, but there were none. She mumbled, "He ... ah, we ... ah Brash ..." Nuroo's glare reduced her to silence.

With his shoulders bowed and his face green, Norlon returned to the fire. "I'm sorry. I couldn't help myself."

Nuroo's fierce expression relaxed. "You did what had to be done before giving in to your nausea. That's all I could ask of you."

Horda watched guilt flutter across Norlon's features. "This is so senseless," he said. "He is so young to suffer such misery."

"Yes he is. Some day you'll learn to separate the wounds and pain from the people who suffer. Just as you'll learn to separate the man Norlon from the Medicine Man. The suffering will still sicken Norlon, but it won't touch the Medicine Man because he cannot allow it to do so, not only for his own sake, but for the sake of those he tends."

Nuroo stared at his son's bowed head. "Norlon will still vomit and howl and kick things. But only in private. They need the Medicine Man's strength as much as they need his skills." He waited until Norlon met his eyes. "My father almost despaired of my learning to separate myself from my station, but I finally did it." He patted his son's shoulder. "You will too."

Norlon nodded gratefully. Horda was surprised learn Nuroo still fought the same battles she and Norlon did — he just hid them more successfully than they did. Undoubtedly it was because he had more practice, and that meant there was hope. She smiled warmly at the Medicine Man. He smiled back, acknowledging her new understanding.

Nuroo turned back to their patient, all business again. "To lower his fever, we must get liquid into him. Norlon, brew some extra strong willow tonic — use three fingers of shredded bark for a small water skin. Sweeten it with two small ladles of cammas molasses.

"Horda, get the large water bag and bathe his face and

chest. The combination of the willow tonic and water should tame the fever demons a little. We don't want them banished completely because they help fight the infection."

Nuroo rubbed his face and looked down at Brash's ravaged shell. Some of the fierce anger seemed to flow back into his body. He headed back to his shelter, leaving Norlon and Horda to carry out his orders.

Though Horda bathed him in the cool water, Brash had not regained consciousness when Nuroo returned, laden with two medium-sized leather pouches and a bundle of dried leaves. The Medicine Man sat beside the fire and opened the first pouch.

"The tonic is cooling," Norlon informed him.

"Good." Nuroo removed a glob from one of the pouches. "Pull the flat fire stone I use to heat pine pitch into the flames."

Though Brash began to whimper and wriggle at her touch, Horda bathed his burning chest once more. Norlon looked up from his work. "How is he?"

"I'm afraid," Horda said quietly. "He seems hotter than ever."

Nuroo's eyes hardened, and he shook his head. "Keep bathing him. I'm fixing a packing to draw the poison away. Perhaps it will help." Brash's arms thrashed feebly, and he opened his eyes just a slit. Nuroo said, "If he's awake, try to get some tonic down him. He needs liquids."

Norlon dipped a horn of the strong willow tonic and lifted the boy's head. "Here, Brash, drink this." Brash mumbled but didn't open his eyes any further. He moved his head from side to side, evading the horn with his remaining strength. "Horda, help me," Norlon called. Horda held Brash's head while Norlon tipped a small amount of the tonic into his mouth. She massaged his throat, forcing him to swallow the liquid. Norlon nodded. "Again." They repeated the process until the horn was completely empty.

Chapter 21

Horda was still bent over the unconscious Brash when Mara, a tiny woman dressed in an elaborately embroidered black tunic and matching moccasins, entered the shelter. A favorite of Horda's, the number one mate of Nuroo, always exuded an aura of comfortable competence. Baked and burned by the suns of many summers, her beauty had faded into the handsome dignity of age. Her dark brown eyes usually snapped and sparkled with delight, but they were now clouded with pain. She walked to Nuroo and touched his arm. "I just heard."

The hard lines of Nuroo's face softened when he looked at her. "Don't worry. Horda and Norlon have been helping me."

"Is there anything you need me to do?"

He nodded. "We need more water to fight the fever demons." He shook his head sadly. "They're consuming Brash's life force. Perhaps the water will slow the demons so he can fight them off."

Mara collected several large water bags and left without another word.

As Horda watched the woman leave, her mind was suddenly filled with thoughts of Meiran. She knew as soon as Mara returned, she would help her bathe the suffering boy, giving no obvious thought to her beautiful tunic and moccasins. Her mother, on the other hand, would never have refused to help, but she'd have found some way to avoid it, especially if she were well dressed. Meiran thought such work beneath her position.

This revelation made Horda's heart jump. *Mama always demanded respect without realizing she had to earn it like Mara does, by truly caring for others. Mother Life, please always let me be like Mara.*

❄

Even as he spoke with his mate, Nuroo's hands didn't pause in their work for an instant. First, he had placed the fist-sized glob of dried lodgepole pine sap on the flat fire stone to soften. "Watch that this doesn't melt completely," he told Norlon.

Next, he chose a large stone cup and dropped in a double handful of the prairie flaxseeds. Then he took several figwort leaves from the bundle and crumbled them into the seeds. He pulverized the seeds and leaves with a pestle made from the front leg bone of a deer. When the leaves and seeds were reduced to a coarse powder, he asked Norlon, "Is the pitch soft enough?"

Instead of replying, Norlon used wooden tongs to fashion the glob into an enormous teardrop shape. Nuroo nodded and held out the stone cup filled the powder. The drop fell into the mixture with a gentle plop. Nuroo continued mixing until it formed a soft ball. "Warm it again," he instructed, passing the cup to his son. The young man dumped the contents onto the flat fire stone amid the flames.

Nuroo examined Brash's wound and shook his head. "I don't want to burn him any more, but the packing must be hot enough to draw the infection."

Norlon nodded and returned to the mixture, cutting it in half and allowing it flow back together. When steam bubbles began to form in it, he tested it with his fingertip. Using a wooden paddle, he scooped the mixture from the flames. "It's ready," he announced.

Nuroo said, "Bring it. It cools quickly."

Norlon held the paddle while his father stirred its contents one more time, lifting some of it so the air could cool it slightly.

Then he nodded and began to pack the gaping wound on Brash's thigh.

Brash's eyes flew open, and he feebly thrashed his limbs. "Shh, shh," crooned Horda. "It's okay. Nuroo's putting medicine on your wound to draw the infection. Then the fever demons will go away and leave you alone. Shh, shh, now. It's okay."

Her words calmed him. Some of the fear disappeared from his eyes, and he lay still. "It hurts," he croaked.

"I know," she said, "but this will help." *Please, don't let me be lying to him, Mother Life.* "You'll soon feel better."

Just then, Mara returned with the water bags and set them beside Brash. Nuroo looked up at her and said, "Please, bring him some more willow water, Mara. It's in the small boiling bag."

She passed a drinking horn of the mixture to Horda, who lifted Brash's head so he could drink. He barely finished the tonic when he started coughing and gagging. "Calm him," ordered Nuroo.

She began to whisper to him again. "Take deep breaths ... Be calm ... Shh." Finally the spasms passed, allowing Mara to begin bathing his head and chest with the cool water.

Almost immediately Brash began shivering. "It's too cold," he complained between his chattering teeth.

"Shh. We must cool your body," Horda told him. "The fever demons think you're a tasty morsel. If we cool your flesh enough, they'll give up and go away. You want them to go away, don't you?"

Gritting his chattering teeth, he nodded. "Good," she said approvingly. "I knew you were strong."

He was strong, but he had been through so much. Finally he couldn't take it any more. "It hurts sho bad. I'm freezin'. Stop! Please, stop!"

Horda's heart twisted. She glanced at Nuroo, who was

wrapping Brash's thigh with strips of washed leather. He looked directly into the boy's eyes. "Son, the only chance you have is if we banish the fever demons. You must let Horda and Mara cool your body." Nuroo signaled Mara to continue bathing his legs and stomach.

Brash bit his lips and closed his eyes. He didn't complain again, but tears streamed down his face and he shivered violently.

Please, Mother Life, don't give up on him after he goes through all this.

Nuroo placed a hand on Brash's burning forehead. He frowned and went back into his shelter, returning quickly with two more medicine pouches. Taking another stone cup, he said, "Brash, we've done all we can to your wound. Now, I'm going to make you a tonic of these."

Brash opened his eyes and looked at the wyethia roots and juniper twigs in Nuroo's hand. Then he appeared to doze. Nuroo continued to talk to him while he shredded the plants with a fine obsidian knife. "I know this tonic doesn't taste very good, but the fever demons hate it too."

Nuroo poured a small amount of hot water from the boiling bag into the cup and gently stirred the mixture. "Are you listening to me? You need to stay awake." He shook Brash gently.

Finally Brash looked up at the Medicine Man. Continuing to stir the concoction, Nuroo smiled encouragement. "That's good. You're doing fine. Can you sit up?"

Brash nodded, and Horda helped him to a sitting position. Nuroo added a little cool water to the brew and handed him the horn. "Drink all of it, please."

Brash gulped the mixture down, began coughing, and immediately vomited up much more liquid than he had just drunk. An even more severe chill rattled his teeth and shook his slight frame.

"I had hoped you could drink this quickly because it tastes like dirty bison hides smell, but I can see that won't work; you're going to have to sip it, okay? Nuroo's voice was soothing. He calmly prepared another mix of wyethia and juniper, but this time he added a ladle of cammas molasses and a sprig of mint to make it more palatable. "Are you ready to try again?" he asked.

Brash nodded doubtfully.

"This time take little sips. Don't try to drink it all at once," cautioned Nuroo.

Brash sipped the mixture. When he started to retch, Nuroo said, "Breathe deeply ... Good ... Take a deep breath ... That's the way." When he had finished the whole thing, Nuroo slipped some mint and a sliver of alum root into his mouth. "Just chew this. Don't swallow the pulp."

Brash chewed obediently, but he retched again as more chills shook his body.

"Wrap him," commanded Nuroo.

Trying to ignore the ominous red flush creeping up his body, Horda wrapped the shivering boy in the warm furs Mara handed her. "You're doing fine, Brash," she crooned. "Just give the medicine a little time to work." *Mother Life, please help him.*

He smiled back then without warning vomited again. "I'm going to the Frozen Wilds, aren't I?" he asked softly.

Mother Life, what am I going to say to this child?

"We all go to the Frozen Wilds someday," she evaded.

"No, I don't mean someday." Brash's voice sounded as small and shrunken as his body looked, but he was insistent. "I mean now. I vomit that medicine, and I'm going to the Frozen Wilds." Thin tears ran down his face, and his body shook with dry sobs and chills.

Nuroo put a gentle hand on Horda's shoulder, lending her strength. He looked Brash right in the eye. "Brash, I refuse to lie to you. You're a very sick young man. Your wound would have been easier to treat when you first injured yourself. We could have done things then to keep you from becoming a feast for the fever demons."

Suddenly looking very tired, Nuroo said, "Anyway, there are a number of things that can help your body heal. We've completed some of them. The medicine is another. It must stay down. It is strong, and you need it. Do you understand me?"

Brash nodded, and Nuroo smiled at him. "Good. You're young and healthy; that's in your favor. You should be able to survive this and live to see your children's children playing around your cook fire."

Horda listened to Nuroo's comforting words and hoped Brash didn't realize how vague they were. She understood Nuroo feared the boy would soon be gone even as he still fought to keep Brash's hope alive. Hope could be powerful medicine.

Brash looked hopefully at Nuroo. "My children's children?" he asked. He thought a moment then added, "Nuroo, do you want me to try to drink that stuff again?"

"Not right now. Right now I want you to sip some sweetened willow tonic. I'll even add some mint."

"I like mint."

"It's good for your stomach," Nuroo said. "If you can keep it down for a while, we'll try the wyethia and juniper again. I suspect part of the problem is the fever demons have burned so much of your juice away that you need plain liquid more than the medicine right now."

Brash nodded solemnly. "I'll try real hard to keep it down."

Horda prayed silently as she fed him sips of the sweetened tonic. The chills had finally stopped, but the fever slashes on his sunken cheeks had spread to paint his skin with an artificially bright flush of health.

"I'm doin' better," he announced weakly. "I haven't vomited."

She nodded. "I know."

"My leg dudn't hardly hurt at all."

"Good." She gave him another sip of the water.

"But my side hurts."

"Where?"

He pushed down the furs and placed his right hand just above his waist. "Here."

"I don't think it's anything to worry about, but I will ask Nuroo just to be sure."

He caught her hand. "I don't want to be alone."

"I'll be right back. I'm just going to talk to Nuroo."

She quickly told him of Brash's newest symptom. Night descended behind Nuroo's eyes. "We must keep the wyethia and juniper down him," he said shortly.

Once more they tried. Once more they failed. Though Brash sobbed throughout, he shed no more tears. Brash clung to her hand. "It's getting dark. I see the sun so I know it isn't, but it looks that way to me. I'm scared, but I don't want to be. I want to be brave. Please stay with me. Please?"

Stroking his sunken cheek, she fought to keep her face from showing her own fears. "I'm right here, Brash. I'm not going anyplace."

"Norlon," Nuroo called, turning away from Horda and the boy.

"Yes, Father."

"Find his parents," Nuroo whispered tightly.

Norlon hurried away. Horda turned her head so Brash wouldn't see her tears.

❀

A short time later, Zaaco and his son Zeephro entered Nuroo's camp. Horda blinked away her tears and nodded at them. "Greetings, Fa, Zeephro."

"Greetings, daughter, Brash." Zaaco's voice rumbled though he tried to speak softly.

"Greetings, Brash. I missed you today." Zeephro moved closer to the furs and took his friend's hand timidly. "Nuroo made us all undress so he could see if we carried secret wounds on our bodies. It was kind of embarrassing; it's a good thing you weren't there." He stopped abruptly, realizing what he had just said.

But Brash seemed not to notice. He opened his eyes and looked at Zeephro. "I really hurt myself at the First Hunt," he admitted. "I guess I shoulda told someone sooner."

It was Zaaco who answered. "Yes, you should have," he said. "It would have sav —" Horda's hand on his arm stopped the words of reproach. She shook her head gently and watched a darkness fall behind her father's eyes. It would not be the last time, she thought. There will be many more such looks before this day ended.

Horda was correct. A few moments later Norlon returned, leading a man and woman. "These are Brash's parents, Juaja and Braso," he told the small group.

The woman fell on Brash, sobbing, and Brash clutched Horda's hand even tighter. "Oh, my child, my child. I knew you were too young for the Rituals. I tried to tell your father, but would he listen to me? No, of course not. I don't know anything, do I? After all, I'm just a lowly woman and can't understand such things." Braso stood back at the entrance, glowering, but he said nothing. Clearly he had heard all this before.

Juaja noticed Horda for the first time. "You may leave now," she said coldly. "I will take care of my son."

"No!" cried Brash, gripping Horda's hand. "I want her to stay."

In answer, Juaja grabbed Brash's other hand. "I'm so sorry, Child. Mama will make it better, you'll see."

Braso clearly had had enough. He took two long strides

over to the furs and roughly pulled his wife away from their son. "Stop coddling him!" he thundered. "All you ever do is make excuses for him. He wouldn't be in this condition if you didn't baby him so."

Brash reacted to his father's words; Horda watched him. This had to stop. She took a deep breath and addressed Juaja. "His age had nothing to do with falling on a stick." The woman's mouth formed an O of surprise.

Then Horda rounded on Braso. "If Brash had allowed us the opportunity to coddle him, he wouldn't be so seriously ill. He wouldn't tell anyone about his wound because he didn't want anyone to think him a coward, especially you." Almost as tall as the posturing bully, she glared into his eyes. "He wanted *you* to be proud of him."

"Well, that's a first. He's always been a mewling, little, ma—"

"Enough!" roared Zaaco, reducing the rest to silence. "This is neither the time nor the place. Nuroo will speak with you; that's why you're here."

Nuroo and Norlon herded the couple to the nearby tree while Horda tried to comfort Brash.

"I knew he'd be angry," he wept. "I told you. He says I'm a worthless girl-child, and maybe he's right."

Zaaco sat on the other side of the boy and stroked his arm. "Let me tell you something," he whispered. "In my life so far, I've had two girl-children, and a whole hand of boy-children." He held up five fingers for Brash to count. "I can tell you from my own experience you aren't a girl-child."

"My fa says I'm a cryin' one because I have my ma wash my cuts," he told the chief.

Horda bit her lip. It was hard to tell whether the boy's external or internal wounds hurt more. She had tended to the obvious ones; now it was time to work on the rest. "Actually, that's the smart thing to do," she said. "Washing wounds and doctoring them when they happen helps keep the fever demons away."

"Listen to her. She's a healer woman and knows these things," Zaaco said. He touched the boy's dull hair. "And if it helps, I'd never consider you a cryin' one because I've never seen you cry without a really good reason."

"I try hard not to. I really want him to be proud of me."

"I can't speak for him, but *I'm* proud of you," he told the boy. Brash smiled, but he didn't speak again. His eyes drifted closed until only a half moon of glazed white showed.

Horda blinked quickly to dry the tears threatening to run down her cheeks. "Thank you, Fa," she mouthed silently.

"Is he asleep?" whispered Zeephro.

"I think so." Horda tried to slip her fingers from Brash's grasp, but he mumbled and tightened his hold. No matter, she thought, she would remain here as long as he needed her. She drew closer to him and made herself as comfortable as she could.

As the sun crawled toward its zenith, Brash's mother returned to sit by his side. His breathing roughened. The fever demons consumed him, causing his chest to rattle and his whole body to flush. Yet Horda marveled that his grip on her hand had never loosened – clearly he possessed inner strength that was not obvious to others. His mother cried quietly, and his father remained nearby staring into the distance.

Horda regretted speaking so harshly with the man, but she regretted his actions toward his son even more. None of this would have happened if Braso hadn't bullied his son into feeling like a coward.

Nuroo brought another horn of wyethia and juniper tonic. "You'll need to move," he quietly told Juaja.

"I'm his mother," snapped Juaja. "Make *her* move."

Once more Horda tried to loosen Brash's grip on her hand. Once more he clutched her tighter and moaned without opening his eyes. She looked at Nuroo helplessly. "Brash wants her near," he said and pushed his way between the woman and her son.

"Brash, you need to wake up," he called to his patient and gently patted his sunken cheeks. Brash mumbled but didn't rouse. "As you did before," Nuroo said to Horda. "I'll open his mouth a little, and you massage his throat." He dribbled a little of the mixture into the boy's mouth. With Horda's help he swallowed, but then immediately began to gag. Nuroo shook his head. "I can do no more."

Juaja immediately began to keen, but Brash never heard. His sleep deepened, bringing him closer and closer to Father Death. Finally the fever demons overwhelmed him, consuming his life force and filling his vessel of time. He exhaled one last time and did not inhale again. He now walked the Frozen Wilds with Father Death.

Horda felt an overwhelming sense of failure. She knew neither Meiran's death nor Brash's was her fault, but she felt guilty about both of them. What kind of a healer would she make if all those in her care died? Horda slipped her hand from his now lifeless grip and hurried away.

The sun had made another turning through the sky, and Brash's body now rested in its new home in the Frozen Wilds. Horda grieved for the man-to-be who was no more. She tried to remind herself the Rituals of Man and Womanhood always resulted in some accidents. Since she was a little girl, Horda had been taught to accept deaths and injuries as part of life, but this Gathering seemed particularly tragic and bloody. Why were there so many? And how many more would walk the Frozen Wilds when Bear Claw learned she chose Mach instead of him?

She tried to dispel the questions, but they wouldn't go; like the ghosts of the dead, they kept returning, begging for answers she didn't seem to have. She wondered if she ever would.

Chapter 22

When Gathering completed four hands of suns, the time of the Bid Ceremony had arrived This was the beginning of the final segment of the Mating Rituals. Walking from her camp to the ceremonial area, Horda knew it was time — time to put the past in the past and look to the future. That was where her new life would be. She pressed her hands against her stomach, trying to still the butterflies fluttering there.

She marveled at the agate and obsidian beading on her new tunic. She remembered how Meiran soaked the leather with klamath weed and alum root twice before it matched the amber of her eyes and hair. The piping calls of the birds and insects blended with the conversations of all the people who had come to Gathering. The world seemed so alive.

Abruptly, though, she felt a lump in her throat. Not everyone was alive. *Oh, Mama, I miss you. Why couldn't you still be here with me?* In the fragrance of flowers, leaves, and seedpods, she could detect the hint of the decay the changing season would bring. So much death, all around. No! This was supposed to be the best Gathering of her life, and she was determined to enjoy it to the fullest.

Horda hurried through the assembled People to reach her place on time. Zaaco already stood on the speaking platform in the Circle of Light with the other young women grouped behind him. The men who would offer bids lined both sides of the area closest to the dais. To Zaaco's right in the place of honor stood

Treema. Her status came not from her position as the Chief's mate, but from the Council, which had chosen her to lead the young women through the Bid Ceremony. Zaaco and Treema smiled encouragingly at Horda as she arrived.

As the sun's first rays pushed above the eastern horizon, music began — the drums and flutes, high willow and low antelope. It was a joyous sound, one filled with the promise of the day. The music faded only when the sun poured its golden light over the edge of the prairie.

Zaaco raised his arms. "Greetings to all," he intoned. "The most joyous rituals of the People of the Frozen Earth are the Ritual of Womanhood and the Ceremony of the Great Traveler." The faintest smile tugged at the corner of his mouth as he saw the looks of surprise from the crowd. He waited a moment before he continued.

"I say this because until these are completed, neither the men nor the young women may move to the Bid Ceremony or the Mating Ceremony."

A small sigh of laughter whispered through the gathered people. Horda looked across the sea of faces and saw Bear Claw standing in his customary place at the back of the crowd; he seemed untouched by the laughter or by the festive mood. As she studied his stern face, her stomach knotted with fear. No, she told herself, she was making the right choice. If he were the slightest bit reasonable, he would understand. But was he reasonable? Perhaps doubt, more than anything, was the source of her fear. She turned her attention back to her father and to the moment.

Zaaco continued, "You all know the People of the Frozen Earth take pride in our family units. We believe our families keep our tribe strong. Because more women than men of our tribe reach this milestone, our men take more than one mate. Not quite half of the young women who stand behind me will be first mates, those who choose and are chosen by the young men just returned from their Great Travels. The rest will become second, third, or even fifth mates, but that does not make them lesser mates. *All* of them will be cherished."

Zaaco looked at the young women briefly then he turned and addressed the men waiting before him. "Men, this is an important step, for you and for our People. These women are the earthly representatives of the benevolent Mother Life. It is the way of our tribe to treat them with care and love and protect them with our lives. Do not choose your mates lightly. For all practical purposes these will be your mates for the rest of your lives."

He turned back to the assembled crowd. Although he spoke to all gathered there, Horda could see Zaaco's eyes fixed on Bear Claw. "From this day forward for the rest of your life, the path of your days will be intertwined with that of your chosen. The wise among you will heed her counsel and accept the words she offers which may go far to lighten your burdens."

Bear Claw's face twisted into an ugly scowl, and he glared back at the old chief. There was a threat implied in those words, and he heard it. Hope flickered in Horda's heart for a brief moment. Perhaps he was wiser than he appeared. Perhaps he'd decide he didn't want her under the conditions Zaaco laid out for him. Perhaps he would simply go back from where he came and leave them all in peace.

Zaaco smoothly broke the eye contact and moved on with the ceremony as if nothing unusual had occurred. He stepped out of the Circle of Light with a gesture to Treema, who took his place.

"The Rituals of Man and Womanhood have explained the roles of men and women in our tribe," she began, looking over the young men and women in turn. "The Mating Rituals will explain each partner's role in the mate. For three turnings of the sun, you and your chosen will study and learn the same things, but you will do so separately. Then you will return to

Gathering and to each other to share what you learned."

Treema turned to the young women. "Love grows between mates. Do not refuse a bid simply because you aren't sure you love the man bidding for you. However, always remember, the acceptance of a bid is a serious matter. Though it's not forbidden, no bid has been returned in my memory. Do not accept a bid unless you're prepared to cherish and care for the man and protect him with all your strength from this day forward for the rest of the time Father Death grants you to walk upon the earth."

Standing straight and tall Treema acknowledged Zaaco when she finished her words. She wondered how much these young ones had heard — they were so wrapped up in the moment. Did they hear anything at all? In truth, though, had she been any different when she was their age? She smiled inwardly, then nodded to the crowd, and stepped from the Circle of Light.

A buzz of expectation rose from the assembly. The time had come for the presentation of the bids, one of the most exciting events of the day. The bids — which included furs, hides, meats, fruits, and vegetables — symbolized the man's ability to clothe, shelter, and feed his mate. Young men just returned from their Great Travels had to depend on their families to supply the bulk of their offerings, but they added whatever hides and food of their own they could manage. The older men frequently presented small representations of their wealth because they were well established, and their abilities were known.

When a woman accepted a bid, she received a promise bouquet, an arrangement of flowers, seedpods, and leaves. Because the men traditionally built the bouquets themselves, most were simply large rather than beautiful. Nevertheless, they served the purpose.

Choices were not formally announced until the Bid Ceremony, but, as in Thuro and Wilda's case, most couples left no doubt about their choices. In accordance with Zaaco's request, Horda's choice had remained a secret, and she knew her father would call her last because he feared the outbursts following her acceptance of Mach. Her hope Bear Claw might have changed his mind grew when she saw his face become a blank mask of boredom as the responsibilities of mating were explained.

Oh, please, Mother Life, let it be so.

Horda was so nervous she was afraid she would lose her morning eat. She heard her father's calm words once more in her mind. "Our scouts found no evidence of other People of the Tall Grass; apparently all their warriors are in our camp. We can defeat them if need be. Don't worry, daughter, we'll take care of you."

Oh, please, let them protect everyone.

"Horda, daughter of Zaaco and Meiran."

Lost in her own thoughts, Horda barely heard her father call her name. Shakily she walked to the center of the Circle of Light and took her place beside the chief.

"Who bids for this woman?" The now familiar words rang out across the assembled.

At once Mach, Emol, and Bear Claw stepped forward. Horda's heart pounded in her throat. *Mother Life, I knew they were all going to bid, but I had hoped. Please give me strength to do what I must.*

"Bring forth your bids," Zaaco commanded.

Mach turned sharply and strode back through the crowd. Emol signaled to one of his band to bring his goods forward while Bear Claw barked a command to his women, who scurried forward.

Emol's man returned first with a small, dirty bundle which he dumped unceremoniously at Horda's feet. Emol frowned his displeasure, and, with much huffing and puffing, knelt to unpack it. His ceremonial tunic stretched tightly across his fat stomach, and the sinew holding some of the beading popped. A bead dropped to the ground and rolled toward Horda. She watched silently as the man pulled the items from the pack — one rabbit pelt minus much of its fur, a badly tanned deer hide with bits of rotting meat still clinging to it, an irregularly shaped lump of flint not much bigger than a little one's fist, and a small food parfleche. Smugly, Emol left the goods in an untidy pile and climbed to his feet, stepping back to allow the others to come forward.

Mach returned a moment later, pulling a travois loaded with bison hides, wolf pelts, and deerskins. His father Mahlo pulled a second, smaller travois laden with foodstuffs while Woda, his mother, carried a large bundle of finely tanned rabbit furs. Finally Ettor, brought a pack with a hand of flint nodules and two hands of fine tools Mach had fashioned. The four of them stepped to the dais and laid the supplies out for Horda to inspect. She gasped with the magnificence of it all.

As Mach and his family stepped back, Bear Claw's women staggered into the assembly area looking as if they would collapse under the weight of their burdens. Four of the women brought packs filled with more woven baskets than Horda could count without a counting cord. She had to concede their workmanship was impressive, far superior to any woven goods the People of the Frozen Earth could produce.

Mother Life. Bear Claw is the only Man of the Tall Grass who has bid for any of our women. He is offering me all the trade goods his people brought to make sure I choose him. What will happen when I choose Mach?

The fifth woman carried a pack smaller than Emol's. She opened it to reveal a strange brownish grey substance. Pinching off a small piece, she offered it to Horda. A sharp, unpleasant smell not unlike spoiled fish assailed Horda's nostrils and caused her stomach to flutter. *Please, don't let me disgrace myself by vomiting in the middle of the Bid Ceremony.*

Horda breathed deeply trying to calm the nausea clawing at the back of her throat. Under other circumstances it would have been quite rude to refuse the offering. Fortunately, however, she was required to inspect all the bids equally; since she hadn't taken anything from the others, she could not do so here.

"Please place all of Bear Claw's bid together," Zaaco instructed the woman. Frowning at the perceived slight, she obeyed him.

With all the goods displayed, Zaaco looked at Horda. "You see before you the bids of three warriors. Have you made your choice?"

"I would speak," wheezed Emol.

Zaaco turned to him. It was highly irregular, but not unheard of, for a bidder to try to sway his chosen with words. "You may speak," Zaaco said, but in a voice that displayed his displeasure.

Emol seemed not to notice. Sweat beaded on his upper lip and trickled down his chin. He wiped it away with his palms and dried them on his already soiled tunic. The loose beading unraveled three more finger widths and allowed four beads to drop to the dust at his feet. He cleared his throat.

"Ah, my offering looks small compared with the bids of these, ah ... " He paused and looked down his fat nose at Mach and Bear Claw. "... other fine warriors, but I assure you this is only a small representation of my wealth. You'll have ..." He eyed Mach's offering. ".... much more — if you choose me. I bring you power because I'm a ranking leader of the People of the Frozen Earth."

Horda stared pointedly at tunic. He pulled at the wrinkles outlining his bulging belly and broke another sinew of beading loose. More beads bounced in the dirt at his feet.

"Do either of you want to speak?" Zaaco asked Mach and Bear Claw. It was only fair to give each an equal chance, but both men shook their heads. "Very well," he said, turning to

Horda. "I ask once again, daughter, have you made your choice?"

Taking a deep breath to calm her nerves, she answered. "Yes, I've made my choice, but first I would speak, too."

"You may speak," Zaaco replied.

Her body felt as if it quivered like a tiny fawn caught in a woman's snare. Her stomach twisted and turned, threatening to jump out her mouth. It had all come down to this one moment. Stiffening her spine, she forced herself to look at Emol, then at Bear Claw, and finally at Mach. When she spoke, her voice sounded strong and clear. "I'm deeply honored these three brave warriors have not only courted but also bid for me. It's a high tribute each of you has paid me." Horda stepped back and was silent.

Grinning, Emol tried once more to smooth the wrinkles from his tight tunic and succeeded only in dislodging two more beads. Mach gave her the slightest wink then returned to the role of stoic warrior. And though Bear Claw stood there as rigid as stone, she saw his icy eyes boldly roam up and down her body, as if calculating the fairness of his bid.

The silence threatened to stretch beyond tolerance. Zaaco coaxed, "Whom have you chosen?"

"Mach." She had made her choice.

An enormous bouquet of wild roses, subalpine larkspur, and figwort blooms mixed with salsify seed heads, small pine boughs with needles and cones, large Aspen leaves, and small dried cattails seemed to walk on its own through the assembled people, finally stopping beside the grinning Mach. She led the laughter as he took the giant bouquet from his small sister, Saba.

"Thanks, Saba," he said. Smiling a snaggle-toothed grin at him, Saba rejoined her mother in the crowd. Mach walked slowly to the Circle of Light. He smiled down at Horda for what seemed a long time before he offered the bouquet to her.

Nobody could mistake Horda's expression for anything other than the love she felt for Mach, and her happiness at having chosen him for her mate. She smiled up at him with all her being and slipped her right arm into the sleeve holder he had attached to the bouquet, sealing their bond. Mach's deep mahogany eyes mirrored his love for his chosen. He held out his hands and engulfed her much smaller one in his grip.

Zaaco said, "I was beginning to think they changed their minds." An appreciative laugh ran through the audience.

Still grinning, Mach looked at the chief and vowed, "Never will I change my mind. We belong to each other for as long as we both shall live." They waited for Zaaco to end the ceremony before they walked away from the Circle of Light, followed by the excited buzz of well wishers.

His face a mask of rage, Emol left his pitiful bid lying on the ground and tried to lose himself in the anonymity of the crowd. Bear Claw, however, did not go quietly. Pointing to his offering, he kicked one of the Women of the Tall Grass. She hurriedly repacked her chief's bid and scuttled back to their encampment. Joined by his now-armed warriors, Bear Claw strode over to Zaaco, his silver eyes burning. "I told you I wanted your daughter."

"And I told you I had no say in her choice of mate," reminded Zaaco tightly.

Bear Claw spat on the ground at Zaaco's feet. "Perhaps you should have. After all, you are the chief ... *and* her father."

Zaaco didn't move a muscle, but five hands of heavily-armed warriors materialized behind him. Startled, Bear Claw couldn't entirely mask his surprise. Taking a step back into the line of warriors and accepting a war axe, Zaaco's eyes glittered as he stated firmly, "It is my daughter's right to choose her own mate."

Bear Claw's eyes flickered over the assembled warriors, inspecting them and weighing his options. These men were bigger, stronger, better armed, and already equal in number to all the warriors he had brought with him. And in the assembly area, more than three times that number stood armed and ready to join the fight against him as soon as the first war axe was thrown.

Bear Claw shrugged, seeming to make a decision. His lips turned up in a parody of a smile. "Very well. I tried your way and lost. I see no reason to remain. We still have our trade goods; I'm sure we can find another band who would appreciate what we have to offer." He made no effort to hide the insult, but Zaaco did not respond. He and his warriors stood their ground and the Chief of the Tall Grass turned and led his people to their camp.

Only when the People of the Tall Grass had left the clearing did Zaaco's fingers relax on the handle of the war axe he held. "Thank you, Mother Life, and you, warriors. May we always be able to divert our enemies in such a peaceful way."

Zeek, one of the assembled warriors, pounded Zaaco on the back and said, "You were right, when Bear Claw realized they didn't have a chance, he turned tail and ran. I doubt he'll ever come back."

"They aren't exactly running," Zaaco remarked, "but I don't believe they'll return." He touched hands with each of the warriors in turn, thanking them for their support and sending them to the feast.

The last warrior had barely departed when Emol huffed up to Zaaco. Without offering the customary polite greetings, he snarled, "This cannot be."

Apparently unruffled, Zaaco responded, "Yes, Emol, I'm having a fine Gathering. I trust yours is also."

"Don't toy with me, Zaaco! I presented Horda a fine flint knife the day I arrived at the Gathering grounds."

"So you did," Zaaco said, a little more forcefully than he intended, "but she received more than two hands' of other gifts also. I lost count."

"Do you truly think I care how many other gifts she

received? Mine was the only one from a ranking leader." Fat blurred the lines of Emol's features, and anger twisted them into a porcine mask. Saliva spewed from his blubbery lips. "Mine was the only one of importance. I bid for her, and she is mine!"

"It is over, Emol. You, Bear Claw, and Mach all bid for her. You'll also notice she rejected Bear Claw's bid when she accepted Mach's."

"This isn't right. You must make her give back the boy's bid."

"She chose Mach."

"She must unchoose him. He's a nobody. Force her to give back his bid."

Zaaco's dark eyes became hot, obsidian knives, and he lashed out at the man with all the power his position. "I was ready to fight Bear Claw and his warriors to ensure my daughter's right to choose her own mate," he said, lifting the heavy war axe he still held. "I'm ready to fight you if you so desire."

Emol took a few steps back and raised his hands. "It's not the way of the People of the Frozen Earth to fight among ourselves."

"Nor is it our way to tell our women whom they choose as their mates. Do not push me!"

"But when a leader chooses a woman, she always accepts," blustered Emol.

"Not always, and Horda didn't."

"But he's only a boy, he has no power. And I'm a leader!" Anger loosened Emol's tongue. "She must mate with me!"

"You hardly lead your own band in out of the rain, Emol. Your shelters are ragged, and your people's clothes are dirty and worn. Frequently you beg for food before the winter blizzards give way to spring breezes. Your people starve in a land where the rest of the bands find plenty."

Emol fidgeted under Zaaco's gaze. "There are difficulties. Our hunting grounds are sparse," he whined. "If she chooses me, we'll join your band. Everything will be better."

"There's nothing wrong with your hunting ground. The difficulty is with the man who says he leads."

A vein bulged on Emol's greasy forehead. "I do my best, but I need help. If I could bring my people to the Inner Band, we'd be a valuable asset, you'd see. You could help —"

Zaaco spoke quietly between gritted teeth. "You presume to join the Inner Band when you don't fulfill your responsibilities to your own band? Such a thing will not happen in my lifetime."

Emol's tiny eyes slitted. His mouth opened and closed, but no more words came.

Still Zaaco pressed on. "Unless you choose to fight me, you'll congratulate the couple and wish them well. Then I'll forget this conversation ever occurred. Do I make myself clear?" When he got no response, he speared Emol with one last glare and headed off to the feast himself.

Emol folded his hands across the soiled leather of his bulging tunic and scowled at Zaaco's back. A malevolent gleam flashed in his little boar eyes. "I may speak the words you want me to speak, old man, but another warrior, more powerful than I, was also angered by her choice. Remember that!"

Chapter 23

Horda carried her bouquet in one hand and clung to Mach's arm with the other as they navigated the turmoil of the assembly area. She appreciated the congratulations and good wishes, but she was feeling overwhelmed by it all. When they finally found themselves alone beside the river, she began to tremble. Mach looked alarmed. "What's the matter?" he whispered anxiously. "Aren't you happy?"

"Of course, I'm happy.".

"Then what's the matter?" He frowned. "Have you decided you don't want to choose me after all?"

She shook her head. "Of course not."

Mach studied her closely. "Are you ill?" he asked. "You look pale."

She shook her head again. "I don't know ... maybe Bear Claw, Emol ... something ... oh, no, I'm going —" She bent over and emptied her stomach into the grass. Mach held on to her, smoothing her hair. She was mortified at her weakness, but she had to admit she felt better once her stomach emptied itself.

"Do you feel better?" he asked, scooping up some water from the river to wash her face.

"Yes." More tears rained down her pale cheeks. "I'm so sorry."

"About what?" She busied herself with tidying up. "Look at me," he commanded. A flush crept up her cheeks, but she reluctantly met his eyes. "You're mine. Sick or well, we belong to each other for as long as we both live, so there's no reason to be embarrassed. You were sick, and I helped you. I'll be sick sometime, and I'm sure you'll help me just the same."

It sounded so simple when he said it.

"I love you no matter what. Nothing you do will ever make me stop," he said firmly.

Tears welled in her eyes again, but this time she smiled through them. "Mother Life has truly blessed us both," she said. "Now come on, I want to eat something before the Rituals of the Mate, and we don't want anyone upset with us because we're here alone."

Mach marveled at her sudden change of direction, but he didn't hesitate to follow her as she headed back toward the feast.

As Mach and Horda sat down at the feast, Emol waddled up to them. "I've been told to give you my congratulations," he muttered, looking anything but pleased.

Rising, Mach smiled his acknowledgment. "Thank you, Emol."

"I trust you're aware of the prize you won."

Horda kept her eyes on her plate; she didn't like where the conversation was headed.

"I'm honored," Mach responded, trying to keep his voice level.

"Honored? Ha. Your power has grown more than you seem to realize."

Bristling Mach said, "I didn't court Horda to increase my power."

"Then you are a f —" He never got to finish his sentence. A strategic cough made him jump as if he had been poked with a hot stick. Now Horda looked up. She could see a vein bulging on Emol's forehead as he tried to control his anger, and it was all she could do to keep from laughing when Emol forced out,

"Horda, please add my good wishes to the others you receive."

The old man hurried away before she or Mach could respond.

"What was that all about?" asked Mach, resuming his seat.

"I think perhaps my father had a hand in his sudden attack of politeness." She smiled at Zaaco, who grinned back with all the innocence of a wolf wearing prairie chicken feathers on its muzzle.

"Oh, I see."

Ravenously hungry now that her stomach had settled, Horda devoured her antelope stew and looked longingly at the remainder of Mach's portion. "Are you going to eat the rest of your stew?"

"I was. Why? Do you want it?"

"Yes."

"I thought you were ill."

"Not any more. For the last day or so I'm either throwing up or starving. It must be all the excitement."

Mach shook his head in bewilderment, but he allowed her to take his stew.

❈

Horda's nausea returned suddenly as Bear Claw approached the couple. Though his fearsome face seemed more relaxed than she'd ever seen it, a sense of foreboding grew until it nearly overwhelmed her. *Relax,* she told herself over and over. *What's done is done.*

Mach stood again to greet their new guest.

"I understand it's the way of the People of the Frozen Earth to offer congratulations to the promised couple." Bear Claw's mouth smiled, but his eyes remained slivers of silver ice.

"Yes, it is," replied Mach warmly.

"Then I congratulate you. Though I won't pretend I don't think your ways are senseless, I have no choice but to accept

249

Horda's decision."

"Thank you, Bear Claw." Horda raised her eyes to his, but she found no more reassurance in his face than she had in his words. In fact, what she saw there — that lustful longing, like a hungry animal — frightened her even more.

"My people and I will be leaving," he added. Though he spoke to both of them, his eyes never left Horda.

Mach seemed not to notice. "Leaving? But Gathering isn't over," he protested.

"We still need women, and since none of yours saw fit to choose our men, we must go elsewhere."

"But none of your m —" Horda jabbed Mach in the ribs. Was he so blind he would provoke this man into action?

"Hopefully you'll find women in another tribe, one closer to your home and your beliefs," she said.

"Possibly," said Bear Claw. "Perhaps we'll meet again." He turned and strode away.

Horda shivered. She feared Bear Claw's words masked his plans. She pushed the last of the stew away.

"I thought you were hungry," teased Mach.

"Not any more."

Mach looked at her more closely seeing her discomfort. "What's wrong?"

"What's wrong?" She shook her head at his stupidity. "Don't you find it hard to believe Bear Claw is just going to walk away after all the threats he made?"

"Don't worry." He gently touched her cheek. "Bear Claw is a warrior. He sees how badly outnumbered his people are, and he knows it's a battle he can't win. You heard him; they're going to look for women elsewhere."

"I hope so."

Joining Mach and Horda again, Zaaco asked, "What do you hope, daughter?"

"I hope Bear Claw really is leaving."

Zaaco watched the retreating backs of the People of the Tall Grass. "Bear Claw knows our warriors are better armed and better trained than his," he echoed Mach's words. "They want to increase their tribe, not destroy it in a hopeless fight."

"Humph," sniffed Horda.

Mach squeezed her cold hand reassuringly, "Exactly what I told her."

Horda still looked doubtful.

"Do you distrust not only my words, daughter, but also those of your chosen?" Horda could hear Zaaco's waning patience as well as his love in his voice. After a moment's hesitation, she shook her head. "Then stop fretting." Zaaco smiled. "You have other things to think about."

Yes, she did, but that didn't quiet the little voice inside her that insisted things were not as they seemed.

Chapter 24

⚙

The sun stood high in the clear blue sky as the feasting came to a close. Bear Claw and his band had headed toward their home to the east, and Horda's heart beat a little easier.

The Mating Rituals were conducted by men and women appointed by the Council to train the future mothers and fathers of the tribe. It was an honor and a huge responsibility.

Only once had her mother been chosen for this role. It wasn't that she lacked position or prestige — she had both. The problem was she believed her position relieved her of certain responsibilities while the People worked toward a society where everyone contributed their fair share to the whole. As a result, she was unable to share the tribe's values fully with the women under her charge, and those women headed into their matings unprepared.

When Zaaco passed her over the following year, Meiran fussed and fretted until he insisted her work with the Council of Elders and the children's sessions kept her much too busy to serve. Horda remembered Meiran's anger when Zaaco first nominated Treema. There had been a lot of yelling in the camp that night, loud enough for everyone to hear. But once again Zaaco had reminded her how busy she was at Gathering, insisting that Treema's nomination was designed to relieve her of an extra burden, and Meiran had relented.

Horda was finally of the age to participate in the Rituals. Once the Bid Ceremony and Feast were completed, the couples, including Horda and Mach, would be separated. The men would travel south while the women traveled north to remote camps for their sessions.

These sessions gave the individuals an opportunity to ask any and all of their questions about the mating experience. They helped them develop a realistic picture of the ways mating would change their lives and assist them in determining methods by which they could make those changes most positive.

Walking beside Mach, Horda turned her attention to the Gathering grounds, where everyone was getting ready for the Rituals. The women were responsible for the sleeping furs. Once these were completed, they passed them to their men. The men were responsible for the actual bowers. They chose the locations and cleared the rocks, stones, weeds, and thorns from each area, making it as beautiful and as comfortable as possible. This was important since the mating bower symbolized the lives the couple would share until their vessels of time were filled.

Though Horda and Mach had carefully avoided mentioning and repeating their night together, she remembered and felt sure he did too. She wondered if any mating would be as pleasing as their forbidden contact. She pressed her hand to her flat stomach and wondered . . .

"Are you still ill?" whispered Mach, noticing her gesture.

She jumped; his voice brought her back to the present. "No, I'm fine," she told him. "I guess nerves or something made me sick. Don't worry."

The log drums began beating, calling the people to the dais in the assembly area of the grounds. "The time has come," Zaaco intoned from his raised position, "for the men and women who will enter into the Ritual of the First Mate to depart for the Mating Rituals."

As the chief explained the details of the Rituals, Horda's attention wandered. She looked at all the women who had accepted bids. She barely knew their names. The tribe was big, but she should do better; she resolved to get to know as many of them as she could before Gathering was over.

One thing she did know — almost two hands of the promised women were widows who chose to accept new mates rather than follow their departed mates into the Frozen Wilds. She wondered — if Mach walked the Frozen Wilds before her, what would she choose? Her chest tightened at the thought.

A movement caught her attention, and she shifted her gaze to see what it was. Abruptly a frown crossed her face. It was Wilda, even now flirting with Thuro. The jingles made by the shells and beads on her braids kept time with her preening movements. Horda longed to poke Wilda to make her behave. But was *she* really any better? Here she was watching the others, and she hadn't heard a word her father said. She forced herself to concentrate on the ritual at hand.

"When two turnings of the sun remain until the Ritual of the First Mate, the young men and women will join together with both sets of teachers." He paused and smiled. "The key word here is together. During that time the couples are encouraged to express their goals and expectations to each other. This time of reconciliation and discussion forces many couples to learn the art of compromise."

Ah, compromise; Zaaco was always telling her that was the key, both to a mating and to being a good leader. Silently she lectured herself not to go into her mating with unrealistic expectations. Mach was just a man, and she was just a woman; they would both have to work hard to remember that. *Mother Life. I love him. Help me to accept him and not try to change him — too much.*

She realized Zaaco was staring at her; he knew her attention was somewhere else. She felt the hated blush on her cheeks and commanded herself to listen.

"The individual members of each couple will spend the last day before the Ritual of the First Mate with their own families, bidding a final farewell to the life each has known and preparing to embrace their new life together." He looked around the assembly then relinquished his place in the Circle of Light, saying, "The leaders will call their groups."

There was ordered chaos as the groups assembled. Mach joined Thuro in Elko's group; it was a good placement, as Elko was one of the favored leaders.

On the other side of the assembly, Treema gathered her group together, a group that included Wilda. There was one spot left, Horda noticed, and Treema was looking around. *Oh, Mother Life, please don't let her call me, too.*

She let out the breath she was holding when Treema called Beil to complete her group. Treema smiled at her and winked. *Was it that obvious how much she disliked Wilda? Probably so.* Before she had time to worry about it, Suka, Elko's number one mate, called her name. *Thank you, Mother Life, for each small favor.*

Two hands of groups of young women stood with their leaders on Zaaco's right while their men stood on his left. Zaaco smiled paternally at them all and said, "Go with Mother Life. Study and prepare yourselves for the most exciting adventure of your lives. We'll see you back here after three turnings of the sun."

That was it; they were on their way. Carrying packs of food and sleeping furs, the groups headed away from the assembly area.

❁

The walk was not arduous, and by the time the sun dropped behind the jagged teeth of the mountains, Suka's group had settled in a small clearing beside one of the streams feeding the River with No End.

"Tomorrow we'll gather wild onions, cattail tubers, and service berries to make a fine eat with the fresh antelope haunch we brought," Suka said, "but tonight we'll stick with pemmi-can and cool water while we learn a little more about each other." She sat beside the small fire and offered cakes of pem-mican, a traveling food made of bison fat, antelope jerky, choke berries, and a little cow parsnip, to the members of her group.

The young women quickly took places around the fire. "I'll begin," said Suka. "Most of you know I'm the number one mate of Elko." She smiled proudly. "You may not agree, but I believe he's the bravest and handsomest warrior in the tribe ..." Mischief made her eyes sparkle. "... except when he's the stupidest man in the world."

Many of the young women gasped at her boldness, but Horda smiled remembering her earlier thoughts about Mach — wonderful and as dense as sand sometimes. Lija, a widow with one finger less than five hands winters who had accepted Trefo's bid, said aloud, "The others may be shocked, Suka, but I wish I'd heard that at my first rituals."

"Me, too," agreed Marmah, another young widow. "It might have made my first mating easier."

Suka looked at the two young women. "Didn't your leader tell you men are sometimes completely stupid?"

"I don't think so," the young women answered almost in unison.

Suka shook her head. "I'm surprised. Did you have the same leader?"

The women looked at each other then at Horda, but neither one answered. Horda understood the look; Meiran had led their group, and the idea that men might be stupid was something she never would have voiced aloud. Horda watched Suka chose her words carefully. "Perhaps stupid is too strong a word. You were told men and women sometimes see the same things in completely different ways, weren't you?"

Lija grinned. "I remember those words, but I never real-ized until now exactly what she meant."

"I remember something like that, but I thought it meant I should try to see things the way he did," said Marmah.

Suka sniffed. "Well, that's not what those words mean at all. Sometimes men need us to help them understand things — they don't always know everything they think they do." She looked around the group and smiled. "Of course, sometimes we need them to help us in the same way — we don't always know as much as we think we do either."

"I'm not sure I understand what you mean," said Aiyana, the youngest woman in their group with only three hands winters, voicing the confusion evident on the others' faces.

"I know I don't understand," added Marmal, a plain young woman with three hands plus four winters. "Orol's wonderful in every way." She looked reproachfully at Suka. "And he's certainly not stupid."

"I didn't mean Elko is truly stupid. Please don't get me wrong." Suka grinned. "But I'd wager anything I own that at least once before next Gathering you'll have thought your men dense for not understanding something that's clear as spring water to you."

Marmal sniffed and rolled her eyes as if she couldn't imagine such a thing, but she didn't say anything else.

Suka laughed softly and said, "What I'm trying to tell you — and I don't seem to be doing a very good job of — is men are different from us. That's a good thing because we need their differences to help us keep our lives in perspective." Suka saw Horda's bright smile and almost imperceptible nod of agreement. "Horda, you seem to agree with me. Would you comment to the group?"

Horda's eyes widened in surprise; she didn't know what to say. She sat silently for a long time before she finally offered, "Umm, I was just remembering Bear Claw's threats upset me today, but Mach dismissed him like he no longer existed. I became frightened and angry and sure Mach was totally stupid to ignore him.

"Mach didn't make fun of me, but I could tell he thought I was being foolish. He reassured me with logic and explained we had far too many warriors for Bear Claw to risk a battle with us, and he made it seem so obvious." She studied the dancing flames before she admitted, "I'm still not sure I agree with him, but I guess he was right. Bear Claw and his people left a span of time before we did."

Then a small smile curved her lips, and her voice gained strength. "Also, something I had eaten upset my stomach, and I was ill — violently ill. Mach helped me and took care of me even though I didn't want him to see me that way. I was embarrassed, but to him it wasn't a problem. I needed help, and he helped me."

Suka nodded. "That's a good example of the differences." Briskly she rubbed her arms, which had suddenly sprouted goose bumps in the crisp air. "Well, it's been a very long day, and I think we should prepare for sleep."

She rose and rallied the women. "Let's spread our furs in the little cave opening over there so we don't have to worry about the fire. I checked the cave when we first arrived, and there are no animals in it."

Horda heard something in Suka's voice that disturbed her — a hesitation, a tremor. Was it fear? She silently watched the older woman shovel dirt on the flames, then scatter the barely cooled ashes over the ground. "You're frightened, aren't you?" she asked at last.

"Me?" Suka used a tree branch to brush away their footprints. "Of course not. What would I be frightened of?"

"Bear Claw."

"Bear Claw?" She put her hand on Horda's shoulder. "Why, child, he and his people are half way home by now. You said it yourself."

Horda stared into the older woman's eyes. "Do you really

believe that?"

"Well, maybe not half way, but certainly far from here. You saw them leave; they went the other way."

"They could turn back."

"Yes, they could, but I'm sure they wouldn't do such a thing. And they don't know the location of these camps, do they?"

Horda shook her head though she was obviously unconvinced.

"Then they couldn't possibly find us here." Suka's mouth smiled even if her eyes did not.

"I don't guess so. But Bear Claw bragged about his great skill as a tracker."

Suka chuckled and shook her head. "I'm trying to reassure you, Horda."

Horda looked around the silent camp. "I know, but it's not working."

"We're safe," Suka said, but she didn't meet Horda's eyes.

Horda nodded her agreement. She looked around the camp again, but there was nothing amiss. Silently she and Suka made their way to the cave to join the others in sleep.

Chapter 25

Horda's eyes popped open. Something woke her, but what? An animal? A cracked twig? She couldn't see anything in the shadowy darkness of the cave. Slowly, cautiously, she raised her head to listen, but all she heard were the breathing and soft snoring of the women. It must have been a dream, she thought, and settled back to sleep.

Bear Claw's fingers bit into the hollow of his careless warrior's neck. The young man's mouth opened as if to scream, but no sound emerged, and he dropped silently to the ground beside the broken twig.

Bear Claw laughed to himself. He had told Zaaco he would have Horda, and he would. Thank the Great Mystery the People of the Frozen Earth were so naïve they believed he would accept defeat easily. Fools, all of them, especially the women; tracking them had been too easy. He'd warned Horda he was a fine tracker, but she obviously hadn't believed him. He'd studied her footprints all through Gathering until he could find them even in the crowded assembly area. Finding them as they made their way to this camp had been child's play.

He shook his head at the pathetic way the women had tried to cover their tracks after they arrived at this place. Much too little and certainly too late. He licked his lips in anticipation. Horda would be his. Soon, very soon.

The moon slipped behind the mountains, and Bear Claw took advantage of the darkness to make his move. One by one, two hands plus two of his warriors, their faces and bodies darkened with diluted war paint, slipped into the cave and waited near the opening while their eyes adjusted to the diminished light. Despite their caution, some of their woven-grass breechcloths sighed like autumn breezes passing through dried grass. Too much noise? Bear Claw used hand signals to tell his men to stop where they were then held his breath. One beat ... two ... but only silence. He signaled them forward.

A woman called out, and the men froze. She turned and resumed the deep even breathing of sleep. The men moved. Bear Claw sensed rather than saw each man take his place beside one of the sleeping women. He trusted they were ready with loosely woven grass blankets and small leather gags. He waited a moment longer, but the soft snores and deep breathing told him all the women still slept.

He whispered the signal, an owl's hoot. As one, the men placed their hands around the women's throats and gently squeezed. The women scratched and fought, but the men squeezed tighter and tighter until the tension drained from the women's bodies, and they relaxed into unconsciousness.

The Men of the Tall Grass dropped the blankets over the women's still bodies, then quickly rolled them into bundles and tied the leather gags in place. Lifting the bundles to their shoulders, they strode from the camp without delay. Bear Claw was elated, and it was only through a great force of will he contained the victory cry that struggled to emerge. It could wait until they were safely away from this place, he told himself; the important thing was he had what he came for — Horda.

❀

Horda opened her eyes slowly, trying to make sense of the world around her. Tiny flint knappers hammered inside her head, and she felt overwhelmed by the smell of ... it was so familiar, but ... Bear Claw! Nausea twisted her insides, and she fought the urge to retch.

Mother Life, Bear Claw had stolen her. Was she the only one, or did he steal the others, too? What would happen to her? To them? Her stomach lurched as she bounced up and down on his shoulder, and her mind whirled as his strong legs carried her farther and farther away from everything she had ever known.

Her thoughts led her in one direction — anger. First and foremost, she was angry at Bear Claw for what he had done, but she couldn't fight. She resorted to silently screaming every oath she'd ever heard while mentally beating him to a bloody pulp. But she was also angry at Mach and Zaaco. She'd tried to tell them Bear Claw wouldn't simply go away, but would they listen to her? Of course not — she was just a frightened woman.

Bear Claw wouldn't dare start a war, they told her. The People of the Frozen Earth had too many warriors and were too strong. They'd defeat Bear Claw's warriors easily, they added. Bear Claw and his people were quietly going home. She didn't need to worry about a thing, they threw in for good measure.

Going home. Humph, they were right in a way. Bear Claw hadn't started a war with the warriors of the Frozen Earth, and she was grateful for that. And *he* was going home; however, *she* was trussed up like a deer carcass and slung over Bear Claw's shoulder while he marched across the land to that home. Nobody had thought about that scenario!

As her thoughts raced from one point to another, the pinkish-grey tints of sunrise allowed her to make out more than just Bear Claw's behind. She raised her head and saw the column of men following them, each carrying a bundle over his shoulder.

Mother Life, they've captured every woman from my group.

Something bothered her about the column, but she couldn't figure out what. She tried to think, but her attention was diverted as tears gathered in her eyes, tears of sadness and anger at their plight. She was determined not to cry openly though; it wouldn't help anybody, especially not herself so she focused on making herself stop. She swallowed the tears, but all that did was set off another wave of the grinding nausea she had tried so hard to forget. Her body heaved with violent retching; she was going to vomit, and she couldn't stop it this time. She squirmed and wiggled until Bear Claw stopped.

Cursing, Bear Claw dropped Horda unceremoniously to the ground, still wrapped in the grass blanket though her arms were loose. She clawed at the gag to remove it; then her stomach violently emptied itself onto her captor's moccasins. His face twisted with rage and disgust. "By the blood of the Great Mystery, you're sick," he accused. "What's wrong with you?"

"I think it was something I ate," she mumbled when she could finally speak.

"I don't want a sickly woman," he spat at her.

"Then take me back."

"Get well," he demanded.

"Just like that?" She laughed a brittle laugh. "Nothing to it. You command, and I obey."

"That's the way of the People of the Tall Grass."

"Tell my stomach because it doesn't seem to hear you." She vomited again.

"You will learn to obey me. Stop this right now!" He slapped her across the face.

She glared up at him with all the hatred she could muster. "I wouldn't, even if I could. Why don't you take me back and save yourself a lot of trouble?"

His eyes grew fierce. "I told you I'd have you, and you will stay."

Mother Life, this is really happening. What can I do? Will I ever see Mach again? She retched and spewed vomit onto Bear Claw's feet once more. With a disgusted snort, he cut the rest of her free from the grass blanket, tied a cord around her neck, and yanked her roughly to her feet. "You will walk."

Then it hit her — the column was too small. She did a quick head count and realized none of the Women of the Tall Grass were present, and a hand of Bear Claw's warriors were missing, as well. She yanked at the cord making Bear Claw turn so she could look him in the eyes. "Where are your women, Bear Claw" She kept her voice neutral, not sure if the women's absence was a good sign or not, but she needed to know.

"I sent them home. They would be a burden on this journey, whining and complaining, and eating all our food. Besides, what do I need them for — I have you all." It was a chilling thought, and Horda had no good response — they were captives, and there didn't appear to be anything they could do about it, at least not now.

The others had remained eerily quiet throughout the exchange as if afraid to anger Bear Claw even more than Horda had done, but now a muffled cry came from one of the bundles. "Wwet mee dowhn," pleaded Suka into her gag. The warrior carrying her over his shoulder at first ignored her pleas then looked to Bear Claw for help as her struggles intensified.

Bear Claw, though, had his gaze firmly locked on Horda, as if waiting to see what she would do. Suka continued to squirm and wiggle and cry out until her captor nearly dropped her. Annoyed, he threw the bundle to the ground and kicked it viciously.

Suka screamed, but she took advantage of her new position to pull off her gag. "Stop! I can help her," she called up to him.

The warrior snarled, "You can't help yourself." He grabbed the bundle and threw the woman back over his shoulder.

"Please, let me help her," begged Suka.

When it didn't look like Horda would cause Bear Claw any trouble, he turned toward the commotion behind him and demanded, "How can you help her?"

"Alum root and mint will settle the stomach. They always

grow near a stream, and there's one nearby. Please let me get some for her."

The sun's first timid fingers were beginning to push the grey away from the eastern rim of the prairie as Bear Claw stopped to consider Suka's words. Horda pulled at the tight cord around her neck; the pressure was only making the retching worse, but Bear Claw seemed not to notice.

Reaching a decision, the chief barked a command, and the column of warriors came to a halt. Pointing to the one carrying Suka, he commanded, "Set the woman free."

A howl of protest answered his words. "But, Bear Claw, she'll run away if I do."

Bear Claw's patience had worn dangerously thin, and he pierced the man with his look. "You fool! Look around you; where will she go? She has no food, no tools, no supplies. She doesn't even have moccasins on her feet."

The warrior said nothing more, just jumped to obey Bear Claw's order. Suka smiled to herself as she squirmed out of the blanket. They were all fools. The People of the Frozen Earth seldom wore moccasins in the summer because the soles of the feet were tougher and more durable than the soles of the moccasins and it would be a waste of good leather. The lack of shoes would not stop her from escaping if she chose.

But her smile dwindled. Bear Claw was right that she had no supplies and no tools or weapons to gather any. She wasn't going anywhere except to get alum root and mint to stop Horda's horrible retching. She'd seldom seen anyone so sick except during the early ... No, no, she wouldn't allow herself to complete the thought.

⊛

"Here." Suka handed Horda a few leaves and a piece of peeled root. "Chew these, but don't swallow the pulp. They're better in hot water, but this will work well enough for now."

Horda took the plants and began to chew, but then another spasm of retching started. "Fight it. Take deep breaths. Keep chewing. Swallow the juice. That's right," Suka soothed, as if treating a sick child. "They won't take long to settle the stomach once you get the juice down."

Breathing deeply against the threatening spasm, Horda chewed and chewed, careful to swallow the juice but not the pulp. She knew this remedy. Women used it for the sickness of early breeding. Early breeding? *Please, Mother Life, no!*

Horda opened her mouth to spit out the pulp, but Suka stopped her. "Not yet. Chew until it's nearly gone, then chew this." She pressed more of the herbs into Horda's hand. "That should be enough for now."

Her primary task accomplished, Suka faced Bear Claw. "Horda and I need to visit the bushes, and I'm sure the others do also. Also, I'd like some water to drink, a chance to wash, and something to eat. We didn't eat much last night, and you brought us away without our morning eat." Without waiting for a reply, she took Horda's hand and started toward the privacy of the bushes near the stream.

Bear Claw stopped her cold. "Come back here!" he thundered. "You will not address me in that way!"

Suka turned slowly, careful to keep her expression calm and reasonable. "I told you we need to visit the bushes. And since we're stopped anyway, you should unwrap the others so they can go, too. I'm sure your warriors will become angry if the women relieve themselves on them, don't you agree?"

Bear Claw's fists clenched and unclenched, and the muscles in his neck corded tightly, but he couldn't fault her logic. He motioned to his warriors to comply. Though none looked happy, they obeyed.

The Women of the Frozen Earth emerged from their blankets like butterflies from cocoons, although not as gracefully. They stretched their cramped muscles, then clumsily stood upright, stamping their feet and wiggling their fingers to get the circulation started again. Horda watched the triumphant smile curve Suka's mouth, and she felt her first real touch of hope since this ordeal began. In letting the women go, Bear Claw was doing exactly what Suka wanted. She quickly averted her eyes from the chief, hoping he didn't notice her expression.

Bear Claw barked another order, and two of his men grudgingly herded the women toward the bushes.

Horda spat out the pulp from the herbs Suka had given her and stuffed the remainder into her mouth. "This stuff really does help," she whispered.

Suka only nodded before muttering, "Make haste, but slowly." She cast fiery eyes at the guards, who had followed them into the bushes. "Have you no decency? Give us a little privacy." The two men hesitated and looked back in Bear Claw's direction, unsure whom to obey. Suka's tone was mocking. "Are the big, strong braves afraid a few unarmed women will attack them?"

One of the men raised his arm as if to strike her, but Suka stood her ground and he relented. The two waited at the bushes' edge while the women walked deeper into their cover.

"We don't have much time," Suka whispered, rattling the leaves and branches to cover her voice, "so listen, all of you. Try to gain their trust so they guard us less, but don't do anything to raise their suspicions. Cry and carry on to slow them down, but don't disobey. Pretend to be resigned to captivity. Follow my lead. We must survive and be ready when our men come for us."

"Hurry up!" Bear Claw's voice was closer than Horda expected; he must be getting impatient. "And no talking in there!"

"We're going as fast as we can, but we're stiff from being tied up so long, and we still must wash our faces and drink," said Suka plaintively. "Also, we're very weak since we're so hungry.

Please feed us now."

But Bear Claw was having none of it. "We'll eat when the sun moves toward night and not before. Now hurry up!"

The women tarried until the warriors grew restless and Bear Claw commanded, "By the blood of the Great Mystery, get them!"

Before the men could move, Suka called out, "We're finished. We're coming back, but the stones make walking difficult." Horda fought not to laugh out loud when Suka winked broadly at her and the others. "Ow! The stones are terrible." The women picked their way out of the bushes as if every leaf and twig caused them great distress.

Horda found she felt almost well by the time the women had reassembled in the clearing, but she watched with dismay as the men prepared to tie the women's hands and feet again.

"Oh, do you really think all those cords are necessary?" Suka whined. Horda glanced at her quickly, afraid the woman might be pushing their luck too far, but she had to admit Suka was convincing; Bear Claw looked more exasperated than angry. "I mean, we couldn't possibly run away. There are wild animals all around, and you've got all these warriors with you, and we're just a bunch of women after all." Ooh, that was a nice touch, Horda thought. All the women nodded their agreement, and some still cried or pretended to.

Horda wiped tears from her own eyes, but unlike most of the other women, hers were tears of fury, not fear. She had known Bear Claw would not give up so easily; why had no one listened to her?

"Fine," Bear Claw spat out, and he motioned for his warriors to pick up the women as they were.

"We'd make better time if we could walk," suggested Suka in a small voice.

Bear Claw glared at her. "I've had just about enough of you, woman!" He thought about it for a moment and signaled his men to put the women back on the ground. "I'll let you walk," he said, as if he was being the most generous person in the world, "but don't try to escape or we'll kill you — all of you."

Suka nodded her understanding. Neither she nor anyone else doubted he would make good on that threat. The men put cords around the women's necks to lead them then started across the rocky terrain.

After they walked in silence for a short time, Suka began to limp — almost imperceptibly at first, then quite noticeably. Horda quickly realized what she was doing and began to do the same, silently signaling the women behind her to join in. Moments later, Suka dropped to the ground, holding her feet and moaning as if in pain. One by one the rest of them followed suit.

The warriors milled about in confusion. "Now what's wrong?" Bear Claw roared, his neck muscles cording up again.

This time Horda took the lead. She choked out, "Our feet. We don't have any moccasins, and the rocks are sharp."

"You wanted to walk," snapped Bear Claw, "so walk! I've had about all I can take of you!"

Suka rubbed her feet and sobbed, "But we didn't realize the rocks were so sharp."

"Well, we don't have any foot coverings to give you," said Bear Claw shortly, looking like he wanted to beat her senseless.

But Suka pressed on. "You don't have any moccasins, and you don't have any food or water I can see," she accused, "yet you drag us all this way. How do you expect us to make it?"

Bear Claw glared at her. "By the Great Mystery, woman!" He stopped, as if realizing she had a valid point, and took a deep breath to calm himself down. "Fine. What do you suggest?"

Horda nearly dropped from surprise when Suka boldly said, "We haven't come very far. We had food, water bags, moccasins, and sleeping furs in our camp. We could go back and get them."

"Go back? You're our captives!" he thundered, as if that explained everything.

"Well, of course, we're your captives," said Suka in as reasonable tone as she could muster. "But do you really want to carry us all the way back to your camp? You've said it's a long way, and your men are going to get very tired themselves with no water or food. Wouldn't it make more sense to use the supplies we brought with us instead of leaving them behind to rot?"

Food, water, and other supplies ripe for the taking, and all within easy reach; that seemed to give Bear Claw pause. The other warriors grumbled among themselves at the situation, and Horda heard snatches of "useless women" and "better to kill them all," but at a sharp look from Bear Claw, they fell silent.

"Perhaps you have a point," Bear Claw granted after a moment. "I'll send one hand of my men back for your supplies."

Horda's heart filled with hope. By the time the warriors retrieved the packs and returned to this place, the sun would have passed the top of its journey across the sky. Then there would be only two more turnings before Mach and the others realized they were missing and began to search for them. Surely she and the others could think of ways to delay the trek even more and buy additional time for them.

"That's a wonderful idea," Suka told him, acting as though the entire concept had been his, "but can they carry everything? We each had a large pack *and* our sleeping furs, and as strong as they are, I'm afraid your men would be overloaded."

Bear Claw seemed to miss the sarcasm in her words. He pointed in the direction from which they'd come. "Carry the women," he told his men. "We'll all go back." Horda smiled at how easily Suka had manipulated Bear Claw. There was hope.

The sun climbed toward its zenith and beat down with a heat rivaling mid-summer as they made their way back to the women's camp. The men became more fatigued, and their burdens seemed heavier with each step. They grumbled, quietly at first, then more and more openly, until Bear Claw flattened the nearest one with a single blow, causing him to drop his bundle.

"Enough!" the chief roared. Horda longed to go to the woman, but her captor picked her up and trudged on.

They traveled the rest of the way to the deserted camp in silence. Now what? she wondered. There must be something else we can do to delay them. Cooking, perhaps?

Suka, it seemed, had the same idea. After quickly retrieving her moccasins from her pack, she took them to the river and proceeded to slowly wash her feet. "What are you doing?" snarled Bear Claw as the other women followed Suka's lead.

"Putting on our moccasins," said Horda innocently. "Isn't that why we came back?"

With her moccasins on, Suka busied herself gathering wood for a cook fire.

"What are you doing now?" demanded Bear Claw.

"I told you long ago that we're hungry."

"We'll eat when sun sets," said Bear Claw coldly.

"Oh, well, if you want us to get sick and weak, then I guess we can wait. It just seems we should eat before we set off on such a long journey," she muttered.

Bear Claw snarled, "By the blood of the Great Mystery, woman, I'm the leader of this group."

"Well, of course you are, we understand that. I just thought you wanted strong women rather than half-starved weaklings, and I figured you and your men might be hungry, too. My mate, Elko, always insists everyone be well fed before we begin a trek." She shrugged. "Never mind, we'll be ready to leave in a short time." She rested one hand on her stomach and sighed pitifully.

Bear Claw looked ready to protest again, but Suka had clearly hit a nerve. From the way his men had grumbled at the mention of food, Horda thought Bear Claw might lose his army if he didn't give in. He threw up his hands in resignation. "Fine. Fix food for all of us, but be quick about it."

"We'll be as quick as we are able," Suka assured him.

Horda smiled knowing they would actually do as much and

work as slowly as they could. Still, she made a show of hurrying over to help.

"I'll get the cook fire going," Suka told her. "You pull some nice wild onions and cattail tubers. We'll fix a dried antelope stew and fry bread."

Horda nodded her head. Dried antelope stew and fry bread would take most of the afternoon to prepare.

Bear Claw apparently knew that, as well. "Enough!" he roared.

Suka and Horda looked at him in feigned surprise.

"Of course, we'll fix enough for everybody," Suka said, deliberately misunderstanding his intent.

"No, you won't," snarled Bear Claw. "You've wasted enough time with all your nonsense. Eat some dried meat and then we'll go."

Suka shrugged. "Oh, I thought you just agreed a nice hot meal would be a good idea."

"We're not waiting for you to prepare stew that takes the rest of the day to cook," declared Bear Claw.

Horda admired the way the older woman pretended innocence under Bear Claw's angry look. She wondered if she would have the nerve to stand up to this man if their places were reversed. In fact, right now she felt as if a swarm of butterflies had taken flight in her stomach. She gently touched her midsection. It felt tender — probably from all the retching — she decided, but she no longer felt ill. She just felt ... hungry ... extremely hungry, and ... she stifled a yawn ... tired ... terribly tired.

"We don't want a meal — hot or otherwise," Bear Claw said, though his warriors grumbled. "You will fix something quickly so we can be on our way."

Suka pretended to consider. "We'll fix porridge and tea. Would that be all right? It doesn't take long, but it should satisfy us fairly well."

"Fine, but no more delays." Bear Claw's eyes flashed fire, but he moved off to allow Suka and the others to prepare the food.

"Ah, Bear Claw," Suka called to his retreating back, "could Horda take three of the women and harvest the vegetables growing by the stream while we make the porridge? We'll need them when we do cook, and it seems a shame to waste this time."

"By the blood of the Great Mystery, woman. Just get on with it. I don't have much patience left!"

❇

The women returned to the camp laden with onions, cattail pods, yampah roots, and pond lily bulbs when Suka called, "The porridge is ready. Come eat quickly." No one had to be asked twice; even Bear Claw hurried over, wolfing down his food like a starving man.

Suka and Horda would have liked to clean all the bowls and wrap them well for the journey, but they wiscly decided they had stalled Bear Claw as long as possible. They made short work of the packing and grouped together once again. "We're ready," Suka announced.

The chief looked over all the women, but when he spoke his words were directed to Suka. "I don't know exactly how you got us back here, old woman, but from here on out I am the one in control."

"Of course, you are," she said simply. "I realize that."

Bear Claw's silver eyes glittered dangerously as he weighed her comment. Horda held her breath while he looked around the empty camp, directly at the signal stones Suka had arranged around the fire pit. *Mother Life, don't let him understand them.* After what seemed a very long time, he raised his arm and motioned to his men. "Aiyahoo! Let's move!" he called.

Horda sighed. There was nothing to left to do but follow and hope they had delayed long enough for the search party to find them.

Chapter 26

By the time sun had sunk behind the mountains and twilight had settled on the land, Horda wished they would stop; not only were her legs tired, but her pack felt almost too heavy to carry. Bear Claw hadn't set a fast pace, and the path he chose led gradually downhill, but they had walked steadily since leaving the women's camp many hours ago. The trek felt even longer than it was because it took them away from the People of the Frozen Earth. For at least the hundredth time that day, Horda wondered if she would ever see her home again.

Finally, as the light became too dim to see the way ahead clearly, Bear Claw motioned everyone to stop. "We'll camp in this clearing. There's water here."

Horda was relieved; she was more tired than she wanted to admit, and the prospect of food and a good night's rest was enticing. "Perhaps we'll make the antelope stew now," she said to Suka.

"How is your stomach?" Suka asked.

"Tender, but I don't feel ill any more." She smiled briefly. "I don't think Bear Claw would appreciate my soiling his moccasins again."

"I'm sure not. Are you hungry?"

"Very." Horda thought for a minute. "You know, it's strange. For the past few turnings of the sun I've been either throwing up or starving. I feel fine when I'm not being violently ill."

Suka frowned but kept silent. She busied herself preparing the evening eat. The antelope stew with wild onions and yampah roots was filling, and Horda was so hungry she thought it was the best thing she'd ever tasted. Afterwards, the women spread their sleeping furs in the shadows at the edge of the fire-light and prepared to go to sleep.

Just as Horda was putting her head down, Bear Claw came up to her, kicking her with the toe of his moccasin. "I'll share your furs."

Her eyes went wide. "You'll what?" She pretended she didn't know what he meant.

"By the blood of the Great Mystery, woman, are you deaf? I'll share your furs, so move over and let me in."

"I belong to Mach."

"Not any more," he announced. His icy eyes glittered. "My men will share the other women, but *you* belong to me."

The panic rose so suddenly within her, Horda was sure she would vomit again. Surely there was something she could do, some way ... "My people do not —" she began.

"We're no longer with your people." Bear Claw spoke with unmistakable finality.

"But —"

His hungry eyes bored into her. "You are mine, and I will have you!"

Frantic, she twisted around, looking for someone — anyone — who would help, but what she found froze her blood. Each of the other women was trapped in her furs, paired with one of their captors. "Oh, pleas —"

She gasped as he covered her mouth with one strong hand and drew her against his massive chest with the other, lowering himself on top of her as he moved. She breathed shallowly, try-ing to avoid the odors of smoke, sweat, and bear grease that emanated from his hot body, but there was no escape. She twisted and turned under his crushing weight, but he pinned her arms down; then his hands fumbled with the lacings of her tunic.

Letting her body go limp, she closed her eyes and drove her teeth into her lower lip. She felt a sharp pain and tasted blood, but she didn't stop. Survival was all that mattered now, and she was determined she *would* survive.

Mother Life gave me to Mach. I will survive, and he will come and take me home. She felt the sting of hot tears in her eyes, and a sob escaped as Bear Claw roughly pushed the tunic from her shoulders. *He will use my body because I cannot stop him, but he cannot touch my soul. That belongs to Mach.*

She closed her eyes and willed herself to think of her chosen. His dark eyes shone in her mind's eye — tender and full of his love. *Please, Mother Life, let Mach still want me after he learns of this.* Silent tears dripped from beneath her closed eyelids, tears of humiliation and pain.

Bear Claw groped and pinched and slobbered and bit. His breathing accelerated to a hoarse rasp, but Horda lay silent and unresponsive. After what seemed like an eternity, Bear Claw pushed her legs apart and thrust himself into her dry body. She cried out in pain — she couldn't help it — but that seemed to encourage her captor to press against her harder, trying to make her scream more.

Quickly reaching his climax, Bear Claw smiled triumphantly. "Now you really are mine." He stretched out beside her and started to snore. When she thought he had fallen asleep, Horda tried to scoot away, but Bear Claw reached over and grabbed a handful of hair, tangling it around his fingers. "Lay still," he commanded.

There was nothing she could do but comply. Lying back in the furs, she curled into a ball of misery. Her skin crawled where the heat of Bear Claw's body touched it. His stink reached out to choke her, making her stomach churn. Hate, once so foreign a thing to her, began to grow, like a living, breathing entity. *I am not his, and I never will be. I'll see him lifeless; I swear it!*

She finally fell asleep, dreaming slow painful deaths for her captor.

※

"Get up, you lazy woman." Bear Claw kicked Horda.

"Ouch!" She bolted upright before realizing she had moved. Once she was awake, though, she made no effort to comply.

"The sun's rising, and it's time to go. Now get up!" He drew back his foot to kick her again.

She rolled out of his reach. "Why are you kicking me?"

"To get you up."

"If you weren't aware, calling works just as well and leaves me more able to make the journey." Her voice dripped with sarcasm.

He scowled. "That's not my way."

Horda struggled to keep her anger under control. She would let it grow, unnoticed until it was powerful enough to wield like a blade. Only then could she defeat this monster. "Maybe your way contributed to the lack of women in your tribe." Her eyes flashed at him before she made her face relax, pasting on as pleasant a smile as she could manage.

Bear Claw turned surly. "You talk too much." He looked like he wanted to kick her again, but she remained out of reach. "Now get up if you plan to eat."

She climbed to her feet and walked to her pack, rummaging for soaproot and the soft leather she used to dry her skin.

"What are you doing?" Bear Claw demanded.

"I'm going to wash."

"Don't bother; it's a waste of time."

"It might make your own women desire you a bit more," she said, unable to resist the jab. She smiled smugly and picked up a water bag. "I need water for the yampah root porridge and flat bread anyway." She walked away before Bear Claw could reply.

Horda met Suka at the spring. Raising her face to the warm sun, Horda said, "I wish Mach would find us today."

Suka frowned. "They won't know we're missing until the sun turns twice more."

"I know, but I can hope, can't I?" Horda scooped the cool water in her hands and washed her face.

"We have more immediate concerns." Suka busied herself filling a waterbag she carried. "Are you ill this morning?" she asked after a moment.

"To be honest, I haven't even thought about my stomach." Pressing her hands to her midsection, Horda considered. "No, it's fine; it must have been nerves or something. In fact, I'm rather hungry."

Suka eyed her skeptically but decided not to pursue the subject, at least not now. She filled another water bag before she asked much more quietly, "Did Bear Claw hurt you?"

Horda felt her face flame. Of course Suka knew — they all knew — but to hear it aloud ... "Not really. I just ache all over."

"I have willow bark in my pack. I'll brew a tonic to ease our pains."

"Willow tonic won't touch my pain." Horda's amber eyes darkened, and she vowed, "I'll see him lifeless."

"Shh. You mustn't say such things aloud." Suka looked around cautiously, but none of the warriors were nearby. "Don't provoke them; we must survive."

"Oh, I intend to survive." Tears glistened in Horda's eyes, but her whisper was fierce. "Oh, Suka, I will survive. I'll see us home where we belong and he ..." She spat in the dirt at her feet, a gesture reminiscent of her captor. "He'll walk in the Outer Darkness ... forever."

"Good. I'm glad you feel that way, because —" She broke off suddenly, as if she couldn't find the right words.

"Because what?" Horda asked.

"Because Aiyana and some of the others are quite despondent, and they need our strength to go on."

"Why? I don't understand."

"They blame themselves for their violations. They fear they won't be allowed to return to the tribe without punishment."

Horda frowned. "That's absurd. We couldn't have stopped those men without killing all of them or ourselves, and neither one was an option."

"I agree, but they're worrying and muttering among themselves nonetheless."

"How can they even think such ridiculous things?" Horda sputtered. "Don't they have the sense the Mother gave a wild goose?"

"Shh." Suka looked again back toward the camp. "We'll discuss this later; just be aware of what's going on. Now, if we all cook together, we can make the morning eat take much, much longer." She grinned.

"I'll hurry slowly."

Bear Claw stomped and growled and fussed during the entire time it took them to prepare the food, but it did no good; the sun was well on its journey before they completed the morning eat and were packed to go.

Horda whispered, "I see no one left without eating."

"I didn't think they would. They like our cooking." Suka helped Horda into her pack then turned for Horda to adjust hers.

"I don't blame them," Horda said. "Did you smell the stuff they eat?"

Suka shook her head.

"Bear Claw offered their traveling food in his bid." She wrinkled her nose. "At least I suppose it was their food. It smelled like rotten fish and looked like bison droppings, and I thought I would embarrass myself by vomiting all over it and his woman. Oh, oh. I see Bear Claw is trying to get our attention."

Bear Claw looked ready to pounce. "Hurry up!" he growled.

Horda rolled her eyes. "We're ready. May we leave?"

Suka looked reprovingly at Horda and whispered, "Be careful of your words. If you anger him, there's no telling what he'll do to you."

Remembering her violent awakening, Horda showed Suka the bruises already darkening her leg. She shrugged. "He wants me; he's made that very clear. So I don't think he'd go to all this trouble just to kill me, and there's not much he can do to me that he hasn't done already."

Suka frowned at her. "Probably not, but there are more of us here, and I wouldn't put it past him to take his anger at you out on one of us."

Horda frowned. "I hadn't thought of that. You're absolutely right, I'll be more careful. I want to see all of us go home."

"We certainly will, and I promise you Bear Claw will be the one suffering before we do."

Horda smiled at Suka's intensity.

"Aiyahoo!" he cried, and the group trudged across the grass toward Bear Claw's home.

Chapter 27

Wilda raced to Thuro and leaped into his arms. "I missed you."

Watching Thuro's embarrassment, Mach fought a smile; it wouldn't do to laugh at his friend in public; it might mar his reputation as a stoic warrior. Wilda's greeting wasn't seemly, but it was the kind he wouldn't mind getting from Horda when she returned. He had missed her these last few days. He scanned the assembled women for her, but she wasn't there. Relax; he told himself, it was still early. The sun hadn't yet reached its highest point, and not everyone had returned.

Mach watched the leaders of the returned groups join Zaaco near the Circle of Light. Counting quickly, he realized he had been wrong; everyone had returned except Suka's group. Some women walk more slowly, he told himself, and maybe they just had more to discuss than the other groups. But as the sun crawled higher, so did his anxiety. And he was not alone. The conversations around him grew louder and more concerned. Everyone was looking in the direction Suka's group had gone. Something was definitely wrong.

When the sun had passed its zenith, Zaaco stepped to the Circle of Light and raised his hands for silence. "I am sure Suka's group is just slightly delayed," he said, keeping his tone light. "You know how our women love to talk." He was greeted with nervous laughter. "However, I believe we should make sure. I have asked Elko to lead a party of four hands of warriors to

281

remind them we still have much to do before Gathering is through."

The crowd laughed again, but it was not a happy sound. Mach pushed through the people clustered in front of him. "I would join them," he called to the chief.

Zaaco nodded. "I thought you would, and we welcome your help."

Thuro strode up beside him and called, "As would I." Zaaco nodded to the young warrior, then stepped down to speak with Elko.

"I didn't expect you to leave Wilda," Mach told his friend, "though I'm glad you're coming, too." Thuro shrugged and clasped his shoulder. Words were not necessary.

"Bear Claw frightened her, and she told me she was afraid. I laughed and told her nothing would happen. How could I have been so wrong?"

"You heard Zaaco; I'm sure they've just been delayed." Thuro gave Mach's shoulder a brotherly pat.

Mach nodded, but he couldn't shake the fear growing in the pit of his stomach. *Oh, Mother Life, please let my fears be wrong and let Horda and the others come back to laugh at my foolishness.*

❁

As they waited for the scout to return, Mach assessed the area near the women's camp site for himself. No smell of smoke lingered in the air. The undergrowth was undisturbed. There were no footsteps or voices, and the birds sang without fear. These were not good signs.

A soft call came from up ahead, and Elko motioned them all forward. They crept on their bellies up the next ridge to find Suka's camp — deserted. Eager to find out what had happened, Mach climbed to his feet, only to be pulled back down by Thuro.

"Stay down," hissed Elko in his direction. Mach felt the

heat rise in his cheeks; he knew better. Using hand signals, Elko directed his men to spread out and surround the encampment, then move in to tighten the trap. They stepped carefully, silently, but no one was there to hear their approach. Once he was certain the camp was really deserted, Elko motioned them all to join him.

Then Mach saw the small pile of signal stones Suka had left behind. Something had definitely gone wrong. "Walk carefully," he told the others, searching for additional clues.

The footprints near the sleeping cave told the story. They were large, heavily indented, and very clear, as if the walkers had been carrying heavy burdens and hadn't worried about covering their tracks. There were smaller barefoot prints, too, moving around the fire as if they cooked and packed. "Bear Claw," Mach hissed loudly. He moved quickly in the direction the footprints led.

"Mach, come back here!" Elko's voice cracked like thunder.

"He took them. We must find them before it's too late," Mach called over his shoulder.

"Then what?"

Mach stopped immediately and turned to the older man, who beckoned him back.

"Use your head, son," Elko admonished. "We need to know more before we do anything. For instance, I find this very strange," Elko said. He pointed to the mingled tracks of men and women near the fire. "What do you see?"

Mach glared at the tracks then shook his head in puzzlement. "It looks like the women cooked here, but everyone ate, even the men." He looked back at the line of tracks left by the shelter. "That can't be. The tracks there show the men surprised them and carried them away."

Thuro ran up to them from the far side of the camp. "There are two sets of tracks beside the stream. It looks a hand of women harvested the vegetables there while a hand of men watched them."

"This doesn't make sense," Mach complained, anxiety for Horda making him even more impatient. "Why are we just standing here? We have to rescue them before it's too late."

Elko's face sobered. "We're all worried, Mach, but they already have a head start of at least two turnings of the sun. And the tracks show they have four hands of warriors and some supplies. So tell me, what are you going to do when you find them?"

A dull red flush climbed the young brave's cheeks, and he sighed. "I don't know."

Elko motioned the rest of the men to join them by the fire pit. When they were all seated, he said, "By the look of the tracks, our women were surprised while they slept and carried off." He pointed to the line of men's tracks Mach found. "But, sometime later, and for some reason we do not know, they returned." He pointed to the women's barefoot tracks mixed with men's tracks.

"The question is why. Now, I know my mate, and I'm guessing she made such a fuss about leaving without her moccasins and supplies that she managed to convince Bear Claw to come back and get them. Once they were here, the women wasted time harvesting vegetables and cooking and packing before they left again. And that time they left signal stones." He pointed to the tracks leaving the cook fire and heading to the east. "When they left that time, you can see the women were burdened, but the men weren't."

Elko lapsed into silence, waiting for the men to consider his words. A murmur of agreement rippled through the group.

"Does anyone have anything to add?" he asked. No one did.

"Fine. Mach, you're the fastest runner here. I want you to go back to Gathering and tell them what has happened."

"But I want —" Elko silenced Mach's protest with a wave

of his hand.

"You'll need to bring us five hands of warriors, weapons, and supplies enough for all of us." A cool breeze whispered through the camp. "Winter comes. We'll need warm clothing, too."

"Surely we'll find them before —"

Elko cut him off. "We can assume nothing, and we must be prepared for whatever awaits. I'm certain the women will leave signs — like this one," he continued, "and do everything in their power to delay their captors so we can catch up. Now we must search the camp here very carefully; they may have left other messages for us."

Realizing the wisdom of the older man's words, Mach quickly departed for the waiting People of the Frozen Earth. Elko divided the remaining warriors into groups, and step by meticulous step, they went through the empty camp, searching for hidden clues.

Mach ran until he reached the Gathering grounds. He was immediately assaulted by a thousand questions: "What's wrong?" "Where are the women?" "Where're the other men?" "What happened?" He didn't know where to start.

Zaaco handed Mach a horn of water. "Give him room," he commanded everyone calmly. "Let Mach drink and catch his breath; then he'll speak."

The chief's tranquil tone caused Mach to feel an urgency to inform everyone of the situation. After all, when they understood what had happened, they would rush to rescue their women from Bear Claw and his men. But he saw something in Zaaco's eyes — a pain much like his own, but tempered by years of experience and wisdom. After a few gulps of the cool water, he tried to speak, but he was still panting so hard he only gasped.

"Take it easy," soothed Zaaco.

Mach took slow, deep breaths and drank more water. Finally he could speak. "The camp is empty, but we found tracks. Bear Claw has them."

The noise from the crowd was deafening, and Zaaco's body jerked as if the words had been a physical blow. Taking a deep breath himself, the old man squared his shoulders. "Tell us what you know."

Mach recounted everything he could remember about the campsite, as well as Elko's plan.

Zaaco nodded, mulling over his words. "I think two hands hands of warriors rather than five —" He trailed off as everyone around him rushed off to their shelters to gather supplies. He hadn't even called for volunteers, but it hadn't been necessary. "You've done well, Mach," he told the warrior. "We'll leave as soon as we're packed."

Still contemplating Mach's words, Zaaco walked slowly to his shelter. Treema followed him inside. "You're going?"

"I have to." He closed his eyes. Horda's frightened face danced behind his eyelids. He had made light of her fears and look what happened. He blamed himself. But that would have to wait; there were more important things to deal with now.

"I know," said Treema. "I'll prepare your food."

Zaaco selected weapons and winter furs. His pack couldn't be too heavy, but he needed so many things. The trip would be long, no matter how good his men were. His old bones ached. No, his heart ached. His daughter was a captive.

Treema interrupted his brooding as she returned to the shelter with a bulging parfleche and a water bag. "You'll hunt along the way, but I packed pemmican and jerky with a few roots and vegetables. You know which plants are edible, so you can get more when these run out." She bustled about the shelter.

"Yes, I know."

"Don't forget to eat some plants every day. They give you strength."

In spite of his grief, he teased. "Yes, Ma."

She stopped, startled by his tone. "I didn't mean —"

He smiled and wrapped her in a comforting hug. "There's so little you can do, and you have to do something. Fretting over me is something; I don't mind." He drank her breath.

She hugged him fiercely and nestled her face against his chest so he wouldn't see her tears. He pretended he didn't hear the quaver in her voice as she said, "Come back, and bring her back to us."

The empty words of comfort that rose quickly to his tongue were smothered by the echo of his own voice trapped in his head. *We'll take care of you. Don't worry.* He couldn't speak the words she wanted to hear, so he settled for "If Mother Life and Father Death will it, I will do both."

Treema crushed her mouth to his. "I love you, old man. Don't leave me alone."

"I love you, Treema, more than I've ever told you." One last hug, one last sharing of breath, and he shouldered his pack and stepped outside. With no one there to hide them from, the tears ran unchecked down Treema's face and dripped on her breast.

Selah, Zaaco's youngest mate, stood patiently near the shelter, waiting for him to emerge. His eyes brightened when he saw her. "Ah, Pet, I wondered where you were."

"I thought you might need these." She held out a new suit of winter clothes complete with the slitted mask he'd need to protect himself from snow blindness.

He laid down his pack to examine the sturdy clothing. He ran his fingers through the sleek fox fur lining the parka, leggings, and moccasins, and admired the stitch work that held everything together. "Thank you," he murmured, caressing her cheek. "You always had a gift for handiwork. He rearranged his pack to make room for the new garments then grinned up at her. "Don't, ah, ever tell anyone, but I completely forgot about a snow mask."

She smiled and traced the line of his jaw as if to memorize it. "Don't forget me," she whispered.

He pulled her against his chest and whispered back, "Never. I love you, Pet, and I don't know what I'd do without you."

She whispered, "I love you, Zaaco. Please, be careful."

"I'm a tough old bird, Selah; it would take a lot to do me in." He drank her breath and touched his lips to hers. "Take care. I'll be back as soon as I can." He patted the rounded mound of her stomach and received a sturdy kick in response. He chuckled. "If nothing else, I have to see the little warrior who takes such delight in punching the chief."

"We'll be waiting." Then Zaaco shouldered his pack once more and headed out of the camp.

Chapter 28

Bear Claw was right about one thing, Horda thought — he was a skilled tracker, and he knew what other trackers would be looking for. As a result, he led his warriors and captives on a zigzagging journey across the prairie, leaving false trails and hiding the real one when he could.

Several times each day the Women of the Frozen Earth left signs for their men, but Bear Claw frequently found them. Sometimes he beat the women when he did; at other times he laughed at their impotent rage and reminded them of his supremacy. But always, always, when he found the signs, he destroyed them. Still, Horda and Suka did not give up. Each sign Bear Claw didn't find fueled their hope of rescue, and they used them to bolster the other women's spirits when they faltered.

Aiyana, in particular, had seemed to give up hope of ever returning to their people. Silent by day, she often woke the entire camp with screaming nightmares, which she refused to discuss with anyone. The men called her "the shrieker," using the name to taunt her at every opportunity. Because Horda suspected the young woman dreamed she would be consumed by the Wrath of Fire for bedding with her captors, she tried to reassure her that would not happen, but it was about as useful as talking to a stone.

Horda's nausea continued. She managed to keep it under control by chewing alum root and mint each morning before she rose, but she could do nothing for the exhaustion that plagued her day and night. Putting one foot before the other sometimes seemed too much to ask of her tired body, but Mach's strong face in her mind's eye and echoes of his gentle words in her heart always granted her enough strength to go on. Each day her hope for a rescue became a little fainter until one day she decided it really didn't matter any more. She would survive, no matter where she ended up.

The counting cord Suka had begun the first night after their capture carried the knots for five hands plus two fingers' turnings of the sun. The sun neared the zenith of five hands plus three when one of the men scouting ahead of the group topped a small knoll and turned to signal silently to the rest. Bear Claw raced up the hill with most of his men, leaving two behind to watch the women. Before reaching the top, he turned back and commanded, "Stay out of the way." As if they had a choice.

"What's happening?" asked Suka in a soft voice.

Horda whispered, "I think the scout found bison." Their food supplies had long since been depleted, and the travelers were usually hungry since little time was allowed for hunting or gathering.

Surprisingly, it was Aiyana who spoke first. "I'm hungry for fresh meat," she said.

Horda smiled at the young woman who had been silent for so much of the journey. "Me, too. Perhaps we'll have a bison hump roast tonight."

A few of the others licked their lips in anticipation.

Although Bear Claw had said to stay out of the way, the guards didn't want to be too far behind the others. They led the women up the hill to get a better view. Below them, the men were creeping across the plains toward an immense herd of bison.

"What are they going to do?" asked Marmal. "They don't have spear throwers or even long spears. How can they kill any of the bison?"

"I don't know," answered Horda. She looked toward the guards, but they were too distracted by the scene to pay any of the women much heed. And it wasn't as if there was anywhere they could run.

Bunched together, they watched the men inch across the plains and form a rough semicircle downwind of the vast herd. Then, as one, the hunters leaped to their feet, shouting and running toward the herd. The frightened animals milled around in confusion for a moment then stampeded breakneck across the plains with the men close behind.

"Mother Life, what's happening?" whispered Horda.

Suka said, "I suppose there's a ravine or gully nearby. They'll run the bison over the edge and butcher the ones that are wounded or killed outright. If the bison don't change direction on them, it might actually work fairly well. Long ago our men hunted like this, but it's very dangerous."

"Why is it more dangerous than stabbing them with the long spears?" asked Horda. She was a healer; she knew very little about hunting.

"Because no one can truly predict which way the bison will run on the open prairie." Almost as if Suka's words called them, the lead animals veered and began to stampede toward the men driving them. The men scattered like dandelion fluff on a summer breeze.

All made it to safety — all but one. He tripped over a depression in the ground and fell beneath the thundering hooves. His helpless screams echoed briefly above the roar of the stampede then ceased, creating a terrible silence in the midst of the maelstrom.

Horrified, the women stared at each other. They all knew how close Father Death was and how quickly he might reach down to claim a victim, but watching it happen was another thing. It chilled them to their marrow. Worse, though, was what followed; none of the Men of the Tall Grass seemed to notice the man's demise, or if they did, they simply didn't care.

�֎

The bison pounded back and forth across the prairie, alternately chasing the Men of the Tall Grass and being chased. Now the men were in desperate pursuit once more. Howling, yelling, and flapping their arms, they tried vainly to turn the raging animals back toward the hidden ravine but instead fell farther and farther behind. Almost as if camas molasses slowed their movements, the women turned to look at each other — the small knoll where they stood now lay in the direct path of the stampede. The women screamed and scattered across the prairie, dropping their packs and other belongings to increase their speed. Suka could see escape was hopeless. The beasts were much faster than the women and much heavier. They could crush someone before she knew what had happened.

"Stop!" Suka screamed to the group. "They're too fast, and we can't get away. The safest place for us is atop the little rise. Come quickly!"

Horda turned when she heard Suka and began urging the women nearest her back the way they had come. Most recognized Suka's wisdom and returned in haste. Three women — Marmal, Angil, and Sidra — dashed farther and farther out onto the prairie, seeking an elusive safety.

Suka spat orders to the women who had congregated at the top of the knoll. "Get on top and hunker down. They won't go to the trouble of climbing with all the flat land around us." *Please, Mother Life, let me be right.*

A short distance away Aiyana dashed headlong into Horda's arms. Horda pulled the frightened young woman toward the knoll, but she resisted turning and twisting in Horda's grasp.

"Let me go," she shouted angrily.

"You'll be killed. Now come on!" Horda pulled the girl by

one arm. Stubbornly Aiyana dug in her heels.

"It doesn't matter."

"You hollow-headed rabbit!" Horda spat at her; true anger rose to mask her fear. "I won't allow you to throw your life away just because you feel sorry for yourself. Now come!" With a mighty shove Horda pushed Aiyana up the small hill into the arms of Suka and scrambled up behind her.

As the women clung together, the earth trembled from the pounding of powerful hooves. The air filled with the bellows of angry beasts and the shrieks of unfortunate men. Clouds of choking dust rose and swirled, first one way, then another until the hill was surrounded. Horda could see the lather streaming from the beasts' heaving flanks as the nearly exhausted animals struggled for air. She could smell the salty, fearful sweat from bodies large and small. Fighting hysteria, the women clung to each other, a tiny island of relative safety in a raging sea of death.

❀

Like any storm, this one reached its peak then faded away, leaving a path of destruction in its wake. Still running, the beasts disappeared across the prairie. One by one the women rose to their feet, looking at each other, almost afraid it was not really over. Horda surveyed the prairie behind them. Three women had run away; now two walked back toward the knoll. *How many men fell beneath the hooves?* She bit her lips and scanned the trampled grasses, searching for the remains of the men and woman.

Bear Claw suddenly appeared in front of Horda. "Are you all right?" he asked between short, shallow breaths.

"Yes," answered Horda.

"The others?"

"Most of the women are well."

"What does that mean?" he demanded.

"Suka realized the knoll was the safest place for us when the stampede came our way. Those who stayed here with us are fine. Three ran; of those, only two returned." She pointed at them a short distance away.

Bear Claw muttered a foul curse and headed toward them. Horda followed close behind him, uncertain what he'd do. The moment he reached them he drew his arm back and began to beat them mercilessly.

"Stop! What are you doing?" shouted Horda.

"They should know better than to try to outrun a stampede," he snarled between blows.

She grabbed his arm and pulled him back. "I said stop!"

Surprised by her audacity more than anything else, he did turn to face her. His icy silver eyes raked up and down her body. Before she could even speak, he raised his arm and slapped her face so hard her head snapped back. "Don't you *ever* question me again!" he growled. He whirled and stalked across the prairie the way he had come.

Shaking, Horda went to the other women. Suka immediately tried to take a look at her face, but she pushed her away. "It's nothing," she said, though her eyes betrayed a boiling anger. "Is everyone else all right?"

Most of the women nodded and began climbing to their feet.

"I was," replied Angil, but she cradled one arm in the other. "I think I broke my arm when *he* knocked me down."

Horda rubbed her temples. *Mother Life, what next?* Taking a deep breath, she motioned to the arm, "Let me see." The woman gingerly lifted it up for inspection. Seeing neither the bone protruding from the flesh nor the telltale bump, Horda gently ran her fingers over the slightly swollen limb. "Why do you think it's broken?"

"I heard a pop, and it hurts."

"Where does it hurt worst?"

Angil pointed to her wrist. Horda lowered her head and

gently rotated Angil's hand, listening for the scrape of bones; it wasn't there. She breathed a small sigh of relief and said, "Wiggle your fingers." Angil winced but managed to move all her fingers.

"Good. It might be cracked, but it's not broken," Horda announced. "Hold it close to your body. I'll wrap it when I get back to my pack. It should be all right in a few turnings of the sun."

"Thank you."

Horda nodded then brought up the topic they were all dreading. "Did you see Marmal?"

Sidra, the other who ran, spoke for the first time. "Marmal and some of the men have gone to the Great Beyond. The bison pounded them into the good earth of the prairie."

"From the knoll, I saw Marmal fall beneath the stampede," offered Parda. "I heard her screams. Then I heard her silence after the animals raced past. She walks with Father Death this day."

Horda looked across the endless prairie, contemplating their situation. It didn't look good. *Please help me, Mother Life. I can't bring them back alone.* Then she turned and followed the others to the knoll to begin tending those who had survived.

❋

Bear Claw's vile oaths purpled the still air. "It's not possible," he shouted. "There must be some bison to butcher."

"Do you see any?" Suka was always the practical one.

"I know some fell."

"Yes, and were trampled into the ground like more than a hand of people. There's not any usable meat on the carcasses."

"I don't believe you," Bear Claw snarled.

Suka threw up her hands. "You find a carcass with meat left on it, and I'll be more than happy to cook it. We're hungry, too, you know."

Bear Claw growled and raised his hand to hit her.

295

Suka stood her ground. "Hitting me won't find us food."

He muttered an oath before shouting to the remaining men, "Go out and inspect all the lifeless bison. There has to be at least one we can use."

Horda said, "I need some of you women to go with me to bring back the people Father Death has claimed so we can prepare them for the Frozen Wilds."

"Leave them," snapped Bear Claw, his patience stretched way too thin to deal with the women right now.

Nevertheless, Horda protested, "But we can't just leave them for —"

"By the blood of the Great Mystery, woman!" Bear Claw wheeled and grabbed her upper arm. "They were stupid enough to get themselves trampled, so you'll leave them where they fell. The scavengers will take care of their remains."

"That's not the way of the People of the Frozen Earth," she shouted.

It might just as well have fallen on deaf ears. "You're part of the People of the Tall Grass now," Bear Claw reminded her acidly, "and what I say goes." It was a sobering thought, and Horda had no response.

Horda was never one to give up easily, though. She used her time tending the others to think, and when she was through, she went out and gathered some of the trampled prairie grasses, twisting them into bundles to build a small fire.

"What are you doing?" Suka asked.

She filled a little basket full of water and set it over the struggling flames before she answered. "Angil's wrist is swollen." She was already digging in her medicine pack. "Ah, I knew I had some skunkweed."

Suka was getting impatient. "And ..." she prompted.

Horda seemed surprised at the question. "And," she went

on, "I need to fix it." She pulled out the skunkweed, dropped a handful of the dried seedpods in the basket, and stirred the concoction. "Angil, watch this," she instructed the other woman. "Let it boil until the water turns dark as a moonless midnight. Add more water if it needs it. When it's done, set it aside to cool. I'll wrap your wrist when I get back."

"Back?" Suka asked. "Are you trying to get us all killed? Don't fool yourself; Bear Claw is capable of killing us."

Horda's amber eyes shone with a fierce light. "Yes he is, but I'm not going to leave Marmal out there alone. If Bear Claw won't let me take her to the Frozen Wilds, the least I can do is make her presentable and sing the songs to ease her journey."

"Bear Claw's going to beat you."

"He's likely to beat us all," Angil complained, holding her arm even tighter.

"I doubt it; it's me he's angry with. But I don't think he'll go after me, either, since I plan to make him think I'm looking for meat."

Suka frowned. "I'm going with you."

"I hoped you would."

The two women made their way across the trampled grass and torn sod of the prairie examining the mangled bison carcasses for usable meat. "Why couldn't one fall at the end of the stampede? Why did all the ones who fell have to be leaders?" asked Horda.

"I don't know."

Then they came to the first man's body — splintered bones, smeared blood, torn flesh, and matted hair. The sight left both women retching. "I don't know what I expected," Horda gasped through painful heaves, "but I never expected this. There's not much left."

Suka swallowed firmly and said, "What can we do?"

"Not much." Horda straightened the remains into a semblance of a body. "Father Death, I'm sorry I can't do more for

297

this, your child. Please accept him and restore him so he may live with you in your kingdom."

"Please," added Suka in a whisper.

"We'll sing the songs to ease his journey when we finish with the rest."

They turned and walked on. They had performed the same small acts and prayed the same brief prayer over two other remains when they found more. "This was Marmal," said Horda. "I can see some of the designs on her tunic."

"I know."

Gently, as though the bones and mangled flesh could still feel pain, Horda straightened the body and covered it with the tattered tunic, then smoothed the hair.

"Father Death, we're sorry we can't do more for your child. Please, ease her journey and heal her injuries. Accept her and restore her so she may happily serve you in your kingdom."

It seemed so little, but it was all they could do this far from home.

❇

After a short time more, Suka said, "We should go back. Bear Claw will be angry."

"He's already angry."

"We still have to feed more than a hand plus one of people with practically no food," said Suka, "and soon the sun will be gone."

Horda looked across the prairie. "There is only one more. It wouldn't be right to leave him."

Suka sighed and followed her. They performed the too-familiar small ritual and prayed the same brief prayer once more. Then turning, they softly sang the funeral songs of the People of the Frozen Earth on their long trek back to the knoll.

Horda and Suka were almost back when they saw it. A large, virtually undamaged, bison carcass lay in a small indentation in the prairie. Together, they turned their eyes heavenward, and Horda whispered, "Thank you, Mother Life, for your bounty in the face of such destruction."

"Bear Claw!" Horda raised her voice. "We've found a bison!" She and Suka continued across the prairie toward where the beast lay.

Bear Claw met them. "Where have you been?" he demanded.

"Looking for meat," Horda answered, "and we found it."

He looked at their empty hands. "Well?"

"You think two women can carry a beast that size? You can follow our steps and get it yourself. Bring the meat to the spring." She pointed the way before she moved on toward the knoll.

"Where are you going?"

Turning back, Horda blinked guileless amber eyes. "Why, Bear Claw, you've told me many times it's the men's place to provide the food for the women cook. I'm going to prepare a fire pit and look for vegetables. We've much to do while you butcher the bison with your big, strong hands." She smiled and hurried away before he could reply.

"You did that quite well," whispered Suka.

"It's a good thing he didn't understand what I really meant." Horda grinned. "Ah, well, we really have a lot to do, but first I must wrap Angil's wrist." She thought a moment then sighed. "I wish I had some snow to pack it."

"The skunkweed seed broth works almost as well," Suka offered.

"Almost, but not quite." Horda shook her head. "But I suppose it's the best I can do for now." They both got busy with the chores that would let them survive — at least one more day.

Chapter 29

Without Suka's counting cord, Horda was certain she wouldn't have been able to tell the passage of time. One day turned into the next then into the one after that, each too similar for her exhausted body to distinguish between them. Her body seemed to move of its own accord — one foot in front of the other through the endless prairie grass.

What worried her more was the nausea that grew more insistent as the days went by, and the time for her moon cycle had passed and now approached again. The healer in her recognized the signs. She still kept trying to justify her symptoms. She knew, though, she wouldn't be able to fool herself much longer.

It was now two hands turning of the sun from the bison stampede. Just as the sun's pink and gold morning rays had blossomed into the white light of noon, the forward scout called back to the ragged column of travelers, shouting, "Smoke!"

Bear Claw and the other men broke into a run leaving the women and the heavy packs behind. Horda watched the men talk excitedly among themselves for a moment. Bear Claw suddenly seemed to miss the women, and he shouted, "Hurry up, you lazy creatures! We are almost home."

Home. Horda felt a momentary thrill of excitement; her breath quickened; her heart beat stronger; and she felt a surge of energy course through her legs. Then she realized her error. This was Bear Claw's home. She looked at the ground while hot anger washed her soul. This was not her home, and it never would be. Was she so desperate for rest she would accept even Bear Claw's camp as a home?

Suka was still thinking clearly. She called back, "We're coming, but the journey's been long, and we're tired. We'll catch up to you as we can." Bear Claw said something they couldn't hear; it obviously wasn't anything pleasant, but he seemed to accept that they would obey and turned back to his men.

Once his back was turned, Suka pulled all the women together, herding them forward, but very, very slowly. "This may be our last chance to talk as a group before we reach the camp, so we must plan as much as we can now. I know it has been many turnings of the sun, but our men are coming, and we must be ready."

Aiyana's eyes filled with tears, and she shook her head, sobbing, "What difference does it make?"

Maybe it was her exhaustion, but Horda found she didn't have any more patience for Aiyana's weeping. "You heard Suka; we have to plan so we'll be ready when our men rescue us."

Aiyana's voice was barely a whisper. "Why would they want to rescue us? Rescue me?"

"Why?" Horda started angrily, but Suka held out a hand to stop her. She had heard the words and understood the pain Aiyana must be feeling. She tried to soften her voice. "They will want to. You must believe."

"I want to believe, but I can't. I just can't any more." She looked directly at Horda. "We're ruined, and it's all your fault!"

It was a thought Horda had many times during their long journey. "You're correct Bear Claw wanted me," she said, as much to the group as to her accuser. "And I'm the one he came after. If I had been alone, it would have ended there, but I was with the rest of you, so he took you, too. I'm sorry."

"Sorry?" spat Aiyana, her weeks of pent-up anger exploding in a blind rage. "Because of you, all our lives are ruined, and all you can say is you're sorry? It's not enough!"

"It *is* enough!" Suka's angry voice stunned the woman into silence. "I know you are angry — we all are — but to blame it on Horda is both petty and cruel. Tell me, can you say Horda enticed Bear Claw into doing what he did?"

Aiyana bowed her head, no longer able to look the others in the eye. "I didn't see her, but she must have, otherwise —"

"Otherwise nothing! We've all seen what kind of man Bear Claw is." Pity and anger warred on Suka's face, and she struggled with a way to end this once and for all. "Horda, did you purposely encourage Bear Claw?" Although her question was addressed to the young woman, she made sure everyone in their group could hear.

"No!"

"Did you want to join with him?"

"No! I have chosen Mach, as everyone knows."

"And didn't you voice your fears about Bear Claw at Gathering?"

"Yes, I did, but everyone felt Bear Claw would depart," Horda replied.

Suka turned back to Aiyana. "Now tell me, do you think there was anything in Horda's behavior that made this happen?"

Finally, Aiyana shook her head.

"Good. Then stop this nonsense and help us plan."

But Aiyana began to sob.

"Now what is it?" Suka asked testily.

"But what if they burn us?"

Suka's stony face melted, and she reached out to hug the young woman. "Don't you understand?"

"I understand both partners are punished when they enter into an unsanctioned joining, and we —"

Suka arched one eyebrow before she said, "I certainly didn't want to join with Rushing Water, sanctioned or unsanctioned, and I don't think any of the others wished to mate with these men. Am I correct?"

The vehemence of their responses made Suka smile.

"I won't be punished for what Rushing Water and the others do to me against my will." She looked at Horda. "Do you expect to be punished for what Bear Claw does to you?"

Horda hesitated a fraction of a second as a wave of guilt washed over her. It was not for what had happened with Bear Claw, but for what had happened with Mach. "No, I do not expect to be punished for Bear Claw's actions," she stated in a firm voice

"So, Aiyana," Suka continued, looking back at the sobbing woman, "do you still expect punishment for the actions of the Men of the Tall Grass?"

To everyone's surprise, she nodded.

Suka caught the younger woman's shoulders and forced her to meet her eyes. "Are you really telling me you believe you'll be punished because these men forced themselves on you?"

"Yes," Aiyana choked out. "We do not stop them; we just let them have their ways with us."

How conceited the young ones were, to think they had so much power. Suka shook her head. "And how do you propose we should stop men bigger and stronger than us who also have more than a four hands of warriors to help them."

"Surely we could do something," Aiyana protested, though a bit weakly this time. "I just feel so guilty."

Horda's heart twisted inside her chest. *Believe it or not, Aiyana, I feel guilty, too.*

Suka nodded and smiled sadly. "I understand your feelings, child. Sometimes we all feel guilty, but nothing that happened has been our fault. If you believe nothing else, believe that. We have to go on." Suka gathered both the young women in her arms and held them close. "It's hard to imagine, but Mother Life must have a reason for thi —"

"What's keeping you?" Bear Claw demanded, snatching Horda from Suka's arms before they could make a plan. He dragged her toward the knoll. As they topped the rise, he gestured toward a smoky smudge and small figures in the distance.

"What am I looking at?" she asked him.

Laughter rumbled deep in his chest — real laughter, the first she'd heard in a long time. "Home."

There was that word again. She was tempted to remind him her home lay far away in the direction from which they'd come. Such words would only anger him. "Oh," was all she said.

But Bear Claw was caught up in the moment. Puffing himself up as much as he could, he caught her hand and hauled her along. "Walk beside me. You're my woman now."

There was nothing to do but force her steps to match his. *Let him think what he will*, she told herself. *I will live to see him regret what he has done.*

Chapter 30

Zaaco's years and responsibilities sat heavily on his shoulders. *First my mate, now my daughter gone. I should have realized Meiran was ill, and I should have known Bear Claw wouldn't give up so easily. How could I be so blind to both?* Tiredly he looked across the grassland for the thousandth time that day, but it showed him nothing except his own exhaustion.

Once more the trail had disappeared. Bear Claw was very skillful at covering his tracks and clever, as well; Zaaco no longer doubted his abilities. The Chief of the People of the Tall Grass had sent him and his men running after trails that twisted and turned, doubled back, or disappeared altogether. It was almost impossible to tell which were real and which were false. Some of the men wanted to ignore the most blatant signs, reasoning those couldn't possibly be correct, but they couldn't do that; it would be just like Bear Claw to mask his trail by putting it in the most obvious place, figuring his pursuers would ignore it. No, they had to check every sign lest they fall into that trap.

Zaaco kept whatever doubts he had about finding the captured women to himself. As chief, the others looked to him for strength and direction, and that's what he gave them. At some point Bear Claw would make a mistake, he told them — after all, he was only human — and they would use it to track him down. They would bring their women home safe and sound and make their captors pay for what they had done. If it sounded like a lie, like nothing more than the wishful thinking of an old and tired man, the others had enough respect for him not to say so.

❁

The rolling prairie lands had nearly swallowed the sun when Bear Claw and his group entered the camp of the People of the Tall Grass.

Horda wrinkled her nose and breathed shallowly through her mouth, trying to block the noxious odors that rolled out in waves to great them — rotting meat, unwashed bodies, human wastes, rancid bear grease, and some others she couldn't begin to identify. How could people choose to live like this? Even the air made her feel dirty.

She forgot all that when she saw the people — two naked toddlers and a pitifully small number of men, women, and youths dressed in dirty, ragged grass aprons. Hollow-eyed and hungry looking, dirtier even than Bear Claw had been when he first entered Gathering, they silently watched the travelers advance. She quickly counted — one hand plus two fingers hands men, three hands less one women, and a hand plus two youths. Surely that couldn't be all, she thought.

"People of the Tall Grass, we have returned." At his booming proclamation, the people broke into a shuffling run toward the travelers.

Horda looked at Bear Claw. "Where are the others?" she asked.

He scowled at her. "What others?"

"The rest of your tribe."

"They went to the Great Beyond last winter."

"All of them?"

"What does it matter?" he asked brusquely. "You're here."

So you keep reminding me, she thought bitterly. *And it does matter*. Only a hand plus two young men and no young women? And only two little ones? Even if she were a willing accomplice in this scheme, she couldn't save them. How could such a thing have happened?

She felt a surge of pity; she could see the answer right in front of her. It had happened because even those that remained looked like they were starving in this time of plenty; the others probably hadn't stood a chance. And now they were heading into winter when food would become even scarcer. What did that mean for the rest? What did it mean for any of them, now that they were here?

As the group advanced, one woman, obviously breeding, broke from the rest and ran to Bear Claw, wrapping him in a fierce embrace. He pulled her dirty arms from around his neck and pushed her out of his way without speaking. The woman screeched and cried at him and pounded her bare breasts, but Bear Claw did not even look at her again, and she finally darted away, sending curses over her shoulder.

Horda watched her go, puzzled by the exchange, but before she could ask Bear Claw about it, he caught her arm again and tugged her toward the shelters. She longed to pull away, but out of the corner of her eye she saw Suka shake her head almost imperceptibly at her, then straighten her shoulders and stride proudly into the camp, looking neither left nor right as she did so. It was a bold display, and Horda admired her for it.

Following Suka's example, she stepped up to Bear Claw's side, fixed an impassive mask on her face, and marched into the camp, trying to ignore the envious looks the assembled People of the Tall Grass cast toward the better-dressed, better-fed Women of the Frozen Earth. She could feel the hostility pouring like a living being from the gathered women; it frightened her, but she kept her shoulders squared and her eyes straight ahead. It wouldn't do to let them know how much their animosity affected her. However, she couldn't control the blushes that painted her face when the men and boys made overtly lewd comments and gestures at her. Bear Claw was their leader; why didn't he stop them?

Horda reached out to Suka with her free hand. The older woman clasped it firmly, but Horda would have been more reassured if Suka's hand hadn't felt as cold as new-fallen snow. She let it go when Bear Claw gave an insistent tug and pulled her toward one of the ragged shelters.

He stopped just outside the shelter and paused. He turned in a full circle inspecting the entire camp. He speared the man nearest him with his gaze. "What have the men done in my absence, Wolf that Walks?"

Horda was surprised. No mention of the journey? Of the men who had lost their lives in the stampede? Just 'what have you been doing?'

"We protected the women as you told us."

"Have you hunted? Winter comes and I don't see any food."

The man ignored his chief's obvious displeasure. "Some."

Bear Claw's voice grew dangerously calm. "Some?"

The man looked to the others for support, but none would meet his gaze. "There wasn't a lot of game around. And we didn't think you wanted the women left alone since you said they were so important."

"But everyone looks hungry. Even the women." Though Bear Claw's tone didn't change, his eyes flashed, and Wolf that Walks began to look nervous.

"Well, there wasn't much game. We had to ration."

Bear Claw moved so fast Horda didn't even register he had done so until his hand made contact with Wolf that Walks' face and blood spurted from the man's nose. "It's too early to ration," he said, enunciating every syllable to bring his point home, "and there is always game if you look for it. Must I do everything around here?"

The others began to back away, leaving Wolf that Walks alone with his chief. The man brought his hand to his bleeding nose and whined, "No. I mean, we tried, but ...but you said you wanted us to protect the women."

"I am the chief of a tribe of fools!" Bear Claw spat. "Go! Hunt now!"

"Now? It's nearly night."

"Then you'll have to move quickly, won't you?"

His sarcasm was lost on the quivering warrior. "But where?"

Bear Claw moved like lightning again. He grabbed Wolf that Walks' hair and twisted until he wrenched tears from the man's eyes. "Perhaps I ought to serve *you* up; you're so little use to me." He let go suddenly, and Wolf that Walks dropped to the ground. "Go to the gully. Perhaps the herds haven't all moved south. And don't return until you have a supply of meat for winter."

"You want me to go alone?"

"Alone?" Bear Claw laughed mirthlessly. "You can't even relieve yourself without someone telling you what to do. Take two hands of men with you."

There was an uncomfortable silence, then Wolf that Walks asked timidly, "Who?"

Bear Claw drew himself up to his full height. "Wolf that Walks, you've hunted for many turnings of the seasons. You know the gully hunting ground that lies less than a turning of the sun away. What's wrong with you?"

"I don't want to displease you," the man sniveled.

"You've already displeased me," Bear Claw snarled. "Now get your men and go before I see to it you'll never walk again!" He turned his back dismissively and motioned Horda inside his lodge.

She'd have preferred walking into the cave of an angry she-bear, but after taking a deep breath of relatively fresh air, she ducked into the smoky, malodorous shelter. Bear Claw followed. Waiting for her eyes to adjust to the semidarkness, she struggled not to cough or gag.

"Ack!" She screamed and jumped back as a dirty pile of tattered furs began to move at her feet. Perhaps a she-bear really had taken refuge in the shelter — with all the garbage around, who would know?

Bear Claw growled and kicked the furs. "Bird Wing, I told you to go away."

The furs stood up, transforming themselves into the woman who had approached Bear Claw outside. "Why?" she snarled, glaring at Horda. "Because you've taken another woman?" Ah, now it all made sense.

"Yes."

"You can't put me aside," she sniffed. "I'm breeding."

"So I've noticed." Bear Claw's eyes glittered like shards of ice in a winter sun; they made Horda shiver. "Even so, I don't have to keep you in my shelter. There aren't enough women to go around, so I'm sure one of the other warriors will provide for you."

"I don't want one of the other warriors," whined the woman, wrapping herself around Bear Claw like a dirty cloak, "I want you. You told me we needed little ones, and now you've got one. It's yours, and you're mine."

"Not any more." He pulled her arms from around his neck and pushed her away with enough force that she stumbled.

"But —"

"Leave and take your dirty things with you. You stink."

"Stink?" Bird Wing sounded affronted.

"Yes, stink. Don't you ever wash, woman?"

"Wash?"

"You're filthy. This camp is filthy. Everything must be cleaned."

"Cleaned?"

"Are you deaf as well as stupid? Stop repeating everything I say! Dirty. Filthy. Disgusting!"

"Cleaning is too much trouble. Why don't we just move?"

"Because I'm tired of the filth," declared Bear Claw, "just as I'm tired of you."

Horda had to swallow the laughter that rose in her throat — Bear Claw complaining about dirt? It was almost too funny to be true.

Eyes widening in surprise, Bird Wing asked, "What happened to you out there?"

"Nothing happened. I simply learned not all people live in dirt as we do."

"So what?" she sneered.

"So they don't sicken and depart as often as we do because of it."

"So suddenly we change the way we've always lived?" scoffed Bird Wing.

"It hasn't always been this way."

Horda was startled; was that a trace of sadness in Bear Claw's angry voice? She wanted to ask Bear Claw what had happened to his tribe, but Bird Wing wasn't finished with him; she scowled and pointed to Horda. "Does this sudden change have anything to do with this new woman of yours?"

Bear Claw drew back his arm, but Bird Wing, clearly used to his behavior, ducked out of the way before he could hit her. "Enough, Bird Wing!" he roared. "Do not question me any more! Leave my shelter at once!"

"Gladly," she retorted. She scurried around the shelter collecting a pitiful pile of dirty belongings then crawled out the opening, spitting on Bear Claw's feet as she did so.

Even through her exhaustion, Horda felt the surge of anger and despair race through her body. Was this dirty, hungry existence all the life she could look forward to? Would she end up like Bird Wing, nothing more than a pile of bones and fur to be discarded at a whim? She stood silent and immobile as if that would make her invisible and these surroundings vanish into a soon-forgotten bad dream.

But it was not to be. "Put down your pack," Bear Claw commanded.

Horda looked at the rotting food scraps and other debris littering the shelter. She didn't want to place her belongings in the trash, but there didn't seem to be any area that was clear.

While she hesitated, Bear Claw stalked around the shelter muttering to himself and kicking rubbish first this way and then that. "I don't remember this camp or the people being so dirty. I don't understand it. What happened to them? They're hungry. They stink. They seem so ... so aimless ..." Suddenly he realized Horda hadn't moved. "I said for you to put down your pack. This is your shelter."

Before she could stop herself, Horda asked, "Where do you want me to put it? On this garbage heap or on that one?" She gestured around the shelter at the entire mess.

Bear Claw scowled at her, but then he lifted the door covering. "Put it outside until this place is cleaned."

Horda ducked out the opening before he changed his mind. She found a relatively clean area, laid down her pack, and sat on it, wondering what to do next. Exhaustion made her bones ache inside her flesh. Hunger gnawed at her stomach despite the nauseating smells blanketing the camp.

Smiling, she listened to Bear Claw bumping around in the shelter. She wondered if he had ever cleaned before. Then her smile died. What would he have in store for her when he found she was doing nothing?

She was surprised when he came outside carrying a huge load of trash. He stalked toward the fire pit in front of his shelter and dumped his burden unceremoniously into the hole. Horda hesitated then asked, "Um, do you really want to do that?"

He frowned. "You want the place clean, so I'll burn the garbage."

"Yes, but there?" She wrinkled her nose.

"Why not?" he demanded.

"Not a good idea. At least, not if you plan to stay in this shelter any time soon. The smell will be terrible, and it will linger."

"You have a better idea?" He spat the words, but she could hear the question beneath.

"Take it a distance away from the camp — a long distance — and dump it for now. Someone can bury it or burn it later."

Bear Claw grunted, but he dutifully picked the pile up again and began to walk away. "I'm hungry," he called over his shoulder. "It's time to eat."

Horda smiled. "Do you want me to cook for you alone or should I join Suka and the others in preparing food for all your people? The ones who didn't accompany you to Gathering look hungry."

Horda thanked Mother Life for the distance separating them because she sensed he would have hit her had she been in reach. Anger, pain, denial, and acceptance flashed across his scarred face in swift succession. "Feed everyone," he finally growled. "Winter nears."

"Yes, it does," she said to herself, "but I don't plan to be here to see it."

Chapter 31

Horda found Suka cleaning the shelter of the warrior who had claimed her. Wrinkling her nose, Suka tied back the flap and fanned her face. "Can you believe people actually live like this?" Horda asked the older woman. "It is a wonder they don't all walk the Frozen Wilds."

Suka placed a finger over her lips. "Shh. The women already resent us for being here, and the men don't care for women who think too much, so it's best we watch our words."

Horda looked around, surprised to find several pairs of dark eyes, including Bird Wing's, peering at them intently. "What are they doing?" she asked.

"Watching me. I'm on display."

"Humph."

"What brings you here? I thought you'd be cleaning your shelter."

"Bear Claw's cleaning."

Suka's eyes widened. "Bear Claw? Really?"

Horda grinned and shrugged her shoulders. "Well, it's stretching it to say he's cleaning. He carried one huge load of trash out of his shelter. Then he told me to come here; we're supposed to cook — for everyone."

"Cook what?"

"I don't know what," Horda answered, "but he wants his people fed. He's upset because they're hungry."

"He should be." Suka frowned. "Is your space this bad?"

Horda appraised this part of the camp. "No, I think ours is worse."

"Remind me not to visit you then," Suka commented dryly. "Okay, if we're going to cook, let's head over there." She pointed to a level space upstream from the main camp. "The water there should be clean. I'll start several cook fires while you get the others. Ask them to bring their stores of food."

Horda surveyed the desolate camp. "What are you going to use for fuel?"

"Wood ..." Suka's voice trailed off as she looked more closely at their surroundings; the only trees were stunted, knobby things that would be difficult to cut. "I don't know. Maybe they have a supply of twisted grass around here somewhere." She sighed. "Do you want to ask Bear Claw or get the others?"

"I'll get the others," said Horda. By the time she had gathered the other Women of the Frozen Earth and returned to Suka's camp, Suka had already built a crackling fire and set a large cooking bag of water over it. Horda wrinkled her nose at the pungent smell of the smoke. "Um, Suka, what are you using for fuel?"

"Don't ask." Suka grimaced. "Believe me, you'll enjoy your eat more if you don't know."

Horda peered at the flames again but didn't question any farther. She said, "I have some bison jerky from the kill two hands turning of the sun ago and a little fresh antelope. Will that help?"

Suka nodded. "I have a haunch of venison from the deer Rushing Water killed yesterday. I also have a bit of the bison hump packed in cow parsnip, but I'd like to save it if I can. I saw some cattails, and there should be yampah root over in that marshy area upstream. It doesn't look like they've harvested any at all."

Zorya said, "Here's some pemmican I saved, and I saw wild onions down the stream a bit."

"There's a bed of pond lilies gone to seed just around the

bend, and I'm sure there are tubers, too," added Singar, another of the young women.

Aiyana held up two small rabbits. "I killed these today. I thought I'd roast them, but we could add them to the stew."

"This should be plenty," Suka told them, "but we have another problem. I brought my largest cooking bag, but I'll need at least four more. Did any of you bring some?"

Horda shook her head and turned to the others. "I didn't; did any of you?"

The young women looked at each other and began to shake their heads. Normally so silent, Aiyana said, "I have one." She took an unusually large and well-crafted bison stomach cooking bag from her pack and handed it to Horda.

"This is beautiful," Horda said.

"I made it for my mating." Aiyana's eyes filled tears. "It wasn't finished when we left for the Rituals, and I thought I might have t ..."

Horda hugged her and offered the bag back out to her. "Surely these people have cooking bags; you should save this."

Gazing at the bag, Aiyana squared her shoulders and looked directly in Horda's eyes. "No. I want us to use it now. It will help us survive so we can go home."

Understanding her determination, Horda simply said, "Thank you."

Watching the exchange, Suka gave thanks of another sort. She believed this was a turning point. It would be a struggle, but they would survive ... they all would survive, and they would return home.

A short span of time later, a small, bent woman inched her way into the group carrying several worn cooking bags. Timidly she held them out to Suka almost as if she expected to be beaten. Suka smiled at the aged woman, the first of the Women of the

Tall Grass to approach them in friendship. "Oh, thank you," she said. "Tell me, who are you? Can you help us prepare this meal?"

Wearing a neat grass apron and a tunic of some tattered but clean leather, the woman pushed back her thin grey hair and stared at Suka with bright black eyes, but she did not speak.

"Do you understand me?" asked Suka gently.

Finally the woman nodded and spoke so softly Suka had to lean close to hear. "I am Unna, healer of the People of the Tall Grass."

"A healer," Suka said delightedly, "just like Horda here. I'm glad to meet you, Unna. I'm Suka, the number one mate of Elko." Suka automatically offered her hand in greeting, but the old woman stepped back, refusing to touch it. Suka's eyes darkened with pain, not at Unna's action, but at her own situation.

She lowered her hand, "I suppose I have not introduced myself properly. I am now the mate of Rushing Water. We need your help, and we appreciate your bringing the cooking bags to us. Do you have any supplies we can use?"

Unna's eyes clouded with fear, and she seemed to fold into herself when Bear Claw approached.

"What are you doing here, old woman?"

Horda could hear the anger in Bear Claw's voice, and when she saw his muscles tense, she was afraid her might hit the cowering woman. Without thinking of the consequences to herself, she stepped between him and the old woman. "Unna kindly brought us some cooking bags. We didn't have enough to prepare an eat for all your people."

Bear Claw spat at Horda's feet. "She's old. She lives when others more worthy walk the Great Beyond."

Anger flushed Horda's cheeks. "I believe Mother Life and Father Death make that decision, not you."

Bear Claw's fists balled at her remarks, and his voice grew deadly calm, and icy. "Do not question me again, woman.

You will learn your place, or I will make you learn it, right here and right now."

Temper tossed Horda's caution to the winds. Amber eyes flashing, she fairly shouted, "Perhaps Unna will teach me what I really need to know."

Even though she knew the punch was coming, Bear Claw moved so quickly she didn't have time to get out of his way. Maybe it was for the best, she told herself; the pain kept her anger hot, and the anger fueled her desire to survive and escape this place. Still, even with her eyes blazing, she made a conscious effort to soften her voice. "Did you ever stop to think maybe the Father and the Mother left her here to help the rest of your tribe survive?"

"She's old and worthless." He said it with a finality that left no room for a response, glaring at the old woman who cowered before him.

"Not totally worthless," said Horda. "I've told you, we can't feed your people without her cooking bags." She pulled the cooking bags out of Suka's hands and waved them beneath his nose. "Now, if you plan to eat before the sun rises on a new morning, leave us to our work."

The slap, although hard enough to make her stumble, was not as bad as she had expected. And then Bear Claw turned on his heel and stalked away, leaving them alone with their work.

Suka reached out to Horda and whispered, "Stupid, stupid." Admiration lightened her eyes but didn't soften her mouth. "Necessary. Brave, even. But stupid. You're going to have to watch yourself in the future."

"Probably," agreed Horda, "but we do need Unna's help now."

"Well, we better get started. Girls, gather what you can find and hurry back." Everyone but Horda, Suka, and Unna rushed from the cook fire.

The moon shone brightly on the prairie before the People of

the Tall Grass sat down to eat the stew and flat bread the Women of the Frozen Earth, with Unna's help, had prepared. The Men and Boys of the Tall Grass devoured their portions with relish while the women sniffed disdainfully and ate cautiously — all except Unna. She fed the little ones three portions each before eating her portion with obvious enjoyment. Horda almost laughed out loud when the old healer snuck her a surreptitious grin.

Only the women who prepared the food realized how thin the stew was — made with more water, ground cattail roots, and pond lily bulbs than meat — but it was hot and filling. So, one meal down. But her real question was, how many more to go?

"These women will poison us with weeds and things. The People of the Tall Grass don't eat this stuff. We need meat," whined Bird Wing, sidling up to Bear Claw as he downed his food.

"Their people eat this kind of food all the time," growled Bear Claw around a mouth full of stew. "Anyway we don't have enough meat to feed us because Wolf that Walks sat around *protecting* you instead of hunting."

"You'd have left us unprotected?"

"I'm sure someone could have stayed behind to guard you," Bear Claw answered bitterly. "I certainly didn't intend for everyone to starve before the winter even walked the land."

His words silenced Bird Wing for the moment; however, her eyes smoldered as she watched Suka offer small baskets of service berries and chokecherries to the group.

"What's that?" Bird Wing croaked nervously.

"A little sweet to end the eat."

"We don't eat those things. They're for the birds, and we're not birds."

"No, but they are very good for people, too, and there are plenty for the birds and for us." Suka's smile froze into a grimace as she watched the men shove their hands into the baskets and gobble up the berries. Not birds, animals, she thought.

Bird Wing's hands curled into claws, and the fire deep in her eyes flamed.

"Enough," Bear Claw growled, swatting Bird Wing as if she were a pesky fly; she barely eluded him. "You can eat or not; I don't care which. But these women come from People who don't know hunger. They can help us survive the winter. You won't hinder them," he added, raising his voice so all could hear. "Not one of you."

Bird Wing glared at the Women of the Frozen Earth before she waddled away from the fire, making a great show of her pregnant belly. One hand of the younger women waited a few heartbeats before abandoning their food to follow in her footsteps. Horda was surprised by the look of regret that softened Bear Claw's face before his usual scowl fell back in place.

The Chief of the Tall Grass rose and announced to those remaining beside the fire, "We must plan for the winter."

A murmur of anticipation ran through the group, but all Horda felt was fear. The People of the Tall Grass appeared to have little saved, and any good plan would require time. They needed the time when the fruits and vegetables were ripe and could be gathered, but that time was mostly passed. They could glean some things, but most of what they needed had gone to waste. They would need time — hot days and warm nights — to prepare any fruits and vegetables they could find for storage. They would need time to hunt large numbers of animals and prepare the meat for food, as well as the furs and hides for clothing and shelters.

Even if they started right this moment, they wouldn't possibly have enough time to do even a small part of what was required. She shivered in fearful anticipation of the long, cold, hungry days to come, because she knew, any rescue party would have to wait until the spring thaws to pick up their trail again.

Horda rose and lost her daily skirmish with nausea before the sun began its journey across the sky the next morning. She found Suka beside a crackling cook fire grinding seeds and roots into coarse meal. "What are you making?"

"A porridge of yampah, cattail roots, and pond lily tubers with a few handfuls of chokecherries and service berries to sweeten it."

Horda grumbled, "It won't be very good without meat."

"You're starting to sound like the women here," Suka reproved. "No, it won't be very good, but I don't happen to have any meat to spare just now. Do you?"

Embarrassed by her own thoughtlessness, Horda shook her head.

"I'm sorry," murmured Suka. "We shouldn't argue, especially not with Bird Wing watching us."

"Bird Wing?"

"Yes, she followed you."

Horda frowned. "Should I ask if she'd like to help us?"

Suka chuckled. "I don't think you'd get a very polite response. I'd just ignore her if I were you; it'll make your life a little easier."

They worked silently for a short time, and when Suka looked back at Bird Wing's hiding place, it was empty. She poked Horda. "She's gone."

"Good, I have enough to worry about," said Horda. "Maybe she'll leave us alone for a time."

"Are you still as sick as you were before we left the Gathering?" Suka asked, changing the topic.

"Yes."

"Do you chew the alum root and mint?"

"It doesn't help until after I vomit."

"I remember those days. There's no sickness quite like it. It usually goes away after three or four moons." Suka smiled. "Of course, it doesn't usually start until after two or three moons, but each time you breed it's different."

Horda grimaced. She couldn't hide it any longer, not from Suka, and not from herself. Suka knew she was breeding. Though Horda had suspected it even before Bear Claw captured them, she had buried the thought to avoid having to deal with the consequences.

Now she would have to deal with them, one way or the other. She felt a wash of shame at what she had done, but she fought it down. It wouldn't help her now. Their first priority had to be getting through the winter, whatever it took.

❋

Bird Wing's eyes gleamed from her new hiding place behind Horda and Suka. Here she could overhear everything they said, and their words would be valuable to her and her little one. She rubbed the mound of her stomach beneath her dirty grass apron. *Oh, little one*, she thought, *I will save these words and use them wisely. They will secure your place in your father's shelter and in the People of the Tall Grass.*

❋

As they continued to prepare the food, Suka changed the subject. "Do you think Bear Claw's plan will work?"

Horda remained silent so long Suka repeated her question. "No, no, I heard you," the younger woman said. "I'm just thinking. Though the best time for gathering food has passed, they don't use most of the vegetables and fruits growing here, so there may be more left than we expect. I think we'll also be able to find many foods even though things are past their prime.

"But none of that is what bothers me. If these were our people, Bear Claw's plan would work because we're all used to cooperating to accomplish what needs to be done." Looking around, Horda shook her head. "I honestly don't know about the People of the Tall Grass. The men were angry he even suggested they help us as if such work were somehow beneath them."

Suka smiled in spite of herself. "They weren't half as angry as the ones he told to gather dung." She wrinkled her nose.

Horda laughed. "You were right not to tell me what you used for fuel. I don't think I could have eaten if I'd known, but I suppose we'll all have to get used to it."

Stirring the coarse meal into a simmering cooking bag, Suka nodded. "We were all famished, and the food really didn't taste any different."

"Not really." But Horda was contemplating a new problem. "Do you think three groups of hunters will be enough?"

Suka shrugged. "The gathering of fruits and vegetables is most important since the frosts will soon destroy everything that's left. The men can continue hunting much longer until the blizzards claim the land."

Horda shivered. "I wonder what the winter will be like here."

"Maybe a little easier. We walked toward the sun."

"But there aren't as many trees to protect us from the wind," Horda pointed out. "And we don't have warm clothes, so I guess we'll have to spend the winter in their hide shelters. It will be aw —"

"We'll do the best we can," Suka put in firmly. "We will use all the hides to make winter clothing, but food is most important right now."

"I wonder what will happen to Bird Wing and her followers," mused Horda.

"Bear Claw said they'd help."

"But will they? Sometimes he seems pretty ... I don't know, aimless as a chief."

Just then Unna crept into the firelight carrying two large, finely woven baskets.

"Greetings, Unna," said Suka warmly. "I trust you spent a restful night."

Unna bowed to the two women and hesitated. "Greetings," she finally whispered.

"These are beautiful baskets." Horda traced the close even weave. "Did you make them?"

The older woman nodded.

"We'll use them for gathering food as soon as we finish the morning eat," said Horda.

Unna shook her head.

Surprised, Horda asked, "Why not?"

"Waterbaskets," murmured Unna.

"Waterbaskets?" Horda had seen and used some of the waterbaskets Bear Claw's people carried to trade, but they were all much smaller than these. She couldn't imagine any straw basket so large holding water.

Unna nodded.

Horda looked at Suka who shrugged and went back to stirring the porridge.

Unna would be more help if she talked to them. "I'm afraid I don't understand," said Horda.

"These baskets hold water. I have other baskets to gather food."

"Do they really hold water?" Horda allowed her doubt to show.

Unna smiled. "Come to the stream with me, and I'll show you."

"Hurry back," said Suka. "I'm about to wake the camp for the eat."

Unna's smile faded, and she withdrew several steps as if fearing pain by association. "Bear Claw doesn't like to be awakened. He'll be angry."

"I'd rather he be angry today than me be hungry when winter comes," said Suka, "and we have much work to do if we're going to be ready." *And we will be ready, no matter what the chief likes or doesn't like about the way we do it.*

Chapter 32

Almost two full moons had passed since the Bid Ceremony, and Mach had lost track of the number of false trails they had followed and abandoned. Two days earlier they had found what looked like a real sign of the women's passage, but a fierce autumn thunderstorm washed it away before they got very far. *Mother Life, would they never get a break?*

In spite of their long, frustratingly fruitless search, Mach believed the women were close by. He had no real evidence to support that, but he had to believe it or he would go insane. Now the sun edged its way toward dusk, and a breeze rippled the dry grasses, causing them to whisper secrets none of the warriors could decode.

He could smell the odor of death drifting faintly on the breeze. Turning into the wind, he lifted his head and sniffed. Still subtle, death spoke more strongly in this direction. Apprehension raced through his body. *Horda does not walk the Frozen Wilds. I'd know. Mother Life gave her to me, and she'd find a way to let me know if Father Death claimed her.*

At last. He crept through the grass seeking the source of the stink. No longer subtle, the stench rose in waves to fill his nostrils and coat his mouth. When he topped the small knoll he had his answer. Bison, more than the fingers of five hands, lay lifeless in a small gully.

A natural stampede? No, something didn't look right for that. He crept closer and found a bit of hope. A few of the bison had been butchered by someone. Choice cuts had been taken from those few carcasses. But the others lay untouched. Every bit of four hands of animals left to rot. That was not the way of the People of the Frozen Earth, but would Bear Claw's people purposely kill so many animals and then leave so much to ruin beneath the autumn sun?

Moving upwind in an effort to escape the stink, he signaled the others by whistling a soft bird call at regular intervals. Soon Zaaco crouched beside him and eyed the destruction. "Perhaps a clue?" Mach offered.

"But why would men kill so many and waste so much."

"I don't know. Perhaps the storm made them flee," suggested Mach.

Zaaco shook his head. "The storm only happened two turnings of the sun ago." He moved down wind a way and sniffed. "This was longer." Zaaco's eyes gleamed. "This is the mistake we've been waiting for. We'll be able to find the trail from here, and it will lead us to our women."

Mach edged down the rotten gully wall toward the destruction, scrambling for purchase every step of the way until he simply jumped the few feet remaining. Zaaco followed a short distance to his right. Mach reached the bottom and looked back. He cried, "Zaaco! Watch out! The side is crumbling." His warning came too late.

Horrified, he watched the side of the gully collapse under the additional weight, and he saw Zaaco stumble and skid, fighting for balance before tumbling to the bottom of the gully in a rain of rocks and dirt.

"Father Death, no!" Mach's scream rent the heavy air. With his blood pounding in his ears, Mach raced to Zaaco, who looked like a child's broken leather doll. *It didn't happen. Please, Father Death, not Zaaco. Don't take him. Please, don't take him.*

Blood trickled from a deep wound on Zaaco's cheek, and his face had bleached an unhealthy shade of grey. One leg lay twisted at an unnatural angle. His eyes were closed. Mach's eyes watered.

The old chief's gone. One misstep and Father Death claimed him. Already he walks the Frozen Wilds. Horda. Oh, Mother Life, how will I tell her when I find her? Mach's heart screamed denials. *He can't be dead. We need him. Horda needs him. What are we going to do?*

Then Zaaco blinked. It was a simple movement, but Mach whooped for joy.

Now he could hear other sounds, footsteps, voices. A moment later Elko called from the top of the gully, "Are you all right?"

"No." Mach wiped his hand across his face to erase the tears he had shed. "I mean, yes, I'm all right. But Zaaco's not; he's hurt."

"Over here. Quickly. We need help. Hurry," called Elko to the other warriors. A shower of gravel told of his descent.

Seeing the chief lying so still beneath the autumn sky, Elko exclaimed, "Father Death!" Neither knew nor cared whether Elko's exclamation was a prayer or a curse. "Where does it hurt, Zaaco?" Elko asked gently.

"All over," said Zaaco with a rueful chuckle. He wiped the trickle of blood from the corner of his mouth with the back of his hand then pressed his fingers to the wound, but otherwise he didn't move. "I seem to have gotten myself into a mess."

Elko ran his hands along the length of Zaaco's leg and smiled. "It could have been much worse. I'm sure the leg's going to be a number of shades of black and blue. It is badly twisted, but the bone is definitely whole."

"Good," mumbled Zaaco.

"Did you hit your head?" Elko examined Zaaco's neck and shoulders.

Now Zaaco turned his head back and forth experimentally. "I don't think so. My cheek burns, but I don't think my head is hurt. Thick-skulled and all that," he added, trying for a touch of humor.

Elko continued to run his hands over the old chief's body, checking for breaks or other wounds, and then examining Zaaco's head. "I don't see any swelling or any sign you were hit. You were lucky, old man."

"Humph," muttered Zaaco. "I doubt I can walk."

"At least not in the Frozen Wilds," retorted Elko.

The other warriors watched the proceedings from the edge of the gully, too shocked to utter a word. Now Elko called them to action. "Don't just stand there. We need some of you to carry Zaaco to the trees. A hide will ease the journey, so bring one down. Now, hurry. We have much to do, and I sense we've found the lost trail, as well."

Zaaco would be fine, and there was real hope of finding the captured women. The men sprang to life once again.

Still dazed, Mach watched the men raise Zaaco from the gully. He followed them to the stream beside the trees, but he stood apart.

Elko took charge. He sent one hand of men off to hunt for fresh meat and directed the others to set up a camp in the small grove. Then he looked around until he spied Mach. "Mach, you will help me."

Mach took a hesitant step forward. "I don't know what to do."

"I do. Come." Mach hurried to his side.

Thuro had started a hot fire and set three bags of water to heat over the flames. Elko nodded his approval then opened the parfleche containing the medicine plants Nuroo had given them for the journey. He handed some soaproot to the others, and the three of them scrubbed their hands with a mixture of the root and some warm water from one of the bags.

Once they were clean, Elko began pulling supplies out of the pack. "Thuro, brew a tonic with these." He handed the young man packets of pipsissewa and willow. "Make it strong."

"How much?" asked Thuro.

"A large horn," replied Elko before turning to the brooding Mach. "Wash the dirt from Zaaco's arms and legs with warm water."

Without speaking, Mach went to work. *Why couldn't I have turned just a little earlier? Why didn't Zaaco climb down the gully in another place? Why can't I save any of the people I love?*

Elko dropped a slender bone needle and a thin string of sinew into one of the cooking bags.

Thuro helped the old man to a sitting position and gave him a large horn of the strong tonic. While Zaaco drank, Elko ground leopard's bane and mugwort into warm water to make a wash for the cut on his face. "Mach, bring the needle and sinew. Then steady Zaaco's head for me." The chief grimaced as Elko cleaned the wound, but otherwise he didn't move. "Old man, you're going to have a scar to rival Bear Claw's."

"I seriously doubt it," said Zaaco trying to laugh. "After all, you aren't planning to rub dirt into my wound, are you?"

Elko chuckled. "Not hardly, but my sewing skills don't come close to Nuroo's. Now bite down on this so you don't get my fingers." He slipped a piece of leather between Zaaco's teeth; when it was securely in place, he closed the gash with more than two hands' count of uneven, but tiny stitches. Mach looked away, unable to watch the needle piercing the skin of Zaaco's face. How strange to be squeamish after all he'd been through. They had put skewers in his body for the Dance of the Sun, but that had seemed somehow different.

"Done," Elko announced with a sigh of satisfaction.

Zaaco took the leather out of his mouth and stared at the deep indentations he'd made in it. "I'm glad."

Elko crumbled dried prairie flaxseeds and mugwort. "I'm

making a packing for your leg and another for your face. Between the tonic and the packing, the swelling and the pain should be under control."

"Humph, it was so careless of me. I should have known better."

Mach soaked strips of leather for the old chief's bruised leg. "No, I should have warned you sooner," he said softly. Zaaco glared at the young warrior, and Mach's heart shriveled. *He blames me. His pain is my fault. Just as Horda's captivity is my fault.*

"You can't blame yourself for everything," Zaaco said sternly.

Mach was about to respond when Elko interrupted, "Is this a private pity party or can anyone join? Move; I'd like to wrap Zaaco's leg."

Zaaco tried to smile but pain stopped him. He patted Mach's leg encouragingly. . "Don't make me laugh, Elko," he muttered.

✸

By the time Elko and Mach finished treating Zaaco's wounds and made him comfortable, the hunting party had returned with four deer. Zeek, one of the older warriors, looked triumphant. "Mother Life smiled. The hunting was easy," he announced. "And we've brought Zaaco the liver and heart of one of the deer — for strength."

"Praises to Mother Life," said Elko. "Mach, cook them quickly, then help Zaaco with his eat."

When the food was prepared, Mach brought a wooden bowl to Zaaco and sat silently beside him. After the chief had taken a few bites, he waved the young man away. "I'm too tired to eat any more," he said closing his eyes. "Let me sleep. You eat the rest."

Mach looked down at the bowl, still filled with fresh meat. The old chief hadn't eaten nearly enough; what if he never regained his strength? What if, despite all their efforts, he went to walk in the Frozen Wilds? *What will I tell Horda when I find her? Will she understand? Will she blame me as I blame myself?*

"Mach, what are you doing?" Elko whispered.

Lost in his thoughts, Mach hadn't heard the older man approach; he jumped and almost dropped the meat. "Um, nothing."

"Then come along. You need to eat, too, and we all need to get some sleep. We'll search for the trail when the sun rises." Elko took the bowl from Mach and waited for him to rise.

"I'm not hungry."

"It doesn't matter. Come on."

Reluctantly Mach followed the older man back to the deserted cook fire. "Are you all right?" Elko asked, giving him a slice of the roasted meat the others had fixed.

"Of course, I'm all right," he snapped. "Why wouldn't I be all right?"

"Why don't you tell me?" Elko replied evenly.

"Tell you what?" Mach's voice began to rise. "Tell you my first mate was kidnapped by a savage brute whom I assured her was no threat to any of us? Tell you now her father is injured because I couldn't warn him fast enough that the gully wasn't safe? What do you want me to tell you?"

Elko waited patiently until Mach finished his tirade. "I see. Why didn't you tell me you were responsible for the all the deaths at Gathering, including Meiran's?" he asked in a conversational tone. "And why didn't you tell me you were responsible for those lifeless bison in the gully? Oh, I almost forgot. Why didn't you tell me you caused my foot to bleed when I climbed down to you and Zaaco?"

Mach glowered. "What are you talking about?"

"What are *you* talking about? You can't take responsibility for all that happens in the world. So, tell me, what are you really talking about?"

A dam broke in Mach's chest, and the words poured out. "Oh, Elko, Horda was scared. She tried to tell me Bear Claw wouldn't give up so easily. She *knew* he intended to do something, but do you know what I did?"

"No, Mach, I don't."

"I told her to let the men worry about Bear Claw. I told her he'd weighed the odds and decided he couldn't win a battle with us. I told her he went home. I told her to trust Zaaco and stop behaving like a woman."

"Did you think Zaaco decided by himself to let Bear Claw leave?"

"I guess I did," Mach admitted.

"He didn't. Suka questioned the full Council about Bear Claw. We questioned all the scouts three times. We discussed all the options. Then we voted — all of us. We all allowed Bear Claw and his people to leave. We all share the guilt. There was nothing more you could have done."

"But she was right. Bear Claw knew he couldn't win a fight, so he just stole Horda and the others from right under our noses."

"We made a mistake, and all of us are paying for it, especially our women." Elko looked out across the dark, lonely prairie. "But when we find them, Bear Claw and his people will pay." Elko's words were soft, but they carried a note of viciousness Mach had never heard him use before.

"I accept my mistake, and I'll do everything I can to make it up to my mate," Mach vowed.

"Good," Elko replied, "that's all you can do." After a moment he said, "Mach, I'm sorry Zaaco's hurt, and I know it's going to be harder to find Bear Claw without him. But you're no more to blame for this than I am. We'll take care of him as we should, not only as our chief, but as a teacher and friend. He doesn't blame you any more than I do."

Mach rubbed his eyes with his fingertips, trying to wipe

away the gritty fatigue. "Elko, I know he doesn't blame me. He told me it was his fault — he was careless — and I've told myself the same things you're telling me. I understand them. I even believe them ... I think. But Zaaco's pain hurts me. And I keep imagining the pain the women are suffering. It hurts me too — right here." He pressed his hands against his chest.

"I know, son. I know." Elko pulled him into a clumsy embrace. Mach leaned against the older man's shoulder and sobbed, finally allowing the tears to wash away some of the pain. After a long moment Elko said softly, "Imagining my mate's pain also causes my heart to hurt."

Mach saw the suffering etched in the new lines on Elko's face then lowered his eyes in shame. *Suka is out there too. How could I have forgotten?* Until that unguarded instant, Mach hadn't realized how deeply Elko grieved for his number one mate.

"It seems each time the sun rises, the pain grows stronger, and I wonder if I'll be able to stand it. But somehow I do because I know we will find them and avenge them. Hold onto that, Mach, as I do. Believe in it if you believe in nothing else."

❖

The morning after Zaaco's fall the men were up bright and early, searching intently for Bear Claw's trail. Hazy sunlight streamed down on them from a blue-white sky.

"It's hot," Mach declared, wiping drops of sweat from his face and swallowing against the sickly sweet smell of the rotting bison meat.

Premo fanned ineffectually at the flies swarming around the lifeless bison. "There's no breeze; that's the problem."

Zeek was staring intently overhead, looking from one direction to the next. "Going to snow ... soon," he said sagely.

"Sure, out of a clear blue sky," hooted Mach, discarding his leggings and tunic.

Zeek smiled indulgently at the youth and continued searching the gully rim for footprints or other clues.

A short time later, Mach approached Zeek on the east side of the gully. He was about to apologize for laughing at the older man's words, but Thuro's cry from the southeastern side prevented him from saying a word.

"Signs! I've found the trail!"

Everyone rushed to Thuro's position, where Elko was already examining the faint markings. "They went that way," he said, pointing ahead, "carrying heavy packs." He stood up, surveyed the prairie, and then cursed. "Oh, Mother Life, the storm; we'll lose this trail."

The others looked up, and there was a babble of confusion. The sky had been clear moments before, but now a storm rolled down on them.

Mach refused to allow something as trivial as weather to interfere with their task — not when they finally had a trail in sight. "No, we won't," he declared, "not if we follow it now. They can't be too far away."

Elko stood to watch the storm boiling over the edge of the horizon and moving fast. "We must find shelter and fuel — quickly. And we must protect Zaaco."

Mach was about to protest further when he saw what had alarmed Elko — dark, leaden clouds gobbling up large chunks of the sky above them. "What should we do?"

Elko spoke quickly. "Mach, put on your leggings and tunic. Everyone, get your parkas; you're going to need them. We'll divide into four groups. Two hands of you, bring as much fuel as you can find in the woods, but don't tarry." To the next group he said, "Bring what food you can find. The third group will move Zaaco and the camp into the gully. The rest of you, help me."

Elko moved quickly to the narrowest section of the gully where he calmly began collecting the largest stones he could find. "We'll cover this area with several of our shelters, weight them down with the stones, and get under them. The sides of the gully offer some protection from the wind, but we'll need to wrap ourselves in the rest of the shelters to give us more protection. And these bison will come in handy; they'll give us fuel if not food."

Mach and Thuro helped Zaaco hobble to the gully and dress in the new winter suit Selah had made for him. The other men hurried to their appointed tasks, bringing the scanty wood, their packs, a few roots and berries, and more stones to secure the shelters and build fire pits in the gully. By the time the first fat snowflakes fell, they had secured their makeshift shelter between the gully walls and had four small fires burning.

A small ledge on the gully wall provided a seat for Zaaco. "Put on all your furs," he commanded when the wind first howled in earnest; with the temperature rapidly falling, nobody questioned the need to do so.

Zaaco nodded approvingly when Elko crawled into the makeshift shelter with a bison hump and some bones. "Well done, Elko," he said. Elko hacked off a piece of fat from the hump and placed it in the meager flames with one of the bones, fanning it higher. Going to the other fire, he repeated the process. Soon the semi-rotten fat crackled and hissed. It sent up malodorous smoke, but no one complained; it gave them warmth and light, both of which they sorely needed.

"Maybe the storm won't last long," said Mach hopefully.

Only the wind answered.

Chapter 33

"She deliberately ruined the cattail root meal," Horda complained over the flames of the morning cook fire.

"Shh." Suka shook her head.

"But I know she put the sand in it," Horda inclined her head toward Bird Wing's usual hiding place.

"Probably, but I can't prove it, can you?"

"Of course not." Horda shoved back the hair curling around her face in the humid morning air.

"Then let it go."

"But I'm so tired of her sneaking around behind us always lis —"

"Let her listen. We need to pick our battles carefully, and this one isn't worth the effort; we have more important things to worry about."

That was certainly true. Suka's counting cord had accumulated two more hands' of knots since the women arrived at the camp of the People of the Tall Grass, and winter sent more hints with each turning of the sun. During each and every one of those days, the Women of the Frozen Earth had worked — often alone — from sunup until long after sunset harvesting and preparing food to feed the people during the long cold moons.

"Have you noticed anything different about Bear Claw?" asked Suka, seemingly changing the topic.

"Besides the fact he abuses his own people more than he does us?"

"Well, there is that. But, no, I meant his attitude. He's helped out quite a lot, and he's tried to make his people help, too. He drives them much harder than he does us."

"He has to drive them harder to get any work out of them," grumbled Horda. "They're the laziest people I've ever seen, and they take longer to do less than anyone I ever knew."

"Yes, but he keeps after them. I've noticed he even washes occasionally."

"Too occasionally," muttered Horda, but there was some truth to Suka's words. Bear Claw did seem dissatisfied with his people, and he pushed them to be more like the People of the Frozen Earth. Instead of reasoning with them when they resisted, he became angry and frustrated — yelling, cursing, and hitting. How could these people survive if their chief didn't lead? Horda frowned; thinking about Bear Claw was making her head hurt, and she had too many other things to worry about right now. "If the weather holds for a few more days, I think we'll have enough food to get through the winter."

Suka nodded, "Yes, so don't cause any trouble you don't have to."

"But she started —"

"You're sounding like a young one right now. So what if she started it? You don't need to help her make it worse."

Horda sighed; Suka was right. She would do her best to control herself whenever Bird Wing was around.

"The sun has burned away the dew," Suka said, "so check the bison jerky. A lot of it should be dry. I have more than a hand of fat bison humps, and Unna and the toddlers picked two hands of baskets of chokecherries and service berries. Oh, and I promised Rain Drop and Storm Cloud we'd make pemmican today."

Under Unna's meager protection, Rain Drop and Storm Cloud, the tribe's two toddlers, had barely existed on the fringes of tribal life. When Horda and Suka had arrived, the little ones had immediately attached themselves to the new women, and now they were thriving. It was a joy to watch them, Horda thought repeatedly.

The only real problem had been the first time Horda tried to bathe them. They had screamed and fought like young wild-cats, almost drowning Horda and themselves in the process. Hearing the commotion, Bear Claw had thundered on the scene; ducking behind Horda, the children had immediately subsided into frightened sniffs and sobs.

Instead of angry, Bear Claw had been highly amused, and his laughter had rung through the entire camp. "Horda, it looks like you've finally met your match."

Turning she smiled at the pink and bronze little ones. "I don't think so," she had said evenly, "I think they've met theirs. If you'll notice, we're all three clean."

Bear Claw's eyes had narrowed at her words, and he had half inclined his head in mocking acquiescence to her logic. "So you are. I'll have to remember the technique."

At Suka's words, the two little ones set down their eating dishes and went to the women. "We he'p gadder food," announced Storm Cloud, a tiny boy of three winters. His body bore scars of what must have been harsh beatings, though his will to survive shined brightly in his eyes.

Suka patted his head. "Yes, you've done a good job."

Storm Cloud continued to prattle to Suka, almost as if she were his mother.

Horda's thoughts returned to the fire when Rain Drop, an even tinier little girl, tugged on her tunic and smiled at her with liquid brown eyes. She knew this child had been beaten though the marks weren't outwardly obvious. "Yes," she said, kneeling down and returning the smile, "you wanted to talk to me?"

Silently Rain Drop nodded. She pointed to Storm Cloud.

Horda shook her head. "Storm Cloud's busy. Why don't you tell me yourself?"

Rain Drop scuffed her toes in the dirt and opened and closed her mouth several times before she grabbed Horda's hand. "I h'ep you," she whispered.

Those were the first words Horda had ever heard her speak — to anyone — and she felt overwhelmed with happiness and gratitude that the little girl spoke them to her.

"Oh, baby, you help me — a lot."

Rain Drop wrapped her spindly arms around Horda's neck then ran to Storm Cloud's side before Horda had a chance to respond in kind.

❈

Suka had been right — most of the jerky had dried out in the warm morning air. As she looked at the large drying racks covered with strips of bison meat, Horda smiled. There wasn't enough here to feed the tribe well for the whole winter, but there was certainly enough to keep them from starving if they were careful. And if the men kept hunting, the women would dry the new meat to add to their stores. They might actually survive the winter if ...

Mother Life, what am I thinking? I don't want the People of the Tall Grass to survive the winter. I don't want them to survive at all after what they've done.

No, that wasn't entirely true. She didn't want the little ones and Unna to suffer; they weren't responsible for any of the horrors the rest of the tribe had caused. She cupped her hands around her still flat stomach, imagining her own little one growing there. She would survive and go home, if not for her own sake then for its. She'd worry about the rest when the time came.

"We haven't had this much food saved ahead since many winters ago before all the old women died off." She jumped at the sound of Bear Claw's voice. He laughed at her agitation. "I frightened you, didn't I?"

"No, you didn't frighten me. I just didn't hear you."

His breath scorched her neck, and it made her skin crawl. "You and your women did a good job."

She stiffened her body against his advance. "Yes, we did, but your people helped."

"Not much," he grumbled.

"Not much, but some. Give them credit for that." She smiled at him in spite of herself. "And give yourself some credit, too. You set an example for them." Mother Life, was she actually praising him?

"I'm not used to that," he confessed. "Usually, I just tell them to do things. Sometimes they do them, but most of the time they don't."

"That doesn't seem like a very good way to run a tribe."

"If I care, I knock a few heads together." His grin was strained. "Then they do what I want. The old men used to follow Umbra, the last leader, a lot more. But things are different now, and my way works."

Horda shook her head and rolled her eyes.

"I know, I know, that's not the way of the People of the Frozen Earth," mimicked Bear Claw.

"No, it's not," she said, "and for good reason. We swat little ones until they learn, but gently, so they understand the lesson. My father wouldn't dream of knocking a few adult heads together to make them do his will."

"It works for us now."

Horda looked deeply into his silver eyes. "Does it? You said yourself they often don't do what you tell them."

Bear Claw's muscles tensed, and he glowered at Horda with a mixture of fury and denial. His jaw worked as he tried to find words to refute her allegations, but he couldn't. She watched him war with himself and braced herself for his abuse in whatever form it came.

"It *does* work," he finally forced out through his clenched teeth, then shaking with rage he spun on his heel and stormed away.

Now, she'd done it. Never mind he knew she was right, he'd make her pay for challenging his sense of the world, if not right this minute, then later tonight when he forced himself into her furs. She went back to collecting the jerky and pushed him from her mind.

✳

A short time later, Bird Wing joined her at the drying racks. Just what she needed, Horda thought bitterly.

"Bear Claw sent me to help you."

"Oh, did he?" she asked acidly, "like you helped with the cattail root flour?"

"What?"

"Never mind," Horda snapped. "I don't need any help."

Bird Wing shrugged. "Suit yourself, but you won't finish. A storm's coming."

"A storm?" Horda raised her head and sniffed the hot, still air. In truth, it did feel like a storm.

Bird Wing pointed to a dark smudge across the northwestern horizon. "Bear Claw thinks we'll get the first snow of the winter."

Horda frowned. "But it's too soon for snow. We haven't finished gathering fruit and vegetables, and the meat isn't dry enough."

Bird Wing smirked. "Tell the Great Mystery."

Horda looked around the vast expanse of prairie to the small group of hide shelters. *Mother Life, these people have almost no fuel for heat or cooking, and their shelters are even flimsier than the summer shelters of my people. How will we survive?*

She looked back to the northwest. While she had stood there thinking, the distant smudge had crawled above the horizon to become a low line of roiling clouds; it was going to be close. She gestured toward the filled baskets. "You can take those to Suka. Then bring more baskets." Bird Wing made a mock gesture of servitude before picking up the filled baskets as slowly as she could and sauntering away.

✸

The coming storm must have frightened Bird Wing more than she let on because now she was hurrying; she returned with a hand of stacked baskets before Horda had filled her one remaining basket with dried meat. Horda grabbed an empty basket from the stack and began frantically separating the meat into two separate piles.

Bird Wing grew impatient. "Never mind that, just hurry! Leave all the meat in one basket."

"We don't want the undried meat to sour the dried meat," Horda explained, her hands still separating while she spoke. "If we don't separate it, all the meat will ruin, and we'll go hungry."

"Takes too much time," muttered Bird Wing, reaching past Horda and sweeping meat off the nearest rack into her basket. "Besides, it doesn't matter. My mother always took time to separate the meat and went on and on about how important it was to keep the meat safe."

"She was right about —"

Bird Wing interrupted. "Shows how little you know. She must not have been right because something happened to the meat she so carefully separated two winters ago. She and most of the other women got sick and died. All that work, and it didn't make any difference."

Horda didn't know what to say — she didn't want to feel any sympathy for Bird Wing, and she suspected Bird Wing wouldn't want it even if she gave it, but it was a terrible story. Before she could reply, four more Women of the Tall Grass, each carrying several large baskets, joined them.

"Suka and the others are gathering those roots and things," announced one of the women. "We'll help you."

Horda opened her mouth to protest when the women began throwing the meat into the baskets without regard for its level of dryness, but a cold wind blew down the prairie, toppling the baskets and chilling her to the bone. The dark clouds had climbed a quarter of the way up the northern sky, turning the day into sudden night. She closed her mouth and joined them, sweeping the meat off the nearest rack into a basket. There wasn't time to worry about anything but getting the meat and themselves inside.

Mother Life, storms rose quickly in the mountains, but this one on the prairie moved faster than any she had ever witnessed. The women had barely grabbed the last of the meat when the wind began to howl in earnest, and the first fat, wet snowflakes were falling when they piled into Bear Claw's shelter at a dead run.

"I never saw a storm strike so quickly." Horda was almost out of breath as she added her basket to the ones arranged around the wall of the shelter.

Bird Wing shrugged. "It happens more often than not."

"I must check on Suka and the others." Horda headed for the shelter opening.

Bird Wing grabbed her arm. "Don't go back outside."

"I have to. They might need help."

"Bear Claw will help them if he's there."

Horda pulled her arm free. "I want to be sure they're safe before the storm gets any worse."

Bird Wing shrugged again and adopted a sage expression; it looked entirely out of place on her grubby features. "You'll get lost. You'll walk the Great Beyond."

"That's ridiculous."

"You saw how fast the storm came. You made it to safety.

You should stay, 'cause it's only going to get worse."

"Maybe you don't care, but I can't leave my friends out there." Horda wrapped a fur around herself and grabbed another to put over her head before she ducked outside the shelter.

Mother Life, how the landscape had transformed itself! Suka's shelter was nothing more than a ghostly image in a swirling maelstrom of white. Horda called out, but the screaming wind stole her words. She clawed her way across the open area to the shelter, grabbed the hide covering the door, and pulled herself inside. She breathed a sigh of relief when she found Suka and the others safe.

"Mother Life, child, what are you doing here?" asked Suka, taking Horda's wet furs. Rain Drop grabbed Horda's hand and pulled her closer to the fire.

"I was afraid you were caught outside."

"Bear Claw sent us inside," announced Storm Cloud.

"He made us quit just before the storm hit," Suka told her. "Everyone's safe, as far as I can tell."

"Did you get all the roots and things?"

Suka shook her head sadly. "We got as much as we could, but it'll be a long hungry winter, I'm afraid."

"Do you know where Bear Claw is?"

"I think he's checking the others. He wants three hands of people in each shelter."

"Three hands?" Horda blinked in surprise. "That's far too many; there won't be room to breathe."

"He said something about it being warmer. You know we don't have much fuel."

"No, no, we don't, I guess you're right." Horda peered out the opening. "I can still see his shelter."

Suka stood beside her. "Just barely."

"Well, since you're safe, I guess I'd better go back so he won't come looking for me and get lost himself."

Lost? Why am I worried about him getting lost? Because I

don't want him lost, I want him lifeless, preferably at my hand and with all our men to witness it.

Suka nodded. "Okay, but I don't trust this storm. I have a supply of sinew. I saved it to sew winter clothes, but I haven't stripped it yet. I think it's long enough to reach to your shelter. I'll tie it to my wrist and you tie it to yours. When you get to your shelter, tug it three times quickly so I'll know you're safe."

Horda smiled as she tied the cord around her wrist. "I'd rather stay here."

The older woman wrapped the furs more tightly around Horda's shoulders. "I'd rather you stayed too, but you should go."

"I'll see you when this is over."

"I'll be waiting."

Horda pulled her furs over her head and plunged into the swirling snow, trailing the cord behind her.

Chapter 34

After giving three sharp tugs on the sinew and receiving Suka's response, Horda carefully loosed the cord from her wrist and retied it to one of the outside shelter supports then ducked inside. Bear Claw slapped her chilled face and knocked her to the ground before she even saw he was there.

"How dare you!" he thundered.

"How dare I what?" She scrambled to her feet and yelled back at him.

"You were safe here in my shelter, but then I find you went right back out again as if this entire storm was just a passing breeze. Do you realize you could have been lost, and that we might not have even found you until the spring thaws, if then?"

"But I wasn't lost. So is my crime here that I went out, or that I didn't die? I always like to know why someone hits me."

"Don't take that tone with me!" He took a deep breath and tried to regain control of the situation. "So why did you go out?" he asked offhandedly.

Horda was not fooled by his demeanor; she realized he did care about her — at least as much as a man of his sort could. "I worried about Suka and the others, so I went to check on them."

"But how did you get there and back? The snow's already blinding."

"I could see their shelter so it wasn't that hard. As soon as I knew they were safe, I came back because the storm's getting worse and I didn't want you out looking for me."

"And," he prompted, trying to cover his surprise.

"And what? I used a cord attached to me and to the other shelter. When I was back, I tied my end to one of the shelter stakes."

"There's a cord between the two shelters?"

"Yes."

He appeared to consider the implications. "So I can go to Rushing Water's shelter without getting lost in the storm?"

"Ah, I don't know for sure that Suka secured the end in her shelter, but she probably did. And anyway, you can leave the end tied here to guide you back safely even if she didn't."

Bear Claw went to the fire and kicked aside the two men sitting nearest. Then he beckoned Horda to his side. "Sit down and tell me what else you know about surviving the winter." His voice was as cold as the wind outside.

He looked angry, Horda thought, but why should that be? Was he angry that he hadn't thought of the rope himself, or was he angry he now required her help, not just for that one thing, but for their very survival? A good chief should recognize when he needed help, but Bear Claw ...

She took the offered seat and thought carefully before she said another word. "Since this is my first winter storm with you, I don't know whether I know anything else you don't. I may only tell you what you already know." She paused, thinking about the caves in which her people passed the winters.

"There's more you want to say. Tell me."

"Well, I wonder how comfortable we'll be in these shelters." To punctuate her words, the wind whistled through a weakened seam.

"Our shelters are much like those of the People of the Frozen Earth," Bear Claw said, as though speaking to a particularly stupid child. "I looked them over while we were at your Gathering."

"Those are our summer shelters."

Bear Claw frowned. "Summer shelters?"

"Yes, we live in those in the warm moons while we hunt and gather. Before the blizzards come, all the bands move into their winter caves."

"You have caves?"

"Yes, each band has a permanent shelter for the cold moons. The caves started as natural formations, I guess, but with the turnings of the seasons, each band enlarged theirs and fixed spaces for each family — storage areas, sleeping areas, and a central assembly area. Oh, and a bath pit, of course."

"A cave?" He seemed stuck on that idea.

"Yes."

"Are you telling me you don't live in hide shelters during the winter?"

"Of course not. It's hard to heat the hide shelters and easy for them to blow away in the blizzards. I'm sure you know that."

Bear Claw's frown darkened, and his attention focused inward. It was true — sometimes the shelters caught fire because they tried too hard to heat them or were careless. And every winter at least one shelter blew away in spite of all the ways they tied them down; some, if not all, of the people inside it froze to death before they found safety. She'd just named the two worst problems his people faced. "Explain!" he commanded.

"Explain what?"

"Explain about the winter caves."

"I'm not sure I can," she said truthfully. "They're just big caves in the sides of the mountains, and the bands live in them. As a band grows larger, they enlarge their cave."

"What happens to the smoke from the fires?"

"There are some holes to the outside. I think some of them occurred naturally, but the men dug most of them. The holes guide the smoke up and out. At least most of it." She grinned ruefully.

"Doesn't the snow block the entrance?"

"No."

"Why not?"

"I don't know why not unless it is because the caves are high, much higher than the ground around them. Most of them are in the sides of the mountains; we have to climb a ways to get to them." She puckered her brow and counted on her fingers. "Actually I've only seen a hand of the winter shelters, aside from our own, and four of them I saw during summer hunts when there was no snow.

"One had a really big opening, but the band had built a wall of wood and hides around it, and their path was kind of protected. Our path usually doesn't get blocked except in two or three places, and the men and boys push the snow away from them before it gets too deep. The snow doesn't collect anywhere else. I don't know why, it just doesn't. I never really thought about it before."

Bear Claw scowled. As uncomfortable and dangerous as the shelters were, he had never considered living anywhere else during the winter, until now. "Caves are dark," he said, trying to find something for which Horda wouldn't have an answer.

"Of course," said Horda. "We use lamps and torches for light."

Bear Claw shook his head. "I don't want to live in a cave."

Horda shrugged. "Nobody said you have to. You asked me to explain, and that's what I was doing."

Bear Claw's face darkened. She stiffened her body, expecting to feel his hand smack across her face, but all he did was look at her with those icy silver eyes. She could feel them bore through her, and she shivered.

"You could help my people."

Horda was confused; wasn't that what she was doing? "I don't understand what you're talking about."

"Your people live better than we do." He made it sound like an accusation.

"Well, yes, we do," she agreed slowly, unsure how she was supposed to respond.

"It isn't fair!"

"Fair has nothing to do with it." A sudden flash of anger and homesickness loosened her tongue. "The People of the Frozen Earth work very hard for what we have."

"My people work hard; you said so yourself."

Horda raised an eyebrow. *Sure, they do, but only when you kick and hit and threaten them. The rest of the time they pretend to work and watch the Women of the Frozen Earth behind their half-closed eyelids. Who're you kidding?* She watched the muscles in Bear Claw's jaw reflect the battle he was waging within his own mind. A feeling almost like sadness flooded her — he really didn't understand the difference between them.

"We do work hard," he repeated.

"I didn't say you didn't. It's just ... your people could do so many more things to make their lives easier."

Suddenly defensive, he snapped, "Our lives are fine the way they are. Don't come in here trying to change us!"

Horda's eyes narrowed. "I'm not trying to change you."

"Of course you are," whined Bird Wing, creeping up beside Bear Claw and clinging to his arm. "You made us gather all those weeds and things, and you're always telling us to wash and clean up, just like my mother and the other women used to — and look where it got them."

"Stay out of this!" Bear Claw backhanded Bird Wing with barely a glance. She scuttled away.

Horda shook her head and fought her own anger. "*You* asked us to help you prepare for the winter, and we did, in the only way we know how, the way we do at home. I'm sorry if we upset you, but we only did what you asked us to do."

"You are insufferable, woman!" Bear Claw roared. "Why did I ever think I wanted you?

Why indeed? Horda thought to herself. Why indeed?

Chapter 35

"Give me that, you old crone." Bird Wing spat at Unna, who clung to the largest basket of dried meat. Unna didn't reply, nor did she relinquish her hold on the basket.

Bird Wing's voice rose, louder and louder, until Bear Claw charged across the shelter. "What in the name of the Great Mystery is going on?"

"I'm hungry," whined Bird Wing, clawing at Bear Claw like a petulant child. "I like the dried meat best. I just want a little, but she won't give it to me."

"You disturbed me for that?" He backhanded Bird Wing and would have hit Unna, too, had she not crouched behind the basket.

Horda raced across the cluttered shelter floor. "What's the problem?"

"She wants this meat," whispered Unna.

Bear Claw demanded, "Give her the basket, old woman, or I will put you out in the storm this instant."

Horda took a deep breath, confronting the chief yet again. "You most certainly will not!"

"What?"

She watched his muscles tense and knew his anger was about ready to erupt again. Though her insides quaked and her knees felt like water, she stood her ground. "She will not give Bird Wing the basket, and you will not put her out."

"I've had it with you, woman ..."

"I'm sure you have," Horda interrupted, "but that meat is well-cured, and it'll last a long time. The meat in the other baskets isn't dry, and if we can't finish drying it before the next blizzard it will sour. Anyway, we should eat the less-dry meat first in case we can't dry it later."

"Fine, have it your way. Eat some of the other meat, Bird Wing," Bear Claw said, "and don't disturb me again."

"It's more trouble. It needs some cooking," whined Bird Wing.

"Then go hungry." Bear Claw returned to his seat beside the fire.

She sniffed disdainfully. "Anyway, we'll eat that meat at the feast."

Horda's head snapped up. Feast? What feast? They barely had enough food as it was.

Bird Wing glared at Horda and Unna who were sorting the meat.

"What feast is she talking about?" whispered Horda, turning her back so Bird Wing wouldn't overhear.

"After the first blizzard, they have a feast and eat all the undried meat before it ruins," breathed Unna.

"All of it?"

"Yes."

"But there are more warm days when it could be preserved. Isn't a feast awfully wasteful?"

Unna nodded. "Of course, it is. This would never have happened in the old days, but times have changed; these young people don't understand what they were taught or choose not to remember it, and we are all paying the price."

"Isn't there anything you can do?"

"I am an old woman," Unna replied, "and of little apparent value to the tribe. I do what I am told."

"As you must, I know." Horda touched her hand sympathetically. "I'm going to set the meat that isn't fully dried outside so the cold air can preserve it until we finish curing it."

Unna nodded. When the baskets were full, Horda took the undried meat and started for the shelter opening.

"Where are you going now?" growled Bear Claw.

"To put this outside."

"Leave it here."

"So it can sour?"

"I told you, we'll eat it soon."

"But we don't need to eat all of it," argued Horda.

"Eating it keeps it from spoiling." Bear Claw smiled at her like she was a not-too-bright child.

"So does putting it outside to freeze until we can finish drying it," replied Horda, using the same artificially sweet tone he had. She could see his jaw muscles tense.

"I told you we'll eat it when the blizzard's over, so put it down and do something useful for a change."

Do something useful? That's all she did around here, useful things, and he was one to talk. She gritted her teeth, trying to rein in her temper; she was not going to give in on this point, no matter what. "Bear Claw, there's enough undried meat here to last more than a moon. It won't spoil if we put it outside to stay cold, and when the sun comes back, we can finish drying it. Winter's just beginning, and we're going to need this and more."

Bear Claw's fists clenched, and he took a menacing step toward her. Before he could do anything, Bird Wing boldly grasped his hand and said, "She's trying to poison us. You know we can't eat meat if the snow's spirit gets in it. That's why she wants the meat outside. She's trying to kill us all."

Horda stared incredulously at her.

"See, she doesn't deny it," Bird Wing crowed triumphantly.

Horda finally found her tongue. "What is she talking about?"

"As if you don't know."

"I certainly don't know what nonsense you're spouting."

Horda emphasized each word. "My people always freeze the undried meat when the blizzards first come. It's true the jerky made from frozen meat doesn't have the same flavor as the fresh, but it fills hungry bellies, and it doesn't poison anyone."

"I don't believe you; the snow spirit is strong," Bear Claw said.

Horda stiffened with anger. "I'm sure it is, Bear Claw, but I don't lie. There's nothing to be afraid of."

As soon as she said it, Horda knew her choice of words had been entirely wrong. Bear Claw's eyes narrowed dangerously, and he moved so close his hot, fetid breath warmed her face. Behind him Bird Wing cackled, but he was so focused on Horda that he didn't even seem to notice.

"I am not the one who should be afraid, woman. Do you know what I believe? I believe you hate me. You hate me so much you would not only kill me, but you would kill the rest of my tribe, too. You'd use the snow spirit to rob me of my power."

Something snapped inside Horda. All these weeks of worry, of suffering, of emptiness, loneliness, and shame came together in a burst of blinding rage, and she lashed out at the man responsible for it all.

"Yes, Bear Claw, I hate you!" Flecks of spittle sprayed his face. "I hate you for taking me away from the people I love, from the life I would have had. I hate you for all that and much, much more, but think about it — as a chief for once. If I poison you, I poison all of us, including myself. Now why would I do that? I want to survive, just as you do, and I can't survive with poisoned meat. And I don't need to rob you of whatever power you think you have; you're doing a fine job of losing it all by yourself."

The two stood nose to nose for a moment that seemed like infinity. Bear Claw moved first. He grabbed her by the hair and yanked. She gasped with the pain and sank to her knees on the cold ground before him.

"You lie," he whispered fiercely. "I will prove you wrong, and then I will make you pay for what you have done." She had no doubt he meant every word.

Still holding her by the hair, Bear Claw dragged Horda toward the door flap. With one hand he pulled a fur across his broad shoulders and threw another at her. He lifted the hide and pushed her out into the snow. "Find the cord," he hissed.

Quickly she located the long sinew beneath the drifted snow and pulled it out. "Now go!" he commanded, and she began to move, placing one hand in front of the other along the cord. Still holding onto her, Bear Claw followed in her wake.

Mother Life, she wished she had her mittens and winter parka. She held the half-cured furs around herself with one hand and shivered. It wasn't nearly as cold as it was going to be, and she was already freezing. She clenched her teeth to stop their chattering. Her feet sank into the soft snow; she'd always hated using snowwalkers, but now she wished she had a pair to make the going easier.

As they approached Rushing Water's shelter, Horda allowed herself a grim chuckle. Suka had lined her own meat baskets outside; it certainly lent some truth to what she had said. Bear Claw didn't spare them a glance before he lifted the door covering and pushed her inside.

Rushing Water jumped to his feet. "Bear Claw, we, ahm, I didn't expect to see you until the storm spirits quieted."

Bear Claw headed for the fire. "I would speak with your woman," he said without preamble. Horda noticed he didn't even have the decency to call Suka by name.

"Um, which one?" Rushing Water asked hesitantly as if afraid to present him with the wrong person.

"The new one, fool. Her!" He pointed sharply in Suka's direction.

Eyes blazing Suka stepped toward the fire. Horda moved to join her, but Bear Claw's arm blocked her way.

"Stay there!" he barked. "By the opening."

Suka stood silently, forcing Bear Claw to make the first move.

"Why are those baskets outside?" he asked abruptly.

Horda watched Suka fight not to balk at his rudeness. Before she could answer, Rushing Water sputtered, "I tried to tell her —"

"Silence!" Rushing Water retreated quickly. "Answer my question, woman,"

Suka smiled graciously. "Some of the meat in our shelter wasn't preserved, so I placed it outside to freeze. When the sun comes back, I'll spread it out once more so it can dry. The jerky won't be quite as good, but it will fill hungry bellies. I'm sure Horda's done the same thing."

Bear Claw's face almost purpled with rage. "What if the snow spirit makes its home in the meat?"

"The what?" Suka asked, looking to Horda for help.

"I tried to tell her, but she wouldn't lis —" sputtered Rushing Water.

Suka looked directly into Bear Claw's eyes. Horda thought he would be wise to respect this woman. "I don't understand what you're talking about. We always freeze meat in our tribe as I'm certain Horda's told you."

Bear Claw returned Suka's glare, but his voice held the hint of genuine curiosity. "And you eat it after it's been frozen?"

"Of course, don't you?"

Rushing Water looked about to say something else, but he stopped as Bear Claw stood abruptly. "I see," was all he said.

"What's this about?" Suka asked him, but at Horda's shake of the head, she stepped back and said nothing more.

"We will leave you to wait out the storm," he told Rushing Water, heading toward the door. "Horda, come!"

Mother Life, I am not a dog, Horda thought. Although Bear Claw's look had become introspective, she could still see the anger rippling beneath the surface, ready to explode. Whether he would acknowledge it or not, Horda knew she had won this skirmish, but she couldn't help feeling the battle was far from over.

Chapter 36

"If we huddle together, we can share our bodies' warmth."
Mach spoke through blue lips.

Elko divided the last of the bison meat and bones for the
fires. "Except for a little wood, this is the last of our fuel."

"I didn't think this storm would last so long," commented
Zaaco to no one in particular.

"It's too early in the winter for such a vicious blizzard."
Thuro shivered and beat his hands against his sides.

Mach grinned at Thuro in spite of his own discomfort.
"Perhaps you should go outside and tell the blizzard spirit to
move on then." Laughter rippled through the crude shelter.

An angry flush painted Thuro's face, and his fists clenched.
"Thanks a lot, Mach. I just meant —"

"To tell us something we already know," taunted Mach.

"Enough!" Zaaco's voice brought an immediate silence to
the shelter. "Contrary to the way it feels, we're not likely to
freeze to death unless we do something stupid, such as fighting among ourselves. So please spare us your childish arguments
and save your energy for survival."

Mach and Thuro shrank into their furs at the thunderous
look on Zaaco's face.

"I don't know, Zaaco, a good fight might warm all of us,"
Zeek said.

The corners of Zaaco's mouth turned upward. "I think we're
all a little tense from being cooped up so long; my apologies. I

do think, however, we need to spend more of our time focusing on how we're going to get through this storm and less on bickering, no matter how entertaining it might be."

The others nodded and murmured their assent.

Elko spoke up. "We need more bison fat and bones."

"I'll go." Mach and Thuro spoke at the same time.

"Good," said Zaaco. "You can both go. Maybe a walk in the snow will cool you down."

Elko nodded. "Take a digging tool and the cord so you don't get lost. And bring back whatever you find that might possibly burn when it's dry."

Glad for any activity, Mach and Thuro hurried outside the meager shelter. Though blanketed by the snow, the bottom of the gully was somewhat protected from the biting wind. Mach looked around until he spotted a large lump in the snow and trudged toward it. "Over there," he called to his friend. "That's probably another carcass."

The snow was packed, but at least it wasn't yet crusted with ice — the work was hard but doable.

"Do you really think we'll find them after all this time?" Thuro asked.

Mach stopped digging and looked at his friend, shocked to hear his own silent question spoken aloud. All his fears rushed through him, chilling his already cold body even more. But he couldn't admit his doubts, not even to Thuro; putting them into words might give them a reality he didn't want to create. "The women depend on us," he replied evasively.

"I know that; that's why we're all here. But Zaaco's injury will slow us, and this blizzard will cover the trail we worked so hard to find. If we can't find it again, we won't be able to track them," said Thuro.

When Mach spoke, his voice was low and vicious, fueled by an angry determination. "Don't ever say that to me again. We'll find them; we have to. And when we do, I'll kill Bear Claw myself for what he's done."

"I'm sorry, Mach, I'm just concerned is all. I shouldn't have said anything. You know I'll do what I can to help."

Mach's normally warm eyes were icy slits. "Say what you like, but when it comes to Bear Claw, just stay out of my way. Then I won't need help-from you or anybody."

✦

She couldn't see the sky in the stuffy, smoke-filled shelter, but Horda knew the blizzard had raged for a full turning of the sun. It was miserable inside. They were certainly warm enough jammed together like winter wood. She lifted her hair from the back of her neck and fanned her face, but it didn't help much. Neither did the alum root and mint. She chewed them faithfully, but the awful nausea still simmered in her stomach.

The smells inside their tiny refuge didn't help. The stench of unwashed bodies, sweat more than a whole summer old, dried blood from the meat, rancid bear grease, and other foul odors she tried not to identify pounded her in waves. She forced herself to breathe shallowly through her mouth. She was just tired, she told herself. Between all the people and the raging storm, she hadn't slept last night. Now her imagination made the odors worse than they actually were because she couldn't get away from them. They turned her stomach.

This sickness will go away of its own accord. She had told herself this over and over, but it never did any good. She still tried to deny she was breeding even though she knew better. In fact, she'd known since her moon cycle failed to appear the first time. And she'd suspected even before the Bid Ceremony. Without thinking, she cupped her hands protectively around her still nearly flat stomach.

Tears burned the back of her throat, and she wondered — would she and Mach be punished for what they'd done? Perhaps when the Men of the Frozen Earth came to rescue them, they'd assume her little one belonged to Bear Claw and wouldn't ask further. Perhaps ... Suddenly a powerful wave of nausea bubbled through her, and she staggered to the shelter opening.

"Where are you going?" Bear Claw barked as soon as he saw her move. He hadn't let her out of his sight for a moment even though there was nowhere for her to go.

Horda didn't pause to answer before she ducked outside into the biting air.

"I told you she tried to poison us," smirked Bird Wing. "See, it didn't work, and she's ill herself."

"Silence, woman!" Bear Claw roared and punched her face with his fist. "Do not ever mention that again or I will poison you myself!" The handfuls of others looked at him questioningly, but no one dared speak; there were some questions better left unanswered. He growled at them all then yanked the flap aside and followed Horda into the snow. "You're still sick," he accused, watching her heave.

She looked up at him. "How could you tell?"

"Don't toy with me." He hesitated a moment. "You didn't do anything to the food, did you?"

She rolled her eyes. Weren't they past this yet? She scooped up a little clean snow to wash the bitter taste from her mouth before she responded. "Bear Claw, I thought we settled that matter yesterday. And anyway, if I were smart enough to poison the food, do you truly think I'd be dumb enough to eat it myself?"

"Then what's wrong?"

"It's very close in the shelter. Actually, it stinks."

"Stinks?"

She nodded, warming to her subject. "Yes, stinks. There are three hands of people in a shelter not really big enough for one hand."

"We crowd together to keep warm," defended Bear Claw, tensing again.

"I know, and it works well" she soothed. "But your people haven't washed since ... since ... oh, I don't know when they washed last, but I can tell it wasn't recently." Turning a definite shade of green, she swallowed hard to keep from vomiting again.

Bear Claw looked suddenly alarmed, and he stepped back quickly. "Will others catch your illness?"

"Unless I'm mistaken, Bird Wing already has my illness."

"That wretch!" he spat. "Did she give it to you? I'll have her thrown in the river for this!" He turned back toward the shelter, but Horda stopped him.

"No, no, she didn't give it to me," she began, but Bear Claw jumped back from her touch as if it would burn him.

"Don't touch me! Have you lost your mind? We lost most of the women of our tribe the last two winters, and I won't have you sicken us again."

Though her face still bore a definite green tinge, Horda smiled. "I'm not sick, and neither is Bird Wing."

"You just said you were. Stop talking in riddles."

"I'm going to have a little one. There, I've said it."

Bear Claw's entire bearing changed in an instant. His face relaxed, and his mouth rounded with surprise. "A little one? Are you sure?" he asked, almost gently.

"Well ... without Nuroo to examine me, no, I'm not totally sure ..." His excitement quickly paled, and she tried to smile reassuringly. It wouldn't do to anger him any more than she already had. "Yes, I believe that's what's wrong with me."

Bear Claw grinned and thumped his chest proudly. "I knew you were the woman for me. Already breeding, imagine that. You'll bear me many fine sons." He lifted her off the ground and hugged her, oblivious to her discomfort.

Horda had to bite her tongue to keep her anger in check. The truth wouldn't do anyone any good right now, but it could do Mach a great deal of harm if it came out.

Bear Claw set her on her feet and grabbed her arm. "Come

back inside out of the cold."

"I'm more comfortable out here," protested Horda.

"No, you could become really ill. You must come inside," he insisted, suddenly very protective.

She opened her mouth to argue, but the cold wind bit through the thin furs she wore. Reluctantly she allowed him to pull her back into the smelly, stifling shelter.

As they entered, Bear Claw puffed up his chest and announced, "Horda doesn't feel well. She carries my son."

Most of the people huddling in the shelter smiled broadly, if not sincerely, at their chief and offered him congratulations. A son. Children. Survival. A few frowned, and Horda could hardly blame them. Even though they knew breeding was the reason Bear Claw had captured these women, the women were still foreigners. And to base one's survival on a foreigner ... well, she would feel the same way they did right now if their places were reversed.

Bird Wing neither smiled nor gasped. She whispered behind her hand to the other Women of the Tall Grass, and they all snickered loud enough for Bear Claw to hear. He rounded on them.

"Share your words," he commanded.

"Gladly," Bird Wing smiled like a cat content after its feathered meal. "I was questioning how you know it's your son this woman carries. Perhaps it belongs to one of her own people. She talked to the older woman about the breeding sickness the first day after you arrived here."

Horda felt a blush creep up her face, but she refused to lower her eyes. *Don't let him question me. Please.*

Bear Claw's eyes narrowed, but he thumped his chest and bragged, "I am her first man. It's my son she carries."

"I," announced Bird Wing haughtily, "carry your son."

"Perhaps," said Bear Claw with a cruel smile.

"Perhaps?" squawked Bird Wing. "Why perhaps?"

"There are many more Men of the Tall Grass than women, and I don't trust you to stick to any man's bed, even my own. Who can say whose child you carry? Now congratulate my mate."

Hatred burned through the tears in Bird Wing's eyes, but she obediently mouthed words of congratulation. No one, even Bear Claw, thought for a moment they were genuine, but it was the act that was important — it was one more way the chief could demonstrate his power. Briefly Horda thought about telling them all Bird Wing was right, the child she carried wasn't Bear Claw's, and she'd be glad to give Bear Claw back to his former mate and go home. She knew it would not only be foolish but dangerous. There was no telling what Bear Claw would do to her — and to the rest of the Women of the Frozen Earth — if he was made out to be such a fool. No, it was best to hold her tongue and bide her time; surely the men would arrive soon and this nightmare would be over.

After all had spoken and Bear Claw had gone to sit by his men and brag about his virility, Bird Wing approached Horda and said in a voice dripping like sweet molasses, "I have some herbs to ease the sickness of breeding. I could give them to you if you want."

The alum root and mint had once helped, but recently they had been useless; Horda tried to remember other herbs she might use, but she couldn't. Giving up, she decided to take Bird Wing up on her offer. "I'd appreciate them," she said graciously. "I used herbs Suka gave me, but they don't help much right now." Her stomach lurched again from the smells and oppressive warmth of the shelter.

"I'll get them. They'll make you feel much better," promised Bird Wing with a lop-sided smile.

Warnings sounded in Horda's mind. *Bird Wing hates me. Why is she suddenly being kind? Still, if there is a chance her herbs will help ...*

"Perhaps you should eat these now. Your face is the color of early spring grass." Bird Wing handed Horda a few dull black berries and three large smooth leaves. "Chew them carefully, then be sure to swallow every bit."

"What are these?" She eyed the offering suspiciously; her healer woman training screamed caution. "They look kind of like black nightshade."

Bird Wing's eyes narrowed. "I ... ah ... am not sure what they're called. I ate them when I was first breeding. They really do help."

Horda looked carefully at the leaves and berries. "Black nightshade's very poisonous," she said evenly.

"It is?" Bird Wing sounded so innocent, but something in her eyes made Horda uncomfortable. "I'm sure they aren't black nightshade then. Eat them, you'll feel better."

Once more Horda's nausea overwhelmed her, and still clutching the berries and leaves, she dashed from the shelter to vomit in the snow. Glaring at Bird Wing, Unna followed her outside.

"Old woman, stay inside," snapped Bird Wing, but Unna paid her no heed.

Mother Life, even my toenails hurt, Horda thought as the retching caused her whole body to spasm violently.

She looked at the berries and leaves clutched in her hand and remembered the relief Suka's herbs once brought. She was desperate, so desperate she was willing to take a chance. She raised her hand to her mouth.

"Don't!" Unna suddenly appeared at Horda's side. "Let me see those," she commanded in an unusually firm voice.

Horda turned to the old woman. "Please, Unna, I'm so sick." She swallowed to keep from retching again.

"I know, but give them to me first." Unna held out her hand.

"Maybe these will help." Desperation made her voice sound weak and whiny.

"They'll help you permanently," said Unna. "If you eat them without proper cooking, you will depart."

"Depart?" Bear Claw growled. He appeared beside the women.

"Yes, depart. These are deadly if not properly prepared." Though Unna lowered her head and refused to look at the chief, her voice was stronger than Horda had ever heard.

A murderous rage twisted Bear Claw's scarred face. He snatched the offending berries and leaves from Unna's hand and shoved the women toward the shelter. Inside he yanked Bird Wing to her feet and shook her until the teeth she had left snapped together. Then he thrust the herbs forcibly into her hand. "Eat these. Now!"

"Why? I'm not ill." All color had drained from her face.

"I said eat them!" he repeated, glaring at her.

Her eyes betrayed her fear, but she tossed her greasy hair and said flippantly, "If your precious Woman of the Frozen Earth doesn't want my help, she doesn't have to accept it. I'm just trying to ease her sickness. I thought you wanted me to help."

"Help her permanently?" The muscles in Bear Claw's arms and neck popped from the tension.

"Of course not." Bird Wing backed away.

"Liar!" Bear Claw roared, catching the woman by the throat. She gurgled weakly then let her body go limp. He growled. "Eat them! Show me they're harmless."

Bird Wing's eyes measured the distance to the fire. Horda watched and knew Bird Wing's plan as surely as if she had spoken her thoughts aloud. Didn't Bear Claw realize?

Bird Wing eyed the herbs then turned and flung them into the fire. "If she doesn't want my help, I won't offer again," she shrieked.

Bear Claw's rage took on a life of its own. He pummeled Bird Wing's face and legs; his fist smashed into her stomach, causing her to double over. He grabbed her hair and dragged her to the shelter opening, much as he had done the day before with Horda, only more violently. "Leave!" he thundered. "And don't you ever return!"

Bird Wing's eyes were already swelling from the beating, but Horda could still see the desperation within them as she realized this time there was no escape; her voice quivered. "I only tried to save you from claiming one of her people for your own. I heard her talking to the older woman. She was already —"

Horda froze waiting for Bird Wing to finish her accusation, but Bear Claw shook Bird Wing violently again, cutting off her words. Bird Wing put her hand to her swelling face. "Please, Bear Claw, don't put me out in the storm. I'll freeze, and so will your child."

But Bear Claw wasn't listening. He grabbed her under the arms and pulled her closer to the shelter opening. "You tried to kill my mate. You're no longer welcome in my shelter, or anyone else's in this tribe!"

Overwhelmed with panic, Bird Wing dug her heels into the dirt floor and shouted, "I'm trying to protect you. I was your mate long before you ever saw her. I heard her tell Rushing Water's woman —"

Horda watched Bear Claw lift the struggling Bird Wing and shake her like a child's doll until she was silent. Then he dropped her to the ground. The blood drained from Horda's face as she felt every eye in the shelter trained on her. *She knows. Mother Life, she knows, and now everyone else suspects what she says is true. If Bear Claw realizes what she said, he'll kill me.*

Horda gritted her teeth to keep them from chattering and forced herself to stay as still as possible so she wouldn't draw the chief's attention and make him question Bird Wing's words. As she stood there, she imagined how she'd feel if Mach ever put her aside for another, and she felt an unwelcome sympathy for Bird Wing. Before she even realized she had uttered a sound, she heard herself say, "Bear Claw, perhaps she didn't realize what they were. Possibly she made an honest mist —" Oh, Mother Life, what had she done?

All eyes were now focused on her. Unna gasped. Bear Claw watched her, torn between astonishment at her actions and the rage he still felt for Bird Wing. It was Bird Wing, who responded first. Smearing the blood on her cheeks, she rose to face Horda.

"Don't make excuses for me, whelp. I'm the young medicine woman of this tribe, and I didn't make a mistake. I know about plants and herbs, just as I know the child you carry does not belong my chief. You are welcome to suffer from the sickness —"

Bear Claw's rage won, and his fist slammed into Bird Wing's face, breaking her nose with a sickening crunch. Blood spurted everywhere, and she wailed piteously before the chief buried his other fist in her stomach, silencing her.

Horda tugged on Bear Claw's arm. "Stop. Please, stop. You'll make her lose the little one."

Bear Claw swatted Horda away and resumed viciously and systematically beating and kicking the injured woman, who now lay in a bloodied heap at his feet, ominously silent. Lifting the cover of the shelter opening, he kicked her inert body into the snow and secured the opening behind her.

"You mustn't leave her outside. She'll freeze," Horda pleaded.

Bear Claw looked into Horda's frightened eyes. Coldly he said, "It doesn't matter; her life is over." Then his brow puckered. "Why are you taking up for her?" he asked curiously. "She tried to kill you, and she lied about you. What are you not telling me?"

Horda stepped back, suddenly panicked. How could she keep from angering him more? She chose her words carefully. "I imagined myself ... in her place."

"Her place?"

Horda nodded. "I'd hate it if Mach put me aside for another."

She should have said nothing, she realized, as rage flashed through his eyes and his balled fist cracked against her cheek. "You may hate me, woman, but I am your life. You're mine, now and always. Don't you ever forget it!"

I will forget about it every chance I get, she told herself vehemently, but she remained outwardly silent. There was nothing more to say.

Chapter 37

The blizzard had raged the entire day and well into a second night. Shortly before sunrise, Mach startled awake. He listened for what had awoken him but heard only silence. That was it — it was quiet out there. "The storm's over," he whispered, afraid to break the spell.

Zaaco woke at the sound of Mach's voice, raised his head, and looked around. "Yes," he said, "it is."

Mach was on his feet, stuffing things in his pack without regard for order. "Good, then let's go."

"Aren't you forgetting something?" Zaaco asked calmly. "In fact, several somethings?"

"I don't think so," Mach replied, looking around the shelter.

"Then let me help you out. First of all, how about a plan?"

"Plan? We have a plan," Mach reminded him.

Zaaco shook his head. "We *had* a plan. Two days of snow covered whatever trail was there, and now we have nothing left to follow."

"We still know which way they went, so why can't we just head in that direction? I'm sure we'll find the trail again once we're on our way."

"Mach, your determination is admirable, but you have to learn patience." He held up his hand to forestall Mach's protest. "Patience, Mach, can be just as important to a hunter or a warrior as action; you need to know when to strike and when to assess. So second of all, what about me? Have you stopped to consider that I can hardly walk? I certainly won't be able to travel with you and keep to your pace."

Mach stared at his moccasins. "Um, I guess I kind of figured we'd pull you on a travois."

"Oh, I see. I know that would make it quite easy to sneak up on Bear Claw and catch him unawares." Mach began to tense up until he saw the smile curving Zaaco's lips and realized how ridiculous he must sound. "I'm glad you'd be willing to take me along, truly I am, but I'd be a hindrance. It would be better for me to stay here."

Mach frowned. "Alone?"

Zaaco chuckled. "I'm careless, but I'm not totally stupid, Mach, no matter what stories you might have heard. I imagine there are two warriors who'd be willing to help the old chief in his time of need."

"I'll stay," he told Zaaco. Although his words were strong, his tone displayed his inner battle.

"No, you won't," said Zaaco firmly.

"You don't trust me?"

"As I said, Mach, I'm not stupid; please give me some credit. It's a question of need — I need to remain here, but you need to follow the trail; you can serve all of us better doing what you do well. Do you understand me?"

Mach was humbled by Zaaco's words, and he understood much better now how and why the man had come to lead the People of the Frozen Earth. He hoped someday he could be even half the chief Zaaco was. He hung his head. "Yes, I do."

"Good," Zaaco said, then raised his voice. "Gather round so you can hear me." He struggled to his feet to give his words the power of his position. "I believe we're close to Bear Claw's camp, and we will not have long to wait before we find our women. My leg is healing, but I cannot walk a long distance yet and will need two warriors to stay with me and bring up the rear."

Zeek and Hubra, two of the older warriors immediately volunteered. Zaaco nodded; they were experienced, but they were old enough they might slow the scouts if they accompanied them. "The rest of you will continue to search for our women. We'll follow your trail after two turnings of the sun so we won't be noticed. If you find them before we catch up to you, come back for us." He paused. "Elko, stand up."

A murmur whispered through the assembled warriors as Elko stood before the chief. Zaaco waited for silence before he raised his hands and spoke. "Elko, I ask you to lead this war party in my stead. Find the People of the Tall Grass. Punish them for what they've done and bring our women home. Do you accept this sacred duty?"

Elko raised his hands to touch Zaaco's. "I accept this sacred duty, and I will do my best to fulfill it." He stepped back among the rest of the men.

Zaaco returned to his seat. "Then be on your way, and may Mother Life grant you success."

The men rushed around the shelter, collecting their belongings and preparing to depart. Elko sent a hand of them outside to scout the area and find out if the trail was still visible. As Mach watched Elko coordinate their efforts, he wondered how Elko could organize so calmly knowing their women were finally near.

His heart warmed at the mere thought of Horda, and he smiled inwardly as he remembered the night they spent together beside the river. But he felt something now he hadn't when they were together — conflict. It had seemed so clear after the Dance of the Sun that they were meant to be together — that Mother Life herself wanted them to be together — so that joining before the ceremony was the most natural and acceptable of actions. But in the eyes of the tribe, in the beliefs they all held dear, it was wrong for them to have done it, and now he felt ashamed. How could he reconcile the two feelings without Horda here to give him support?

Horda, sweet, funny, gentle Horda, was suffering. He knew it as clearly as he knew his own name, and that was almost too much for him to bear. As the image of Bear Claw's scarred face burned in his mind, Mach's anger ignited. Instead of trying to dampen it, he allowed his anger to fan the flames until they fairly consumed him.

A little voice in the back of his mind reminded him to respect life — all life, even Bear Claw's — but he refused to listen. When he found Bear Claw and his people, he would tear them limb from limb with his bare hands. He would make them suffer as much as they had made him and his own people suffer, and he would revel in their screams of agony. Surely, that would not be wrong in the eyes of Mother Life or the People. It would be just punishment for what Bear Claw had done.

Mother Life, why did Elko move so slowly? He must have snow water in his veins to be so calm and controlled. They had to move now, to pick up the trail before it disappeared forever under the melting snow. Determined to get them moving, Mach focused back on the present and discovered all the men were gathered around Elko; he alone stood apart.

"... when the sun comes up. It feels like the air is already warming." Elko looked at Mach questioningly.

Embarrassed to be caught unawares, Mach pretended he knew what Elko had said. "Yep, I'm ready to go."

"Do you have snowwalkers?"

"Snowwalkers?" Mach looked blank. "Of course not."

"Then how can you say you're ready?"

"Well, I meant I ..." Mach's voice trailed off as the other men began to chuckle.

"Okay, I guess I was thinking ahead," he admitted, unwilling to divulge what was really going on in his mind. Why was that? Was it because such thoughts were wrong? Some part of him agreed, and it made him even more uncomfortable. "What did you say, Elko?"

Aware only of the young warrior's impatience, Elko had to smile at his inattention, but he hid it behind a faked cough so as not to cause more distress. "The snow's deep but soft, and we'll make better progress if we use snowwalkers. We can make them with the hides of the bison carcasses and some of the green wood we found at the watering hole. They won't be very sturdy, but we probably won't need them long anyway."

Mach nodded.

"Let's get started. Two hands of you go for the wood. Bring a supply of wood for Zaaco and his men to burn while we're gone, as well. The rest of us will prepare the bison skins. The faster we get this done, the faster we'll be on our way."

Faster was good, Mach thought to himself as he rushed to get the supplies they would need.

❋

By the time the sun's first pink tints brightened the snow fields to full light, the men had provisioned Zaaco's camp and fashioned primitive snowwalkers for everyone. They were ready to set out.

Elko pointed toward the southeast. "We know they went in that direction, but we don't know whether they went over the little rises or around them. They could have traveled almost due east or," looking at the lay of the land, he frowned, "almost due south."

Mach opened his mouth but closed it without speaking. *Patience, I must learn patience. Elko is in charge now, and I need to let the man finish before I butt in.*

"The problem is, we don't know how far they traveled in whatever direction they went, nor do we know how the land lies there. Surprise is going to be the most important thing. We can't go blundering into their camp like a herd of blind bison, or it may end up in disaster."

Mach frowned. He hadn't thought of any of those things, and he knew he should have. He was letting his desire to get Horda back and take vengeance for her capture cloud his judgment, and it was making him overlook important details. Grudgingly he conceded to himself Elko might be moving as quickly as was prudent.

"Do any of you have suggestions how we should proceed?" Elko was asking. The silence stretched. "Mach, you looked like you wanted to say something earlier."

"I did, but I hadn't thought it through," Mach admitted.

"When you're ready, please share your thoughts with us."

Mach opened his mouth to decline, feeling abashed by his previous failures, but Zaaco poked him firmly in the ribs with a piece of wood. Finally he said, "I thought we could spread out and search a wider area than if we stayed all bunched up together. The land's flat enough we could probably see each other if we were four or even five hands of arm's lengths apart."

Elko nodded. "That's true, but you hesitated. Why wouldn't this be a good plan?"

"Well, the land provides little cover. It will be difficult to hide ourselves even if we're not spread out. We won't have the element of surprise."

"True," agreed Elko, "but that raises a good question."

"What do you mean?" Mach asked, not following his reasoning.

"If we have to cross the flat land, how can we hide ourselves in plain view?"

Despite his attempt to remain patient and controlled, Mach's temper flared. "I don't know or I'd ..." He subsided when Elko arched one eyebrow at him. "Sorry," he muttered.

"I was just thinking," mused Thuro, "that each of us has a shelter."

Now Elko looked puzzled. "And . . ." he coaxed.

"And the insides of them are sort of white."

"How would that help?"

Thuro coughed softly. "Well, I don't know if this will work, but couldn't we sort of disguise ourselves as lumps of whi ..., well, not quite white, but sort of white snow. We could drape our shelters over ourselves like capes and creep along ... maybe?" He looked at the others, hesitantly hopeful.

"Of course," several of the men said together, suddenly understanding.

"That's a great idea!" Mach clapped Thuro on the shoulder. "If we move slowly enough, they shouldn't even notice we're not part of the natural landscape or drifts of snow. And we can brush our paths with branches until the snow melts."

"You've both done well," Elko said. With the proper training and experience, the People of the Frozen Earth will have fine leaders in those two. "We'll probably need our shelters for warmth for a while anyway, so it shouldn't be too hard to use them to conceal our movements, too."

Elko tied on his snowwalkers and reached for his pack. "Don't forget your snow masks," he instructed. "The snow will be blinding even if it is melting quickly." Elko looked the men over. "The sun has begun its journey for the day. It is time to continue ours."

"Wait," said Mach.

Elko looked at him questioningly.

"I ... ah ... thought of something." He fidgeted with his mask, pushing it up his forehead while he spoke. "Don't we need to discuss what we'll do when we find Bear Claw and his people? How will we communicate? We may not have the opportunity to talk about it then."

Zaaco coughed to cover his chuckle at Elko's surprised look. Quickly regaining his composure, Elko asked, "What do you recommend?"

"I think we need to plan," Mach echoed Elko's earlier words.

"Well, we can't use bird calls to signal since there don't

seem to be any birds around right now," said Thuro.

"No, we can't," agreed Elko.

"We can't use hand signals because they might be too visible and give us away," offered Premo.

"Probably," Elko conceded.

Cryon said, "I heard some coyotes before the blizzard started."

"I did, too, but there are too many of us to pass such a signal from man to man. It would be out of place," said Thuro.

Mach frowned with concentration. "Yes, there are," he said slowly, "but two or three calls should be enough to alert all of us without Bear Claw becoming suspicious, don't you think?"

Elko considered. "Probably. When we hear the signal, we'll double back to meet and decide what to do."

"Um, there's one more thing," Mach said awkwardly as if afraid he was pushing his position too hard. "If the snow hasn't melted by the time we find them, we'll need to cover our tracks when we back up also."

"We can smooth them away with our branches, the same as before," Elko responded. "It should work just as well, I'd think."

The other men quickly nodded. Mach thought briefly before he replied, "I guess."

Elko stared at Mach. "But you aren't sure."

"Are you?" the young man challenged.

Zaaco chuckled at the exchange. Swallowing his own grin, Elko declared, "No, I'm not, but it'll certainly be easier if we can. There are things we cannot know in advance; no matter how carefully we plan. Flexibility is just as important as patience. Why don't we travel a little way and see how this works? Then we'll decide if we need to change." He lowered his snow mask and adjusted the eye coverings.

Mach fastened his own snow mask. "That sounds fine."

"Then unless anyone has anything else to add, we're ready to go. Zaaco, will you ask the Spirits' protection for us?"

Zaaco raised his arms and intoned, "Mother Life, guide these men on their journey and give them the strength and courage to find our women and bring them back to us. Father Death, spare our men and take our enemies into your kingdom where they will face your judgment for the crimes they have committed."

He lowered his arms and nodded to Elko, who signaled the men. They picked up their packs and draped their shelters over their heads, setting off into the unknown.

Chapter 38

A dream of Mach, of flowers, and of home — this was the first good dream Horda could remember clearly since her capture. She drifted in the pleasant haze of memories, unaware of anything that had not appeared in her sleep.

As she tried to move, the present came crashing back in a sudden, painful wave — Bear Claw, Bird Wing, fists, blood, and an ache so deep it touched her soul. An involuntary whimper escaped her lips. She flexed her face muscles. They hurt, but not as much as she expected — just a gentle ache; she would have to thank Unna for the horn of willow tonic that let her sleep so her body could heal.

Unna was such a mystery in many ways. Tiny, frail, little old Unna wouldn't so much as say a word to Bear Claw and cringed every time he walked nearby, but she openly defied him to tend to her face. And Unna, who bore the insults and abuse of the tribe daily, had exposed Bird Wing's plot at the risk of her own life. Who would have thought Unna capable of such miraculous feats? She was a more powerful healer — and leader — than anyone gave her credit for.

Horda tried to open her eyes but couldn't. Could it be she was really dead? That Bird Wing did kill her? That everything she thought now was a remnant of her previous life and was no more substantial than the dream she thought she just had? She could hear a voice, becoming louder as she struggled to adjust to her surroundings. Was it Father Death? No, it couldn't be, it was a woman's voice, but whose?

"Horda, wake up. Wake up!"

Unna. It was Unna's voice — she must still be alive.

Unna shook Horda, bringing her fully awake. "The blizzard's over, and we've much to do today. Wake up."

"I can't wake up," she whimpered, her voice edged with panic. "I can't open my eyes. I can't wake up."

"What nonsense. You're awake, girl. You can't open your eyes because of the packing I put on them to help the swelling." Unna chuckled softly and peeled the damp squawroot leaves off Horda's face. "Now, open your eyes, child."

Horda forced her eyes open, then immediately closed them against the light streaming in.

Unna caught her chin and turned her face to and fro, inspecting the blackened eye. She clucked, "Nothing works for swelling like squawroot — except snow. And squawroot doesn't work as well without the snow. Your eye's almost normal."

Horda blinked experimentally then covered her good eye. "It really doesn't hurt ... much, and I can see out of it."

"Good, Bear Claw did enough damage without you having to worry about your sight."

Tears filled Horda's eyes — tears of rage and guilt. "He killed her, didn't he? Bear Claw killed Bird Wing because of me."

Unna shook her head. "I don't believe this. Look at me." Horda lowered her eyes.

"No, I said look at me!" Reluctantly the young woman obeyed. Unna spoke firmly, with an authority she didn't show anyone else. "You didn't cause Bird Wing's death."

Horda struggled to rise from her sleeping furs. "You mean she survived?"

Unna placed her hand on Horda's shoulder and pushed her back. "No, I don't mean she survived."

"I'm sorry, Unna, I'm so sorry. I didn't mean for this to happen."

"Of course, you didn't!" Unna said forcefully. "But by blood of the Great Mystery, girl, I don't understand you one bit. She tried to poison you. Then she tried to turn Bear Claw against you by telling him about your little one."

"I know, but ... aaaaa" Horda's guilt was replaced by fear. Bird Wing had opened a door that couldn't be closed again. The Women of the Frozen Earth would remember now she was already sick at the Bid Ceremony. The People of the Tall Grass would realize, too, she was sick long before she arrived at this place.

"But nothing! Bird Wing was bad." Unna spat on the floor of the shelter — this gesture made Horda think of Bear Claw and she didn't want anything of this kind woman to remind her of him. "Always causing trouble. Though she claimed to be a medicine woman, more often than not those in her care embraced the Great Mystery. Humph! Last winter when food was scarce, many hungry little ones ate the bl —" She broke off suddenly when Bear Claw stepped into the shelter.

Horda barely acknowledged the chief's presence while she dressed. As she crawled to her feet, Unna pressed several small pieces of alum root and some dried mint leaves into her hand. Smiling gratefully, Horda chewed them before stepping around Bear Claw and slipping out into the crisp, morning air. Ah, freedom.

It was a rude awakening. Just outside the shelter, blood stained and frozen stiff, Bird Wing's body lay in a twisted heap.

As a healer woman, she had seen death many times, including the recent passings of Meiran and Brash. But this — this hit her almost as if it were Bear Claw's fist smashing against her face again. This was cruel, violent, senseless. No matter how bad Bird Wing had been she had not deserved such a death and neither had her unborn child.

Yet a part of Horda was thankful. Bird Wing laid there, not her. Bear Claw hadn't believed the woman's hurtful words even if they were the truth, and he had taken out his anger on the messenger. *Thank you, Mother Life for sparing me, even at the cost of another. May this never go any farther so I can return home and live the rest of my life among those I love.* She repeated the words, hoping they would soothe the pain. She stumbled across the camp to find Suka.

She didn't have far to go. Suka was already plowing through the deep but melting snow to meet her friend.

"Horda, isn't it a lovely day? We can put the rest of the meat out to dry if this weather holds. We'll —." Suka stopped in mid-sentence when she saw Horda's battered, tear-stained face. She caught the younger woman in her arms and held her tightly as she sobbed out her grief. Once the sobs subsided, Suka pushed back the fur so she could better examine Horda's face. "What happened? Tell me what happened."

"She walks the Frozen Wilds, but she told Bear Claw the little one I carry does not belong to him, and now she's lying frozen stiff back there in the snow."

Suka looked thoroughly confused. Best to start with the first part and work her way through. "Who's dead?"

"Bird Wing."

"Bird Wing? Was she the one who did this to your face?"

"No, no, that was Bear Claw." Horda's words tumbled over each other like water over stones in a flood. "He found out I'm breeding and told the entire shelter he was going to have a little one, and she gave me some poison berries and told him my little one doesn't belong to him and he b —"

Suka grabbed Horda's shoulders and made her look at her. "Slow down, child, so I can understand your words."

"I'm sorry." Drawing a deep breath and gulping back her tears, Horda explained everything that happened, slowly and in detail.

Suka listened patiently until Horda ran out of words. "Well, I have to say Unna's right; Bird Wing caused her own death. But how did Bear Claw learn you're breeding?"

"I ... told him." Once more Horda explained.

"And what did he do?"

Horda said sourly, "He grinned and thumped his chest and bragged and hovered over me. I hate to say it, but it reminded me a bit of Fa, and the way he behaves when one of his mates is breeding."

"Yes, but what did he do when Bird Wing said your little one wasn't his?" Suka's voice took on a note of urgency.

"I told you. He beat her and put her out in the blizzard."

"You didn't cause Bird Wing's death," Suka said again. They both knew Bear Claw would eventually realize Bird Wing's words were true.

Slowly Horda nodded, "I know, but now the words have been spoken aloud. Everyone knows, and I can't —"

"Knows what?" Suka demanded. "They know nothing."

"They know Mach and I —"

"Were promised and should have mated more than two moons ago."

Horda nodded miserably. "Should have, but — "

"But nothing," Suka hissed. "Do not speak those words aloud; they have no place here. Bear Claw kidnapped you and stole you away from your chosen. He joined with you without your consent and gave you the impossible job of finding food for his lazy people. Did you ask him to do any of these things?"

Horda shook her head.

"No, of course you didn't. And you certainly didn't ask him to put a little one in you. So keep quiet; you have nothing to answer for. We'll get through this."

"Will we?" Horda asked. "I'm beginning to wonder."

"Yes," answered Suka fiercely, "we will. We'll all go home and live the lives Mother Life intended. I'll be the number one

mate of Elko, and you'll be the number one mate of Mach."
Suka forced a smile. "And we're the ones who'll lead the men
who think they lead the People of the Frozen Earth."

"Oh, Mother Life, I hope so."

"Good," Suka announced. "It's time for our men to find
us."

"What do you mean?"

Suka shaded her eyes with one hand and gestured with the
other toward the gently rolling prairie to the west. "I mean, by
my reckoning, our men should be coming over those hills any day
now." She seemed to look inward. "I'm tired of being a captive.
I'm ready to go home, and I'll give Elko a piece of my mind if he
makes us wait much longer."

Horda smiled at Suka's tone. "I don't see any hills."

"Well, neither do I, but I can pretend I do. Hills make for
good cover." Suka lowered her voice in case any others were
listening. "I believe our men are close."

Horda felt a thrill of anticipation. "Why?"

"I don't know why. I just do." Suka turned and raised her
voice, as if they were discussing nothing more than a cooking bag
or the change in weather. "Ah, here's Bear Claw now. Greetings,
Bear Claw. Since the storm has passed, Horda and I would like
to prepare the morning eat here in the open."

Bear Claw ignored Suka and gazed intently at Horda. "How
do you feel?"

"Me?" Something was wrong. He never worried about how
she felt; he hadn't even come by last night when Unna was treating the wounds he inflicted. "Ah, I guess I'm fine," she said evasively.

"Are you still sick in your stomach? Are you going to throw
up again?" His eyes seemed to look straight through Horda. It
was very disquieting.

"Not now, no. Now, I'm just hungry." *Mother Life, help me.
He knows the little one I carry is not his.*

Suka tried to diffuse the tension. "I asked if we —"

"I heard you, woman. I don't care where you cook, just get it done." He held Horda in his gaze for another moment, scrutinizing her from head to toe, then turned on his heel and stalked away, leaving her to wonder what would come next.

Chapter 39

Creeping cautiously through the snow was cold, wet, and body-numbing. Mach was bone tired. His legs burned from dragging the unwieldy snowwalkers through snow turning liquid beneath them. His arms ached from constantly sweeping his tracks away behind him. Already in its downward journey toward night, the sun still reflected brilliantly off the whiteness and made his eyes smart behind the snow mask.

At the top of a gentle incline, he slipped the mask up and rubbed his face, careful not to open his eyes. Surely Elko would call a rest soon. He was about to say something to that effect when he heard a sound, the unmistakable, lonely howl of a coyote. He quickly replaced his mask and squinted through the slits at the distant horizon. He couldn't see anything, so he began inching back down the rise. Halting partway down, he gazed at the line of trees filling a small dip in the otherwise flat view

He reminded himself to be careful; many people's lives were at stake. It might not be anything, but if it were Bear Claw's camp, they might have lookouts, and he didn't want to risk being seen before they were ready to make their move.

Frustrated, he raised his snow mask and stared intently at the smudges on the horizon. He realized his mistake when his eyes began to throb and tear, and he quickly eased the mask back into place. There was no question it hampered his normal vision, but without it the snowfield blinded him. He blinked his burning eyes and cursed himself for a fool. Another coyote call brought his attention to the present. Carefully smoothing the snow in front of him by touch, he backed down the incline to join the others.

At the bottom, he bumped into Thuro. "Did you see?" he asked.

"See what?"

"I thought I saw some smoke above those trees or bushes over there." Mach patted a thin coat of snow on his eyes to ease the burning.

"Where?" Thuro asked.

"Almost straight ahead."

"Are you sure?"

"No, I lifted my mask to get a better look," Mach admitted.

"And couldn't see a thing," finished Thuro. "For a smart man, you do some pretty stupid things."

"I know," agreed Mach, rubbing the snow off his burning eyes and grinning, "but usually I have you to blame."

"Thanks," Thuro said sarcastically.

"How are we doing?" Elko had come up behind the two, as quiet as ever in his traditional sneak-up mode. "Except for being cold and wet with aching legs and trouble seeing through your snow masks, of course?"

In spite of himself, Mach grinned. He admired Elko's technique; the man acknowledged all their major complaints.

Trefo, the warrior who had chosen Lija, scuttled up beside Thuro. A thin, quiet man, he scuffed the snow at his feet for a moment before he found the courage to speak. "I'm not sure, but I thought I saw smoke on the far horizon. I couldn't see well enough through the slits to tell for sure."

Thuro clasped Mach's shoulder. Elko saw the gesture and said, "Did either of you see anything?"

Mach rubbed his eyes once more. Elko watched him, knowing the cause of his distress, but he did not scold. The burning would soon pass, and there was no greater teacher than experience — he had made the same mistake when he was Mach's age and had never repeated it.

Thuro poked Mach again. "Answer him."

Mach said, "I also thought I saw some smoke, right above those trees or bushes that fill the notch in the horizon. It was almost as far as I could see, so I'm not sure either."

"Did anyone else see anything?"

The warriors looked at one another. An older man named Ferno said, "I thought I saw a smudge in the sky, but like the others, I decided I imagined it. Perhaps I didn't."

Elko nodded. "With three possible sightings, it's likely we're near an encampment, possibly Bear Claw's. That means we must be even more cautious to avoid giving ourselves away. Remember, we have one major advantage: surprise; if we lose that, we may lose everything." He waited for his words to sink in, but it was clear everyone already knew how much was at stake.

"Good," he continued. "Thuro, your eyes are probably the best here. Slip up to the top of the rise and tell us what you see."

Thuro didn't speak, but he looked hesitant. Mach whispered, so low no one else could hear his words, "There is a dip almost straight across from where I was. That's where I thought I saw the smoke." Thuro nodded his appreciation and crawled up the rise.

✦

Dropping the new parka she was sewing, Horda shaded her eyes and peered across the plains mottled with patches of melting snow. After conspiring with the gentle breeze to melt the snow left by the blizzard, the warm sun was sliding beneath the gentle roll of the horizon in a soft orange and lavender haze. Horda ignored the chattering of the Women of the Frozen Earth who sat around her, working leather and sewing winter clothing;

388

she found listening put her more on edge than she already was.

"By my reckoning, our men should be coming over those hills any day now." Suka's words echoed in Horda's memory. Could they really be true? Would Mach come for her and take her away from this place, back to her home? Home. Would she ever feel safe there again after what she'd been through? Maybe that's what was really troubling her, but she had no answers.

She blinked and rubbed her eyes. They were tired and gritty from all the close-up work, so she must be imagining the things they saw now. It wasn't possible for mounds of snow to move. A cold wind pierced her thin furs, and she shivered. To make matters worse, her stomach rumbled so noisily the women stopped their talking and laughed.

"Hungry?" asked Suka.

Horda nodded. She rolled her sinew and stowed her needle and awl in her sewing pack. The time had come to prepare the evening eat for these people anyway, so she had best get to it. Why? A little part of her mind asked plaintively. Of all the Women of the Tall Grass, only Unna helped them willingly; the others went out of their way to make the lives of the Women of the Frozen Earth difficult and degrading. They helped only when they were forced to, then they did as little as they could get away with. And the men made no secret of how little they liked or respected them, abusing them whenever they got the chance. Why should she help any of them?

Because her survival was tied to their survival, and she wanted to survive, for herself, for Mach, and for their little one not yet born. Because she would not let a thug and bully like Bear Claw determine the outcome of her life. Because she was better than they were, and she wouldn't allow herself to stoop to their level. They might not appreciate anything she did, but that was their problem, not hers.

Climbing to her feet, she met Bear Claw. His face was totally unreadable — not a good sign. At least if he were scowling, yelling, or spitting, she would know what to expect; this way she hadn't a clue.

"If you'll excuse me, I must help the others with the evening eat." She tried to step around him.

He shifted to block her path. "Are you in a hurry?"

"It grows late." She rubbed her arms suddenly covered with goose bumps. "Now the sun sets, and it grows colder. We need to eat and get inside."

"The others will prepare the food."

"They need my help, and I have nothing more important to do right now."

Oh, that was the wrong thing to say; she knew it as soon as the words left her mouth. "You are talking to me." His tone matched the ice in his eyes.

"I'm sorry," she said truthfully. "I didn't mean to upset you."

He traced the line of her jaw. His hand was gentle like the calm before the storm. "But you did," he said. "You know, you almost had me convinced." Then his fingers clenched her chin, forcing her face to meet his. Tears filled her eyes. She struggled, but she couldn't break away. "But you lied," he accused.

"I don't know what you're talking about," she said brusquely, trying to cover her fear with bravado.

"Of course, you do. Little Horda isn't stupid, is she? But in spite of what you say, you *are* afraid of me." He pushed her away, hard; she stumbled but didn't fall.

"I am not afraid of you." She looked him straight in the eye, but she had to lace her fingers together behind her back so he wouldn't notice their trembling.

"You should be."

The soft, almost gentle tone of his voice frightened her even more. She tried to laugh, but it sounded more like a sob. "I already told you, I don't know what you're talking about."

"I think you do." He reached out and grasped her shoulders now, pulling her toward him again. Brutally, his fingers dug into her flesh until she gasped from the pain.

"After all your talk about your precious Rituals of Mating and the Wrath of Fire, I didn't even question, but I should have, shouldn't I? Do you think I'm that much of a fool?" He spat into the snow. The women around them grew very quiet. Many backed away. But all of them watched; they were afraid to look but somehow even more afraid to look away.

Horda was so frightened she couldn't answer. *Now he believes Bird Wing. Mother Life, there's no hiding it now.*

Her silence only seemed to fuel his anger, and he shook her hard. "Well, I'm not! The little one you carry does not belong to me," he spat. "Does it?"

Horda licked her lips, which had gone suddenly dry. "How ... How can you ask such a thing?"

She didn't see the first blow coming, but she felt its force against her stomach. She tried to double over, but Bear Claw held her upright so the next blow hit the same spot. *Mother Life, he is going to kill the little one within me.* She had to protect it, protect herself, but she knew there was nothing she could do.

And there wasn't. Punctuating each word with a punch, Bear Claw spat, "Because — I — was — not — your — first — man." He hit her again and again.. *Mother Life, am I going to end up like Bird Wing?*

Bear Claw suddenly released her, and she dropped to the ground, rolling herself protectively around her stomach. But it wasn't over yet. Bear Claw drove his foot into her back, her side, her legs, or whichever part of her body was most exposed.

"You suffered the sickness of early breeding when I captured you," he snarled, "but you said 'I think it was something I ate.' You knew, but you lied to me. Can you deny it?" He pulled her to her feet though she could barely stand on her own.

She was angry, frightened, outraged. She would have loved to spit in his face and tell him what she really thought, but she didn't have the strength, and she knew he would kill her if she did. And ... and it was almost as if he wanted her to deny it. So she tried to form the words he wanted to hear, to somehow explain it all away, but her lips seemed to be made of stone.

"Of course, you can't!" he roared then he punched her so hard she stumbled away to land in a heap at Aiyana and Lija's feet. "You'd rather have that weak, mewling pup than this chief. You're useless, even for a woman!"

She lay on the ground gasping and terrified of the silence that had suddenly descended. She tried to remain perfectly still, afraid the slightest movement would start his beating all over again, and he'd finally kill her ... and her little one. But there was only silence; when she risked a glance upward, she realized he had gone away, leaving her there like so much discarded trash. Now her fingers tightened reflexively over her stomach, which was awash with pain such as she'd never felt in her entire life.

Father Death, please don't take me. I still have so much life to live, and I want to go home.

She clung to the pain as if to life itself, using it to remain in the here and now. And then it began to squeeze tighter and tighter, causing her breath to come in raspy gasps, she finally understood — she might not be departing, but her little one already walked the Frozen Wilds. It was almost too much to bear. She moaned once before allowing the darkness to take her away.

Chapter 40

"Someone, build up the fire and heat water," commanded Unna, rummaging in her medicine bag.

Suka was impressed. The timid old crone was gone and in her place stood a confident medicine woman. She must have been quite a formidable woman when she was younger; her current status was a waste of talent. Ayianna tended the fire while Suka arranged Horda's limp body carefully on the bed of furs in Unna's tent.

"I often assist in the delivery of little ones, but I'm not a medicine woman," Suka admitted.

"Well, I am." Unna's voice was clear and strong.

"Tell me, what I should do."

"Take off her clothes so we can see how much damage he's done." Unna continued to rifle her pack. "But be careful. Let her remain unconscious if she can; that way she won't feel the pain." Unna selected two kinds of dried leaves and a packet of bark, sniffed each small bundle, and set them aside. She rummaged again. "Do you have any dried buckthorn blooms, Suka?"

"Ah, I don't think so. I'm sorry."

"I need some." Unna frowned. "Isn't Horda a trained medicine woman?"

"Yes," answered Suka. "Perhaps she has some in her pack."

Unna turned to one of the young women. "Zorya, can you find Horda's medicine pack?"

"Where is it?"

"It's in Bear Claw's shelter, so be careful, especially if he's there." Unna's eyes glittered fiercely. "Try not to let him see you take it; there's no telling what he'd do." Zorya nodded and left.

After selecting a hand of leaves from one bunch of her herbs, two leaves from the other, and several small pieces of bark, Unna took a bone pestle and ground them into a coarse powder. When she finished, she went to the fire. Aiyana was there, offering her a horn of steaming water and a large piece of soaproot. "Thank you, child."

Aiyana said, "I thought maybe I could help."

"Of course you can. It's been a long time since anyone even offered to help me with my medicine, and I appreciate it." Unna looked at the water in the horn, spilled half of it back into the water bag, then poured the ground leaves and bark into the horn, swirling them around. She pointed to a large waterbasket. "I'm going to need one of those baskets of hot water soon."

Just then, Zorya hurried into the shelter carrying Horda's medicine pack.

"Good, I'm ready for that." Unna handed the concoction she had made to Zorya and took the pack from her. "Did you have any trouble getting it?"

She shook her head. "No. No one was in the shelter. Bear Claw and the rest of your people are all by the stream."

"Why?" Suka demanded, but Unna only shook her head. *Her* people, yes, but clearly she didn't approve.

"I don't know, but they're building a big fire."

"And I'll bet all the baskets of uncured meat are gone," Unna said wearily.

"The feast?" Suka growled. The stupidity was almost inconceivable. "How dare he!"

"He can, so he dares," whispered Unna fiercely. "There's nothing you can do about it. Now lower your voice so you don't disturb Horda. She has enough trouble right now without having to worry about waking up." She pulled out a handful of dried blossoms from Horda's pack and sniffed them. "Ah, this is what I wanted. Here."

She handed the flowers to Aiyana who stood close by holding the horn of herbed water. "Put these in one of those small waterbaskets and fill it half full of hot water. Then set it over the fire. When it comes to a rolling boil, take it off the fire and allow it to cool just a little. Then bring it to me so I can mix it with this." She retrieved the horn of medicine and stirred it again while the others made themselves useful with their assigned tasks.

❋

Horda's face felt hot, but she could also sense a cool breeze reaching out to caress it. She floated in a haze, somewhere above the clouds. But where was Mach? He should be up here with her; he'd promised to walk with her in the clouds. Light as air, she began to smile at the thought of him, but there was a flash of lightning, thunder, pain. Oh, such pain! It ripped through the haze and brought her crashing down to ... where was she? She was confused, disoriented, and very afraid. Then another stab of pain ripped through her and brought the memories with it. *Oh, Mother Life, what has he done to me?*

She heard the soft drone of voices nearby, but she couldn't summon the strength to open her eyes to see who was speaking. They must have brought her to the shelter while she was unconscious. As she lay there, the sounds began to separate, and she could hear Suka's voice close by, making soothing sounds, and Unna's farther away, giving instructions. It sounded like Unna, only it didn't — too strong, too authoritative. It confused her even more.

"Ah, she's coming around," she heard the Woman of the Tall Grass say. "Come, Horda, drink this." A pair of hands raised her head and thrust the drinking horn to her lips.

Even in her weakened state, Horda wrinkled her nose at

395

the acrid smell rising from the horn. "What is it?" she croaked, surprised by the roughness of her own voice.

"Medicine; what do you think?" Unna asked with feigned exasperation. "My word, the worst patients are always the medicine women."

"I'm not a medicine woman," wheezed Horda. "I'm a healer woman."

"Same difference," said Unna, but she sounded pleased Horda was well enough to complain about such things. "If you must know, it's a tonic of white alder bark, willow, and buckthorn blooms with two lobelia leaves for good measure. Are you satisfied? Will you drink it now?"

Horda wanted to nod her agreement, but it took too much energy. Instead, she let Unna and Suka help her; she managed to drink about half of the bitter tonic before another pain twisted her insides and caused her to cry out.

"Don't fight the pain. Work with it," counseled Suka. "Breathe ..."

"I am breathing," snapped Horda.

Unna swallowed a smile. "That's good, but try breathing like this." She demonstrated short panting breaths. "It will help you get through the pain better."

While Horda concentrated on breathing, Suka finished undressing her.

"That's good," Unna encouraged. "Now drink the rest of this." She thrust the horn under Horda's nose again, keeping up a stream of supportive chatter. "You're going to be fine. Uncomfortable, but fine."

Briefly Horda wondered what she meant by the "uncomfortable" part, but before she could ask, she floated away into a pleasant haze. Though the pains didn't go away, she didn't quite feel them anymore. She knew Suka and Unna were cleaning her body. The warm water felt good, like a cradle, and she let herself fall into the sensation.

She had no sense of time; she couldn't tell how long it had been when she felt a particularly sharp pain shoot through her, causing her to cry out even through the haze. Vaguely she felt the hands on her, heard a voice telling her to push. She tried — she thought she did, but she wasn't sure. After that, the pains lessened greatly. She almost smiled in relief until something inside her told her the little one was gone from her body. She struggled to open her eyes, to see what Bear Claw had taken from her.

The room spun around her, but she could see the figures closest to her. Suka was wrapping the tiny thing that would have been a little one and its placenta in a clean fawn skin while Unna cleaned and examined her once more.

"She doesn't seem damaged," the medicine woman said.

"Mother Life watched over her," said Suka.

"She's special."

"I know, and I thank you for saving her." Suka smoothed the dirty, matted hair back from Horda's battered face.

Unaccustomed to such compliments, Unna was embarrassed. Her response was to reach for her medicine pack and say, "Lija, take a basket and find some clean snow. Aiyana, bring more fuel because we don't want her to catch a chill. Zorya, find me some of the fat we saved. It's time we treated the rest of her wounds."

❀

Suka listened while the sounds of revelry gradually faded. Burning with impotent anger, she had watched through a slit in the shelter opening as Bear Claw and his people devoured the supplies from his shelter. She dreamed of storming across the camp to stop their wasteful excess though she admitted to herself she'd have had more success trying to stop a blizzard.

The camp grew silent as the People of the Tall Grass fell into satiated slumber. Thankfully the noisy carousing hadn't disturbed Horda; tonight she needed all the rest she could get. But tomorrow? *What will Bear Claw do tomorrow? What if he wakes up and decides he isn't finished punishing Horda and the rest of us? Oh, Elko, please hurry.*

Careful not to disturb the other women sleeping in the shelter, Suka retrieved her store of tools. She eyed the bone scrapers used to clean meat and fur from hides. After hopefully fingering the edge of one, she set them all aside with a sigh. They weren't sharp enough and the women weren't strong enough to do real damage unless the men sat still and waited to be hacked to pieces. She smiled bitterly at her ridiculous thought.

Then she lifted the crude flint knife Bear Claw had given her to butcher bison and other large animals. Gently she ran the pad of her right thumb across the sharp face of the blade; a cold smile curved her lips when blood beaded along the slice in her thumb. She laid it aside and picked up the two smaller blades she used to separate the meat from the bones. After testing their edges she put them aside. She thought sourly of the fine chert blade she'd broken filleting the meat Bear Claw and his people so carelessly devoured. *Stop thinking about what can't be changed and start planning for what can.*

She continued looking around the crowded shelter in the dim firelight then stopped suddenly when she saw that Rushing Water, Wolf that Walks, and three of the other warriors had left their hunting packs by their sleeping furs. No, they couldn't have been that careless or stupid, she thought — but they had been. Laughter bubbled in her throat as she removed the knives, war axes, and other weapons from the packs and silently made plans about which of the Women of the Frozen Earth should get which weapon. Oh, yes, the Women of the Frozen Earth could hurt the People of the Tall Grass. More than a little.

But ... another thought intruded on her glee. Her plan would certainly assure the deaths of many, if not all, the Women of the Frozen Earth. Did she have the right to ask that of them? Did the damage they could cause justify the price they would pay?

With an exasperated sigh, she set the weapons aside and peered out the shelter opening to see if anyone was in sight, but it was completely silent. She needed to breathe fresh air before she suffocated, so she slipped outside and picked her way around the patches of slushy snow until the shelter blocked her from view of the rest of the camp.

Taking a deep breath of crisp air, she looked at the stars glittering like shiny crystals in the cold night sky. Campfires in the Frozen Wilds. She smiled and touched the small beaded leather pouch she always wore around her neck, a reminder of home.

Long ago, when Elko began to court her, he gave her the small sack and a crystal he had found. She remembered how his eyes had danced in his solemn face when he held up the bit of stone so the firelight could make it sparkle. With the dignity only a warrior with four hands of winters could muster, he explained Mother Life or Father Death, he wasn't quite sure which, had trapped a bit of fire from the sky in the cool stone, just for her. She had laughed at him, and he had feigned great hurt until she touched her lips to his — for the very first time.

She still wore the little pouch with its tiny fire around her neck, and she knew she always would. Just touching it brought Elko close and helped her stay strong. She had to be strong now. If he were here, Elko could save them, but he wasn't; she and the other women would have to save themselves.

"Thwo-whoo, thwo-whoo." It was the soft cry of an owl, close by. Elko called her that way, and she found herself searching the darkness for him. How silly, like a little girl. She had been thinking of him and was now imagining his call because she needed him so desperately.

"Thwo-whoo, thwo-whoo." Closer now, but where? She jumped back in alarm as the mound of snow in front of her transformed into a man. It took her just a moment to realize this was no illusion. She threw herself into Elko's arms, clinging to the reality with desperate hope.

"Oh, Elko, I knew you'd find us, but I was afraid you'd be too late." Tears of joy and pain streamed down her face.

"Shh, shh," he soothed, gently wiping away her tears. "I'm here now, but we don't want to come this far and have our reunion give us away." He crushed his mouth against hers and held her so tightly she could feel the beating of his heart.

She looked into his eyes and whispered, "Bear Claw almost beat Horda to death this afternoon."

"I saw, but we were too far away to stop him, and it would have given us away if we had tried. I'm so sorry. Is she all right? Are the rest of you?"

"She'll be okay, but Marmal walks the Frozen Wilds with Father Death."

"Bear Claw, too?" Elko could barely contain his rage.

"No, she was trampled when she tried to outrun a bison stampede."

Elko relaxed, but only marginally; his eyes kept sweeping the camp for danger. "I'm sorry we couldn't find you sooner; maybe we could have prevented that, too."

"You're here now. Oh, Elko, I was so scared." Tears flooded her eyes once more, and sobbing, she burrowed her head into the hollow of his neck.

He hugged her tightly until she had cried herself out. Then he raised her head so he could look into her eyes. "Tell me more of what's happened. We need to know if we're going to get everyone out of here safely."

So much had happened; where should she start? "Bear Claw was obsessed with Horda until now," she told her mate, "but I don't know what he plans next. None of his people have come near this shelter since we carried her inside. Yesterday he beat Bird Wing, one of his own women, and put her out in the blizzard to freeze, and she was carrying a little one. Today he turned his anger on Horda, and then he and his people all went down to the river to feast on their winter supplies — they won't have anything left when winter truly comes. I don't care about the adults, but the children will starve!"

Elko's face darkened. "Where are the children now?" he asked.

"With us."

"All of them?"

"There are only two. They attached themselves to Horda and me when we arrived, and I think everyone here was glad to be rid of them. They're in the shelter with us."

Elko rubbed his forehead pensively. "Only two. No wonder Bear Claw was so desperate."

Taking a deep breath, she pushed on, letting all her fears and anger drain into her words; it felt so good to have someone listen. "They don't care about the little ones, Elko. They treat anyone weaker than themselves badly; the men hit the women, the women hit the children, the children hit each other. Unna said they used to be a strong people, a proud people, but most of the tribe died off in the sickness two winters ago. Bear Claw and his young followers took over, but they didn't value the same things the elders did, and this is the result." She waved her hand to encompass the raggedness around them.

Elko opened his mouth to speak, but Suka placed her fingers on his lips. "There's one more thing you should know. Bear Claw killed Bird Wing, who carried his little one, because she tried to kill Horda with poison berries when Bear Claw learned Horda was also breeding. But when he realized the little one Horda carried wasn't his, then he beat her so savagely she lost it."

Elko's rage vibrated through his body, and the force of his words left no room for doubt about his intentions. "I'm sorry we weren't here to protect you before, Suka, but that has changed. The People of the Tall Grass will answer to us for what they did. We will destroy them as surely as they tried to destroy us."

"I never doubted you would." Her hand gently smoothed the angry lines pleating his forehead.

He caught her hand and brought it to his lips. "Are all the Women of the Frozen Earth in this one shelter?"

"Yes."

"You're sure?"

"Of course, I'm sure, Elko. In case you've forgotten, there aren't so many of us I would lose count."

"I'm sorry." His laugh was genuine, and he hugged her again. "How many People of the Tall Grass are there?"

"Two hands' hands plus four hands."

"So few?"

"One hand plus two fingers hands warriors and a hand plus two fingers youths."

"We had two hands hands warriors."

"Had?" Suka felt the bottom of her stomach drop out. "Some walk the Frozen Wilds?"

He shook his head. "No, nothing like that; do not be concerned. It's only Zaaco fell and hurt his leg before the blizzard. He'll recover, but we left two warriors with him at the bison gully."

"I'm relieved. Can you tell me what you are planning?"

Elko shook his head. "We haven't decided for sure. We tried to watch, to get a sense of these people's movements, but we had to pull back too many times; we were afraid they would see us. We searched for a plan that would spare the children, but since we now know they're safe with you, I can tell you our job will be easier. We've sworn to wipe the People of the Tall Grass off the face of the earth, and we will."

She shivered. Watching her closely, he asked, "Are there some who helped you? Some you think should be spared?"

She nodded. "Yes, one — Unna. They treat her worse than they treat us."

His eyes questioned her.

"She's a medicine woman. She helped Horda."

"A medicine woman?"

"Yes."

"Still they treat her badly?"

"She has many winters and much wisdom, but I told you things have changed here. She refused to depart just because Bear Claw thought she should, and they hold it against her."

Elko's mouth set in a grim line. "Very well. Go inside and stay there until I come for you. Don't come out, and don't allow any of the others to come out either. No matter what you hear." He started to walk away, then turned back. Grabbing Suka in his arms, he shared her breath and hugged her once more. "I missed you, Suka."

She wrapped her arms around his solid warmth and clung to him.

He touched his lips to hers and turned. Then he stopped and asked, "Do you have any fat?"

Surprised, she said, "What?"

"Fat," he said, "you know, bison humps or something — even pemmican. Fat burns hotter than wood."

"There isn't much wood in this place."

"I know," he said. "We burned fat and bison bones during the blizzard."

A smile arced across her face. "They use the droppings of animals for fuel."

Elko grimaced. "We aren't that desperate, but fat would be useful to block the shelter entrances."

"They aren't inside the shelters, Elko."

"What?"

"I told you — they had a feast. They sat around eating much of the food we stored for winter and drinking something they brew that intoxicates them. They're asleep or passed out in that little grove of trees beside the spring. All of them except Unna and the little ones."

"Are you sure?"

She nodded. "Oh! I almost forgot. The men who slept in my shelter left their weapons behind."

"So they're unarmed?"

She nodded again.

He shook his head in amazement.

"I told you they're different from us. I can't imagine you ever doing such a stupid thing." She laughed. Lifting the small pouch suspended around her neck, she touched it first to his lips then her own. It was time for him to go.

He took one last look at her before he faded into the darkness. Suka slipped back inside the shelter, only then realizing Elko had never questioned whose child Horda had carried.

Chapter 41

"See the shelter?" Elko indicated the structure a short distance away. "All our women are inside that one shelter, along with two children and one old medicine woman from their tribe. All the others had some kind of feast and are sleeping in that grove; there are only a few more than came to our Gathering.

"I hope they enjoyed their meal," Mach whispered fiercely to Thuro, "because it was their last."

Elko overheard the comment and fixed the two young warriors with a stern look; both shifted uneasily beneath his gaze. "Actually, I was hoping they'd be in the shelters. We could surround them easily, burn them out, and then pick them off as they tried to escape. There wouldn't be much danger to us or to our women."

"But they're not in their shelters, so what are we going to do?" asked Thuro, trying to get back in Elko's good graces.

"We have almost four warriors with us for every three of theirs." A murmur passed through the group; that wasn't many at all. Elko waited for them to quiet and then continued. "They also have a few women and just over a hand of youths." He decided not to tell them they might be unarmed; he didn't want them to take their victory for granted.

"Are we just going to slip up to them and slit their throats?" asked Mach.

"Basically, though I seriously doubt it'll be that easy. The ground is flat by the river, so we'll have to move very carefully."

The men nodded their understanding, but as Mach glanced around, he could see something in their eyes — not hesitation exactly, more like regret. He could understand; he felt it, too. Everyone there was determined to complete the mission; it was the reason they had come, and no one questioned that. It was just that taking life was not a trivial thing, and here they were preparing to wipe out an entire tribe with the exception of two children and an old woman. How could they not feel regret?

"What if they wake up and discover us before we are ready?" Trefo asked. It was a good question.

Elko said, "We'll still have the advantage of surprise, and we'll just have to fight harder to kill all of them instead of being killed ourselves."

Elko waited patiently while the men thought about this information. He could not rush them, but he could help them prepare themselves for what lay ahead. Taking a deep breath, he sought them out one by one, his eyes locking on each man's for a moment before moving on. "You all know why we're here," he began, "and *I* know you're all committed to this. I can feel many of you hesitate at the scale of what we're about to do. The People of the Frozen Earth are peaceful people, for the most part, and this is anything but a peaceful raid."

His voice began to rise with the passion of his words. "You've all heard Suka's account of what has happened here, the beatings, the violence, the deaths. You are all angry, and rightly so; just as I am. So, yes, we are here to rescue our women. Yes, we are here to exact vengeance on those who captured and abused them. But if those are the only reasons we are here, we can count ourselves no better than those we will kill tonight."

Mach looked at Elko in astonishment; what could he possibly mean? What other reasons could there possibly be? An excited buzz rippled through the crowd; clearly the other men were just as puzzled by his words.

Elko gave them a moment to wonder then continued. "Suka

has told me the People of the Tall Grass were once a proud people, but they have sunk into this loathsome state because they did not care to stop it. The People of the Frozen Earth are still a proud people. We are here because we not only want to survive, but we want to survive *well*. We care about who we are. We want to reward the just and punish the evil and know we can distinguish between the two. The fact you hesitate about taking these lives, even after all they've done, tells me you do care, and I applaud you for that.

"But we have a choice to make now, one that will decide our future, not just as men standing here, but also as a tribe. Will we allow evil to flourish amongst us, to wear us down until we, like the People of the Tall Grass, no longer care about who we are? Or will we take action, here and now, to ensure our children and our children's children have a safe and peaceful world to grow up in? The choice is up to you."

How small-minded I have been, Mach thought. There really is so much more at stake than my mate and our happiness. If I am ever a leader, I hope one day to be as worthy a leader as Elko. I will remember his words for all of my days, teaching them not only to my own little ones, but to all the tribe's little ones, too.

The group buzzed with anticipation, with conviction. Elko waited until every eye was once again on him then gave each man his task, some to come up behind the enemy, some to circle around the grove to the river's other bank, ensuring no one could escape that way, and some to stay behind and protect the women and children. Every task was important, and no one grumbled about the assignment he'd been given. "There's just one more thing," Elko informed them. "Night is our ally in surprise; we need this finished before the sun begins its journey across the sky."

There were no more words left to say; the time had come for action. The warriors melted into the starlit darkness to engage the enemy.

❋

"I'm glad they have strong bladders and don't need to get up," whispered Thuro from his position beside the small grove. It was addressed to no one in particular, and no one replied.

The "ready" signal, the owl's soft churring "Whoo," made its way around the circle. Elko took a deep breath as it came back to him. *Mother Life, forgive us for any wrong we are about to commit.*

His eyes fixed firmly on the sleepers; he raised his axe above his head and slowly lowered it. The Warriors of the Frozen Earth erupted like locusts from their hiding places, a mighty war cry issuing from each and every throat.

Fuzzy headed and sated from their revelries, the People of the Tall Grass were slow to respond. They woke in confusion, stumbled to their feet, and headed this way and that; the men groped for weapons most had left somewhere else.

The battle was unquestionably one-sided, and its outcome was decided the moment the Warriors of the Frozen Earth moved to attack. Their heavy war axes, long spears, and daggers made short work of their unarmed victims, felling men and women alike without pause.

After the initial assault, Mach, stripped of his winter furs, stood back from the battle. He had come for one reason — to kill the man who had taken his world from him. But it wouldn't do just to take his life; first, he would make him understand who had come for him.

But where was Bear Claw? He was not yet among the dead, and in the melee, Mach couldn't identify his nemesis. His eyes searched the area until ... there! Bear Claw was standing on the edge of the field, looking disbelievingly at the carnage around him. Mach clenched his fists around his spear and war axe waiting for Bear Claw to join the fight.

But he never did. Instead, he pulled his tattered bearskin

cloak around his body and inched away, fleeing the scene like a coward. A hand of Elko's warriors saw this and began to chase him. "He's mine!" Mach shouted with such ferocity the others pulled back.

Throwing his weapons aside, Mach pounded after Bear Claw and made a flying body tackle, crushing the smaller man into the mud. Then he leaped to his feet and dropped into the classic fighter's stance. "Stand up and fight me, coward!"

Bear Claw coughed on the dirt he had eaten, but he wouldn't stand. Mach grabbed him by the shoulders and heaved him to his feet. "You're quick to use your fists against women. See how well — you — do — against — me." He didn't give Bear Claw a chance to pull himself together but instead pummeled him with a flurry of blows to his face, neck, and chest.

Bear Claw reeled and blood streamed from his mouth and nose, he spat a broken tooth at Mach's feet. He took a swing at Mach, but his reflexes were still dulled from the night's revelry; the blow missed Mach's midsection, and the force of his swing cost Bear Claw his precarious balance. He dropped to his knees in the dirt, panting.

Mach's anger only burned hotter. "Get up!" he roared, stepping forward to kick the fallen Bear Claw in the stomach. Thuro started to pull him away, but Elko restrained him. "Leave them alone," The chief told him. "One way or the other, Bear Claw is finished, and Mach needs this more than he knows."

Mach once again dragged his adversary to his feet. Bear Claw took another swing and finally connected with his body. Mach staggered back with a grunt of pain, and then ducked inside to pound Bear Claw's stomach and chest. Bear Claw crumpled to the ground, and Mach placed punishing kicks to his kidneys and back before hauling him to his feet for another pounding.

Mach connected blow after blow, sending blood and sweat spraying in every direction. He was so blinded by his rage he barely paused to draw breath until Elko walked forward and placed a hand on his back. "Enough," the elder told him.

"But he still lives!" Mach shouted, swinging past Elko to land a solid blow on the side of Bear Claw's chin, cracking his jaw bone like dry stick.

Bear Claw moaned, and a thread of bloody spittle studded with pieces of broken teeth trickled out of his sagging mouth.

Mach would have pulled him to his feet again, but this time Elko stood in his path. "Are you an honorable man or a savage?" he asked forcefully. "You are angry, but he is unarmed."

Mach cursed under his breath; his anger had almost destroyed him. But it would end here, he told himself. He relaxed his muscles, and Elko stepped away from him.

He faced his opponent again but from a few paces away. "I vowed to kill you slowly and imagined many painful tortures." His voice was now under control. "Even against all I have been taught, I dreamed of beating you to death with my bare hands. But Elko is right — to do such things would only lower me to your level, and that I will not do." He spat in the dirt at Bear Claw's feet. "Look around you, Bear Claw of the Tall Grass. Go to the Frozen Wilds knowing because of your actions the People of the Frozen Earth this day came and destroyed your tribe."

He took his spear from Thuro's outstretched hand. Panic-stricken, with tears streaming from his swollen eyes, Bear Claw raised his empty hands and babbled incoherent pleas. Mach glared at the unarmed warrior. "Give him a weapon!" he commanded.

Thuro handed Bear Claw a spear, the twin to the one in Mach's hand, but the chief dropped it to the ground.

"Pick it up," Mach ordered.

Bear Claw wiped his nose, smearing blood across his battered face. Taking a deep breath he lifted his chin, "M'unarmed," he mumbled, "G'me mercy."

"Mercy?" Mach fairly roared. "Did you show our unarmed

women mercy when you beat them? Did you show your own mate mercy when you beat her and threw her into the snow to freeze?"

"She tried to kill your woman," slurred Bear Claw. "I only protected Horda for you."

"Then you tried to kill her. I know what happened," Mach spat. "Now pick up the spear and depart like a warrior."

Bear Claw flailed, reaching awkwardly for the spear. The moment his hand made contact with it and he stood, Mach drove his own spear home.

Dropping his weapon, Bear Claw grasped the spear's shaft, now the only thing that held him upright. Blood gushed from his mouth, and his icy silver eyes stared into nothingness. Only then did Mach allow Bear Claw to crumple to the ground, still clutching the shaft of the spear that filled his cup of time.

"The People of the Tall Grass are no more." The battle was over, and Mach felt both exuberant and empty; it was a strange mix. But now that it really was over, there was only one thing he wanted — Horda. Along with the other Men of the Frozen Earth, he hurried into the camp to find his mate.

❄

Aiyana jumped to her feet and started to the shelter opening when she heard the men coming into the camp. "Sit down," Suka said sternly from Horda's side.

"But, I want to see," pleaded the youngest of the women, suddenly more alive than anyone had seen her for weeks.

Patiently Suka said, "I've told you, Elko said to stay inside until he came for us."

"Elko?" The word was little more than a croak, but it was a wonderful sound to Suka's ears; Horda was awake at last. She reached out and grasped Suka's hand, her eyes bright. "Our men are here?" she whispered.

"Yes."

"And Mach?"

Suka nodded. "He's here, too."

Horda brightened visibly. "What about my father?"

Suka smoothed the hair back from Horda's battered face and evaded the question. "I believe the voices outside mean our captivity is over."

"You're going home," Horda said.

Tears filled Suka's eyes, but she fought them down. "*We're going home*," she said. "Everything will be all right now." *Mother Life, please don't let me be lying, not after all we've been through.*

Suka turned away so Horda wouldn't see her tears, but Aiyana noticed, and they confused her. She sat down beside Lija, who was talking quietly to Zorya. "Horda and Suka told us we'd get to go home," Aiyana said hesitantly.

"Yes," said Lija. "You know they did, so why are you asking?"

"I don't understand. Why is Suka crying now? Isn't she happy?"

Lija turned and saw Suka fighting tears even as she tended Horda. She understood, but it was not an easy thing to say.

Aiyana, although a woman in the tribe's eyes, still remained childlike in many ways; she clearly had not grasped the situation. "Then what's wrong with her?" she pressed.

"Keep your voice down," Lija hissed. Then she whispered, "Think about it."

"Horda?"

"Yes, Horda," said Lija quietly.

Aiyana's mouth made a little round O of dismay. "But she helped me see that it wasn't my ..."

"Yes, Horda helped you," Lija interrupted. "She helped all of us, even more than Suka did."

"Did they lie to us?" Now Aiyana's eyes were wide with fear, and tears welled to the surface. "Are we going to be punished for what those men did to us?"

"No," said Lija shortly, "we're not." She still didn't get it. After all Horda had just gone through, the woman still couldn't see what was right in front of her face.

"Then why is Suka crying?" persisted Aiyana.

It was Zorya who, exasperated, finally muttered, "You figure it out, Aiyana. There's nothing more we can say right now."

❇

Elko fumbled with the shelter opening. "You can come out now. It is over."

The tent suddenly filled with a mixture of frenzied excitement and fearful hesitation. This was the moment the women all had been waiting for — their men finally rescuing them. But while they couldn't wait to get out the door and into the men's arms, they were also unsure of how they would be received. Would the men still want them? Would they love them? Would the past remain in the past, or would it forever color their future? There was no way to tell without plunging ahead, and that's exactly what they did.

Suka stayed with Unna near Horda's side, but the rest of the Women of the Frozen Earth almost ran over each other in their haste to get outside. A smile lightened Suka's tear-stained face when little Aiyana, despite all her fears, flung herself into her chosen Premo's arms and plastered his face with kisses. "I knew you'd be here," she shrieked excitedly. His arms tight around her was all the answer she needed from him right now; the rest would come in its own time.

Elko and Mach threaded their way through the happy reunions and into the shelter. Suka shook Horda's shoulder to rouse her. "Mach's here," she said gently, and Horda's eyes lightened her bruised face.

As Mach hesitantly made his way to Horda's side, Unna gestured toward the opening. Suka rose, taking Elko's hand tightly in hers, and together they herded the others away from the shelter. Unna closed the shelter opening and sat down before it. "Go with your man," she said. "I'll keep watch to see they're not disturbed."

Suka smiled her gratitude and started to head away, but Elko stopped and faced the old woman. "Greetings, Unna, I am Elko. Suka is my first mate. She has told me much about you." Elko politely held out his hand to her.

Unna didn't know what to make of the gesture, and her face registered both her surprise and suspicion. Nevertheless, she climbed to her feet and took his proffered hand although she said nothing.

"You will have an honored place beside the cook fires of my band as long as you need it."

She cocked her head quizzically. "He means we'll take care of you for the rest of your life," Suka explained.

Now Unna fixed Elko with a piercing look. "Why?"

Elko was taken aback. "Why? I don't understand what you mean."

Unna looked pointedly at the destruction before her. "Although I do not grieve for any of them, you destroyed all the members of my tribe except me and two little ones. And now you tell us we are welcome. I want to know why."

Elko nodded appreciatively. "Suka told me you were wise. We spared the children because they're not responsible for the actions of the adults. We spared you because we're grateful to you for helping our women. And we welcome you at our cook fires because you are a good person and a valued one. If your own people could not see that, it was their loss."

Unna smiled her appreciation. "Your women helped me more than I could ever have helped them, but I am grateful for your words and for your invitation. All of the women are good women, but Suka is one of the very best."

"I'm aware of that," he said solemnly.

She cocked her head and looked up at him. "And if she chose you, I suspect you're a good man."

Elko didn't know how to respond, and his face flushed with embarrassment. Suka quickly intervened. "He is," she said, hugging him, "a very good man."

Unna's smile widened to show the gaps of missing teeth. "Everyone's too busy to bother you now, so perhaps you should take this time for yourselves." She gestured to the shelter behind her. "As I said, I will protect them."

"Thank you." Elko took Suka's hand and walked away into the night.

❋

Oh, no, not already, Suka thought. They had all been together only a short time when Premo asked what many of the others clearly wanted to but hadn't yet. "What caused Bear Claw to beat Horda so?"

Without the slightest hesitation, Aiyana said, "We don't know for sure, unless it was because she looked at the sunset instead of preparing the evening eat."

Premo's face darkened. "He beat her for not cooking?"

Suka jumped in, trying to avert a full-blown discussion of the topic. "He beat her for a lot of reasons, but that's over now. I want to think about going home."

The others agreed, and everyone began chattering at the same time about the journey back and what they would do once they arrived at their camp. Elko looked pointedly at Suka, but he said nothing, giving everyone the chance to enjoy the moment.

It was over now, Suka thought to herself, but in some ways Horda's problems were just beginning.

Chapter 42

Sitting on the furs beside Horda, Mach looked at the blood that stained his hands — he should have cleaned them before he came, but he had been in a rush to see his mate and any further delay had seemed unreasonable. Once he looked at her bruised and battered face he forgot everything but his beloved and her pain.

"This was all my fault, Horda. I should have listened to you when you told me your fears, but I never believed he would ... that is ... Anyhow, I wanted to tell you I'm sorry for all the pain I caused you, but it's over now. The People of the Tall Grass are lifeless — all except the old medicine woman and the two little ones. Elko tells me they are special."

She stared at his cherished face. She spoke so softly he leaned closer to hear her. "They are special and so are you. Throughout this whole ordeal, I held on to my memories of you. They helped me survive and gave me the courage to go on even when I didn't think I could draw another breath. But now I'm afraid."

Mach smoothed her hair from her face and murmured reassuringly. "There's no reason to be afraid. Suka says you're going to be fine, and we'll be leaving for home soon. We'll be at the foothills before the winter blizzards really begin, and there's plenty of fuel and shelter there."

Horda shifted on the furs, agitated by his lack of understanding. "No, no, you don't understand. I know I must face my punishment now, but I'm afraid you'll be punished for my actions, and I don't want that." He stared at her blankly; she wasn't making any sense. He was about to ask her what she was talking about when she burst out, "Don't you know why Bear Claw beat me?"

He shook his head. "I saw the way he treated his people at Gathering, and I've heard from the others that he beat you for any reason or even no reason at all. I supposed you simply displeased him some way."

"Oh, yes, I displeased him. I surely displeased him." She pulled her hand away from his but continued to study his face.

He looked back at her, smiling. "So what did you do? Burn his porridge one time too many?" He had hoped the joke would make her laugh and ease the tension, but all it did was make her more upset. "I'm sorry, I shouldn't have said that. It's just that all the time we searched for you I was afraid Bear Claw would kill you, but here you are. You do look a little the worse for wear, but Suka says you'll —"

"I'm a lot the worse for wear," she told him, her voice raspy. *Mother Life, how could she find the words to say what she must?* "Mach, Bear Claw beat me because I carried a little one."

"A little one?" He rubbed his free hand across his face, trying to absorb the information. "We all knew ... I mean, *I* knew in my head he would probably use you, but I never thought about a little one. It must have been terrible; I'm sorry I couldn't protect you from that."

Exasperated, she struggled to sit up, realizing she was going to have to say everything whether she wanted to or not. "Mach, it wasn't his little one. That's why he beat me."

"Not his? You mean he allowed the others ..." He looked aghast at the thought.

"Do you have no sense at all?" she asked him, completely frustrated. "No, he didn't allow any of his other men near me. I was his personal property." She squeezed her eyes tight, but one tear still escaped and followed a lonely trail down her left cheek. "The little one belonged to … you."

"Me?" His eyes widened, his expression running from shocked surprise to bewildered amazement.

"Yes."

"Are you sure?"

Now that it was out in the open, she couldn't prevent the tears from flowing freely. "Bear Claw was sure."

Mach was still struggling to absorb what she was telling him. She was to have a little one; the little one was his; the little one was gone; and it was Bear Claw's fault. "Why did he decide the little one wasn't his?" he finally asked.

"I was sick from the morning he captured me." She carefully avoided looking in his eyes, afraid of what she might find there.

"And?" he prompted.

"And he realized he wasn't the first man to join with me."

"You were sick before the Bid Ceremony — either vomiting or starving," Mach said, suddenly remembering. "You told me it was nerves or something you ate, but it wasn't, was it?"

"Hardly half a moon had passed since Lonzar almost drowned; I knew, but I kept telling myself nothing was wrong."

Mach's voice became soft — memories suddenly awakened. "My mother often told about the time she carried Ettor. She joked that she suffered the sickness of early breeding from the morning after he was conceived. Though I had little more than a hand of winters, I remember that terrible time. I thought she was departing because she was so sick for so long — right up to the day of his birth. It was just that nothing helped for more than a day or two.

"Then when she carried Saba, no one even realized she was breeding until Ileea noticed how round she had grown." The hint of a smile lightened his face. "That's the first time I really noticed the looks my mother and father exchange. I was almost halfway through the Rituals of Manhood — I hadn't even started to think about the Mating Ritual, but I suddenly realized they shared something special, something I wanted to share with someone when the time came. Something I know I want to share with you, no matter what."

"But now — " she began.

"Now what?" he demanded.

"Now things have changed; don't you understand? I chose to join with you though I knew the taboo, and look what happened. I do not want you to take the blame for my actions, but I must pay for what I've done."

Mach turned her head so she had to look at him, and his voice took on a hard edge. "That's nonsense, and you should know it. We made the decision to mate together, and together we will face the future. And in any case, we would have celebrated the Ritual of the First Mate two moons past if Bear Claw hadn't captured you."

"But he did capture me, and we didn't celebrate the Ritual."

"Don't push me away, Horda. Mother Life gave us to each other, so I say we will face the future as she intended, together."

"Then we may taste the Wrath of Fire together," she said in anguish, "and I can't bear for that to happen. You're the future of our tribe, and you must not depart."

"And you should?" he asked.

She frowned. "Don't you understand? We'll be punished."

"You don't know that."

"Sappha and Dion were."

He grimaced. "Don't compare us to them. He was a lecherous bully, cruel to his own mates but always flirting and posturing with other women."

"And what was her excuse? That her mate Garo didn't please her? No one listened, and they were burned."

"It's not the same. They were each mated to another."

"Yes, they were."

"Anyway, they were caught," he said, desperately trying to

find a way out of this.

"So were we."

He sighed, but he couldn't deny there was some truth to her words. "I can't remember a promised couple being burned," he said, "though I can remember a number of big and well-developed little ones at the Gatherings after their parents celebrated the Ritual of the First Mate."

Her eyes widened in surprise. "I didn't think anyone else noticed."

"Oh, I noticed all right. I even commented on Lonzar's size at his first Gathering. I remember my mother scolding me. She said it was 'impolite' to say such things, but when I asked her why, all she did was glare at me and tell me not to ask questions about things I didn't understand." His laughter sounded sad. "I understand now."

Horda nodded miserably. "But it still isn't the same. His parents did celebrate the Ritual of the First Mate, long before his birth. We didn't. I must confess and take my punishment."

He gripped her hands tightly. "Horda, I don't know what's going to happen, but whatever happens there is no *I* anymore. *We* are in this together."

Tears filled her eyes. "I need to talk to my father. Didn't he come with you? I thought he would."

"He's, um, not here." Mach looked away.

"What's wrong?" She cried. *Oh, Mother Life, was there no end to the misery?*

"Shh, shh," he soothed. "Calm down." Slowly he explained what had happened.

As he spoke, Unna, drawn by Horda's outburst, poked her head into the shelter. "Is everything all right here?" she asked, studying them both.

"I'm sorry," Horda told her. "Mach told me my father wasn't here, and I jumped to the wrong conclusion."

"I knew she would ask, and I should have chosen my words

more carefully," Mach wilted under Unna's gaze. Horda marveled at Unna; only a short time ago she could not have imagined she possessed such strength.

"Yes, you should have," she admonished, "but it seems no harm was done." She turned her attention to Horda. "I look forward to meeting the special man who raised a special daughter like you."

Horda's eyes teared again. "He is very special, but I'm not."

"Very special." Her tone left no room for argument. "You made a mistake. Now you've paid for it.".".

But Horda shook her head, unconvinced.

"Yes, you have," Unna insisted. "You think about my words." She extended a hand to Mach. "Come; we should let her rest, and you, young man, should go clean up. I'm surprised she let you stay in such a state. She always fussed about how dirty Bear Claw and his people were, and I have to tell you, you smell like one of them."

Mach looked down at the blood, dirt, and sweat staining his body and clothes as if he were seeing them for the first time. "Um, yeah, I guess I should," he mumbled.

"It's a wonder you didn't scare poor Horda out of her wits coming in here like that." Horda smiled at the two of them even as she lay back against the furs and closed her eyes. Unna's chatter sounded wonderful, and it was so good to see Mach again.

Unna pushed Mach out the door and said, "Give me time to settle my patient, and I'll bring you soaproot and warm water. Now shoo," she commanded.

Mach took a brief look back at Horda then headed out into the camp.

Unna brought her attention back to Horda, who suddenly looked very small and fragile after the strains of the day. "Do you need anything?"

"I don't think so."

Unna placed a practiced hand on her brow. "You're too

warm. I don't want the fever demon taking hold of you. I prepared some willow tonic earlier, and I want you to drink it." She bustled about the shelter.

"I don't think I need any," protested Horda.

"For now, you're the patient," said Unna, supporting her head and holding the horn to her lips. "I'm the medicine woman."

Horda drank a couple of swallows, then looked accusing.

Unna grinned then said, "Okay, so I slipped in a little lobelia and bitterroot. Drink it anyway."

Horda arched an eyebrow, "And?"

"And a few ground up pipsissewa leaves and seeds."

"You're a devious one," Horda said playfully through her fatigue, but she obediently drank every drop.

Unna sat beside her. "Good, now I want to talk to you for a little."

Horda feigned a yawn. "I'm really tired, and I don't feel like talking." She yawned again for good measure.

"This won't take long." Unna took Horda's hand. "You've suffered a great deal, but I want you to make me a promise."

"What kind of a promise?"

"Promise me you won't go confessing any sins, real or imagined, until you're better."

"I'm not sure I can promise that."

Unna's voice took on the tone of command. "I've lived many turnings of the seasons, and I know good people sometimes make mistakes. You and these other Women of the Frozen Earth are good women. I don't know your men well yet, but I sense they are also good."

"They destroyed your tribe."

Sadness darkened the old woman's eyes. "Yes, they did, but they had their reasons, and I understand them. I think you know my tribe wasn't always the one you saw. We had laws and codes of behavior similar to those of the People of the Frozen Earth, and they made us strong — a force to be reckoned with. When I was a young woman, only a few of my people were like Bear Claw, selfish and petty and hungry for power. As I grew older that changed, so slowly at first it was hard to notice, and when we did, it was too late to stop. Most of the old ones died two winters ago, and it left only the young ones who didn't know any better and who didn't want to know. Your men didn't destroy my tribe, child; they destroyed themselves."

Horda took the old woman's hand. "I'm still sorry it happened."

"And that is one of the reasons you are better than they ever were. They wished the Great Mystery would claim me. To them, I was an unwanted burden, a reminder of the old ways. I am old, but I know many things, and I could have helped them, but they wouldn't let me. If your men had not come, Bear Claw would have ended my life during the coming winter, telling himself and everyone else it was for the good of the tribe. Everyone would have agreed with him, too." Unna shook her head and brought her full attention back to the present. "But we were talking about you — not me."

Horda fought to keep from smiling. She had tried to side-track the old woman, but Unna was too smart to fall for that. "What good will my silence do?" she asked faintly.

"It will give you time to heal and realize your worth."

"But won't my silence be a lie? A transgression, just like my action?"

"I just told you to keep your mouth shut, not to lie," snapped Unna. "And if you decide to go through with this when you've given yourself time to reflect, you may find the words to convince the others of your worth."

"But it is wrong to join —"

"Unless I miss my guess," Unna interrupted, "you were absolutely sure you were going to be joined with Mach before you gave yourself to him. Isn't that so?" Horda nodded, and

Unna pressed on. "And such matings aren't really what that rule's meant to stop, are they?"

Horda shook her head. "I don't think so, but —"

"But nothing." Unna's voice took on a new intensity. "Listen to me carefully, child. Any fool can choose to die — you need look no farther than my own people to see how true that is. But it takes a great person to choose to live and live well. You've told me much of your people's greatness, and I've seen some of it myself; now it's up to you to prove it. It's not enough to choose the right path, but you must choose it for the right reasons. Promise me you'll think about both before you say a word."

"I promise," Horda whispered.

"Good. Then I'll leave you to rest." Picking up her pack and the cooking bag of hot water from the fire, Unna turned and walked out of the shelter.

❀

Mach was waiting outside the shelter when she emerged. "May I speak with you?" he asked her.

Unna smiled, unaccustomed both to the talk and to the courtesy this man extended to her. "Of course," she answered.

He hesitated a moment, uncertain how to begin. "Um, I wanted to tell you ... I'm not sorry Bear Claw's lifeless," he finally got out, "but I am sorry we destroyed your tribe. That's a terrible burden for you to bear."

"As I told your mate, my tribe had destroyed itself long ago; you merely disposed of the bodies."

He sighed. "Then perhaps I should apologize for not arriving earlier. Maybe we could have saved them."

She eyed him intently for a moment then offered, "To have been saved, my tribe would have had to have wanted to be saved. They didn't care, so nothing you could have done would have changed anything."

"Thank you for your kindness," he said, but there was a

hesitation in his voice, as though he wanted to say something more but didn't know how.

Unna waited.

"I, ah, also want to thank you for what you said about Horda being special."

"I spoke the truth." Unna thrust the heavy cooking bag into his hand and rummaged through her pack for the soaproot she had promised him.

"I know that, but I was afraid after what she told me, you and Suka might not think so."

Unna looked up at him, a mixture of curiosity and offense flashing behind her eyes. She chose her words carefully. "I cannot speak for Suka, but I believe what's important isn't the mistake she made some moons back — it's the woman she was during this ordeal, the woman she is now, and the woman she will become in the future. So why would I not think she's special?"

"You're right, of course. Again my apologies."

But Unna wasn't through with him yet. "The same is true for you. You made a mistake, too." He opened his mouth to protest, but she cut him off with a wave of her hand. "As a medicine woman, I can tell you it takes two to mate. Do you disagree?"

Mach colored slightly. "Um, no, I don't."

She smiled. "I didn't think so. But it pleased me to see how quickly she defended you. She loves you, you know."

Mach smiled back. "I'd give my life for her."

"You've proven that, but that's not the point here. The point is if you're going to give your life, you must make sure it is for the right reasons. Don't throw it away."

Mach looked thoroughly confused.

"Horda has promised not to confess anything until she's given serious thought to the words we spoke." Her eyes bored into his. "Now I want a promise from you. I want you to speak with her about those things and reflect on them before you say anything to anyone else about what occurred. Will you promise me that?" He opened his mouth to argue, but Unna would have none of it. "Promise me now, or I will not let you rest until you do. There is too much at stake to risk a hasty action from either one of you."

How had this woman become so wise? "I promise," he told her.

"Good." She gestured to the tiny tents dotting the area. "Do you have one of those shelters in your pack?"

"Yes." He raised his eyebrows at her quick change of subject.

"I'll set it up for you while you wash — over there." She pointed to a small tree away from the carnage and held out a large piece of soaproot then reached for his pack.

"I can set up my own shelter."

"I know you can," she poked a bony finger into his chest, "but you are tired, and I will set it up for you."

Reluctantly he took the soaproot and handed her his pack. "Thank you."

"You're welcome." A promising young fellow, she thought then turned her attention to the task at hand.

Chapter 43

Unable to lie still any longer, Mach crawled out of his small shelter. It was still dark, the deep, soul-wrenching blackness that came each night between the set of the moon and the rise of the sun. And standing beneath the endless sky of the prairie, Mach felt very small.

He rotated his shoulders and winced at the pain shooting through the muscles; he'd been too distracted right after the battle to notice. He'd give two of his teeth for a long soak in the bath pit back at the band's winter shelter; he could almost feel the hot water soothing his aches and pains. But such luxuries would have to wait.

As he stood lost in thought, the stars winked out, and the black of the night sky leached away to reveal the pink-tinged grey beneath. The prairie grass smelled fresh, despite the morning cold, and he could hear small animals rustling within it.

If he closed his eyes, he could pretend everything was as it should be. Their women were all safe. The People of the Tall Grass were no more. Beautiful Horda was his. They were all going home — or were they?

But the morning breeze brought ugly reminders of what had happened the night before — the salty scent of blood from the grove, the silence of a camp that the morning before had held an entire tribe. And try as he might, he couldn't forget the image of Horda's beautiful face, now battered and bruised.

These things stirred up such terrible thoughts and feelings

within him — rage, desire, hate, guilt — he was ashamed. He had enjoyed killing Bear Claw, and he couldn't pretend he wouldn't enjoy killing him again if he had the chance. Nor could he pretend he was sorry he'd joined with Horda before the Ritual. Yet he felt guilty, so guilty he believed he deserved the Wrath of Fire, no matter what Unna said.

"Mach." Elko was calling him from a short distance away; how many times had he tried before Mach heard him?

"Yes?"

"I don't think we should move the camp right now, so we'll need to clean the grove."

There was so much death around him; now that he looked, he could see the extent of the destruction he and his people had caused, and he felt sick. "What are we going to do with the bodies?" he asked Elko quietly, afraid if he raised his voice the ghosts of all the dead might rise to haunt him.

Elko gestured behind him. "There is a pit of sorts over there. We can put them in that and cover them with fat and branches. Then we can burn the whole thing."

Without speaking, Mach picked up the first corpse he came to, carried it down to the pit, and laid it carefully, almost gently, on the ground and closed its eyes. Then he went back for another, and another, doing the same thing each time. As the two worked, Elko watched him carefully, noting the troubled expression on his face, but he said nothing until they were done.

"You look troubled, Mach," he said. "You know we did what was necessary."

"I know that," Mach snapped.

"I'm sure you do." Elko waited a moment, but Mach said nothing further.

"But there is something troubling you." He suggested, letting the question hang in the space between them.

"When I think of Bear Claw ..." His voice trailed off; how could he put this in words?

"Your stomach tenses, and you wish him alive so you could punish him some more. Am I right?" Elko took his silence as assent. "At least, that's the way I would feel, and I'm sure most of the others would tell you the same thing."

"Yes, but I enjoyed it," Mach protested. "What kind of a man does that make me?"

"A very human one," Elko answered. "You can't help the way you feel, only what you do about it. And remember Bear Claw was a terrible person, Mach; he deserved his punishment, not just for what he did to Horda, but for what he did to his own tribe. That remains true whether you enjoyed killing him or not. Do you remember I told you he killed one of his own women during the blizzard?"

Elko waited patiently until Mach nodded. "I didn't tell you she carried his child. He beat her viciously then kicked her outside the shelter into the storm. She either froze or bled to death."

"Unna told me they destroyed themselves." Mach's empty eyes looked at a place Elko could not see, and they filled with a rage that could consume a person's soul. "Bear Claw begged me for mercy, but he had done so much bad that I wanted to —"

"I know, son, I know." Elko grasped Mach's shoulder. "But I've watched you grow from an infant to a man. You have a number of faults, but I know you don't take pleasure in hurting people — especially people who are weaker than you and don't deserve to be hurt. You are not the type of man who would enjoy dealing with others the way you dealt with Bear Claw. Learn from this experience, as you do from all others, and move forward with your life."

"Forward, yes, but to what?" Mach asked, a terrible sorrow in his voice.

Elko knew why, but he would have to wait for the young man to bring it up first. "Mach, if you need to talk more, the others can get along without us for a while longer."

But in an instant, Mach's expression changed, his eyes

became as unreadable as Bear Claw's often had been. "Thank you, no. I promised Unna I'd wait." And with that he simply walked away.

❀

Suka bustled around the cook fire. "Where were you?" she demanded as Elko approached.

"We ... ah ... went for a walk," said Elko. He cast a meaningful look toward Mach.

Suka nodded and squeezed Elko's hand, then drew back as she realized how dirty it was. "You should wash. Unna prepared several large waterbaskets of hot water for the men when they finished cleaning the camp. I hope there's still some left." She gestured toward the little tree where the baskets were. "There's soaproot with the water. We don't have much left, but you need it. When you're done you can eat."

Elko watched Suka flit from one thing to the next, her hands constantly in motion, and he raised his eyebrows. "What's the matter?"

"Nothing's the matter. We have a lot to do, in case you haven't noticed, and I'm very busy. Now go wash."

Mach longed to ask about Horda, but Suka seemed so distracted, he was afraid there was more going on than she said. Instead, he and Elko walked to the tree and obediently washed the dirt and gore from their hands and bodies.

When they returned to the cook fire, they found Suka with a faint tear in her eye. She handed her mate a horn of steaming liquid and said, "I carried these wild rose blossoms when we left Gathering for the Mating Rituals. I saved them until I could serve the tea to you, Elko."

Elko leaned down and touched his lips to hers. "Thank you. You always knew what I liked."

She smiled then turned to dip a horn for Mach.

Mach nodded his thanks and glanced around while Suka

filled two shallow wooden bowls with yampah and cattail tuber porridge. "I chopped pemmican into the porridge. I knew you'd enjoy the richness of the fat."

"I'll just enjoy you doing the cooking instead of me," teased Elko, tracing a fingertip down the line of her jaw. "I never was very good at it."

Suka laughed and spoke conspiratorially to Mach. "He understates his lack of talent. Oh, Mother Life, I can't believe I forgot to tell you to fetch your utensils." She darted to a large cooking bag hanging near the fire and used wooden tongs to lift two carved horn spoons from the hot water then dried them on a small piece of leather. "You can use these. I'm sure Thuro and I don't mind, but you'll have to bring your own to evening eat if you eat on time." She held out the spoons to Mach and Elko.

Instead of the utensil, Elko took her hand and pulled her close. "Stop flitting about like a hummingbird and join us."

Suka pulled her hand loose and frowned, looking toward the shelter. "I told you, I'm busy now. Eat." She thrust the utensil into his hand, dipped some of the wild rose tea into one of Unna's little waterbaskets, and scurried into the shelter.

Elko shook his head in amusement then obediently began eating; Mach, however, stared morosely into his bowl of porridge. Unna had said to think about her words, and since then he had been unable to do anything but think about them. His mind was filled with horrible images of the Wrath of Fire devouring every part of his body and his spirit, and he didn't know how to rid himself of them, or even that he should.

Unable to endure Mach's troubled silence, Elko said, "Ah, Suka said Unna was the Medicine Woman of the People of the Tall Grass."

Mach nodded, but he was only half listening. Silently he cursed himself. He'd known what would happen if anyone found out — but he hadn't thought anyone would find out.

"Suka has some healer skills but not much training. Suka said Unna did a good job, but I don't know. Perhaps Horda can help in her own treatment."

The mention of Horda's name brought Mach back to the present. "What? Is she all right?"

"I assume she is, or Suka would have said something."

But Mach's stomach twisted itself into knots. Here he worried about being punished while Horda lay injured inside the shelter. *Please, Father Death, don't take her. Leave her so she can taste the Wrath of Fire. Oh, that didn't come out right.*

Elko reached out and touched the younger man's hand. "I'm sure she'll be all right."

"It really won't make much difference in the end," said Mach bitterly. He immediately regretted his words. "I'm sorry," he said. "It's just ...." His voice trailed off; he didn't know what else to say. He settled for watching Suka and Unna bustle in and out of the shelter.

Finally Suka returned to the fire. Mach looked at her with a pleading expression. "I assume you want to know how Horda is," she said, a touch of exasperation in her voice, "but like a man you refuse to ask."

Mach merely nodded.

"Well, she had a little fever last night, but Unna dosed her with willow and some other things. She seems better, but she's very weak, which is not unusual after all she went through." Suka laughed softly. "Earlier she made a fuss about bathing and washing her hair, but Unna wouldn't let her, so we sponged her and rubbed her scalp with rose water. She's not satisfied, but she's tired enough to quit fussing."

Elko set his empty bowl on the ground and rubbed his hands together. "That's good news."

Mach let out a huge sigh. "So she's all right?" His half-question, half-assertion spoke volumes.

"She's not all right yet, Mach, but she's certainly improving."

He was about to ask more questions, but Unna came out of the shelter and approached them. "Horda's ready to see you," she informed Mach.

Mach jumped to his feet, spilling his forgotten porridge and horn of wild rose tea. "Oh, I didn't mean to ..."

Suka took the bowl and spoon out of his hands. "Don't worry about it."

"I'll ah ...." He looked at the mess at his feet and then at Suka.

Shaking her head, she pointed toward the shelter. "Horda is waiting for you."

A bright grin lighted his face, and he fairly tripped over his own feet as he sprinted for the shelter, shouting a "Thanks, Suka!" over his shoulder as he went.

"That boy has it bad," Elko laughed with a lop-sided grin.

"Worse than you realize," said Suka softly, more to herself than to either of them. Unna nodded, then left the two of them alone.

"What are you mumbling about now, woman?" Elko demanded.

"They should have celebrated the Ritual of the First Mate more than two moons ago."

He shrugged. "So they'll celebrate it when we get home."

"Oh, Elko, I love you, but sometimes you're so dense."

"Why? Because I refuse to accuse Mach and Horda — even to you?"

"What are we going to do?"

"Nothing. There's really nothing to do unless they — or someone else — makes an issue out of it, and I know I won't. I agree what they did was wrong, sort of, but if they celebrate the Rituals without confessing they were premature ..."

"Unna has asked both of them to keep quiet for now, but I'm not sure they will."

"I sent a hand of men for Zaaco today," Elko said. "They'll

be back tomorrow, and we'll see what happens then."

"What do you think he'll do if he finds out?"

Elko rubbed his face. "I told you I don't know. I don't want to be in charge."

She smiled encouragingly. "You're doing a good job."

"Well, to be honest, I'm scared to death. The best young warrior we've had for many turnings of the seasons is involved in an unsanctified joining. He may confess to me, — me, of all people — and if that happens, I'll have to help make a decision. But I don't know what to do because I don't believe they deserve to be burned even if they do confess. They aren't the first to do this, and they won't be the last. And if Bear Claw hadn't captured you all, we wouldn't be worrying about this in the first place." He scowled and cursed Bear Claw roundly.

"But he did, and don't forget we also have two hands' of other promised couples to get back to the Gathering ground and a limited number of very small shelters."

"So now we'll be burning all the couples. Or feeling guilty for burning Mach and Horda for something the rest of them will probably do before we get them home anyway."

Suka interrupted him. "I've been thinking. The other couples celebrated the Ritual of the First Mate back at Gathering after you left, didn't they?"

He nodded, "I suppose so. Zaaco told the Council to finish the Gathering and get everybody settled before winter. Thuro was the only one of the other promised men who came with us." He grinned in spite of himself. "Wilda worked herself into a rage. She threw a terrible fit."

"Ooh, wonderful Wilda. I'm sure she did."

He chuckled. "If Bear Claw had wanted her, we wouldn't be here."

"No, but others would be."

"No, they wouldn't," he said firmly. "I'd have suggested we let him have her, and Zaaco would have agreed. We'd have given

Bear Claw a travois of prime furs and two baskets of pemmican to take her off our hands."

"That's a terrible thing to say," she admonished, but she had to admit it was an amusing thought.

"So what was it you were saying?" He sobered quickly; this was too important an issue to make light of.

"Well, Zaaco will be here tomorrow."

"What does that have to do with anything?"

"Still dense, aren't you? What I'm saying is since these couples should have celebrated the Ritual of the First Mate a long time ago, I think they should celebrate it now, and Zaaco can lead it."

He blinked. "How will that help Mach and Horda?"

"Maybe if they can be mated officially before we return, they won't feel like they need to confess." Her voice trailed to silence at his skeptical look.

"Do you really think that would help?"

"I don't know. Do you have a better idea?"

"No, I don't," Elko admitted. "I hate that rule, more so now than ever."

"So do I, but I understand it. I even support it most of the time, but not now. I don't think they deserve to be burned because they joined a few days before a ceremony they would have attended otherwise."

"No more than we do," he said softly.

"No." She touched his arm. "No more than we do. I've never regretted our decision."

"Nor have I."

"Hmm," Suka said, suddenly thoughtful. "The Wrath of Fire hasn't ever been used for premature joining of couples who later went through the Ritual of the First Mate, has it?"

"Not that I know of. All the cases we've ever heard about are of people who joined with someone else's mate or undertook some kind of perversion. I can't believe Mach and Horda will be burned just because they anticipated the Ritual of the First Mate by a few days. But I'm not the chief — what if Zaaco feels differently?"

She sighed. "It's more difficult because she's his daughter. He'll have trouble making an exception."

"We'll have to convince him if we can't keep them from confessing," he said.

She nodded. "Then that's where we start. Mach's your job, and I'll take Horda. Let's see if we can sort this out before the others arrive."

Chapter 44

Suka stood outside the shelter for a long time before she entered. *Please, Mother Life, give me the right words to say.*

She lifted the door covering, but Unna stopped her. She placed a finger to her lips and rose from her place beside Horda, motioning Suka back outside. "She's finally fallen asleep, and I don't want to wake her."

"Of course not," Suka whispered. "I'm glad she's able to rest."

Unna shook her head in exasperation. "This girl has sand for brains. She keeps insisting she must confess. Perhaps that mate of hers can talk some sense into her."

"I was going to sit with her and try myself," Suka said, "but if she's asleep ..."

"You can sit with her, but best to let her be right now; tomorrow will come soon enough."

Suka nodded her agreement then slipped into the shelter as quietly as she could.

After Bear Claw's feast, they needed meat, and Elko had taken advantage of the bright sun and the melting snow. He organized the men into hunting parties to bring back game before they set out for home. After so many weeks focused on tracking their women, Mach found this routine activity exhilarating. Still, he chafed at being away from Horda for even a second, and the moment they returned, laden with fresh kill, he hurried to her tent and slipped inside.

Suka was there when he arrived, sitting beside his mate. She motioned him to be silent, but she needn't have bothered. Horda stirred on the furs, shaking off the last of her slumber. Her smile was radiant when she caught sight of him.

Suka still wanted to talk to Horda, preferably before the younger woman could speak with Mach, but it was clear the two of them wanted to be together, and she would be intruding. "I guess I'll leave you two to catch up," she said.

"Thanks," Mach replied gratefully, and Suka took her leave. There was much he wanted to say to Horda, but once they were alone, Mach didn't know where to begin.

It was Horda who broke the silence. "I'm so sorry, Mach."

"Sorry for what? You have nothing to be sorry for."

"For the position I've put you in."

"I told you we are in this together," Mach said firmly, "and I meant it. We'll figure out something."

"I already have," Horda told him quietly. "I am going to confess.

"You can't," Mach protested. "And I know Unna told you ..."

Horda interrupted him. "It's because of what Unna said I know I must. Everyone knows the truth, Mach, no matter if I speak about it or not — Bird Wing and Bear Claw saw to that. If I don't confess, the truth will lie there and fester like Brash's wound, turning uglier and more painful each day.

"They won't say it openly, but there are many who would claim I got away with it because of my privileged status as the daughter of the chief. My mother, if she had been in this position, might have chosen to remain silent; for all I loved her, I would not have respected her for making that choice.

"Unna said I should choose the right path for the *right reasons*. Before, I wanted to confess because I felt such guilt, but that would have been wrong because I would only have been thinking about you and me. This decision has consequences larger than ourselves; it affects the entire tribe.

"Our laws and our values are what make us strong; they are what made us different from and better than the People of the Tall Grass. If I don't stand by them now, when it really matters, I will be showing everyone that who we are does not matter, and *that* is the lie. Do you understand?"

Her eyes were shining with her conviction, and Mach found he had fallen in love with her all over again. "I do understand," he told her. "In fact, Elko said something similar right before we attacked the camp, and I wondered at the wisdom behind it." He paused for a moment then said, "If it's not too selfish to admit, I want to live, to mate with you and raise our little ones together, to grow old together. I do not want to taste the Wrath of Fire, nor do I want to see you endure such pain."

Horda said, "I want nothing more than to be with you forever; my heart aches to make that true. But we need to set the example. If the Council votes to let us live, we will never have to hide or hang our heads with shame; if they don't, others will know we received justice, and the tribe will be stronger for it."

He nodded his agreement, and she smiled affectionately at him. He took her hands in his and held them tightly. No matter what happened, he thought, they were together, and that's what really mattered.

❉

The sun had climbed high in the sky, and Suka was busy with her chores when she noticed movement on the horizon. Still skittish from the weeks of captivity, her heart skipped a beat, but within moments she could make out the figures — they were only the Men of the Frozen Earth, returned from retrieving Zaaco and pulling him into the camp on a travois. How did they get here so soon?

"Greetings, Zaaco," she said, a smile on her face. "Since you are here earlier than we expected, I trust your injuries are healing well."

Zaaco reached out to touch her hand. "Greetings, Suka. The pain is almost gone, but I still walk slowly. Yesterday afternoon most of the snow had melted, so I insisted we follow the trail of our men, and when we met the men Elko sent today, they insisted we'd make better time if I rode. So —"

She laughed. It felt good to laugh, and it was good to see him again.

But she sobered as Zaaco caught her hand and spoke earnestly. "I wish we could have found you sooner. I trust you have no lasting injuries from your captivity."

"You came as quickly as you could, and I am fine." She dared not say anything more until he asked.

"Where's Elko?"

"He went hunting with some of the young men, and now he's butchering the carcasses. Bear Claw and his people ate much of the meat we had for the winter last night."

Zaaco frowned. "They were unusual people."

"They were, but that is over." Suka was surprised she dared cut off the chief that way, but it hurt too much to think about. That surprised her, too, the depth of her own pain. She would have to reflect on that more later.

Zaaco let the topic go. "I felt my daughter needed me," he said. "That's why I started on the trail yesterday. The men told me little except Bear Claw beat her. How is she?"

"Oh, Zaaco." Suka blinked rapidly to stop the tears threatening to fill her eyes; it would be unseemly to cry now. "She needs you very much."

Zaaco waved the men away and struggled to his feet. "Can you tell me about it?" he asked softly.

Suka chose her words carefully. She wouldn't lie, but she didn't want to tell the whole truth — what to say? "She heals physically, but she feels the need to confess the child —"

Zaaco nodded, taking her hand and holding it tightly; she was grateful for his understanding. "I was afraid of this. Tell me what you know," he commanded. As she explained, Zaaco listened silently allowing only his eyes to betray his pain. When she had finished, he said simply, "I must speak with my daughter."

"I would speak with you first," she said. "Forgive my forwardness, but I believe we must celebrate the Ritual of the Mate before we leave this place. I hope you will agree with me."

Zaaco's expression was unreadable. "I will consider your words. Now, where is my daughter?"

Suka pointed to the shelter where Horda lay, and the old chief hobbled toward it. *Mother Life, please let it go well*, Suka prayed. *After all we've been through, we need something good so we can move on with our lives.*

❋

Zaaco walked outside into the lavender light of sunset to find Elko. Suka had said he was butchering the meat, so the best place would probably be near the stream. He was correct.

"Greetings, Zaaco," Elko called at his approach. "It is good to see you moving around again."

"I agree," Zaaco replied. "I see your hunt was successful."

"Yes, we were fortunate."

Out of small talk, the silence grew.

"I guess we, ah, need to talk," Elko finally said.

Zaaco glanced around the crowded work area. "I agree, but privately."

"Shall I send them away?"

Zaaco snorted. "I can walk."

Elko smiled and pointed up stream. "A walk beside the water?"

Zaaco headed off with only the slightest limp, and Elko followed him. When a good distance separated them from the others, Zaaco said, "I need your help." Though he didn't say what about, they both knew what he meant.

Elko started. "But why are you asking me?"

"Because I don't know what to do," Zaaco said impatiently. "Why else? I hoped you might have a suggestion."

"If they confess —"

Zaaco cut him off. "My daughter already confessed to me. I asked her why they didn't just go through the Ritual of the First Mate and keep their mouths shut, but she insisted she didn't want to live in fear the rest of her life, and I must agree." He rubbed his eyes, suddenly looking old. "But I blame Bear Claw; it's as much his fault as theirs."

"True," agreed Elko, "but that doesn't change the fact we have to act."

"I know, but I'm of two minds. As chief, I recognize the necessity of calling them to task. But I'm also a father, and I'm afraid of what would happen should a Band Council find them guilty. I don't think I could bear to lose her — lose them both — again."

Elko's heart felt like it was tearing in two. He had rarely known Zaaco to be so open with his feelings, and it hurt to know there was little he could do to reassure him. Words were inadequate now, and so he kept silent.

Zaaco thought a moment longer. "Throughout these long weeks all I could hope for was to find her alive and well, and now it seems Mother Life has played a cruel joke on me. But I don't see I have a choice. After two turnings of the sun, we'll celebrate the Ritual of the First Mate. All those who choose to participate here and not wait until our return home may do so, and the ceremony will be binding. But first, we'll name a Band Council and hope for the best."

"What if the Council finds them guilty?" Elko asked his voice barely above a whisper.

"You know the taboo isn't meant for cases like this."

"I know it, and you know it, but the rule is unsanctified joining, regardless of the cause. So what if the Council finds them guilty?"

"Then they will taste the Wrath of Fire, and there will be nothing you or I can do to prevent it."

❋

The sunset's colors had faded first to grey and then black, and the stars sparkled in the dark bowl of the night sky. Everyone was seated around the cook fire, talking and finishing the evening eat when Zaaco rose before them, raising his arms and calling for silence. As the last of the voices trailed off, he said formally, "It is necessary that I appoint a Band Council to help me, the Chief of the People of the Frozen Earth, decide a matter of grave importance. Tomorrow when the sun reaches its highest point in the sky, the Council will meet in the shelter we call Suka's."

A collective gasp made its way around the circle of men and women — calling such a Council signaled something grave indeed. Zaaco waited until all were silent once more before he continued, "Unna, the former Medicine Woman of the People of the Tall Grass, is the oldest member of this band. She has by her support and assistance shown herself worthy to be called a Woman of the Frozen Earth, and I therefore name her to the Council."

There was a murmur of assent from the group, then silence again. "Suka and Angil are the next oldest women in our band, so they will also serve on the Council along with Zeek, Cryon, and Elko, the oldest warriors in the band besides myself."

Unna looked thoroughly confused, and she poked Suka in the ribs. "What's he talking about?"

"You've been named to the Council to try Mach and Horda," whispered Suka.

"Me? But I don't think they should be burned."

"You have to listen to their words before you decide," Suka murmured.

"Fine. I'll listen to their words then I'll decide those two young people do not deserve to be burned."

"I agree with you, but the others may not."

"Humph," snorted Unna. "Why wouldn't they?"

"For one thing, Angil and Cryon were very close to the last couple who tasted the Wrath of Fire for unsanctified mating."

"A promised couple?"

"No, they were joined to others."

"How long ago?"

"Two Gatherings."

Unna frowned and shook her head. "Well, I guess it's better to have them on the Council so they know exactly what's happening than on the outside wondering and causing mischief."

Suka nodded. "I just hope it helps."

Chapter 45

The morning was crisp and sunny. Horda convinced Unna to allow her to walk outside with Mach. As the sun reached its zenith, the members of the Band Council filed toward Suka's shelter. Watching them disappear into the structure, Horda's heart beat faster; for all her assertion this was the right path, she was still afraid. Mach stood and helped her to her feet. "It's time," he said taking her cold hand in his. She leaned on him, as much for moral support as for physical, and they walked together to meet their fate.

Inside the shelter, the Council members were already seated in a semi-circle around the fire pit. Two seats of piled furs, separated from the others, awaited them. Horda's feet felt cold though her toes burned. It was almost as if she already tasted the Wrath of Fire, she thought. She tried to get a sense of the Council members' moods, but it was difficult to know if what she saw was real or merely a product of her own fears.

"Greetings, Mach, Horda," Zaaco said formally, keeping his face as impassive as possible. "We are ready for you." He motioned to the seats; Mach helped Horda to hers before sitting down himself.

"You know why we are gathered here," Zaaco intoned, "but you may not know the decision of the Band Council must be unanimous. If it's not, you will have to appear before the Council of Elders when we return to the Inner Band. Do you understand?"

Mach and Horda nodded their understanding.

"Good," Zaaco said. "Then we shall begin. Horda, you may speak first."

Still shaky from her ordeal, Horda rose to her feet. Her voice, though, was firm and clear. She recounted to the Council, in as much detail as she could, everything that happened from the time she told Bear Claw she was breeding to the time he beat her.

Cryon was the first to respond. "It's simple. She admits the little one was Mach's not Bear Claw's, which means she entered into an unsanctified joining with Mach. The rule is clear. They should taste the Wrath of —"

"That is not all," Horda interrupted.

A buzz ran through the crowd. "Not all?" Cryon demanded, incredulous.

"Not all?" echoed Angil. "Isn't it enough you admitted your little one belonged to a man who was not your mate?"

"No, that is not all, and it is not enough." She opened the small pouch on her necklace and shook the dried flowers from it into her hand. Then she told the rest of the story, from the vision she and Mach had shared during the Dance of the Sun to their actual mating. "I believe Mother Life chose us for each other and sanctified our mating on the day of the Dance of the Sun."

"Bah!" Cryon spit into the fire pit. "You could have found the flowers anywhere." It was clear where he stood on the verdict.

"But I didn't."

"No, she didn't," said Zaaco slowly, as if suddenly remembering an important fact. "I found them on her tunic after the Dance of the Sun. I would have thrown them away, but she told me she wanted to keep them."

Zeek held out his hand. "Let me look at the flowers."

Reluctantly Horda handed them to the older man. He gazed

at them. "These are truly forget-me-nots and tiny primroses," he said quietly handing them back to Horda.

"Yes, they are," agreed Horda and Zaaco at the same time.

"She showed them to me the night we mated," Mach interjected.

"Anyone can dry early flowers and pretend they were a gift from the Mother," cried Angil.

"Yes, they can," admitted Zaaco. "Though the time for their blooming was several moons past, the flowers were fresh when I found them on her shoulder."

Still angry but not willing to argue with the chief, Cryon contented himself with glaring at the young couple.

"Cryon, why do the People of the Frozen Earth have the rule about unsanctified mating?" asked Unna suddenly.

The question caught him off guard, and he turned his glare on the old woman. "We have the rule to keep our families strong and committed to each other. It is wrong for people to hop from sleeping fur to sleeping fur, joining with anyone who catches their eyes."

Unna nodded. "I don't think anyone here questions that," she said, "but tell me, were Horda and Mach hopping from sleeping fur to sleeping fur with anyone who caught their eyes?"

"They entered into an unsanctified joining," he answered stubbornly, refusing to acknowledge her point.

"Yes, they did, and they admitted as much" Angil complained. "And they haven't even said they were sorry."

Mach could no longer hold his peace. "Horda is mine. Mother Life gave her to me at the Dance of the Sun, and I'm committed to her just as she's committed to me. We were not to blame that Bear Claw kidnapped her and the others before the Rituals, but if we're given the chance now, we'll gladly celebrate them and form a strong family."

The arguments raged back and forth through the long afternoon. Finally Cryon's temper blazed out of control. He shouted,

"Zaaco, you want us to spare them because she's your daughter, and he's your hand picked young hero."

"That's right," Angil agreed angrily. "You make an example of others, but you want to make an exception of your daughter."

So there it was — the real source of Angil and Cryon's anger. Their friend and sister had tasted the Wrath of Fire, sent there in part at Zaaco's hand. Now they would punish his daughter in the same way.

Zeek's soft, firm voice cut into the terrible silence that had descended. "Horda and Mach's situation is not the same as Dion and Sappho's, Cryon, and it's wrong of you to imply it is."

Tears welled in Angil's eyes. "It is the same," she declared hotly.

"No, it's not," Zeek said again firmly. "Cryon, I know Dion was your special friend, but your lives took different paths. You only saw him at Gatherings after he became a man, not at his shelter with his mates, but I did. I lived in the same band with him for two hands' turnings of the seasons. He treated his mates carelessly and didn't take good care of them. We suspected he hit them, but we could never prove it."

"Of course, you couldn't," growled Cryon, "because he didn't. He was a good m —"

"No, he wasn't," Zeek continued, his voice rising to be heard, "and it is wrong of you to tell us so. You weren't there to see that he never provided quite enough food or furs or attention for his mates or his children. You weren't there to see how lazy he was, lazy, but smart. Smart enough not to get himself banished though many of the members of the band who were there to see recognized him for what he was. His only commitment was to himself and his own pleasure. He deserved to taste the Wrath of Fire."

"And what about my sister?" cried Angil. "Did Sappho deserve to be burned? Her mate treated her badly, and she was unhappy with him. Was that her fault?"

"Ah, Sappho," said Suka softly. "Suddenly when she's caught in another man's furs, her mate treats her badly, and she is unhappy with him."

Angil grabbed onto Suka's words. "Yes, that's exactly my point. She had many complaints, but the Council didn't listen. They burned her anyway."

Zaaco stared at the young widow. "The Council listened, and we reminded her she could have come to us earlier. We would have released her from her mating."

Angil's face tightened. "But you burned her anyway."

"We listened, and we asked." Now it was Elko's soft voice that vibrated through the quiet shelter. "We sought one person to verify Sappho's claims against her mate. One person who would testify she told them of her problems with him before she stood before us. No one came forward," he said softly, "not even you."

"We belonged to different bands. We didn't see each other except at Gathering," Angil protested feebly.

"It was late in the Gathering, and you and your sister spent much time together for nearly a moon before that time," reminded Suka gently.

Angil began to sob. "She knew Dion wasn't a good man, but he made her laugh. She just wanted to enjoy his attention for a little while, was that so wrong?"

"She was mated to another," said Elko quietly. "He deserved her attention. So, yes, it was wrong, and, yes, she deserved the punishment she received. However, neither of these two has committed such a crime."

Angil wiped the tears from her face with the backs of her hands. "She was my sister, and I loved her very much."

"No one doubts that," Zaaco said gently.

Angil sniffed. "It was ... it still is ... hard to admit that she, like Dion, was only committed to herself and her own pleasure." Zaaco opened his mouth to speak again, but Angil stopped him. "I would say more."

He nodded, and she said, "I saw Horda throughout our captivity. She hated Bear Claw with every fiber of her being, and I believe she endured him only to make the lives of the other women easier. She survived because she never let herself doubt Mach would find her and take her home." A single tear trickled down her cheek. "If commitment is the measure by which Mach and Horda should be judged, then I say they do not deserve to be burned. Allow them to mate and get on with their lives."

Zaaco looked toward Cryon. "Cryon, you seem to be the only one unconvinced."

"You'll never convince me," he spat. "They deserve to be burned as surely as Dion and Sappho did."

"Cryon, your loyalty to your friend is admirable, especially since he felt no such loyalty to you."

Cryon looked at Zaaco defiantly. "I do not believe you. He was a good man, and he didn't deserve to be burned."

"Dion agreed with you completely," Zaaco told him. "He even used you to try to escape the flames, though his words could have condemned you to them with him."

"I, ah, don't understand," muttered Cryon.

"Then I'll tell you what your friend Dion told the Council. He said the rule was old and useless. He said none of the men believed in it anymore. He said everyone joined with women who weren't their mates. And he even said you were guilty of the same crime he was. Now, have you anything else to say?"

Cryon was clearly uncomfortable at this new scrutiny, but just as clearly he wasn't ready to give up or give in. "If he accused me, why wasn't I called before the Council?"

Zaaco smiled. "Because when we questioned him more closely, Dion admitted the only women he knew you joined with later became your mates. He insisted you told him you joined with each of them before the Rituals.

"Of course, we couldn't prove his words, and we didn't

even try because the women he named were all three your mates, and you seemed committed to them."

Cryon breathed an almost audible sigh of relief.

Zaaco's dark eyes searched Cryon's face. "But I do recall at least one of your daughters was sitting alone at her first Gathering. She was quite advanced for only three moons. I remember Meiran commenting she looked more like she had a hand or even a hand plus one moon."

"We celebrated the Rituals many moons before her birth," mumbled Cryon in a strangled voice.

"As would Mach and Horda have done if Bear Claw had not intervened. Do you not see the similarity?" asked Zaaco. "I believe the captivity and the loss of the little one have been punishment enough for whatever crime these two have committed. Does anyone else have more to say?"

Horda held her breath in the silence. Cryon glared sullenly at his moccasins, but he didn't say another word.

"Then I call for the vote," said Zaaco. "Either they should taste the Wrath of Fire, or they should celebrate the Rituals of the First Mate. Unna?"

Unna flashed a grin at Horda. "Celebrate the Rituals of the First Mate."

"Suka?"

"Celebrate the Rituals of the First Mate." She looked at Horda and smiled.

"Angil?"

"I already told you," she muttered. "Celebrate the Rituals of the First Mate."

"Elko?"

He looked at Mach. "Celebrate the Rituals."

"Zeek?"

Zeek cast a smile across the circle at Mach and Horda. "Celebrate the Rituals."

"Cryon?"

The silence stretched, and Horda's heart beat so hard she feared it would burst from her chest. She clasped her hands tightly in her lap. *Oh, please, Mother Life. I'll spend the rest of my life trying to be worthy of Mach if you'll see fit to let me live it.*

After what seemed an eternity, Cryon raised his head and looked at her and Mach. "I vote they should celebrate the Rituals of the First Mate."

Horda released the breath she hadn't realized she'd been holding and threw herself into Mach's arms.

He hugged her tightly against his chest then released her to look toward the Council members. "Tomorrow we will celebrate the Rituals of the First Mate with the others," he announced.

Horda smiled. "At last, we truly become one. We will see the future together."

AND THE NEW DAY WILL DAWN ...

Scott Monroe

About the Author

A story-teller and writer since she could talk and hold a pencil, Grace Anne Schaefer taught English and reading for thirty-two years. She lives in central Texas with her husband Kenn, also a writer. Their grown daughter Anja teaches high school English. Grace Anne — who collects Beanie babies, Santa Clauses, and dust bunnies — looks forward to the dawn of her own new day.

From:
As Shadows Fall
People of the Frozen Earth
Book Two

Shock flashed through Horda, making her fingers tingle.

The Council doesn't do such things. My father wouldn't do such a thing to me. Would he?

Squeezing her eyes shut she took deep breaths until her anger trickled away.

Oh, please, Mother Life, wake me from this nightmare.

She peeked through her eyelashes and found herself still in the midst of the Gathering assembly. The jagged purple teeth of the high mountains to the west still ate at the sky while the brown grasses of the plains to the east rolled away to the edge of the world. The lazy breeze tweaked her nose and gently swirled the smoke from the assembly fire hurrying on its way to the other world. The crisp smells of pine, cedar, and sage mingled with the tart odor of grasses trampled beneath the feet of the People.

Opening her eyes, she looked up at her mate, Mach. The late summer sun's golden rays cast red and blue highlights in his waist-length ebony hair and glistened on the his broad bronzed shoulders. His scars from the Dance of the Sun had faded to pale lines across his pectoral muscles. Her fingers itched to trace the lines of his chest — anything to make the words she had heard go away. *I was dreaming.* She tried to pretend she hadn't heard the words that would change her life forever.

She watched Mach whisper some comment to Thuro, his taller, but thinner, darker, and quieter best friend. Their eyes snapped and sparked like children who have just been given more camas molasses candy than they can hold in both hands. Her father Zaaco's words hadn't upset them.

"Did you know anything about this?" Thuro's voice betrayed his awe.

Mach shook his head. "Just what I told you yesterday. That the People are forming a new band mostly of younger warriors. I had no idea they were naming us the leaders. I can't believe it."

Thuro grinned.